THE ULTIMATE SPIDER-MAN

From Putnam/Byron Preiss Multimedia:
SPIDER-MAN: THE VENOM FACTOR by Diane Duane

From Berkley/Byron Preiss Multimedia:
THE ULTIMATE SPIDER-MAN, Stan Lee, Editor

THE ULTIMATE SPIDER-MAN

STAN LEE, EDITOR

BYRON PREISS MULTIMEDIA COMPANY, INC.
NEW YORK

BERKLEY BOOKS, NEW YORK

Special thanks to Lou Aronica, Jacky Sach, and Michelle Kennedy at Berkley;
Julia Molino, Michael Hobson, Tom DeFalco, Danny Fingeroth, and Eric Fein
at Marvel; and especially Deborah Valcourt, John Betancourt, and Keith R.A.
DeCandido at BPMC for service above and beyond.

THE ULTIMATE SPIDER-MAN

A Berkley Book
A Byron Preiss Multimedia Company, Inc., Book

PRINTING HISTORY
Berkley trade paperback edition / December 1994

ISBN: 0-425-14610-3

BERKLEY®
Berkley Books are published by The Berkley Publishing Group,
200 Madison Avenue, New York, New York 10016.
BERKLEY and the "B" design
are trademarks belonging to Berkley Publishing Corporation.

PRINTED IN THE UNITED STATES OF AMERICA

10 9 8 7 6 5 4 3 2 1

CONTENTS

To Steve Ditko, who was there at the beginning

INTRODUCTION

STAN LEE

Illustration by Jack Kirby and Steve Ditko

I've written more introductions to more books and articles about Spidey than I can count. So, when the time came to write *this* intro, the first thought that crossed my mind was, "How can I do this differently? What can I discuss that hasn't been covered a zillion times before?"

The easy way would be to tell about all the great treats in store for you on the pages that follow. But you'll discover them soon enough yourself.

Or, I could rhapsodize about our wondrous web-swinger's worldwide popularity, the proliferation of toys, games, trading cards, cartoons, film projects and seemingly countless comic book titles. But you might think we were bragging.

Therefore, let me offer you instead an aspect of Spider-Man which will undoubtedly prove monumentally important to historians, archivists and dedicated scholars of popular culture. I urge you to pay close attention; there may be an exam.

Time and again people have asked, "How did you come up with the idea for Spider-Man?" At first, I replied as honestly as possible, "I really don't remember." After all, no one at Marvel expected Spidey to become a cultural icon. Had we known, I'd have paid more attention. But, at that time, he was just one of many, many characters that were being continuously hatched, published, abandoned, and forgotten if they didn't catch on.

However, my guileless response inevitably brought a look of sheer disappointment to the interrogator's face. I realized people simply didn't believe me. How could someone not remember how he thought up a character? Especially a character as prominent as Spider-Man.

So, with the very best of intentions, not wanting to offend any fans who really cared about such matters, I cooked up an answer to the "How did you create Spidey?" query. I'll share that answer with you right now, but with one caveat: I've told this to so many people, so many times, that I've actually started to believe it. So I no longer know if it's true or not!

Now then, with that puzzling preamble out of the way, here's how I created the concept of Spider-Man, sort of . . .

It was early in the year 1962. In our cramped but colorful little bullpen at Marvel Comics, buoyed by our triumphant creations of *The Fantastic Four* and *The Incredible Hulk*, we decided to try for another superhero title, to see if we could strike pay dirt three times in a row.

One of the first critical decisions that must be made when creating a new superhero is—what power should he or she have? The thought kept running through my mind that we already had heroes who were super strong, were able to fly, had the ability to change shape, and could turn invisible. There seemed to be nothing left. But I had to come up with something.

What power, I kept asking myself, could I give to a new superhero that would be original and dramatic?

At first, the answer didn't come. I just sat there, elbows on my cluttered desk, scratching my head, rubbing my chin, tapping my fingers against the typewriter, bending paper clip after paper clip, staring out the window, looking up at the ceiling, examining the wallpaper on the wall, doing all the ridiculous things any writer does when waiting for an idea to strike.

Then, while staring blankly ahead of me, I became aware of a small insect crawling on the outside of my window. I kept watching it, almost hypnotized by its slow, seemingly effortless progress as it adhered to the slippery glass as if by magic.

Back and forth it crawled, silently, easily, never for an instant losing its footing. I found myself wondering, what makes it stick to the glass? Why is it that all sorts of insects have the ability to crawl on walls, ceilings, anything at all, and they can do it upside down, defying gravity as if it doesn't exist?

Well, I'm sure you can see what this is leading up to. At some point I thought to myself, "Hey, what if a superhero had the ability of an insect? What if he could crawl on walls or even walk upside down on ceilings? Wouldn't that be a hoot!"

Best of all, as far as I knew, there had never been such a comic book character. He'd be a true original.

And so the hard part was done. I had found the superpower I'd been seeking. The next prerequisite was a name. The first thought that hit me was Insect Man, but it just didn't sound heroic enough. Next, I rolled Mosquito Man around on my tongue. Close, but no cigar. Fly Man? Not quite. Then suddenly, inspiration struck. Spider Man! Wow, that really sounded dramatic to me, plus it seemed to have a desirable touch of menace. So Spider Man it was.

However, the name still needed one other element—a hyphen. I didn't want to take any chance, not the slightest chance in the world, that a reader looking at the title quickly might mistake it for Superman. So I added the quintessential hyphen, and lo, the Spider-Man we all know and love was born!

Oh, I forgot to mention that I've always been a sucker for adjectives (i.e.: The *Fantastic* Four, The *Incredible* Hulk,

The *Invincible* Iron Man, The *Uncanny* X-Men, The *Mighty* Thor). Well, I certainly wasn't going to let my favorite hero of all go through life adjectiveless. So I decided to call him The *Amazing* Spider-Man. No special reason why I chose the word "amazing." I simply liked the sound of it.

Now that we had our title and Spidey had his super-power, all that remained was for the brilliant artist Steve Ditko to give our wondrous web-swinger his look, style, and unique visual appeal, while also contributing mightily in the plotting of our extravagant little epics. Steve did it. The fans bought it. The rest is history.

Later, when Steve went on to other projects, the awesomely talented John Romita brought his own dazzling interpretation to Spidey, lifting our wondrous wall-crawler to still greater heights of popularity and fame.

After all these years, I seem to remember it happening that way. It could have happened that way. It should have happened that way. And it probably did.

And now that you've been thoroughly briefed and indoctrinated, it's time to turn the page to see what all the fuss is about. Your friendly neighborhood Spider-Man has a surfeit of surprises for you, and you know how arachnids hate to be kept waiting!

Excelsior!

Stan

Stan Lee

S P I D E R - M A N

STAN LEE AND PETER DAVID

Illustration by John Romita Sr.

The fist was a blur. The impact, however, had more substance.

Many times when Peter Parker had perused comic books in his youth—back in the days when he had time for such trivialities, before he found his leisure moments utterly consumed by science texts and the like—he had read the phrase, "He never knew what hit him." It was such a jazzy phrase, one that implied action and violence at breakneck speed. In his previous seventeen-plus years of existence, however, it had never quite had any real, personal meaning before.

Peter Parker never knew what hit him.

Oh, intellectually, he did. It was a fist. A curled, brutish fist about the size of a glazed ham, with thick bristling hair protruding from the knuckles. It would not have seemed out of line to Peter if the fist's owner, upon finishing with Parker, decided to grab a screaming blonde, scale the Empire State Building, and commence swiping at army planes.

Peter spun, his glasses flying off his head to thud on the floor of the alley. The glasses' erstwhile owner joined them a moment later. His normally immaculately groomed brown hair was disheveled. His crisp white shirt and blue sweater were now soiled by the blood that was trickling from his split lip. He heard a high-pitched, crack-voiced shrieking and was confused enough at that moment to wonder whose it was. Then the shrieks turned to genuine words.

"Take it!" the old woman was crying. "Here, take it!" She was shoving money into the hands of the man who had just sent Peter Parker crashing to the ground. Peter couldn't quite see anything, what with the combination of his missing glasses and the world swirling around him. What he was able to make out, though, were the hands of his aunt, May Parker, trembling. Out of fear? Out of rage? Both? No matter. She was shoving the money from her just-cashed Social Security check into the hands of the brute who had nearly decapitated her nephew with just one punch. The brute had an associate standing nearby. The latter's purpose was a mystery to Peter. What did the first guy need backup for?

The injured teenager ran his hands along the ground, found his glasses, and put them on. There was smeared dirt on them, and they hung lopsidedly on his face.

Peter's assailant was clutching the money in his ham hock fist. He smiled raggedly, a line of green discoloration where his teeth met the gum lines. Peter wanted to crow, *Ha! At least I'll still have my teeth five years from now,* but decided that wouldn't be the wisest course . . . particularly since the brute might engage in some on-the-spot dentistry to make sure that Peter's teeth predeceased his own.

"Thanks for your time," grunted the other, who was as wide as his associate but about a head shorter. Whereas Peter's assailant had not uttered a word, the second guy had actually strung a whole sentence together. Clearly he was the brains of the outfit.

The two of them moved away into the shadows that had belched them out moments ago, intercepting Peter Parker and his aunt upon their departure from the check-cashing place.

Peter tried to pull himself to his feet, but he couldn't get his legs to work. And then Aunt May was there, and heaven knows she didn't have the strength to haul him up, but she braced him. "Peter, stay where you are! I'll get a doctor!" said the gray-haired woman. "Don't—!"

"No, I'm fine. No doctor. I'm fine." Shoving his back against the wall, he pulled himself to standing.

"But . . . but look at you!" stammered Aunt May. "Look what he did! A doctor will—!"

"*No doctor!*" he said with greater force than he would have liked. He didn't tell her that he was embarrassed, humiliated. That he didn't want to have to explain to someone how he was so weak that he never even got a punch in. He didn't want to deal with his own guilt, because Aunt May should have just been able to deposit the check in her bank account, but she needed the cash immediately because Peter needed some supplies for a science project. She'd wanted to help him and she wound up losing all the money because of it. All the rage and frustration and guilt that surged through Peter had collapsed down into one, terse, angry, "*No doctor!*"

Aunt May seemed taken aback at first. But then her face softened, and she nodded. She touched his cheek gingerly and said, "All right, Peter. I understand." Indeed, it seemed as if she did. She checked her urge to mother him (an understandable one, since she had raised him almost from infancy) and stepped back, allowing Peter to haul himself up.

She shrugged her narrow shoulders. "Who needs doctors and their inflated bills anyway?" she scoffed. "I'll take you home, get you patched up just fine myself. Heaven knows your Uncle Ben got into enough scrapes when he was a young man, and I was always there for him. Just as I'll always be here for you, Peter."

They emerged into the sunlight. New York passersby didn't even afford the disheveled youth a glance. Peter looked at Aunt May, and even though the motion hurt his mouth, he couldn't help but smile. This old, frail woman saying that she would always be there to help him and lend him support.

Somehow he had the funny feeling that she might very well be capable of it. A flapper in her glory days, someone whose gentle exterior belied a possibly sordid past . . . if there was anyone capable of outliving Peter Parker, then his aunt (and by extension, his uncle) seemed more than capable.

Especially if he kept going as he had been.

As onlookers watched in amazement, the metal arms worked in perfect unison. The radioactive isotopes were gently slid back into place with movements as precise and deft as if they were being handled by human hands.

Doctor Otto Octavius was feeling rather pleased with himself. Not that the scientist would have let any indication of his private amusement show to anyone else.

He was odd looking, to put it mildly. He was relatively short, and rather stocky. His eyes being light sensitive, he wore thick prescription sunglasses. His black/brown hair was in a sort of bowl cut, which prompted some of his students at Empire State University to nickname him "Moe," after the popular Stooge. But it was his breakthrough in the creation of Waldos—mechanical arms used to handle radioactive material while protected by shielding—that had caused him to acquire the more widely bandied nickname of Dr. Octopus ("Doc Ock," to the overly familiar). At first the name had annoyed him, but after consideration—and the inherent recognition of his achievement—he grudgingly became somewhat enamored of it. "Dr. Octopus" it had become.

At that moment he was making use of the device that had led to his new designation. Wrapped around his midsection was a metal bracket with dials and control mechanisms that he handled so expertly he barely had to give them any thought. Extending from the bracket, two on either side, were the metal arms. Heavy shielding separated the far ends of the arms from Octopus. Each of those far ends had claw-like attachments which were strong enough to crush bones, but by the same token, could be manipulated gently enough to thread a needle.

The final isotopes replaced, Doc Ock sighed slightly, as he always did when it came time to disengage himself from his favorite "toy." He undid the fastenings and stepped out of the bracket.

"Amazing," a voice murmured from behind him.

He turned to face the dean of science for Empire State University, a fairly affable man named Henry Martin who, by the unfortunate happenstance of his job title, had to go through his scholastic career bearing the inauspicious tag of Dean Martin. Amused students alternated between singing "That's Amore" whenever he was in earshot, or else calling out "Hey Deeeaaan" in raucous imitation of Jerry Lewis. Neither tactic endeared the student body of E.S.U. to him, and he couldn't wait to finally hit an incoming generation of students who'd never heard of the damned actor/singer.

"You've seen me at work before, Dean," replied Octavius mildly.

"True, Otto, but you never fail to impress. I swear, sometimes I think you operate those things by thought alone."

Octavius nodded thoughtfully. "That would certainly be

the next step, wouldn't it? As soon as I finish on the current project . . ."

Dean Martin tried to repress a smile. "The antigravity business again? Otto . . . let's not go over that again."

"I'm telling you, Dean, that you're being far too dismissive. By severing the gravimetric lines—"

Martin waved impatiently. "Look, Otto, I'm not ruling out that you might be on the edge of a breakthrough, all right? With you, anything is possible. I freely admit that. What I want to know is, have you given any thought to my request?"

"The demonstration?" Octavius made a rude noise. "Am I some sort of a sideshow freak that you should invite people in and put me on display?"

"Otto, be reasonable," said Martin. "Our teaching demands of you have been incredibly small . . . much less so than any other teacher or researcher on campus. Do us this, though. Enrollment has been down, and by opening up a demonstration to high schoolers who are considering what college to go to . . ."

"The long and short of it," said Octavius patiently, "is that you want me to be the center attraction of a science fiction dog-and-pony show. Come to E.S.U. and see—"

"—the incredible brilliance of men like Doctor Otto Octavius," Martin said quickly. Dropping his voice in an almost seductive air, he said, "Is that so bad, really? Do you deserve any less?"

Octavius stroked his chubby chin thoughtfully for a moment. "When you put it that way . . ."

"It's the only way *to* put it, Otto," said Martin. "Look . . . instead of dragging on discussions, let's just do it. I can have it scheduled for two days from now. What do you say?''

Octavius sighed with the air of a man greatly put upon, having to tolerate the demands and needs of far inferior beings. Then he made an impatient wave. "Fine. Whatever you say. But," he raised a warning finger, "I will take this opportunity to discuss my work in antigravity. I warn you now, so you won't complain about filling their little mutton-heads with 'wild speculations.' "

"If it's good enough for you, Otto, it's good enough for me," said Dean Martin. Privately he figured, What the hell. Anti-grav gimmicks. The ignorant kids would eat it up.

And as they walked away from the lab area, neither of them noticed the tiny spider that was calmly going about its business spinning a web . . . on the inside of the isotope room . . .

In the corner of her sensibly furnished Forest Hills living room, May Parker swung her broom and brushed away some cobwebs that had clustered toward a corner of the ceiling. A spider scuttled away from the center, and she gave it a solid whack with her broom. She craned her neck slightly to catch a glimpse of it and make certain that it was good and squished, and then she nodded approvingly.

Her husband, Ben, adjusted the color on his brand new 13-inch television screen, and glanced over his shoulder affectionately at his wife of forty-three years. "You sure gave him what-for, May," he said.

She shuddered. "I just can't stand spiders, that's all. Disgusting creatures." She glanced at the clock on the wall and then called upstairs, "Peter! Shouldn't you be on your way?''

That was the most authoritarian May Parker ever got with him. Someone else might have barked, "Peter! You're going to be late for school! Get moving!" Not May, though. A gentle prodding, a nudge, was the most she could muster . . . at least, when it came to Peter.

For her husband, however, she could manage more.

Peter Parker darted down the stairs. He had his books slung over his shoulder. His glasses were still slightly skewed from the altercation the other day, but it was nothing he couldn't live with. He certainly had no intention of telling Aunt May and Uncle Ben that he now needed his glasses repaired. After all, the damage had come about as a result of an attempt to do something nice for him in the first place.

Besides, she seemed busy at the moment.

"Ben," she sighed in exasperation, "how often have we talked about this?"

The target of her ire was not her husband specifically, but rather what he had on the television. It was a wrestling match—two sweaty men, clad in garish tights and outlandish costumes, slamming into each other with such force that their considerable muscles quivered with the impact.

"There's nothing wrong with it, May!" said Ben defensively, as he had so many times before. "They're professionals."

"Professional fakers is more like it," said May. "It's all make-believe, and they're all on the same payroll. Everyone knows that."

"Not true," Ben retorted. "For instance, every Wednesday is open ring night. Anyone can take a shot at the champ and win a thousand dollars! Does that sound fixed to you?"

May saw that Peter was watching the screen fixedly, and

that was all the additional impetus she needed. She moved firmly to the dial and, over her husband's protests, switched to the early morning news. "If you want violence, Ben Parker," she said tartly, "then I guess you'll just have to be satisfied with what you can find of it in the real world, instead of men playacting it for money."

Ben grumbled disconsolately to his nephew, "You understand, don't you, Peter?"

Peter, who didn't, said, "Sure, Uncle Ben."

Ben smiled slightly at that and punched Peter affectionately in the arm. "If I were still a young man, you'd see me in the wrestling ring, Peter. I'm no stranger to a good mixing-it-up, let me tell you. Why, I was quite the specimen in my youth. What do you think got your aunt to take an interest in me, eh?"

"Pity," said May archly. "Just pity. Nothing more." But there was amusement in her eyes, which she quickly covered as she looked at Peter and made an abrupt shooing gesture. That was all that Peter needed to know that he'd best be on his way.

He paused only long enough for his lips to brush Aunt May's cheek. Uncle Ben sat in desultory fashion in front of the TV. On the early morning news program, there was a report about an upcoming peace conference at the United Nations, and Ben was nodding approvingly. "If the governments are finally starting to get themselves together," Ben said, "we might actually have a shot at making it into the next century." He looked up at Peter, who was running out of the kitchen, hurriedly shoving a Nutri-Bar into his shirt pocket for consumption later on. "Our generation's made a muddle of it, Peter. I'm trusting yours to clean up after us. And I have every intention of being around to see it happen.''

"Absolutely, Uncle Ben," said Peter. He ran out the door with a hurried, "Bye!"

He hurried down the sidewalk, and it was at that moment that his glasses slipped precipitously. He tried to skid to a halt and catch himself, but wasn't successful, as the glasses flew off his face.

Then Peter collided with a brick wall.

Unfortunately, this brick wall was mobile, and had a name. A name which was now being shouted by a teenage girl. *"Flash!"* cried out the attractive blonde, whose own name was Liz Allen and whose lot in life, at this particular moment, was to be the slightly unwilling apple of the aforementioned Flash's piglike eye.

Flash's surname was Thompson, and he had taken an instant dislike to Peter Parker from the moment they'd landed in third grade together. Peter quickly became notorious for test scores that blew grade curves to hell and back. When it came to grades, Flash needed all the help he could get, and Peter Parker certainly provided none at all. Thompson was carrot-topped and carrot-brained, having been blessed with the build of a mountain range and roughly the same IQ. (Rumor had it that, upon the moment of his birth, Flash Thompson had high-fived the delivering doctor and walked out of the operating room under his own steam.)

Peter thudded to the ground, having discommoded Flash Thompson only so far as his pride was concerned. Unfortunately, that was pretty far.

On his hands and knees, Peter tried to scoop up his glasses, and then his dismayed ears heard a distinctive crunch as Flash Thompson crushed the plastic lenses underfoot. He chuckled in that Neanderthal way that some intellects do, when they are the type that garner amusement from the misfortune of others.

Liz, however, was not amused. "Flash, that was mean!" she told him.

Flash looked at her. She could have started spouting fluent Irdu and not garnered a more bewildered look from the athlete. He cracked a lopsided grin. "Aw, Liz, it was just a joke," said Thompson, which was his usual line. If Flash Thompson had crashed the Hindenberg, his explanation would have been that it was just a joke. "Besides, he banged into me," Thompson added.

"It was an accident, wasn't it, Peter?" asked Liz.

Peter nodded. What he would really have liked to do was leap to his feet and slug Flash so hard that it knocked him silly for a week. Unfortunately, the impact would more likely have broken Parker's knuckles and have no effect on Thompson whatsoever. So he contented himself with saying numbly, "Yeah. Just an accident."

"Help him up, Flash."

Flash grunted (which, for him, constituted witty repartee), grabbed Peter by the forearm and yanked him to his feet as if he weighed nothing. Then he looked sullenly at Liz. "You're always sticking up for Parker the pantywaist. Whose side are you on, anyway?"

"Mine," said Liz primly.

"Well, fine, then why don't you walk to school with *him* then?" retorted Flash, apparently unaware that his response was something of a nonsequitur. The reason, of course, was that he hadn't really paid attention to what Liz had said. Feeling friendless, he decided to have a snit, and stalked away down the sidewalk to school so that he could commiserate over the unfairness of a world where useless brains like Peter Parker existed in order to make normal guys feel dumb.

"I'm sorry, Peter. Are you okay?" She was dusting off the front of his sweater vest.

Peter was mildly conflicted. On the one hand, he hated Liz Allen fussing over him. On the other hand . . . he kind of liked it. He stopped his knee-jerk response of "I feel fine" and said, instead, "Well, my head sort of hurts."

"Ohhh! How's this?" She reached up and rubbed his temples gently.

"Feels great," he said, and that was certainly no exaggeration.

From two blocks away, Flash Thompson glanced over his shoulder, and his beetle brow furrowed even more.

Even from that distance, Liz could see the jealousy on his face. And wouldn't it be just delightful to teach him a lesson, just to show him that pushing people around was not acceptable behavior?

"Peter," she said, as they slowly started toward school, "tell me . . . what do you do for fun?"

Peter Parker's jaw sagged so profoundly in astonishment that he almost tripped over it.

The *Daily Bugle* routinely had two meetings to discuss how the news day was shaping up. They were overseen by J. Jonah Jameson, the man who was nominally the publisher but spent much more time in the regular pursuit of the other job he'd kept for himself, editor in chief. His staffers were assembled, seated or standing, leaning against walls, consulting notepads or scraps of paper on clipboards.

Jameson—privately known to some as Old Brillo Head—had bristling steel gray hair that was whitening at the temples. He also had the kind of mustache that Adolf Hitler had once sported. Most other males on the face of the planet had shaved theirs once Hitler had achieved his infamy. Jameson, however, felt no need to allow his own sartorial preferences to be usurped. The mustache stayed.

A cigar was clenched, as always, between his yellowing teeth.

As publisher, Jameson's bottom line was financial. As editor in chief, his bottom line was the news. Both were his mistresses, and he loved them equally. He had ink in his veins and money on his brains.

"Give me good news," he told his staffers. This didn't mean "good" news, per se. It meant stories that would appeal to the lowest common denominator and, hence, the highest possible sales figures.

The science editor, Brad Newman, said, "Science demonstration. Doctor Octavius—Doc Octopus, they call him. Demonstrating an antigravity device."

"Science. Dry as dust. Nothing personal, Newman," said Jameson. "Send a shutterbug down there; those nutty metal arms are worth a shot. Forget it otherwise unless the crazy device really works and he lifts a building or something. Metro . . . anything?"

Joe Robertson, the city editor, said, "Big news is the peace summit."

" 'Peace.' " Jameson chomped furiously on his cigar. "Peace doesn't sell papers. Give me a fresh angle. Something people can grumble about."

Robertson rubbed the top of his short-cropped, white

curly hair. He sighed. "We could focus on the cost to the taxpayers."

Jameson looked interested. "Yeah?"

Max Frey, the international editor, pointed a pencil at Robertson. "You mean like overtime for cops? That kind of thing?"

"Security's always a nightmare with these sorts of things. Costs will be through the roof."

"Run with it," said Jameson. He was grinning, which always meant problems for someone. "I want hard numbers, and squirming officials."

Jameson's secretary, who was taking notes, mumbled something. Jameson's head snapped around. "What was that, Miss Brant?"

Betty Brant looked up, like a deer caught in headlights. "The . . . uh . . . I said, 'The Price of Peace.' I thought that would make a good headline. I'm sorry." She looked down.

Jameson nodded thoughtfully. "The Price of Peace. I like it."

Betty smiled.

Joe Robertson sighed. He wondered if there was anything that Jameson wouldn't do for a headline. And he wondered why he was even bothering to wonder.

"A science exhibit?"

Peter squinted, to see if Liz Allen's expression matched the disbelief in her voice. Sadly, it did. Still, the subject had been broached, and he couldn't exactly back down. He cleared his throat and said, "Well . . . yes. A science exhibit, at E.S.U. Not an exhibit, actually. A demonstration."

They were standing in a corridor of the high school, near Liz's locker. Liz pulled the books for that night's homework out of her locker and dropped them into her backpack. She did so at random, since she hadn't paid attention to what the day's assignments were. "Couldn't we just, like, go to a mall, or maybe . . . you know . . . hang out?"

Peter stared at her as if she'd sprung a third eye. "'Hang out?' Just stand around? Not accomplish anything?"

"Well . . . yeah," she said brightly.

"But . . . but why?"

She was about to answer, but suddenly her attitude seemed to shift. Very quickly, she said, "Um, look, Peter . . . maybe some other time, okay?" She closed the locker door with a clang and darted away.

At first he didn't understand why . . . but then some sixth sense made him turn and glance over his shoulder. Sure enough, standing nearby, snickering, was Flash Thompson. Flash shook his head and walked away without saying anything. He didn't have to. The message was clear, even to the nearsighted Peter Parker.

He sighed, knowing he had blown it, not entirely sure how, or what he should have done differently. Then he headed out to the science exhibit.

The spider was quite small, and extremely curious for such a minuscule creature.

The glowing warmth of the radioactive isotopes had prompted the insect to give the materials a closer look. It had crawled closer and closer, leaving the relative safety of its web, attracted for reasons it could not even begin to comprehend. On its most basic, fundamental level, it might have wondered whether the radiant green material might be some sort of sustenance. A change from the usual regimen of flies and such.

The gleaming metal arms of Dr. Octopus withdrew the isotope from the protective cannister, heedless of the tiny creature's presence. Nor was Octavius particularly heeding of the students who were seated nearby, like mindless fans at a football game. Dean Martin was droning on and on about Doctor Octavius's scientific know-how, and the various opportunities for learning and growth that existed at Empire State University.

What an absurd situation to be in. A scientist of his intellect, serving as a shill to induce brainless students to waste their money attending E.S.U. A waste because ultimately they would not remember or understand most of what they learned. Furthermore, the degree they believed would be their passport to riches would, ultimately, avail them nothing. Thousands of students would be foisted onto the job market with identical degrees. Thousands of faceless drones, each indistinguishable from the other.

Pathetic. All of them.

Distracted as he was, Doc Ock kept the isotope out of its protective covering for seconds longer than he ordinarily would have. Since the isotope was separated by heavy shielding from Octopus, and the onlookers, there was no harmful effect from the radiation.

The spider, however, was not separated.

Nor was it spared.

The radiation suffused the arachnid. The creature staggered, not understanding the mutating forces that permeated every cell of its structure. It had lowered itself down toward the isotope on a web line, but now it was so disconcerted that it slipped off the web line and landed on the nearest available surface.

Which just happened to be an arm of Dr. Octopus.

There was a tiny space in the juncture where the claw grips were joined with the ends of the arms, and it was into that juncture that the spider now crawled. Its only concern at that point was to try and put as much distance as possible between itself and the odd glowing object which had filled the creature with a distant burning sensation.

The spider skittered through the interior of the arm, dodging between the whirring servos that operated the tentacles. The spider was, naturally, unable to fully understand that it had changed. That it was moving with far greater speed or surety than it had ever known before. It didn't care about any of that. All that mattered was the fundamental, instinctive desire for self-preservation.

Peter Parker watched, squinted, then jotted down a few notes on a pad of paper.

He was marvelling at the dexterity and confidence with which Doctor Octavius was manipulating the arms, but that had only captured part of his attention. He was also turning over in his mind the notion that he might be able to turn this outing into something more than a visit to a science demonstration. Perhaps he could write it up as an article or something for the *Daily Bugle*.

What had set his thoughts in that direction was the presence of a photographer wearing a "Press" tag that identified him as Lance Bannon of the *Daily Bugle*. Bannon was clicking away. Peter glanced around but wasn't able to make out anyone else from the *Bugle*, which meant they thought the story was important enough for photo coverage, but they couldn't spare a reporter. Maybe the *Bugle* was shorthanded. Maybe they could use the help.

Peter could definitely make use of the money that such freelancing would bring in.

He also admitted to a bit of smug satisfaction. He envisioned Liz Allen reading the newspaper, seeing his byline, and his responding with some nonchalant comment such as "Why yes, of course I work for the *Bugle*. Did I forget to tell you? I was *covering* that science expo. Maybe you'll want to come along with me on my next news assignment. I could even quote you, get your name in the paper . . . if you're the type who gets excited about that sort of thing, of course."

Peter suspected that she was.

He was so distracted by his momentary reverie that he didn't even hear Octopus grunt, as if startled. Then a quick movement of one of Octopus's arms caught the corner of his eye.

That was when something bit him.

Dr. Octopus was at a delicate moment in his maneuvering, a fact which Dean Martin made certain to impress upon the crowd.

"By employing the isotope to the previously existing compound," Martin was saying, "Doctor Octavius is hoping to provide technology that is actually capable of severing the gravimetric bonds that—"

"You mean antigravity?" asked one student, making no attempt to hide his skepticism.

Octavius did not pay heed to the annoying student. He was busy in his work, because now would not be the appropriate time for a mishap. In fact, just to be absolutely safe,

Octavius looked down at the control dials of his chest plate, figuring that he would manipulate them manually.

That was when the spider emerged from his chest plate and start to crawl along his upper left tentacle.

Doctor Otto Octavius hated spiders.

Not fear, for there was nothing that Doc Ock feared. But hated. Disgusting, crawling things whose every movement filled Octavius with loathing for no reason that he could quite articulate. But there was no need for him to explain himself. He was, after all, Otto Octavius.

And he hated spiders. Loathed them. Despised them.

Casually, but with a sort of grim satisfaction, Octopus made a quick snap of the tentacle and the spider flew off.

The lapse was unfortunate, however, because in making that gesture with his tentacle, Octopus momentarily forgot about the isotope that he was handling.

At the far end of the tentacle, behind the protective shielding, the isotope slipped out of the gripper claw and crashed to the floor.

"Oops," said Dr. Octopus.

The spider, hot, confused and—although it didn't quite realize it—in its death throes, sailed through the air and landed on the hand of a human.

If such a fundamentally simple creature could ever have a sense of its impending mortality, then the spider had one at that moment. Its relatively brief life span had just been further truncated, and somehow the spider perceived that. Perhaps there was even a realization that humans had somehow been responsible for its imminent demise.

That being the case, something as close as possible to rage that the creature could muster filled its irradiated and mutating body. The spider lashed out, sank its fangs into the nearest being upon whom it could vent its ire.

It was the spider's last act.

In terms of significance, it was fairly impressive.

"Ow!" muttered Peter Parker as he looked down.

There was a spider on his hand. For the briefest of moments, it appeared to have been glowing softly, but Peter thought he might have imagined it. What he had not imagined, however, was the pain the spider had caused him.

The damned thing had bitten him.

Peter snapped his hand at the wrist, and the spider landed on the ground between his feet. The spider had made no effort to get away . . . unsurprisingly, since it had died mere instants after sinking its fangs into Peter Parker.

Then he heard an alarmed squawk from Dean Martin, and the dean was saying, "People . . . we're asking everyone to leave now. There's no serious danger, but safety precautions must be observed." He clapped his hands together. "Quickly! Quickly!"

Peter glanced over at the news photographer. Bannon, apparently realizing that something was going on, tried to push his way closer toward Octopus. Martin interposed himself with his not-inconsiderable bulk.

The students, meantime, knew that something was up. Nor were they fools. When someone handling radioactive material suddenly says, "Oops," that is generally a good time to put some distance between oneself and the person. This the students did, with impressive urgency, almost to the point of a panicked stampede.

Peter Parker wanted to try and move toward the news photographer, to see how he was handling the situation.

But he was swept away in the crush of bodies as near-frantic students poured out of the science exhibit.

And then the floor seemed to tilt around him, and Peter felt a momentary wave of nausea. He staggered back, unable to put any resistance against the crowd. The next thing he knew, he was outside, looking around in confusion.

Having afforded themselves a measure of safety by exiting the building, the students were clustered around outside, milling about, trading speculation as to what was happening inside.

Then Peter felt a second wave of nausea, and this time there was no stopping it. Not wanting to embarrass himself in front of the crowd, he ran across the street and darted down an alleyway to find someplace relatively private where he could be sick.

"Clear out! Evacuate the building!" Dean Martin was shouting.

The radioactive isotope was seeping into the circuitry of Octavius's machine, sending the energy levels leaping to the top of the scales. The shielding still protected against radiation leaks, but the safety it provided was going to be transitory at best.

Dr. Octopus wasn't leaving.

"I can handle this!" he snarled to Martin, manipulating the machine's manual overrides.

Martin yanked at Octavius's arm, and was surprised at the strength in the shorter man. Doc Ock shoved him firmly and Martin stumbled back.

The room was suddenly filled with a warning Klaxon as the machine's final safety overrides failed, eaten away by the radioactive isotope that was running rampant through the machinery.

Doc Ock didn't seem to notice. "I can handle this," he continued to mutter, and Dean Martin abruptly realized that the only thing he was going to accomplish by trying to save Otto Octavius was both of them dying. With a muttered curse, Martin ran out the door, the howl of the alarms ringing in his ears.

Throat raw, a foul taste in his mouth, and confused at the sickness that suddenly raged through him, Peter Parker was by this point blocks away from the E.S.U. Science Center. Then he felt another wave of nausea, and he ran down yet another alley. Finding a "private" spot, he heaved until his stomach was empty. Peter gasped, sucking great lungfuls of air in, and then he stood up.

And felt fine.

He was surprised. Perhaps the last round of vomiting had taken the last of whatever had gotten into him out.

He rubbed his hand where the spider had bitten him. For a moment he had thought that perhaps it had been some sort of poisonous spider. Still, he didn't think so. He was hardly an expert in the field, but this one had just looked like your ordinary garden variety spider.

Nevertheless, if it had indeed injected some sort of toxin into him, well . . . it was certainly gone now. He felt fine.

No. He felt better than fine.

He thumped his chest, invigorated. "I feel great," he said to no one in particular.

"How nice for ya," somebody answered.

He turned, and couldn't believe it.

It was the two guys. The two muggers from the other

day, standing at the entranceway to the alley.

"Aw no," he muttered.

The taller of the two gazed at Peter for a moment, and then recognition crossed his lined face. "Oh yeah!" he said, except it came out sounding like "A-yuh!" He continued, "I remember you. With the old broad."

Peter started to back up, which was a mistake since it was a dead-end alleyway. The two thugs advanced on him.

The shorter-but-wider of the two, sounding almost apologetic, said, "Problem is, we spent all the money. Got any more on ya?"

They didn't wait for him to answer as the taller one came in fast.

The fist was a blur.

The impact, however, was nonexistent because it never reached its target.

Peter brushed aside the punch. A three-year-old kid might as well have thrown it for all that it bothered Peter Parker.

The thug stared at his fist in surprise, as if it had betrayed him.

Peter looked at his own arm in equal astonishment.

This time the thug left nothing to chance, but instead grabbed at Peter.

This move was actually less successful than the previous one.

Peter darted between the thug's outstretched arms and then, operating solely on instinct, smashed a punch straight into the thug's chest since it was the closest place to strike. He'd read once that a good shot to the solar plexus will rock even the most formidable opponent.

The thug shrieked, and Peter heard something crack

beneath the impact. For one giddy, insane moment, the bookish, weak-armed high school senior thought that he had broken one of the guy's ribs.

He was wrong.

He'd broken three.

The thug went down, screeching and clutching his chest, and now true horror surged through Peter Parker, because he was not aggressive, not warlike, and not at all sure what he was doing. He didn't have time to think, though, because the second of the two thugs came at him. The second was the more vicious, and the more combat-experienced.

He was also the more fortunate, because there was an energy flooding through Peter Parker that the teen had only the barest idea how to control.

Peter drove a clumsy uppercut to his opponent's chin.

If Peter had been of a more fearsome disposition . . . if he had been the type to rejoice in the pain of others . . . if, God help them, he had been homicidal, or had been a slower learner in terms of regulating his strength . . . then his attacker's head would likely have landed somewhere in the vicinity of the Verrazano Narrows toll plaza.

As it was, the guy spun like a top, and was unconscious long before he hit the ground.

Peter stood over him for a moment. He felt empowered, in a manner beyond merely the physical strength that he seemed to have acquired as if by magic. He moved toward the first man, who was moaning on the ground.

He spoke in a voice that didn't sound like his own. It was tougher, more confident . . . even a bit snide.

"Sure you haven't got any of that money left?" he asked.

Without a word the mugger shoved a hand into his

jacket pocket, and pulled out some crumbled bills. It was his aunt's, all right. It was still tucked into the money clip that Ben had given her on their twentieth anniversary, just as it had been when the two thugs had victimized May and her nephew.

Neither of them would be in shape to do much victimizing for a while, however. As soon as he had forked over the money to Peter, the thug released his tenuous hold on consciousness and passed out.

Peter looked from one to the other. Now that the pressure, the "high" of the moment, was gone, confusion and uncertainty was settling back into its customary home in the Parker psyche. He stumbled out from the alleyway. He looked around, trying to figure out what to do, and then he spotted a pay phone. Quickly he went to it, punched in "911," and reported that an ambulance was going to be required.

Then, without a backward glance, he darted down the street.

That was when, from blocks away, he heard an explosion.

"Everyone get back!" Dean Martin was shouting. "The authorities have been called!" Indeed they had; not only had he phoned the fire department and the police, but also the Nuclear Safety Commission. Because if there were radioactive materials running rampant, the fire department wasn't equipped to deal with it.

And that was when the upper section of the E.S.U. science center blew.

People ran, covering their heads as debris rained down. In the crowd, Lance Bannon tried to get photographs, but he was having trouble getting any sort of angle where the events would be clear.

Half a dozen E.S.U. students, who had never liked Dr. Octopus, applauded.

Confused and suddenly disoriented once again, Peter Parker started down the street.

His thoughts were still racing. Where had that strength come from? How had he suddenly been able to dispatch those muggers with such ease? What was this bizarre sensation running through him, that on the one hand made him feel as if he could conquer the world, and on the other hand scared the daylights out of him?

He started to cross the street, paying no heed whatsoever to the world around him. He was in such shock over what had happened that he was having difficulty absorbing it all.

As a result, the warning siren from the racing police car didn't make an impression on him, nor did the sound of screeching tires as the black and white car, on its way to crowd control at E.S.U., whipped around the corner.

But something else warned him. There was a buzzing sensation in the back of his head that sent him into action before he had the time to consciously assess the information being provided him.

He moved instinctively and immediately, and he had to because the cop car was practically right on top of him.

Peter Parker leaped, so fast, so far, that he had disappeared from the cop car's path before his presence had fully registered on the driver or his partner. The cop at the wheel blinked, certain that there had been some sort of blur in front of them. But there was nothing there now.

Nor was there the sickening thud of the car hitting or running over a body. Clearly everything was fine.

The police car continued on its way. And neither of the cops in the car happened to glance to their right, about forty feet up in the air. There was no reason that they should have.

If they *had*, though, they would have seen Peter Parker clinging to the side of the building.

His fingers were not seeking purchase in the brick work, or seeking out a ledge. He just hung there, adhering by the power of his fingers alone.

Peter looked down.

Forty feet below, the sidewalk beckoned to him. If he could have attributed human emotions to inanimate concrete, he would have said that the ground seemed rather annoyed that he was defying gravity.

Part of him wanted to immediately reclaim the safety of the ground; to forget what had happened to him, the things that he found himself doing. But, at his core, Peter Parker was a scientist. And a scientist, when faced with unknown circumstances, has an irresistible urge to explore them.

Not feeling brave enough to break contact with the wall, Peter slid his right hand up it. His shoes provided no security at all. Whatever was giving him this ability, it wasn't going through the thick soles of his loafers.

You'll need thinner material to cover your feet, something in his mind told him. And then something else asked, with legitimate curiosity, *Need it for what?*

He told his collective mind to shut up, since he was otherwise occupied.

At this point, he didn't need his feet, really. The

strength in his arms was such that he was able to pull himself up with that alone.

He clambered up the side of the building on his hands and knees, cautiously, as if he were moving along the surface of an iced-over pond. He was not permitting himself to address the possibility that whatever had happened to him might "un-happen" at any moment, and the fall he faced would be terminal.

With each moment he became more and more confident, moving faster and faster. Within seconds he had reached the flat rooftop.

"The spider," he whispered, although there was no one around to hear. "The spider bite . . . that must have done it somehow. It . . . it must have been affected by some sort of radiation at the science exhibit . . ."

That reminded him.

He looked off into the distance. He felt only the mildest surprise that his eyes focused perfectly on the smoke billowing from the E.S.U. science center. Why shouldn't his vision have cleared up? On a day when two thugs became his punching bags and a building turned into his personal jungle gym . . . well, heck, why *shouldn't* he suddenly discover he no longer had a need for glasses? That was par for the course, wasn't it?

He wanted to head back to the science center to see what had happened. But already police were cordoning off the street, stopping pedestrians, telling them that no one was being allowed around the area.

Unsurprisingly, no blockades had been erected on the rooftops of the city.

Peter glanced over to the next building. A gap of twenty feet separated him.

He took off his shoes, intertwined the laces, and looped them through his belt. He flexed his toes, knowing instinctively that they possessed the same adhesive power that his fingers did.

He did a few squat thrusts, the type that in gym class had always left him breathless. Now he just felt exhilarated.

Then he ran, his quick sure strides eating up distance. As he approached the edge of the roof, he leaped, not sure how to judge the distance. For one brief moment he thought perhaps his newfound confidence might also be the end of him.

He cleared the twenty feet and kept going, landing so far over on the next roof that he almost skidded off the far side. He repositioned himself, got ready, than ran and jumped again to the next roof, and the one after that.

Minutes later he had reached the area of Empire State University. He gasped in amazement as he saw the smoking ruins where, only a short time ago (and yet, in many ways, a lifetime ago) he had been attending the science exhibit.

Police were pushing people back, keeping them away. With his new and improved vision, Peter could see a frustrated Lance Bannon arguing with the cops. Bannon had just been climbing a tree to try and get some sort of a decent angle, and was being yanked downward by a short-tempered police officer.

Peter felt the money clip with the money still lodged in his pocket. Then he glanced down.

At the bottom of the building he was standing on, there was a drugstore.

A plan was already forming in his mind. It meant using Aunt May's money, but he quickly rationalized that she had already figured she'd never see it again anyway. Besides, if this worked, he would be able to pay her back with interest.

Moments later he was standing in front of the cashier at the drugstore. She was looking past him out the window. "What happened over there?" she asked. "At the university? Something not good, I think."

"Definitely," said Peter, not up for small talk. He pointed at a "sure-shot" camera with a simple zoom lens. "One of those, please. And some film."

"Comes with film," she said. "Anything else?"

He pictured himself dashing back up a wall, in an area crawling with cops who might spot him this time. His luck couldn't hold out forever.

"Panty hose," he said.

"What size?" she asked.

"Huh?"

"Who are they for?" she said patiently.

"Me," Peter Parker said.

To her credit, the cashier said nothing.

Dr. Octopus was alive, to the surprise of all concerned. He was being carted out on a stretcher, and it was at that point that Dean Martin became rather alarmed. Because Octopus's metal arms were still attached to him. And they were moving, twisting and writhing as if in response to the pain that he was enduring.

His hands were nowhere near the dials on his control panel. And then, to his horror, Martin noticed that there were areas of Octavius's body where the edge of the metal plating actually seemed to have *fused* with his flesh. It was all Martin could do to choke down the gagging reflex.

Nevertheless he ran alongside the stretcher as it was

moved out toward the ambulance. Octopus's skin was covered with ash. He was muttering, "Who did it . . . who . . ."

"You'll be all right, Otto," Martin kept saying.

"Sabotaged . . . had to be . . ." said Octavius. "Should have been able to stop it . . . should have . . . couldn't have been my fault . . . must have been sabotaged . . ." His voice was weak, and he sounded delirious.

"We'll be looking into it," said Martin.

Octavius shook his head, and looked away from Martin.

All eyes in the immediate area were focused on Dr. Octopus and the freakish nature of his accident. Consequently, no one was looking where Octopus himself was gazing. He was looking at a building across the way. On the side of the building was a man, clinging as if by magic.

Octopus squinted, unsure that his eyes weren't lying to him.

It was hard to make out anything, but the man seemed to be aiming something at him. Yes . . . a camera. He was taking his picture. And then the man seemed to become aware that Octopus was looking right at him. Apparently unnerved, the man lowered his camera.

He had no face. Just flesh.

Then he turned his back and climbed up the side of the building like a human spider.

Spider . . .

In his fevered, semi-coherent mind, Octopus made a tortured connection. There had been a spider at the exhibit. And now there was some sort of . . . of faceless spider man outside, waiting for him, looking down at him, chortling at him.

"The spider man," murmured Octopus, his head snapping around. "He and his friends . . . they did this . . . they did . . ."

He kept muttering that all the way to the hospital.

"It's urgent that I see him!" Peter Parker told the guard in the *Daily Bugle* lobby.

The guard, a heavyset man with the rather unforgiving name of "Stone" etched on his nameplate, slowly shook his head.

"I've got photos they'll want to see," Peter said, waving his camera. "And they've gotta have deadlines and stuff, right?"

"Yeah. They've got deadlines and stuff. What they don't have is time for some high school kid who thinks he's a photographer," said Stone. "Now *scram!*"

Peter bit his lower lip. He could always just climb the side of the building and try to sneak in. But he had the mental image of a newspaper crawling with reporters at every turn . . . and a reporter who caught a glimpse of him entering through a 35th story window would give him all sorts of publicity that he wasn't sure he was ready for.

The nervous and flighty student that Peter Parker had been would have been out the door by this point. But the new sense of puissance granted him by the miracle of the spider's bite was already working changes in his personality.

Plus, he felt driven by his own personal deadline: his speed and sky-high detour had gotten him back to the *Bugle* before the official photographer could make it back. If he had a hope of getting his own material looked at, it was going to have to be done very, very soon.

He raised his voice so that it ricocheted off the marble walls of the lobby. "Fine," he said forcefully. "That's your call, then. I'll bring these over to the *Daily Globe,* and when J. Jonah Jameson is furious that the *Globe* has shots the *Bugle* doesn't, why then—"

For just a second he ran out of steam, and then his gaze caught an attractive brunette woman who had paused by the elevators, apparently lending a curious ear to Peter's declaration.

He pointed at her and said, "Miss! Excuse me! Do you ever see Mr. Jameson?" He knew Jameson's name because, well, everyone in town knew Jameson's name. The publisher was inextricably linked with his newspaper in the public eye, and to know one was to know the other.

The young woman smiled wanly. "Every now and then," she said.

"Well, please let him know that Stone here just guaranteed that the *Daily Globe* is going to have better shots of the explosion out at Empire State University's science center than you will."

Her gaze flickered from the young man to the guard, who suddenly seemed to have developed a thin bead of sweat on his upper lip, and then back to the young man.

"Tony," she said the guard, "how about I take responsibility for him, okay?" She wasn't waiting for the guard's approval, but was already sliding her hand around the crook of Peter's elbow.

The guard was aware that he had lost control of the situation, and actually seemed a bit relieved. "Whatever you say, Miss Brant."

"First name is Betty," she told Peter. "Betty Brant. And you are . . . ?"

"Peter Parker." He was finding it hard to tear his attention away from her smile, which seemed dazzling and in danger of filling up the elevator that they had just stepped into. Betty Brant pushed a button, the doors closed, and the elevator started up. "Uhm, what do you do at the *Bugle*?"

"I'm Mr. Jameson's assistant," she said.

"Oh," was all he could think of to say.

"So let's see the pictures."

He held up the camera.

"They're not developed?"

"No. I, uh, came straight here, and—"

She pursed her lips a moment, and then pushed a button on the elevator control panel that was several floors lower than the first one she'd pushed before. "Okay. We'll stop at the lab first. Get them developed, see if we've got anything. Believe me . . . you don't want to go to Mr. Jameson if you have nothing."

"Thanks," said Peter gratefully. "Are you this nice to every would-be photographer?"

She shrugged, and that incredible smile of hers widened. "I just have a feeling about you, that's all."

J. Jonah Jameson expertly studied the contact sheets with a magnifying glass. Standing in the doorway, Peter Parker didn't know what to do with his hands. He tried folding his arms, then he shoved his hands in his pockets, then he crossed them again.

Jameson's cigar travelled from one side of his mouth to the other as if it had decided, on its own, to embark on the trip.

Betty was standing just outside. Then Peter looked up as a tall, sturdily built, white-haired black man elbowed his way in. " 'Scuse me, son," he said to Parker, then turned to Jameson. "Bannon's here. He's got photos from the E.S.U. explosion. The scientist, Octavius, is still in surgery."

"Bannon's here, huh? Send him in, Robbie."

Bannon entered, his camera swinging from around his neck. He tossed the contact sheet onto Jameson's desk, glancing briefly and with not much interest at Parker. Jameson quickly skimmed Bannon's sheet.

"These stink," he said succinctly.

"The shots before the explosion are good," replied Bannon.

"The shots before the explosion aren't news," Jameson shot back. "They're filler. When this was just a filler story, they were fine. Now it's a news story, and they stink."

"The cops weren't letting anyone get good shots."

"Don't whine at me, Bannon. You're annoying when you whine. Also, the cops didn't seem to impede this young man."

This time Bannon looked more closely at Peter Parker. He didn't say anything, though. Just glared.

"Meet . . ." He paused and frowned. "What'd you say your name was again, kid?"

"Peter Parker, sir."

"Bannon, this is Peter Parker, future has-been. Parker, this is Lance Bannon, future never-was."

Lance Bannon's jaw worked back and forth as if he were chewing on gravel, but no words came out. Then he stormed out the door. Jameson ignored him, intent on the photos.

"Your ability to make people feel good about themselves continues unabated," said the one Jameson had called "Robbie."

"Bannon was getting too cocky and too lazy. That's a

dangerous combination. He had it coming," he said without looking up, and then continued, "Parker, this is Joe Robertson, my city editor. He'll work with you to get you set up on our voucher system."

Robertson extended a hand. "Folks call me Robbie."

"Pleased to meet you, Robbie." It was an odd sensation for Peter. He had never addressed any man over the age of thirty in any way other than his surname preceded by "Mister."

Robertson grunted as Peter shook his hand. "Some grip you got there, son."

"Sorry," said Peter, easing up automatically and mentally chewing himself out for letting himself get carried away.

"You didn't take these out a window," said Jameson suddenly. "At first I presumed you did, but now I see the angle's not right. Not for that building, and I know that building because the *Bugle* used to have an office there. You took these from right near the building corner. But it's not so high up that you were on the roof. What'd you do, climb out on the ledge?"

Peter wasn't the world's best liar, and he certainly didn't want to try and carry off a lie in front of a newspaper publisher and his city editor. They ate far more experienced liars than he for breakfast. So he just shrugged and said, "I did what I had to in order to get the photos."

Of course, what that meant in his case was pull panty hose over his head, scale the building, and squeeze off as many shots as he could. It had gone amazingly smoothly, all things considered. Although that moment when Otto Octavius seemed to be looking right in his direction—almost, it seemed, right into his masked eyes—Peter had felt extremely disconcerted.

Jameson nodded approvingly. But then he demanded, "What the hell kind of camera did you use? Certainly not one with a professional telephoto lens. This looks like something that was taken with a camera you bought in a drug store."

Suddenly Peter felt nervous. "I thought you liked them."

"I like the angle, and I like the resourcefulness it took. At least you had the brains to use 35 millimeter. Robbie, get Parker his check immediately, and a check cashing card. Make sure the check contains an advance against his next work for us as well. I want him to have some money quickly so that he can buy a decent camera, and enough money that he can get all the proper attachments."

"Thanks, Mr. Jameson!" said Peter eagerly. "That's—that's very generous of you—"

"Generous! *Generous!?*" thundered Jameson, thudding his fist so hard on the desk that the phone jangled. He grabbed the receiver and barked "Hello!" before realizing that there was no one there. He hung up again, muttered a curse about the phone system, and then turned his piercing gaze back on Parker. Then he did something that chilled Peter to the bone: he smiled.

"Parker . . . we need to come to an *understanding* up front. Are you listening? Because this is very important. Get this straight, Parker: I'm not generous. I'm not your mommy. I'm not a sweetheart, a softy, a philanthropist, a loan company, a confidant, a shoulder to cry on, a father confessor, a Dutch uncle, a maiden aunt, a sob sister, or . . . God forbid . . . a nice guy. I don't care about you. It's nothing personal. I don't care about Joe Robertson, and he's been my right arm for years. Miss Brant is the sweetest person in the newsroom, and I don't care about her either. I'm the most abusive boss she's ever had. That *anyone's* ever had. Isn't that right, Miss Brant?''

"Yes, sir. You're the pits," said Betty gamely.

"Damned right," Jonah nodded. "No one can ever bring me up on charges of discrimination or sexual harassment, because I harass everyone, regardless of race, color, creed, gender, or national origin. And it's all because the only thing I care about in the world is this newspaper. That's it. Nothing else. Zero. Zip. Nada. And getting you some decent equipment will serve two purposes. First, it will get better pictures for my paper. And second, it will give you a feeling of indebtedness, which means you won't play games like, say, going crosstown to those dopes at the *Globe* and trying to play them against me. Because you're one of those types who develops loyalties to people, aren't you?''

"Uh . . . I guess, yessir," stammered Peter.

"Shut up, Parker, I was speaking rhetorically. You see, Parker, I've targeted a weakness in you, and if there's a weakness, then I'll exploit it. The fact that I know that weakness is there means that I can tell you that you should, in fact, never develop loyalty to people. People will betray you. Every time. No exception. Sooner or later, they disappoint you. I can tell you this with impunity because I know you'll ignore it. The fact is, Parker, that these four walls and the printing press downstairs, they don't ever let me down. I'm good to them, they're good to me. And you're going to be good to them, and you're going to be good to me, Parker." He leaned forward, his face almost in Peter's, his mustache bristling. *"You know why?"*

In a very small voice, Peter said, "Because I'm intimidated by you?"

Jonah clapped him on the shoulder. "*Now* we have an *understanding.* Welcome to the *Bugle* family. Now get your ass out of my office."

Peter got it out.

At St. Joseph's hospital, Doctor Sean Flynn was heading toward the room of Doctor Otto Octavius. He was not looking forward to giving the Doctor the news . . . namely that the tentacles, at this point, were not removable. That somehow the combination of the explosion, the radiation, and who knew what other elements, had definitely fused the control panel to Octavius's body. Perhaps, down the road, extensive plastic surgery could do the job. But the short term was not promising.

Then Flynn heard a crash.

He had been walking slowly and calmly down the corridor, but now he picked up the pace, because the crash had come from Octavius's room. It had been very loud, very pronounced, and the floor under Flynn had shaken when the noise had been made.

He threw open the door to the recovery room in which Octavius had been lying after his operation.

Dr. Octopus was gone.

Along with the far wall.

A steady breeze was blowing in, and Dr. Octopus was nowhere in sight.

In the quiet Forest Hills home, May Parker called up the stairs, "Peter! What are you up to, dear?"

"Just stuff, Aunt May," Peter called back down.

"That's nice," said May. She didn't have to add that he should be sure to get his homework done, since Peter was always conscientious about such things.

She had no idea that, at that moment, homework was the furthest thing from Peter's mind.

She also had no idea that Peter had entered the house twice. The first time had been by scaling the wall outside his bedroom, since he had no desire to answer his aunt's inevitable questions when he came in toting shopping bags filled not only with top flight camera equipment, but also a blue bodysuit, red cloth, sewing equipment, plus some assorted hardware.

He had stashed the bags in his bedroom and was about to clamber back out the window when something made him pull back. A tingling, like ants congregating around his cerebral cortex, and it prevented him from exiting before he fully understood why. He peered out cautiously and saw two women passing by on the sidewalk. "Whewww," he said, pleased at the luck. If he climbed out the window when they were happening by, they would have spotted him for sure.

Then he realized that it was more than luck. Somehow he seemed to have acquired a sort of internal warning device, a type of accelerated sixth sense. That, along with the other remarkable changes that the bite of the radioactive spider had wrought.

He just hoped that leukemia wasn't going to be another of them.

No.

No, he refused to think about that, or deal with that. Not even the notoriously lousy Parker luck could bring such incredible, miraculous happpenstance to his life . . . and then poison his blood to boot. It made no sense, and he would not dwell on it any further.

The tingling in his head was gone. Nevertheless he waited until his eyes were satisfied that no one was around. Then, noiselessly, he went down the way he 'd gone up. He dusted himself off, entered the house through the more mundane front door, and tried to act as normal as possible . . . all things considered.

Between his vastly improved eye-hand coordination, and the unnatural speed he'd acquired, the work went quickly. He laced black threads through the red cloth, intersecting vertically and horizontally. That took the longest. After that, it was short work to cut the material and attach it to the blue bodysuit.

The mask took him a bit longer, but not much. Form fitting, to be sure, but he was concerned about the eye holes. He stared into the mirror, and somehow there was nothing about his eyes that seemed likely to strike terror into anyone. Not to mention the fact that he was still rather nervous about what he was doing, and he doubted he'd be able to hide any fear reflected in his eyes . . .

Reflected. That had been the key.

He'd picked up some mylar at the same store where his uncle had once purchased virtually the only thing that Peter cared about: his microscope. The mylar was silvery on one side, flat and unburnished on the other. He could see out, whereas others could not see in. Within minutes he had sliced out wedge-shaped pieces and fitted them into the grooves from which he was constructing the eye pieces.

It took him far less time than he thought. Once the costume was done, he set it aside and started working on the other accoutrement that he had conceived. If he was going to do this thing, he was going to go all the way with it.

The adhesive was a mixture he'd already been working on, but had back-burnered because he'd hit a snag. The intention had been to submit it for a science fair. He'd hoped it would be the sort of thing that would garner attention; perhaps even a Westinghouse scholarship or something that would ease the financial burden when it was time for college.

It was a super adhesive.

The problem he'd run into was that it was only temporary. It stuck like nothing else on the market, but after a couple of hours, it dissolved into wisp-thin threads.

This drawback, however, had no impact on the use to which he intended to put it.

He started work on the launcher, and was already coming up with excuses that he would give his aunt and uncle as to where he would be off to. Probably he'd just tell them that he was out with the kids. Aunt May and Uncle Ben would be thrilled; they told him so often that he should get out and socialize (which he did so rarely) that there was no way they'd challenge him when he said he was doing that very thing.

And he was indeed going out.

But socializing was not on the agenda.

Crusher Hogan had the size, shape, and IQ of a cement mixer. In his line of work, the first two attributes were all that counted.

Hogan stalked the middle of the ring, shouting, waving his arms, hurling taunts at the crowd who was shouting back at him just as eagerly. The Empire Arena was thick with the smell of sweat and machismo.

Even with his microphone, the referee was having trouble making himself heard. He had just done a ten-count on a T-shirt–clad bruiser who'd gotten the snot kicked out of him in under thirty seconds. He was being hauled out of the ring by several of his friends who, the ref suspected, had put him up to it.

Crusher Hogan played to the TV cameras. He flexed his bronzed muscles, and the lights reflected brightly off his shaved head. "Is that the best you wimps can do?!" he shouted. "Some idiot trucker and his pals taking their shots at me? I'm gonna be the reigning champ for all time! No one can beat me! No one can touch me! Y'hear me? Y'hear me, all you wimps? Ya better! Ya better,'cause none of you got a prayer!"

"Come on, now!" called out the ref. "Anyone else looking for their shot at fame and fortune? Who wants to take on Crusher Hogan? Huh? Who's next?"

Unseen by both the ref and Hogan, a gossamer thread suddenly swirled down from the darkened ceiling of the arena. Several people in the crowd saw it, though, and started pointing and shouting. But there was so much yelling going on that neither of the ring's occupants was fully cognizant of what the crowd was trying to tell them.

And then, lowering itself hand over hand until it was dangling a mere six feet above the ring, there came a figure clad in blue and red. Now the crowd was going completely nuts, and finally the ref picked up on the fact that they were signaling for him to turn around. He did so, and gaped.

There was a scrawny runt in a leotard and mask standing in the middle of the ring.

The ref laughed.

"Better get out of the ring, fella, 'fore Crusher notices you and breaks you like a pretzel," he said.

This prompted Crusher Hogan to look back at the ref, and now he saw the newcomer as well. "Where'd *that* come from?" he demanded, chuckling derisively.

"What's your name, pal?" asked the ref, shoving the microphone forward.

"Spider-Man."

The voice sounded youthful, but surprisingly confident. "Well, Spider-Man," said the ref. "You think you can last three minutes with Crusher Hogan and win a thousand dollars?"

Spider-Man looked Hogan up and down. Hogan folded arms across his chest that were the size of jackhammers.

"Does it have to be three minutes?" asked Spider-Man.

It was a slow night, and the ref tried to milk the moment since this kid had clearly started to realize he was in over his head. "That's the rules of the game, pal!" said the ref.

"So you're saying I have to beat up on him for three solid minutes?" Spider-Man actually sounded concerned. "That sounds kind of mean. What if he gives up sooner?"

This prompted a major roar from the crowd. Hogan laughed, a noise like a steam engine. The ref was pleased that this had happened; it had certainly livened up an otherwise predictable evening.

"If the champ cuts it short himself," said the ref, "then you win."

"Ohhh yeah, I'm really gonna give up before you hurt me too much," bellowed Hogan.

"Your concern for your fellow man is touching," said the ref. "Hope, for your sake, that Crusher's feeling as merciful. Okay, boys! To your respective corners!''

Spider-Man moved to the far corner of the ring. His masked face was, of course, unreadable. Hogan presumed that Spider-Man was nervous under the mask.

He was right, in a manner of speaking.

Spider-Man was nervous that he was going to cripple the guy.

The bell clanged, and Crusher Hogan lumbered forward with full confidence. Spider-Man walked toward the center of the ring, his arms akimbo, not striking any particular sort of wrestling stance.

Crusher lunged at him. He was prepared for his diminutive foe to back up, to come forward, or to try and get either to his left or right.

Spider-Man vaulted over his head, somersaulting in mid-air and landing directly behind the astounded wrestler. Hogan whirled, not entirely sure what had just happened. He swung a massive arm, but Spider-Man ducked under it, grabbed him by the back of the knee, and tossed him easily to the mat.

The crowd shouted its approval. There was the great Crusher Hogan, being flipped around like a poker chip by a beanpole about one-eighth his size.

Hogan was on his feet immediately, swinging his arms again and again. This time Spider-Man didn't even bother to somersault. He simply dodged this way and that, making Hogan look as if he were moving in slow motion.

"*Stand still!*" shouted an infuriated Hogan.

Spider-Man shrugged. "Okay," he said.

He stood perfectly still.

Crusher Hogan grabbed him by the waist, with the intention of hoisting him in the air, twirling him around in

Crusher Hogan's famous propeller spin, and then probably climaxing with hurling him right out of the ring.

It was a commendable plan, but did not get much beyond the grabbing part. Because when Hogan endeavored to lift, he found Spider-Man had become the proverbial immovable object.

What he did not know, could not know, was that Spider-Man was adhering to the floor with his feet. No one realized, of course. Instead it simply seemed as if the apparently scrawny, undersized guy in the blue and red tights actually weighed somewhere in the neighborhood of half a ton.

Up until that point, Crusher Hogan had simply assumed that he was dealing with some gymnastic smart-ass. But it was at that particular moment, when he was unable to budge Spider-Man from the spot, that the truth began to seep through to Hogan's pea brain.

He began to understand that there was something extraordinary—even unnatural—about his opponent. For the first time in his professional career, Crusher Hogan knew fear.

He didn't know it for long.

Spider-Man picked him up as if he was weightless and then leaped nearly ten feet into the air. Crusher Hogan shrieked as the ring was left below.

Even laden down with his burden as he was, Spider-Man could have jumped two, three times that height without any appreciable effort. But he had a gut feeling that to do so might freak out the audience, who would become aware that they were seeing feats performed by someone who was more than human.

"Give up?" asked Spider-Man in midair.

"No! Never!" shouted Crusher Hogan.

"Okay."

They landed, every bone in Hogan's body shaking, his jaw feeling like it was going to slam through the back of his head, his brain bouncing around inside his skull.

Spider-Man did it again.

And again.

By the time Spider-Man was ready for his fourth launch, Crusher Hogan—who wasn't the greatest when it came to heights anyway—was shrieking, "*Okay! Okay! I give up. I give up!*"

The entire fight had taken forty-five seconds. Crusher Hogan had gone into it full of confidence, and was exiting it on his hands and knees, crawling out of the ring and hugging the ground as if to reassure himself that it would never leave him.

Spider-Man stood in the middle of the ring, allowing the ref to hold his fist over his head. "Ladies and gentlemen!" shouted the ref. "I give you . . . Spider-Man! No . . . not just Spider-Man! The A-maaaaaazing Spider-Man!"

I'm gonna take Flash Thompson's head off was all Spider-Man could think.

"Just like you asked," said Mr. Melvin. "In cash. We don't like to do it this way, you understand."

Melvin was the owner and operator of the Empire Arena, where Spider-Man had just taken his star attraction and reduced him to a screaming, sobbing wreck in under a minute. But Melvin was a quick, canny operator. Hogan meant nothing to him beyond a name to slap on the marquis. And "Spider-Man" was just as marketable a name, if not more so.

Spider-Man thumbed through the wad of bills. "It's the

way *I* like to do things," he said flatly.

Melvin nodded and scratched the bristling beard that he had grown in order to hide his double chin. "Have you got an agent? A manager? Somebody?"

"Just me at the moment," said Spider-Man.

"How'd you like to sign on with me?"

It had been what Spider-Man had been waiting for. This was it: He'd embarked on a road to fame and wealth. And this guy would be his ticket in.

Except . . .

You can do better, a voice whispered to him.

"There's a lot I can do for you," said Melvin.

But Spider-Man wasn't listening. Why should he, after all? This was the first guy to make him an offer. Perhaps he could, indeed, do better. He wasn't just some slob off the street. He was the Amazing Spider-Man, for crying out loud. He could probably have his pick of managers. Of fights.

All his life, as long as he could remember, he'd been pushed around, shoved around. Had to struggle for money, for respect. The only thing that had come easily to him were his grades, and even those seemed to have cost him more than they'd gained.

But that was over now. It was all over. A new life was opening up for him, and there was no way that he was just going to go rushing into it. No, he was going to savor every moment.

"I'll think about it," he said.

"I wouldn't think too long," Melvin said. "You've got a golden opportunity here . . ."

Under his mask, Spider-Man smirked. He was not able to keep the self-satisfied tone out of his voice, either. "Save your 'golden opportunities,' Melvin," he said. "We both

know that, anytime I feel like it, I could come back here
and you'd be falling all over yourself to represent me. So
don't act like there's any sort of time limit, okay?''

Melvin's eyes narrowed. ''Trying to play hardball with
me?''

''No,'' replied Spider-Man. ''Just telling you that I've
spent a lot of years with people pushing me around. And
that's not going to be happening anymore. Gimme some
room, and we might wind up being the best of friends. Get
on my back, and I'll shrug you right off. Clear?''

''Crystal,'' said Melvin.

Spider-Man nodded once and then headed out into the
corridor. He stood in the doorway of Melvin's office a moment longer, double-checking the wad of bills in his hand.

Then he heard a shout. A howl of ''Stop, thief!''

Dashing down the corridor was a square-jawed, pasty-
faced man in a brown leather jacket and watchcap. He had
a metal box tucked under his arm, and Spider-Man immediately recognized it for what it was: a cash box. Considering the speed with which he was moving, and the
consternation from the people who were in pursuit, it probably contained the day's gate receipts.

''Stop him! Somebody stop him!'' Rounding the far corner was a security guard, pounding after the fleeing thief
as quickly as he could.

The thief ran past Spider-Man, slowing down momentarily to gape at the costumed youth. Spider-Man stared
straight into his face. Involuntarily, he started to take a step
forward to stop the thief.

Then he thought better of it.

At the far end of the corridor was an elevator. The doors
were just closing when the thief gracefully insinuated his

body between them. The elevator closed and, seconds later, headed down toward street level.

The guard pulled up to the elevator, huffing, furious and frustrated. He knew that it was over. By the time he got down to street level, the thief would be long gone.

He spun and faced Spider-Man, who was watching him with a sort of bland curiosity. "Thanks for nothing, pal!" he shouted. "All you had to do was trip him, or slow him down . . . even for a second! That's all I needed!"

"What you needed was to be better at your job in the first place," retorted Spider-Man. "You let some clown grab the receipts, and then you're mad at me because I didn't do your job for you? I'd adjust your attitude if I were you, pal."

"You're the one whose attitude could use a makeover, 'pal,' " the guard said, and stalked away.

Spider-Man shrugged.

Not his problem. Not his problem at all.

Liz Allen yawned.

On the playground basketball court, Flash Thompson and his bully boy pals were moving smoothly, passing the ball with experience and confidence. It was a simple pickup game, but with Flash Thompson, every physical challenge was an opportunity to prove just how wonderful he really was.

It was old hat for Liz.

Flash drove in fast for a lay-up, and the kid guarding him tried to block. Flash slammed into him and the kid went down, landing badly on his ankle. He let out a yelp even as Thompson jumped up and slam-dunked the ball through the hoop.

"I'm all right! I'm okay!" the kid yelled in annoyance as others came out to help him off the court. He tried to walk it off, but it was clear that—although nothing was broken—he wasn't up for some continued basketball play.

"We need another guy!" called Flash.

No one seemed particularly anxious to volunteer.

Then Liz Allen spotted a familiar figure, hurrying quickly past on his way home. "Peter!" she called.

Peter Parker broke his stride momentarily and, smiling, waved.

Thompson looked from one to the other, and then smiled that derisive smile of his. "Hey, Parker! We need another man!" He paused and then added, "Y'know any?"

This caused a raucous laugh from his friends, and Peter felt his face go red with anger.

And then, just like that, he suddenly realized that he was only blushing from habit. That there was no need to react that way.

"I'm sure Peter has more important things to do than play a silly game," Liz said defensively, but Peter could tell—or at least thought he could—that there was a tinge of embarrassment in her voice.

And to the astonishment of everyone, Peter Parker pulled off his sweater vest and said, "Let's go."

It was a lab that the school did not know about, because Otto Octavius had arranged for the lease under an assumed name. At the time that he had done so, it had been his natural paranoia at work; he wanted somewhere that he could go where he could work in complete privacy. He would not have to be concerned about annoying students, jealous teachers, or anyone else.

It was serving him well now. When he had escaped from the hospital, it had prompted an immediate manhunt to be launched. Stakeouts had been created around all of his usual haunts, and if he had indeed gone to his home, or back to the school—or what was left of the school—then a major battle would very likely have ensued.

But Doc Ock was in his "secret" lab in one of the more rundown sections of Chelsea. The exterior was so dilapidated that there was no chance of anyone thinking that anything of value could possibly be inside. Even if they had leaped to that assumption, Octopus had sufficient alarms and safeguards built in to discourage any unfortunate potential burglars.

Dr. Octopus, at that moment, was engaged in a rather odd endeavor.

He was trying to unclench his hands.

Not his biological hands. Rather, the gripper claws that were at the ends of his tentacles.

Ever since the explosion, they had locked into their clenched position, as if grabbing on to something. It had been extremely irritating for Octopus, who was manipulating the dials on his control pad and not having any success at all.

Finally, exasperated, he dropped his hands to his sides and looked in annoyance at the ends of his arms.

He wanted to inspect the claws more closely.

To his shock, they moved toward him on their own.

In the moments after the explosion, Octopus's metal arms had been a mass of seething, twisted metal. He had not been fully aware of that, however, since he'd been barely conscious and delirious. Now, though, he was fully awake and cognizant. Enough, in fact, to have used the strength in his metal arms to smash down the hospital walls and propel him through the air to this hideaway.

But when he'd been doing all that, he had been—as always—maneuvering the various control dials on the chest panel. Now, though, he had simply *thought* about the tentacles moving toward him, and they had done so immediately. And it felt as natural and automatic as if it were his own flesh and blood arms making the movement.

"I don't believe it," he whispered.

His tentacles scratched the top of his head thoughtfully without his being aware of it at first. Then he realized what was happening, and laughed. The tentacles jiggled in sympathetic amusement.

He commanded the tentacles to move in intricate patterns, and they did so instantly. "Incredible," he kept saying to himself.

Then he brought the tentacles up to the front of his face, staring at the claws. The dials to open the claws had been damaged, but now he merely commanded them to open with the slightest movement of his lips.

They relaxed immediately.

There were pieces of glowing material trapped in the claws. Whether it was remains of the machine, or some sort of bizarre synthesis of metal and the radioactive isotope, he couldn't be sure. The pieces glistened from the twilight overhead that was filtering in through the filthy skylight.

The moment the fast-fading sunlight struck the mysterious material, it floated out of the claws' grasp. Floated, then picked up speed and, seconds later, nestled securely against the ceiling.

"I'll be damned," said Dr. Octopus.

He started to reach for the phone on impulse . . . and

then stopped. Was he out of his mind? Was he supposed to contact the university and tell them what he had discovered? That his experiments had actually borne fruit. And what would they do then? They would come and arrest him, try and drag him back to that hospital, keep him prisoner . . .

His still-feverish brain worked faster and faster, becoming more out of control in its imaginings. That damnable Dean Martin would steal his discovery, that was it. Perhaps . . . perhaps he was in league with the spider man who had caused the experiment to go awry in the first place. Yes, that was it! It made so much sense!

All the incredible things, the uses, to which this material could be put . . . Martin would probably hog it all, to try and generate money to rebuild the destroyed science center.

That's what it always came down to, wasn't it? Otto Octavius, a man of science, pursuing various avenues of research purely for the sheer joy of exploration. And then cretins like Martin come along and profit off his discoveries, while keeping him locked away in some hospital.

"To hell with that," murmured Octavius. "If there's going to be profit made off this . . . I'll be the one who makes it."

Flash Thompson lunged at the ball, air burning in his lungs, face burning as well.

And there went Puny Parker again, dribbling clumsily, tripping and yet somehow tripping just far enough away from Flash that the ball remained elusively out of the athlete's reach. If Flash hadn't known better, he would have thought that Parker was doing it on purpose, somehow.

Worse, that he was holding back. But he knew that couldn't be it. It simply couldn't be.

But that's what it had been like, game after game, ever since Parker took the court. His pathetic attempts to play basketball had resulted in much laughter and amusement from the players and spectators, but none of them were seeing what Thompson alone was noticing.

No one managed to get the ball away from Parker. Not ever. Oh, they came close, and when he passed to another player it was always clumsy, with no style at all—but the pass always found its way to its target.

When Parker was covering someone, they never got a shot off.

And when Parker shot—on those rare occasions when he did shoot—it was in a clumsy, half-baked manner. No artistry, no professionalism—and yet the ball always went in, as if it had eyes.

Peter Parker was every inch the stumbling, bumbling nerd, playing basketball for the first time in his sheltered, pampered, namby-pamby life.

And yet Flash Thompson couldn't shake the feeling that Parker was just screwing around. That he was toying with them. That there were four other guys on Parker's side, and—in point of fact—he didn't need them.

The suspicion fueled Thompson's anger. There was Parker, dribbling the ball, as his teammates shouted for him to pass it.

Game point hinged, and Parker moved to pass. That was when Flash Thompson suddenly charged him, full bore, as if the game had suddenly switched from hoops to football.

He was coming in behind Parker. There was no way that Parker could have seen him. And yet suddenly Peter doubled over. Thompson came in too quickly, unable to check his momentum, and collided with Parker.

Peter didn't budge from the spot but, instead, straightened up at the exact instance that Thompson was off-balance atop him. He slammed into Flash, and the larger boy somersaulted over Parker, thudding to the ground and getting the wind knocked out of him in the process. With his shot clear, Peter Parker made one of his patented, clumsy throws—and the ball swished through the hoop.

The cheer from the other guys on Parker's side was drowned out by the bull elephant roar of Flash Thompson, lunging to his feet, blood trickling from his scraped knees.

"*You fouled me, ya little creep!*" he shouted.

Peter permitted a small smile. "Well, you're much more experienced at this stuff than me, Flash, but since you're the one who plowed into *me*, I don't think you're right."

"No way, man, do-over! I was fouled!"

And Peter couldn't resist. "You were foul before the game even started."

Thompson lunged at him, and Peter stepped back, his fist cocked. He'd had his fun, but now it was time to let Flash Thompson know, once and for all, that his years of tormenting Peter Parker had come to an end.

That was when Liz Allen interposed herself between them, pushing at Flash. "Stop it! *Stop it*, Flash! You'll hurt him!"

"Outta the way!"

"*No!*"

"Out of his way, Liz, I'm not afraid of him," said Peter.

"Well, you *should* be!" shot back Flash.

The arguing continued, and then it became harder and harder for the participants to make themselves heard because of the sirens that were overwhelming then. Eventually Peter, Flash, and Liz's attention was drawn away from the immediate problem in favor of what seemed far more spectacular fare.

Several police cars shot past, their red lights spinning, their sirens howling. An ambulance came in their wake. "Wow," murmured one kid. "I bet somebody got killed or something."

Peter watched the police cars turn off, and then realized with a dim awareness that they were heading in the general direction of his house.

Something began to tingle in the back of his head. Not that warning sense he'd noticed earlier, but something else, a general feeling of unease.

He started heading after the police cars.

Flash Thompson jumped into his path. "Okay, Parker, right here, right now! Let's go!"

Peter was barely aware of him, for the sense of dread was practically overwhelming.

"What'sa matter, Parker? Chicken?" demanded Flash.

"Flash, leave him alone!" pleaded Liz.

Peter darted around him, so fast that it seemed to Flash as if Parker had simply vanished. He turned in time to see Peter charging out the playground exit.

"Ha!" shouted Flash, feeling his world settling back down into its normal, preferable status quo. "I knew he was gutless! I knew it!"

Liz thumped him on the chest in irritation.

The sidewalk seemed to blur under Peter's feet as he ran full speed. Passersby barely saw him, he was moving so quickly.

Peter rounded the corner, all the while trying to convince himself that he was imagining it. That he was paranoid. That the police cars had not, in fact, settled in front of his nice, normal, safe, two story A-frame house.

The houses all around were bathed in red light, as if blood was seeping out of the walls.

Barricades had been set up around his house.

Aunt May was there, sobbing onto the shoulder of a man that Peter took to be a plainclothes cop. There were several uniforms as well . . .

. . . and a body, covered by a white sheet, being carted out on a stretcher to the ambulance. A large blotch of red stained the middle of the sheet.

Peter's legs moved without his consent or awareness, because his brain had shut down. He headed toward the barricade, still trying to tell himself that there had to be some nice, normal reason for all of this. That matters were not as they appeared. That perhaps the oil burner had backed up, as it had once a couple years ago. Or maybe they'd won the lottery, that was it, yes, it had to be. His pocket was bulging with hundred dollar bills, and now it was going to turn out that they were, in fact, millionaires.

He got to the barricade and a burly cop got in his path. The cop started to say, "Please step back," but he didn't get the first word out because Peter—functioning on autopilot—simply shoved the cop aside as if he were weightless.

The cop yelped in anger and started to reach for his billy club, and then May spotted Peter and shrieked his name. That was when the last of the nice little fantasies Peter was desperately entertaining fell completely away, as his white-haired aunt fell sobbing into his arms.

She was moaning something repeatedly—"Ben . . . Ben . . ."

The cop whom Peter had shoved, endeavoring to recapture his dignity, said, "This is your nephew, ma'am?"

May didn't hear. Peter turned to him and murmured, "Wh-what happened?"

"Burglar," said the cop. "Saw just some old folks were living here, figured they'd be easy pickings."

"Ben . . . tried to stop him." May looked up at Peter, eyes red and lifeless, as if her soul had died. "Tried wrestling the gun away—animals, Peter, my God, they're animals—the world's full of animals . . ."

The plainclothes detective, a pleasant-looking, brown-haired man, was holding up a piece of paper. "Mrs. Parker," he said gently, "is this a complete list of everything he got?"

May nodded numbly.

"Just grabbed what was nearby and ran, huh." He skimmed the list. "Microscope, huh?"

Peter moaned.

The detective turned to Peter. "Don't worry, son. We'll find the man who did this."

"As soon as you hear," said Peter, unsure of what to say or do, "please . . . tell me . . . if there's anything I can do . . ."

"Just let us do our job," said the detective, and then smiled, not unkindly. He handed Peter a card. "I'm Sergeant Stan Carter. Feel free to call me if anything else is found missing."

"Yessir," said Peter numbly. He felt removed from his body, as if he were watching events that were happening to someone else.

Carter turned to Aunt May. "I'm sorry for your loss, Mrs. Parker. Frankly . . . you're lucky to be alive."

She looked up at him and, incredibly, started to laugh. "Lucky? *Lucky?!*" And the laughter then degenerated into hysterical sobs, as Peter helped her toward the home where the population had just been reduced by one third.

Peter leaped for the phone . . . literally.

Aunt May had just fallen asleep, finally, on the living room couch, after agreeing to take several tranquilizers. She had not been able to bring herself to go up to her bedroom; she was not ready to face an empty bed.

The police had cleared out their forensic tools hours earlier. Peter was tiptoeing around, puttering about, uncertain what to do but convinced that he should be doing *something.*

The jangle of the phone seemed abnormally loud, and Peter—who was in the kitchen at the time—soared through the air, propelled by the superhuman strength in his legs. He landed surefootedly next to the phone and grabbed up the receiver, his head snapping around to check Aunt May and make sure that she hadn't been disturbed by the ringing.

She lay there, unmoving, dead to the world . . .

The phrasing, even though it was unspoken, made him wince. "Hello?" he said.

"This is Sergeant Carter," came a gruff voice. "I thought you'd want to know . . . we got him."

Peter could scarcely believe it. "He's—he's in jail?"

"Not quite. But he will be shortly. The jerk had the bad luck to try and pawn the stuff at a shop where we had an ongoing surveillance set up. Tried to pawn your micro-

scope, son. Between that and the description your aunt provided, that nailed him immediately. He caught a break and
eluded our uniformed officers, but—''

"He got away? *He got away?!*"

"Calm down, son," said Carter. "He took refuge in an
old warehouse, down by Corona near the big oil tanks. He's
holed up there, but the place is surrounded. He's not going
anywhere, believe me. Look, I wouldn't be calling you if I
thought there was a chance he'd get away. This is good
news, son, and I just thought you'd be real anxious to hear
it."

"Yes, sir," Peter said. "Yes . . . thank you."

"Be sure to tell your aunt."

"She's sleeping now, but I will, soon as she wakes up."

Peter put the phone down, and stared at his slumbering
aunt. Stared at the woman who had been a mother to him
for as long as he could remember.

He thought about Uncle Ben, sitting in his favorite
chair, talking about what it was like when he was a young
man, and speculating about the bright future that Peter had
waiting for him.

And he thought about the thief, who had entered their
lives and destroyed their peaceful existence with a few well-
placed bullets.

Peter's fingers curled into a trembling fist. He imagined
it smashing into the thief's face, pulping it, and the pleasure that that would bring.

What if the guy shot some policemen while trying to
escape? What if he was responsible for more deaths? Or
even worse . . . what if Carter's confidence was misplaced?
Things could go wrong. He could still get away.

No.

No, he wasn't going to get away.

Josh Kaplan, manager of the All That Glitters Jewelry store, was preparing to close up for the evening. It was a cool night, and—looking around to make sure nobody was minding his business for him—he reached under the counter and took a quick swig from a small container of booze.

He saw a shadow appear at the front door. "We're closed!" he called.

The gated door exploded as what appeared to be long metal pipes smashed through it, caving it inward with no hesitation.

Kaplan gasped, guarding his face against the flying glass. When he dared to peek through his upraised arms, he saw a roundish, rather odd looking man stepping into the store. And there seemed to be snakes coming out of him from all sides. Metal snakes. Kaplan was sure, at that moment, that he was hallucinating.

"Now you're open," said Dr. Octopus.

He raised a bizarre, wide-barreled object that bore a resemblance to a gun, and aimed it at Kaplan.

"*No! Don't kill me!*" cried out Kaplan. Even as he pleaded, however, his toe edged toward the alarm button on the floor.

"I'm not going to kill you," replied Octopus. "This is just an experiment. But don't you worry. It won't be on the final exam."

He fired the gun. Pulling the trigger exposed a miniature radiant stimulation chamber, firing ionized particles through the miraculous metal that lodged in the gun's housing.

A beam, invisible to the naked eye, blasted out of the end of the gun and struck Kaplan. His toe was still half an inch away from the button, a second later, it was eight feet plus half an inch away as Kaplan hurtled upward and slammed against the ceiling.

Octopus calmly began to smash his mechanical arms through the cabinets, removing the contents. They went about their business almost as if they had minds of their own. Octopus, in the meantime, had removed a stopwatch from his pocket and proceeded to watch the seconds tick away.

"Stop your whimpering, sir," said Octopus in an annoyed and warning tone. "Judging by your mass, and the amount of exposure you received, I would calculate that you will return to earth in precisely two minutes, thirty-seven seconds. Once that happens, I would appreciate it if you'd be certain to let the police, and the news media, know the full details of our encounter. I want them to know what they're up against. And more important"—he smiled ruthlessly—"I want them to know that I don't care if they know."

"Don't lemme fall!" cried out Kaplan. "I'll—I'll break something!"

Dr. Octopus sighed.

"You're probably right," he said. "But then . . . we all have to make sacrifices in the name of science."

"Keep that spotlight there!" Lieutenant Hunt of S.W.A.T. directed his men. Obediently, a searchlight swept across one of the street level entrances. There were three, and all were covered. "And keep those damned news cameras back!"

Carrying out his orders, several cops shooed back a TV camera, as the reporter kept a continuous barrage of chatter going for the benefit of the cameraman.

Hunt put the loudspeaker to his face and called, "Attention! You cannot escape! Come out with your hands up!"

From one of the boarded-over windows, bullets were spit out at a rapid clip, sending policemen dodging back behind their vehicles for protection.

"Does anyone have a clear shot?" Hunt spoke into his walkie-talkie. He got back several quick responses in the negative. Their intended prisoner was keeping himself out of the S.W.A.T. team's direct sight line.

The newswoman looked around in frustration, trying to see someplace for the cameraman to focus on. She could have killed the cops for making her job so difficult . . .

Then she spotted him.

Her eyes narrowed, and she tapped her cameraman on the shoulder. "Chucky . . . bring it around. That rooftop across the street . . . zoom in. What do you see?"

The cameraman obeyed her instructions, looking through the viewfinder. He squinted. "What the hell—?"

"What? What?"

"It's—it's some nut in a costume. Crouching on the ledge."

"What's he doing?"

"Just watching . . . he . . . wait. He stuck his arm out . . . like he's pointing at the warehouse."

The newswoman frowned. "Pointing and doing what?"

"I dunno. Just—" And then he gasped. "*Jesus! He jumped!*"

The newswoman had no idea what was going on, but she knew a story when she hit one, and footage of some lunatic jumper—even though it was unrelated to the story of the standoff that she was covering—would nevertheless be worthwhile. "Follow him down!" she said, not caring a bit about the fact that a fellow human being was plunging to his death. To her, he was just another story.

She had no idea just how big a story he was about to become. She got her first inkling when the cameraman said, "He's . . . *he's not falling! He's . . . flying!*"

Crouched on the rooftop, Spider-Man looked across the street at the warehouse. Cops had ringed the place. But the creep could hole up there for ages, perhaps cost more lives . . .

He'd been through all the logical reasons to take matters into his own hands. And through all the illogical ones as well. There was no longer any point in rehashing them. Now . . . now he was just going to do it.

Peter's breath sounded loud inside his mask. His heart was thudding against his chest.

Someone had seen him. There was that buzzing in his head again, similar to when the women had walked past earlier, but less severe . . . probably because whoever was looking at him posed no danger. This spider-sense of his was clearly capable of putting across degrees of severity for whatever hazards it was warning him about.

He chose to ignore it. He had more important things to be concerned about than someone in the crowd below eyeballing him.

He stretched out a hand and fired a webline. It was super-strong, but thin as always. To anyone below, thanks to the darkness of the sky and the slenderness of the thread, it would be invisible.

The webline arched across the street, propelled by the launcher on his wrist. The wind took it slightly, and it landed several inches to the left of where he'd originally aimed it. Nevertheless, it still adhered solidly; an experimental tug assured him of that. He scooted over a few inches to adjust for the new trajectory.

For one brief moment he hesitated, and then he saw, in his mind's eye, Uncle Ben going down before the weapon of his assailant. And Spider-Man hesitated no longer.

He leaped.

He started to descend, and then the webline snapped taut and swung through his parabolic arc. His speed increased with each passing second.

He was going to hit the wall.

He'd misjudged and was going to go splat against the wall, since the window he was aiming for was going to wind up a couple of feet above his head.

In mid-swing, he corrected his height on the webline, pulling himself up hand over hand several more feet to compensate.

By this point, more people in the street had spotted him. There were shouts and pointed fingers, and shrieks of astonishment. He ignored them all. He was focused entirely on the window that he was hurtling toward fast, way too fast, he wasn't going to be ready for it and then there was no more time to prepare.

Spider-Man smashed through the boarded-up window feet first. The wood was solid, but through the combination of his speed and his strength, Spider-Man splintered it as if it were balsa. Pieces flew everywhere and Spider-Man landed inside the warehouse, automatically somersaulting and moving just in case his target was waiting for him.

But he was quickly coming to trust his spider-sense over his eyes, and his spider-sense was telling him that there was no one aiming anything at him. The darkness was overwhelming, but it didn't bother him much. Sure, the murderer had had more time to allow his eyes to adjust. But he could have had a cat's night vision and it would still have been peanuts compared to Spider-Man's spider-sense.

Spider-Man skittered along a wall, moving with caution but confidence. From downstairs he heard creaking floorboards. His target was moving. He was willing to bet, though, that the wall and ceiling weren't going to creak at all.

Staying with the wall, he moved out into a corridor. There was a stairway leading down. No other way to go. His spider-sense was screaming now; his target was downstairs. The chances were that he'd make a perfect target the moment he showed his masked face in walking down the stairs.

He'd brought his camera, outfitted with a special lens and loaded with infrared film.

These pictures weren't for J. Jonah Jameson. These were going to be for himself. He wanted to look back at them, to see with grim satisfaction the expression of the bastard when Peter put him down.

He gripped the camera firmly with one hand, crouched at the top of the stairs . . .

. . . and launched himself downward.

He came down so fast that the thug downstairs hadn't been expecting it. No sane person would come down stairs that way. By the time that the thug realized what was happening, Spider-Man's momentum had already carried him three quarters of the way down.

The thug opened fire.

The bullets cut across the air just behind Spider-Man as, head first, he arrived at the bottom of the stairs. One hand was still clutching the camera, and the other was extended. In a dazzling display of strength, he landed on the one hand and did a hand spring, a flip in the air, and then a leap that carried him toward a high corner of the room.

The thug had completely lost sight of him. The warehouse still had boxes in it, left over from an old customer who'd never paid up. The thug, still not realizing what he was dealing with, figured that the intruder was a nutso cowboy cop hiding among the crates somewhere.

He was wrong on both counts.

Spider-Man quickly webbed the camera to the ceiling, aiming it downward. Then he set the timer for five second intervals.

He skittered away from the camera, wanting to make sure that no stray bullets blasted it apart. That would be just his luck, to lose the camera and valuable film to flying ammo.

"You're through," he called down. He couldn't see the thug. It didn't matter. With his spider-sense acting like a beacon, it could just as easily have been a fully lit room.

The thug whirled, not sure where the voice was coming from, and let fire. Bullets sliced across the room, thudding into crates, kicking up dust.

He ceased firing, to see if his bullets had had any effect.

"You killed a good man. An innocent man. And you're going to pay for it," Spider-Man called to him, and then he was already moving as the thug opened fire again. Plaster rained down as the bullets chewed up the ceiling, but

Spider-Man was no longer remotely in the vicinity of where the thug was firing.

Suddenly the intensity of his spider-sense lessened tremendously, as if a major portion of the danger had passed.

He's out of ammo, thought Spider-Man, and he didn't even think about the fact that he was staking his life to this strange, totally incomprehensible sixth sense of his. Instead, utterly fearless, he launched himself through the air, descending toward the criminal like a great bird of prey.

Out of the corner of his eye, the thug spotted him, turned, and squeezed the trigger.

Nothing. He'd emptied his clip.

Before he could even contemplate trying to reload, Spider-Man plowed into him.

They went down, a tangle of arms and legs, and the thug brought the gun butt up and slammed it against the side of Spider-Man's head. The world seemed to fuzz out around Spider-Man for a moment from the impact; he'd known it was coming, but at such close quarters he'd been unable to do anything to protect himself.

The thug coiled his legs under Spider-Man's chest and shoved, driving him back. He brought the gun around and swung it at the staggering figure again.

Not this time.

Spider-Man caught it, his strength far greater than the thug's. He yanked it away, almost breaking the gun in half out of sheer rage, and then realized that the police might need it for forensic evidence. He settled for tossing it aside, and then he advanced on the thug.

The thug, his face in shadows, swung a fist.

Spider-Man brushed it aside as if it were a feather punch, and then drove a fierce roundhouse that seemed to originate somewhere around his ankles. It landed with such bruising force that he would have caved in the thug's skull if he hadn't pulled the punch at the last second. As it was, two of the thug's teeth flew out of his head, along with about a quarter of a pint of blood from his nose.

He went down, unconscious, and Spider-Man felt nothing but rage. He grabbed the insensate thief by the front of his jacket and hauled the thug to his feet. He didn't want it to be over so quickly. He wanted to pound on him some more, to make him realize what he had done, to make him sorry, to make him hurt just for a few minutes the way that Aunt May was going to be hurting for the rest of her life, the way that he . . .

Then Spider-Man squinted, his eyes finally adjusting to the darkness. The thief had been wearing a cap, but the impact had knocked it off . . . indeed, almost knocked his entire head off.

And the face . . . that face . . .

He knew it. Knew it in an instant.

It was the guy. The guy from the wrestling place, the one stealing the gate receipts. The guy that Spider-Man had stood by and allowed to get away.

His hands went numb, and the thief slid from his grasp and dropped to the floor.

"Oh my God," whispered Spider-Man, but it was Peter Parker who was speaking from beneath the mask.

He backed away, his world swirling around him.

And now his mind's eye was playing a far different scene. There was his Uncle Ben going down before a stream of bullets, but now it was Peter himself who was pulling the trigger.

For that was, in essence, what he had done. By standing

aside and doing nothing, by allowing the thief to escape, he was indirectly—even directly—responsible for the death of his uncle.

He'd had the power in his hands to allow his uncle to live, and he had let it slip through his fingers.

He was barely aware of his retrieving the camera. Then he went back to the thug. He fired a webline, because he couldn't even bring himself to touch the guy now. Moments later he was striding across the vacant warehouse, dragging the thug behind him.

He paused at the warehouse door long enough to pick up a large crate. It felt like it weighed a ton. Spider-Man didn't care. He didn't care about anything except just putting an end to the nightmare . . . a nightmare that he really knew was only just beginning.

With a slight grunt, he hurled the crate at the door. It crashed into it, the crate shattered, but the door flew open from the impact. He stepped back, pausing to see if the cops would start firing automatically, but his spider-sense told him what several seconds of waiting subsequently confirmed: the cops were holding their fire. They had seen Spider-Man go in, and they weren't sure what was happening, but they weren't going to jump the gun either.

Good for them.

At least there were some people in the world, Spider-Man thought bleakly, who had some sense.

He picked up the thug and unceremoniously threw him through the door as if he were a sack of wheat. The thug hit the ground outside, making a slight squishy sound from the impact. For a moment, Spider-Man wondered if he'd killed the guy. For a moment, he didn't care.

Floodlights were bathing the front door now, and Spider-Man stepped through, knowing full well now that he was in no danger. No one was going to put a bullet through him.

No.

That would be too easy. Too merciful.

The reflective material in his mask protected him from the glare of the lights as he heard a cop bellowing through a loudspeaker, "Don't move! *Don't move! Stay right where you are!*"

He did not particularly feel like obeying.

He turned his back on the cops and proceeded to scale the building.

He heard shouts of amazement, and some futile bellowing from the cops, but what were they going to do? Shoot at him? With his back to them, and him clearly not carrying a weapon of any sort? No way.

He even heard some applause. He ignored it. He ignored everyone and everything except the breaking of his heart.

He reached the top of the building, fired a webline and—disregarding the cheers and shouts of the crowd—swung away into the night.

Dr. Octopus turned on the TV news at eleven P.M. He fully expected to be the lead item.

He gaped in fury.

There, on the screen . . .

It was the spider man. The man he'd never met, and yet—his nemesis.

The wall-crawling creature who was trying to discredit him.

To belittle him. To steal his thunder.

To destroy him.

Dr. Octopus had never done anything to this man.

He changed to another channel. To all the channels.

Spider-Man was on every single one. The media was going nuts for this mystery man who scaled walls, hurtled through the air, battled criminals . . .

He stuck with one of the channels, and they finally got around to mentioning him. He was the fifth item, not the first.

And he wasn't exactly the item.

". . . after the clerk gave a description of an antigravity gun that the police termed 'far-fetched,' police tested the alcohol content of his blood and found it far above the legal limit," said the anchorman with a smile. "The mysterious 'snake-armed man' is currently believed to be a figment of the clerk's overactive imagination, although an investigation is being made into the damage done to the store. In international news, plans for the peace conference at the United Nations proceed with—"

In a fit of pique, Dr. Octopus smashed the TV to pieces.

The next day, Spider-Man was all over the news.

Peter Parker didn't care. He was at the funeral parlor.

"We have a full range of caskets at reasonable prices," began the mortician.

"He gets the best of everything," said Peter tonelessly. "That's all. That's what he deserves. That's what he gets. End of discussion."

The mortician tried to smile sympathetically, which was a craft he had long ago perfected. "Son . . . let's not kid each other. That's a lot of money, which I doubt you have."

"Tell me the cost. The whole thing."

"The whole thing? Soup to nuts? Sixteen hundred dollars."

"Fine," said Peter, and he turned and left without another word.

He went home, got the camera, removed the film, and was at the *Daily Bugle* within the hour. This time the guard let him right up.

He could hear Jonah Jameson bellowing from across the newsroom, demanding to know the story about this Spider-Man character. There were two things that Jameson hated: being scooped, and being scooped by TV news, for which he had nothing but contempt.

"Oh, Peter!" said Betty from her desk. "I wouldn't go in right now if I were—!"

Peter walked past her, and pushed open the door to Jameson's office. Jameson was busy shouting at Joe Robertson, who didn't look particularly discomfited. Nevertheless they both stopped and stared wordlessly at Parker.

"Well?!? What the hell do you want?!" demanded Jameson.

There was no expression in Peter's face as he flipped the roll of film onto Jameson's desk. "Six hundred dollars," he said, "for the first photographs of Spider-Man. It's shots from last night, him catching that guy."

Jameson's cigar fell out of his mouth into his coffee. He grabbed the roll. "Are you *serious?* Shots of this Spider-Man character nailing the creepo?"

Peter nodded.

"So . . . you weren't a fluke after all." Then his eyes narrowed craftily. "But six hundred dollars . . . that's above norm, even for front page stuff like this. Plus, you owe us for the advance . . ."

"Six hundred, or I'm gone," said Peter in a voice without inflection.

Jameson slammed his fist down, this time knocking his ashtray off the desk. "Don't dictate terms to me, Parker! I don't take well to it! Not at all! What does a punk kid like you need six hundred bucks for, anyway?!"

"To bury the man the creepo murdered."

Jameson's mouth opened, and then closed without saying anything.

Joe Robertson looked at Peter, then glanced at a piece of paper on Jameson's desk . . . an obit.

"Ben Parker," said Robertson softly. "Leaving behind a wife and nephew." His gaze flickered to Peter. "You the nephew, Peter?"

Jameson snorted, "He's obviously not the wife, Robertson," but there was a different tone in his voice. He paused a moment, and then said, "Pay the man."

Robbie nodded and went out. Peter stood there a moment, shifting from one foot to the next, and then he turned to go as well.

"Parker . . ."

Peter turned.

Jameson tried to think of something to say.

Nothing came to mind except, "Good job."

Peter Parker nodded, and then walked out of Jameson's office.

He returned to the funeral parlor precisely at 1 P.M. He had with him the money from the *Daily Bugle*, plus the $1,000 he'd won wrestling. In total, it was just enough to pay for his uncle's funeral.

* * *

Peter Parker sat in the cafeteria at school, picking aimlessly at the food in front of him. Usually Aunt May packed him lunch, but lately—for obvious reasons—her attempts to get back into her usual routine were somewhat half-hearted. Peter had told her not to worry about it. He was old enough, after all, to take care of his own lunch. But peanut butter and jelly sandwiches, which were pretty much the extent of his culinary expertise, wore thin after a couple of days, and this day he opted for the cafeteria lunch . . . not that that was much of a bargain in terms of sustenance.

He noticed that someone had stopped directly across from him. He looked up. It was Liz Allen, standing there and holding her tray.

"Mind if I sit down here, Peter?"

He shrugged and gestured for her to do so.

"I heard about your uncle," she said softly as she settled opposite him. "I'm really sorry. We all are."

"Uh huh," said Peter, making no effort to keep the bitterness he felt out of his voice. " 'We all?' I bet Flash is just broken up about it."

"Oh, you know how he is," she said dismissively. "The things he cares about . . . well, Lord, who knows how his mind works? Right now he's obsessing about this Spider-Man character."

This actually brought Peter the first feeling other than grief that he'd had in days. "No kidding," he said.

"Oh, he thinks Spider-Man is the greatest hero in the world. He's creepy, if you ask me. Although . . . he did catch the man who killed your uncle. So you must be grateful to him."

Peter shrugged.

Then he sensed, rather than saw, someone coming up

behind him, and then the danger inside his head shouted a warning.

Peter, driven entirely by reflex, dodged to one side, just in time to see food spilling past him and Flash Thompson's voice saying, in heavy sarcasm, "Oops!"

In an instant it was clear what had happened. Thompson had spotted Parker having lunch with Liz, and decided to get back at him by "accidentally" spilling his tray loaded with food all over Peter Parker.

Problem was, Peter had avoided the cascade in time. And without his body there to intercept the flow of food, that meant that all of it—soup, soda, ketchup-laden hamburger and runny mashed potatos—spilled across the table and onto the next available target.

Which happened to be Liz Allen.

Flash repeated his statement of "Oops," except this time his chagrin was genuine. It was also useless, because Liz was absolutely boiling. Her white blouse was now multicolored, and her expression was one of sheer fury.

"You did that on purpose, *you creep!*" she shouted. All eyes in the cafeteria were upon her. "You did that *on purpose!*"

"It was just a joke!" Flash tried to explain, but somehow that didn't seem to mollify Liz.

The lunchroom teacher was advancing on the scene of the accident. Although naturally Peter felt badly for Liz, somehow the prospect of Flash landing in trouble because of a misfired attempt to humiliate Peter was a happenstance Peter considered to be most amusing.

That was when one of Flash's cronies suddenly dashed into the lunchroom. He was carrying a transistor radio with a set of headphones plugged in. And he was shouting,

"Flash! Flash! Spider-Man's on the radio!"

This news, of course, was greeted with enthusiasm by Flash Thompson, albeit considerable—and well-concealed—surprise by Peter Parker. "What happened? What's he doing?" demanded Flash.

"He's not on exactly! But they're talking about him!"

"Mr. Thompson," the teacher said severely, determined to remind Flash that he was still in difficulty.

It didn't register on Flash, who was only capable of concentrating on one thing at a time. "Let's hear!" he said.

The crony yanked the earphone jack out of the radio, and now the broadcast was audible to all.

". . . and the man identified as Doctor Otto Octavius—and presently calling himself Dr. Octopus," the broadcaster was saying urgently, "has stated that if Spider-Man does not present himself within the hour, then Octopus will take retaliatory steps. Spider-Man's presence is an additional demand to the five million dollars that Octopus has also—"

"What's going on? Where is this happening?" demanded Flash.

"You won't believe it," replied the kid. "You won't. I swear it."

The United Nations was a series of buildings situated near the East River in Manhattan. The imposing Secretariat Building was probably the best known. If the average tourist (and there were many) was facing the Secretariat Building, one would see the Dag Hammarskjold Library to the right, and the General Assembly Building to the left . . .

On a typical day.

This, however, was not a typical day. There were two indicators of that status: first, the massive assemblage of police, soldiers, and reporters, all vying for space in the plaza; and second, the fact that the General Assembly Building was hovering several hundred feet in the air.

Within the building, in the great auditorium that housed the General Assembly itself, Dr. Octopus stalked back and forth, his arms snaking about like the top of the Medusa's head. Delegates from all over the world were united in fear.

"You don't have much time!" Octopus was shouting. Around the floor of the auditorium, various guards lay unconscious—remnants of Doc Ock's arrival at the General Assembly Building a short time before. He was waving his anti-grav gun around and snarling, "Unless the polarity of the anti-grav particles is gradually reversed—and soon—this entire building will crash to the ground! Is that what you want? Is that what all of you want?" Then he smiled and said sarcastically, "Perhaps you'd all like to put it to a vote."

"Doctor," said one of the undersecretaries, being careful to address Octopus by that title since the secretary-general had disdained to do so and was now lying unconscious along with the guards. "Doctor . . . putting it to a vote would be pointless. Obviously we wish to live. However, you must be reasonable . . ."

"And you must be insane," snapped back Octopus, "if you think that I have any interest in anything you have to say!" His tentacle lashed out toward the undersecretary, who barely dodged before the tentacle hammered down and shattered the podium in front of him.

He spun to face the TV cameras which had been recording the General Assembly activities that day, which was the kickoff for the peace conference that was to have addressed the problems of war throughout the world. Ironically, the conference itself had apparently turned into a war zone.

"I want my money!" Octopus shouted to the cameras. "And I want Spider-Man! And if they're not here soon—"

"I can't account for the money . . . so I guess you'll have to settle for me."

Doc Ock's head whipped around.

Clinging to the ceiling was Spider-Man: the only individual in the room who had to be concerned that, if he survived the next five minutes, he would probably get stuck with detention for slipping out of school and going into the city without permission.

Getting from Queens to Manhattan had been a matter of a twenty-minute subway ride.

Getting from the ground to the floating United Nations building had been something else again. Climbing around on buildings in Queens a few stories high had been one thing. Now, though, Spider-Man was scaling skyscrapers. As he did so, an occasional wave of fear would pass through him. He still didn't understand this power, after all. What if it gave out on him suddenly? Disappeared as abruptly as it had arrived? At any time, the building surface could suddenly become slick and untenable, and Spider-Man could go sliding off, screaming, to his death.

What would Aunt May say when required to identify the pulped remains of the bloody mass that had been her nephew?

He couldn't think about it. Down that way definitely lay madness.

He'd gotten within range of the floating General Assembly Building, still unable to believe what his eyes were telling him. With his webline, it was the work of minutes to attach a line to the building and swing across the space, hauling himself up and in to the besieged structure.

It was no great trick finding Dr. Octopus; his was the only voice in earshot, and he was ranting and raving fairly loudly.

Spider-Man crawled across the ceiling, listening to Octopus shouting about something or other. From the police reports he'd heard, from everything the news was saying, Dr. Octopus had gone completely off the deep end. Word from the hospital was that his mechanical arms had actually become fused to his body. That might be enough to drive anyone over the edge. In a way, Doc Ock's fate evoked pity from Spider-Man. Despite Octavius's terrorism, despite the insanity of developing some sort of anti-grav gizmo that had actually sent a United Nations building sky-high, Spider-Man couldn't summon any hatred for this man . . . or even anger.

The reason for that was simple. After the events of the past week, there was no anger left in the teenager . . . except, perhaps, the anger directed at himself. He felt like an emotional washcloth, utterly wrung out.

Then he noticed something, and he felt an even greater chill than when he'd first seen the building floating. That, at least, he was prepared for . . . as insane as the development may have been.

But what he was seeing now stunned him. Dr. Octopus was talking, gesturing . . . and his hands were nowhere near the dials and controls on his chest plate. Indeed, he was now wearing a loose-fitting green tunic over the plate, so the dials weren't even accessible. On top of that he was wearing a white lab coat, giving him an almost studious air that was in direct contrast to the situation. The arms were moving, mirroring and imitating Octopus's every gesture. They were responding to his mental commands, had become a literal extension of his own mind.

Despite the inconvenience such a change would have caused, Spider-Man couldn't help but think how handy it would have been if one of the alterations that the spider bite had prompted in him would have been the sprouting of a few extra arms. Because this was going to be difficult.

Hanging on to the ceiling and observing wasn't getting him anywhere. Octopus was ranting about wanting money, wanting Spider-Man . . . it was time to get the show on the road.

"I can't account for the money . . . so I guess you'll have to settle for me."

"At last!" Octopus cried out. "We meet, face to face . . . or face to mask! My greatest enemy!" His metal arms hoisted him upward.

Warily Spider-Man backed up. "What are you talking about?" demanded Spider-Man. "Since when am I your enemy?"

"Don't deny it! You were behind the accident that did this" —and he thumped his chest— "to me!"

Spider-Man watched the movements of the tentacles. It seemed that they were everywhere, and it was getting hard for his spider-sense to keep track of them all.

"I didn't do anything to you! The accident was just that—an accident!"

"Do you expect me to believe you?"

"I'd held out a vague hope for it, yeah," retorted Spider-Man. He spoke with a flippancy he did not feel, but the last thing he was going to do was let Octopus be aware of just how petrified he was. And yet, the flippancy somehow came naturally to him. As if the costume, in providing anonymity, somehow gave rise to a devil-may-care attitude that precluded caring about annoying people. Indeed, an attitude that rejoiced in annoying people.

However, annoying someone who had hundreds of people terrified for their lives was probably not the brightest move Spider-Man could make.

"Hope," said Octopus, "is one thing you do not have." And with no further preamble, his tentacles lashed out at Spider-Man.

Spider-Man dropped off the ceiling and, as he plummeted, fired his webbing straight at Dr. Octopus's face.

The webbing plastered itself over Doc Ock's glasses, obscuring his vision and sticking to his face with steel-hard adhesion.

Doc Ock howled, trying to pull it off himself. Spider-Man hit the ground, ricocheted off it and headed straight for Ock himself.

He got close, but that was all.

The arms were all around, and one of them reached up and deflected Spider-Man's leap. The moment the arm knew where he was, it wrapped itself around his legs, immobilizing him. Before Spider-Man could move, another mechanical arm had ensnared his upper torso, and now Spider-Man was in danger of being torn apart.

This is what happens when you go up against a real opponent, a voice in his head warned him. *You're going to die now. You're going to die, he's going to do to you what that thug did to Uncle Ben, and it will all have come full circle . . .*

Driven by desperation and franticness, Spider-Man exerted his strength and pushed his way clear of the mechanical arms. As Octopus struggled with the webbing over his face, Spider-Man leaped and dodged. The arms pursued him relentlessly.

He anchored himself to the ceiling, grabbed two arms as they approached and then, with almost balletic movements, tied them together. The tentacles were too thick around, and the metal too dense, for the knot to hold. But just for a moment they were immobilized.

Doc Ock twisted around, still yanking at the webbing.

Then Spider-Man saw it. Under the lab coat, hanging from Octopus's belt—a gun, but one that was unlike any that Spider-Man had ever seen.

It had to be the device that had caused the building to rise into the air. At least he hoped it was.

The other two tentacles speared out toward where Spider-Man was, but he wasn't there anymore. Instead he was hurtling through the air, firing a webline to snag the gun. He yanked, pulling it free of the belt, just as Dr. Octopus pulled the webbing clear of his face, taking half the skin with it.

Dr. Octopus shrieked in pain and indignation; if he'd had his tentacles around Spider-Man, Spider-Man would very likely have died at that instant.

"*Give me that!*" shouted Dr. Octopus.

Spider-Man had the gun in his hands. It was covered with an array of buttons and regulating switches; it wasn't anything like a simple handgun. This thing had to be operated by someone who knew what he was doing, and Spider-Man hadn't had the time to try and figure it out yet. Plus, his major concern was to get Octopus clear of the people who might get hurt.

No more innocents were going to die because Spider-Man failed to think ahead. No more.

It was at this moment that Spider-Man was most vulnerable, because Octopus could easily grab any of the delegates and threaten to kill him unless Spider-Man gave him back the gun.

Octopus had one major weakness, though: he was nuts. By definition, that meant that he might not be thinking in the most rational means available.

"Come and get it!" challenged Spider-Man. "Or are you afraid?"

With a roar, Octopus came after him, his arms propelling him forward like a torpedo.

Spider-Man vaulted the distance between himself and the nearest exit. He charged out, and right behind him came the infuriated Dr. Octopus.

On the roof of a skyscraper, Lance Bannon adjusted his telephoto lens. He had managed to slip past police barricades, hundreds of soldiers, and cops trying to keep everyone away. He, Lance Bannon, had managed to snag himself a ringside seat.

He peered through his viewfinder, and then he saw something . . . something on the outside wall of the rectangular building.

It was Spider-Man.

"*Yes!*" shouted Bannon triumphantly. "Ha! Eat my dust, Peter Parker! I'd like to see you try and get closer to the action than this!"

He'd managed to lose Octopus through the twists and turns of the building corridors, but he didn't know how much time he was going to have. Hurriedly he studied the controls of the gun, divining the correct usage, praying that he knew what the hell he was doing.

There were two dials that he hadn't figured out yet: one blue, one red. One of them, he was certain, when adjusted properly would slowly reverse the polarity of the ions, and lower the building gently to the ground. The other would do it all at once, sending the building hurtling downward to an inglorious and fatal termination.

Then he realized—his spider-sense could be an additional guide.

He turned the blue dial, aimed the gun at the building, started to squeeze the trigger . . . and his spider-sense screamed at him. He eased up immediately, for the message was clear. If the gun was adjusted in that manner, then extreme danger was going to follow. A safe descent was not dangerous. Ergo, a rapid descent was more likely.

He turned the blue dial back, and then adjusted the red dial. He aimed it and, once again, his finger began to depress the trigger. This time there was no warning sensations in his head. This time . . .

And suddenly his spider-sense went off again. He eased up on the trigger . . . but the warnings were still there . . .

The wall to his immediate right shattered, pounded apart by the impact of the tentacles, and Dr. Octopus emerged. He spotted Spider-Man immediately and shouted, "*Give me that! It's mine!*" His tentacles descended on Spider-Man.

Spider-Man charged up the side of the building. Dr. Octopus was right behind him, his vicious tentacles hauling him up.

Spider-Man made it to the rooftop and suddenly one of

the tentacles lashed out at his right. He spun out of the way, but now another tagged him from behind, crashing against his arm. The impact was fearsome, and despite the incredible adhesion ability of his fingers, the gun nevertheless flew from Spider-Man's hand. It clattered across the roof.

He fired his webbing to snag it, but the tentacles got in the way. "Fine then!" shouted Spider-Man and fired more webbing, cocooning three of Doc Ock's tentacles.

The tentacles struggled with the webbing and lashed toward Spider-Man, a fearsome metal club. Spider-Man dodged them as the tentacles smashed this way and that, sending pieces of the roof flying.

Then the tentacles exerted themselves, and the webbing snapped. They writhed free and came at him again.

One of them snagged his left wrist, the vicious pincer-like claws immobilizing his arm. He tried to yank free, but then his right wrist was caught, and before he knew it, his ankles were likewise ensnared.

He was helpless, utterly helpless, all four limbs paralyzed by the strength of the tentacles.

Dr. Octopus laughed chillingly and drew Spider-Man toward him.

"So," sneered Octopus, "the Amazing Spider-Man turns out to be not so amazing after all."

"The most amazing thing here is that you think you're something special," retorted Spider-Man. "You're nothing, Octopus. Just a demented creep."

"You dare insult me!" said Octopus. "I'll kill you for that!"

"Fine. I'll be dead, but you won't be any less of a demented creep."

At that second, the building shifted under them. Far below, the crowd screamed.

The antigravity charge with which Octopus had shot the building was starting to wear off.

The slight jostle threw Octopus slightly off balance, rocking him on his heels.

It was enough.

Spider-Man suddenly twisted around and, with his increased strength, yanked his right arm free of the tentacle that had trapped it. He brought his right arm over, snagged the tentacle that had caught his left arm and with a powerful twist of his arm, which threatened to dislocate his shoulder, pulled that free as well.

Then he grabbed Ock's upper right tentacle with both arms and, incredibly, started dragging himself forward, hand over hand, down the length of Octopus's tentacle.

The tentacle writhed under his grip, and his feet were still trapped, but the strength in Spider-Man's arms was more than a match, and the fury that was building in him was forcing him to overcome, to ignore the pain that was ripping through his lower body as Octopus tried to pry him off. Octopus brought his other, free tentacle over and started to club viciously at the teenager. Spider-Man ignored it, ignored the screaming of his muscles, ignored everything except the fact that he was getting closer to Octopus, and closer—he was five feet away, now four, and every inch that he was traversing was costing him dearly, but he would not be stopped, could not be stopped.

Octopus couldn't believe it. He saw Spider-Man's flesh shake under the pounding, heard the grunts of anguish, and still his foe kept coming, kept coming. And now three feet away, and Spider-Man was almost on top of him . . .

"You're mad!" howled Octopus, unable to accept that any but an insane person would sustain this sort of punishment.

And Spider-Man wrapped both of his hands around the base of the upper right tentacle, where it connected with the control plate under Ock's shirt.

"I'm not mad," shot back Spider-Man. "I'm just really pissed off."

He pulled with all his strength.

The right tentacle ripped out of its base, sparks flying everywhere.

Octopus howled with such pain, such anguish, that it was Spider-Man's first inkling of just how completely man and machine had become linked. There was no blood, but there just as well might have been, because for Dr. Octopus it was the mental and physical equivalent of Spider-Man ripping out one of his own flesh-and-blood arms.

The edges of his lab coat caught fire from the sparks, and Doc Ock dropped to the ground, rolling and thrashing about to try and extinguish them.

Spider-Man leaped clear, scooped up the antigravity gun. He felt the building jostle again, and then he pointed the gun downward and fired.

The entire General Assembly Building was bathed in a greenish light. The shuddering settled down and slowly, gently, the General Assembly Building began to settle toward the ground . . .

And that was when the roof was ripped out from under Spider-Man.

He leaped clear of it, spun, and saw Octopus coming toward him.

He had three tentacles left, and he was utterly berserk.

The tentacles were coming in too fast, too furiously, and for all his speed, Spider-Man could barely stay ahead of them. No matter which way he dodged, the metal arms were there, cutting him off, hounding him, pursuing him across the length of the roof.

One tripped him up, and another cracked across his head. Spider-Man went down, clutching the anti-grav gun. The tentacles whipped past him, and he back flipped out of the way . . .

And one of the tentacle's gripper claws snagged him around the throat. Another wrapped around both his arms, and although Doc Ock's arms never tired, Spider-Man most definitely did.

"*I'll kill you!*" howled Dr. Octopus, shaking Spider-Man as a dog would a bone.

Spider-Man felt the world blacking out in front of him, even as his desperate fingers blindly twisted the dials on the gun. Only his hands were free, but with those hands he raised the gun and, uttering a quick prayer, fired.

The ray enveloped Dr. Octopus. Octopus let out a startled yelp—and rose into the air. Unlike the hapless jeweler, Octopus had no ceiling to stop him. And, unlike the anti-grav charge he had unleashed at the building, this blast wasn't carefully modulated for mass and density.

He soared heavenward at high velocity . . .

. . . and then stopped.

Because his arms were still choking Spider-Man.

Spider-Man's feet were adhering him to the roof. The costumed teenager frantically pulled at the claw, trying to pry it loose. He felt his throat collapsing, his larynx being crushed under the steady pressure.

And then his feet were ripped loose from the roof.

It wasn't that he had lost his grip. Pieces of the roof were sticking to the undersides of his feet. It had been the section of the roof that had given way.

Spider-Man and Dr. Octopus soared at an angle across the Manhattan sky, sailing out over the East River. Spider-Man had still been clutching onto the ray gun, but now he needed both hands or he didn't have a hope in hell.

He let go of the gun, and it spiralled down and away.

Dr. Octopus shouted his fury, but there was nothing he could do. The gun was already far out of his reach, and falling faster and farther with every passing second.

Spider-Man fired his webbing. Some of it Octopus managed to deflect with an arm, but some got onto his shirt. Spider-Man yanked with all his strength, and Octopus—with nothing to grab onto—shot through the air and crashed into Spider-Man.

If the claw on his tentacle had been mechanically controlled, the impact would not have affected it. But it was tied in with Octopus's nervous system, and when he was jolted, so was the claw. It loosened just slightly, but it was enough for Spider-Man to pry it off. Spider-Man gasped, sucking in air greedily.

The two foes twisted and struggled in midair, each jockeying for a solid position, each trying to get the upper hand on the other. Spider-Man couldn't get a clear punch at Octopus because the arms kept getting in the way, but Spider-Man in turn was clambering all over the place so that Octopus couldn't get another firm grip on him.

Octopus saw an opening and, with his biological right arm, slugged Spider-Man in the chin. Spider-Man's head snapped back, the strength of the crazed scientist momentarily catching him off guard.

"*Hah!*" shouted Doc Ock, and then a fierce punch from Spider-Man sent him spiralling backward. Spider-Man was still in the clutches of the tentacles, though, and besides, he was also in midair. There was nowhere, he realized, for him to go.

As it turned out, he was wrong.

Because at that moment, the brief anti-grav charge that he'd hit Doc Ock with wore off.

Dr. Octopus plummeted, and along with him went the Amazing Spider-Man. Down, down they spiralled toward the East River. Doc Ock was still trying to kill him, still struggling, still cursing at him.

Then Spider-Man saw an opening and took it; his fist speared forward and slugged Doc Ock square in the chest with all his strength. He felt something give under the impact, the metal of the chest plate.

Dr. Octopus screamed and this time his arms reflexively shoved Spider-Man away. They were also spasmodic, though, as if the "life" that they'd possessed was ebbing out of them.

Spider-Man, free of Octopus, spun in midair, managed to pull his body into a dive position, and hit the water clean. He plunged down, slowing his descent. Then he twisted around and kicked upward with a powerful scissor movement of his legs. He started toward the surface . . .

And then he saw something, some yards away under the water.

It was Dr. Octopus.

He had survived the fall.

The landing was another matter, however.

His three remaining metal arms were hanging lifelessly at his side, dead weight, rapidly dragging him down like three large anchors. He was thrashing about, having ripped away his shirt, and he was now desperately, frantically, trying to pull the metal harness off his body. It remained fused to his skin, however, and wasn't going anywhere except down, along with him.

In the dimness of the water, he still somehow managed to spot Spider-Man. Despite his attempts to kill Spider-Man; to extort the world; to potentially commit mass murder—despite all of it, Octopus was now nothing more than a terrified human being. He reached up through the darkness, his fingers clutching at the water, reaching toward Spider-Man who was too far away to do anything.

And then he was gone, dragged out of sight to the inky blackness of the river bottom.

For a moment Spider-Man almost went after him, but the air was already growing stale in his lungs. He felt the pounding against his chest, the need for fresh air.

He kicked upward, and somehow the surface seemed much, much too far away. He realized with bleak certainty that he was not going to make it. That he and Dr. Octopus were going to share the same watery grave. And he kept thinking that up to, and even past, the moment when he broke the surface.

"Look at this!" Flash Thompson was shaking a copy of the *Daily Bugle.*

It was the next day, in detention hall. Flash was there because Flash was usually there. A number of his cronies were there as well. Sitting off to the side, staring into space, was Peter Parker.

"Can you believe this Jameson jerk?" demanded Flash, and then proceeded to read, " 'The Spider-Men of this world are precisely what are not needed. Costumed vigilantees who not only denigrate the efforts of trained law-enforcement officials, but also serve to exacerbate the antisocial tendencies of pathetic wretches like Otto Octavius. If it were not for Spider-Man and his activities, the so-called Dr. Octopus would not have been motivated to take actions that resulted in an international incident.' And look at this headline! *'Spider-Man: Threat or Menace?'* '' Thompson threw the newspaper down onto the table in disgust. "This is such crap! Where does Jameson get off? He makes it sound like Doc Ock is somebody we should feel sorry for, while Spidey is a crook or something.''

Peter couldn't help himself. He looked up and said in amusement, " 'Spidey?' You his pal or something, Flash?''

"I could be!'' declared Flash forcefully. "He and I, we could be buds. 'Cause Spider-Man is my kind of guy.''

"How do you know that, Flash?''

"Because,'' Flash said confidently, "he's the exact opposite of you, and I can't stand you, so I know he and I would get along great.'' Then he smirked. A couple of his pals high-fived him.

"I guess I can't argue with that,'' said Peter.

" 'Cause you know I'm right.''

"No, because I don't know enough one-syllable words to keep a conversation with you going.''

Flash, naturally, rejoindered with a snappy, "Huh?''

One of the other guys had picked up the paper and continued to read. " 'Whatever bizarre gifts or abilities this masked adventurer may have, he must realize that our helpless city is not his playground to do as he pleases. Just because he has powers—whether by Divine Providence or, more likely, through clever trickery—these powers must be used wisely. Thus far, nothing we've seen in Spider-Man's showboating, crowd-endangering stunts indicates that he is capable of doing so.' "

"What does he know?" said Flash.

"Maybe a little," Peter said.

Flash made a dismissive gesture, but Peter wasn't even listening anymore.

He was thinking about Aunt May, still walking around the house as if she were in a fog.

He was thinking of the gentle white-haired man who was no longer waiting to greet him with a smile or a gentle joke.

He was thinking of the thug who had destroyed their lives, and who had run past Spider-Man while the so-called "hero" had been revelling in his new-found sense of smugness and capriciousness.

He had been given—by Divine Providence—a great power. And his first impulse was to trivialize it, to use it purely for monetary gain and self-aggrandizement. He had given no thought to how his abilities could be used for the betterment of others. And for this sin, for this selfishness, it had been his uncle who had paid.

And who might it be next time?

There could never be a next time. He knew that with utter certainty. He could never again, through inaction or complacency, allow an innocent person to suffer.

Because he had learned, the hard way, for now and for ever, that with great power . . . comes great responsibility.

S U I T S

TOM DE HAVEN AND DEAN WESLEY SMITH

Illustration by Steve Ditko

NOTE: This story takes place concurrently with the events chronicled in the comic book The Amazing Spider-Man #7 *(December 1963) by Stan Lee & Steve Ditko, and takes place very shortly after Peter Parker becomes Spider-Man.*

The two-fisted uppercut rocked Spider-Man off the edge of the building's parapet and into the cold winter air eighty stories above the street. The first thought fighting its way through the haze of pain from the blow was that he needed to learn to totally trust his spider-sense. It had tried to warn him that the Vulture was coming, but he hadn't listened. It might have been a fatal mistake.

"This time," the Vulture said, "the victory is mine." The Vulture's cackling laugh echoed through the thin cold air. As they both dropped through the air, toward the almost empty street below, the Vulture pounded Spidey's head and face with steel-hard fists.

With one last massive blow to Spider-Man's head and a sharp snap of his huge wings, the Vulture stopped in the air and watched Spider-Man fall.

"Happy landings, Spider-Man," he shouted, and again his laugh echoed through the streets, filling the air with a coldness far beyond the freezing temperature and black sky.

Twisting around in midair Spidey fought to clear his head. He didn't need his spider-sense going wild to tell him he had to break his fall somehow. Quickly he aimed a web-shooter at the edge of a nearby building and fired. His vision was blurred and his head ached from the pounding the Vulture had given him. His shot missed, the webbing trailing uselessly behind him like the tail of a kite.

Did he have time for another try? And even if his webbing did catch, would it hold at this speed? And would his arms hold if he did manage to snag the side of a building?

Twisting around instantly, his head clearing except for the spider-sense warning filling his every cell, he shot a web at the corner of a passing building.

It caught, just barely enough.

The snap of the web against his arm sent pain through his shoulder, but somehow he hung on. The webbing swung him sharply around the corner of the building and sent him bouncing across a lower rooftop like a kid's ball kicked across a smooth floor.

He curled and rolled with the momentum as jabs of pain shot through his left arm and shoulder.

Then it was over.

With an impact that knocked the breath out of him, his body slammed against a brick wall and finally stopped, upside down.

His first thought was a cheerful, "I'm alive."

But as he started to move, he quickly realized he wasn't much more than that.

Staggering to his feet, the pain in his arm and shoulder almost making him black out, he ducked inside the stairway door and quickly webbed himself to the wall above the door. If he kept quiet the Vulture wouldn't spot him. There was no way with his hurt arm he would have a chance fighting him again.

Twenty agonizing minutes later his spider-sense told him the Vulture had moved on. With a whimper of pain he slipped off the wall and moved slowly down the dark, musty-smelling stairs. He'd have to take his chances in the street instead of above it. With the pain in his arm throbbing like someone was poking him with a hot branding iron, there was no way he could swing on webbing—at least not tonight. And maybe not for some nights to come, even though he healed fast with his new spider powers.

On the way across town, working from shadow to shadow, his thoughts were as black as the night. This Spider-Man thing just wasn't worth the grief and pain. Maybe he should just hang it up altogether. Maybe old J. Jonah Jameson was right. Maybe he was a public menace. Maybe he should just finish school like any other normal guy and let someone else do the fighting. Who had elected him to the job, anyhow? Hadn't the world got along just fine without him just a year ago? Sure it had. And it would survive without Spider-Man next year if it had to.

Pain shot through his arm and shoulder as he brushed against the edge of a building. He stopped and sucked down a deep breath of icy night air. He certainly would have some time to think about quitting now.

And time to think about just how close he had come to being killed.

Aunt May replaced the phone with a soft click in its cradle and then stood silently staring at it.

Peter, his left arm in a sling, had been doing homework at the dining room table. Two days had passed since the Vulture had almost killed him. He had decided to quit being Spider-Man at least ten different times in those two days. On a date with Betty Brant the night before she had said how much she didn't like Spider-Man, even quoting some of J. Jonah Jameson's words from a recent editorial. If she ever found out he was Spider-Man, he'd never see her again, which left him even more convinced he should hang up the suit.

"You all right?" Peter asked Aunt May after a moment

of her standing silently over the phone.

She stirred and then nodded, her thin frame and bony shoulders always seeming tired and stooped under by a perpetual heavy weight. "That was Mary-Alice."

"Last minute planning for your trip?" Peter asked, then glanced down at the math book in front of him. His aunt and her friend Mary-Alice had been planning a trip to Atlantic City for months, and at times it seemed that it was all Aunt May could talk about. Aunt May had won the free bus tickets to Atlantic City a few months back from a contest at her favorite grocery store. Ever since, she had saved nickels and quarters in a jar so she would have some extra gambling money. They planned on leaving in the morning and Peter would have bet anything that Aunt May had had her bag packed for two days.

Aunt May sighed. "Mary-Alice slipped and broke her hip this afternoon. She's all right. They say she'll be out of the hospital in a few days, and good as new in a few months." After another moment she took a deep, shuddering breath, moved over, and slumped down into a chair across from Peter at the dining room table.

"That's really sad," Peter said. "I know how much you were looking forward to this trip."

Aunt May just nodded and didn't say a word. All the color and life that planning for this trip had brought to her face was now gone, replaced by a pale, sickly white: The same look she had worn for months after his uncle was killed.

"Can't you find someone to take Mary-Alice's place?"

Aunt May shook her head slowly, seeming to think about it for a few moments. "Not on this short notice."

"And you can't get the tickets rescheduled?"

Again Aunt May shook her head.

Peter glanced down at the homework in front of him, and then back at his aunt. His grades had been suffering a bit for the last year since he became Spider-Man. But there were no tests in the next few days, and he could take the homework with him. On top of that it might not hurt him to get out of the city for a few days. He was already thought of as a skinny, weak wimp at school and his excuse that he had hurt his arm playing volleyball hadn't slowed the taunts at all. It would be good to give his arm time to heal and get rid of the sling. Besides, a trip with Aunt May would give him time to think about his future—and Spider-Man's future.

"I'd love to go with you," Peter said.

His aunt, somewhat startled, looked up at him. "Oh, Peter, that's nice, but you have school."

"No tests and nothing really important going on. I'm sure if you write them a note they wouldn't care at all. And I'll take my homework with me and actually do it, I promise."

Slowly some pinks and reds flowed back into Aunt May's cheeks as she thought about Peter's offer. With only a glance at the phone she laughed and said yes. She clapped her hands together as though she was applauding a good stage show. "Oh, won't this be fun?"

Then she jumped to her feet and headed for the stairs. "We'd better get you packed."

The Port Authority smelled of cleaning solution and diesel, mixed with the occasional stray smell of some greasy food cooking. Peter had his bag and one of Aunt May's in his good hand as they stepped out through the glass doors and headed for the line of people leading to their bus. He'd left his sling at home, but still held his left arm across his chest to protect it.

Aunt May was a few steps ahead of him carrying one small bag and clutching her purse and the tickets in her other hand. She was as excited as a freshman on the first day of high school. Since his uncle's murder, she hadn't smiled much. It was good to see her happy again, even if it meant a long bus trip and a boring few days in Atlantic City for him.

They ended up in the middle of the bus with Aunt May on one side of the aisle and Peter on the other. Aunt May sat next to another elderly woman dressed in a flower-print suit very much like her own. The lady looked almost as excited as Aunt May did. Aunt May introduced herself and Peter, and from that point on the two women talked non-stop.

That was just fine with Peter. He settled back and watched the few remaining passengers get on. One of the last was a middle-aged man with dark black hair and huge arms. He stood only about five-foot-two and his clothes looked like he had slept in them. He carried a small satchel that looked well-worn.

The bus driver said something to the man and the guy nodded, then glanced toward the back of the bus with a look as though he was taking everything and everyone in at once. The man's eyes snapped Peter to attention. They were dark, almost black, and set deep into his head. Wrinkles surrounded them and a feeling of immense sadness radiated from those dark windows. But beyond that they were the eyes of a man who had seen the world and knew what he was looking at. Those eyes didn't match the man's outward appearance at all.

He started slowly down the aisle, paying little or no attention to the other passengers. As he got closer, Peter noticed a slight tingling in his spider-sense that caused him to sit up just a little straighter. After the Vulture had knocked him off that building there was no way he would ever ignore his spider-sense again.

Slightly in front of Peter, the man suddenly stopped and looked directly into Peter's eyes. For a moment Peter could read the sudden puzzlement on the man's face as he studied Peter.

But then, just as quickly, the man smiled, started forward again, and as he reached Peter's seat he lightly squeezed Peter on the shoulder.

"Hey, brother," is all he said as he moved on toward the back and found a seat next to an elderly man.

Peter had no idea at all what the guy saw or why he'd called him brother, but for the rest of the trip he kept glancing back at the man and every time he did, the guy would smile and give Peter a little salute.

And with every salute, Peter's spider-sense tingled.

It was a very long bus trip.

By the time they reached Atlantic City, Aunt May had made plans with her newfound friend and as soon as they were checked into the hotel, she went off on the first planned excursion, with Peter making the excuse that he would rather stay behind if she didn't mind and just do some homework.

Their hotel room was what Peter would call comfortable: two fairly big beds, nice thick carpet that looked new, and a large television set. But after an hour of alternating between boring television and even more boring math, Peter found himself wandering among the loud bells, bright lights, and loud talking of the casino.

For some reason the whole atmosphere of the place disturbed Peter. He knew that most of the people's laughter was forced, that many of those here couldn't afford to be in this room, and for many this room was an addiction as deadly as any drug.

Mirrored ceilings and bubbles spaced evenly throughout left no doubt that everyone was being constantly watched, and that twisted Peter's stomach. He was much more used to the silence of the night, high over the streets of New York, where being watched by anyone usually spelt danger.

With the thought of danger, Peter became aware of the slight warning his spider-sense was giving him, hidden under the loud noise of the casino.

Leaning against an open slot machine and doing his best to just blend in, he studied the room until he spotted the man from the bus sitting at a poker table. And from the looks of it the guy was losing, and losing bad.

After a moment, as if he could sense Peter watching him, the guy turned around and looked directly at Peter. He waved for Peter to come over and again ignoring the very slight warning from his spider-sense, Peter moved between the blackjack tables to the poker area.

"Hang around for a minute," the guy said as Peter stopped near the padded rail of the poker section. His voice was deep and assured, not at all matching the disheveled look of his clothes and rough beard. "You might bring me some luck."

Peter just shrugged and watched for two hands as the guy won two pots, and then scraped his chips into his hand and stood.

"Thanks," he said to Peter. "Looks like I came out ahead for a change." Holding the chips up he asked, "Can I buy you lunch?"

Peter shook his head. "Thanks, just ate." He hadn't, but he didn't want to get stuck at a table with this guy for an hour, especially if the guy was a crazy.

"Well," the guy said. "let's take a walk. We should get to know one another." He stuck out his hand. "My name is Damon. Damon Hooks."

Peter shook the guy's hand with his good arm and introduced himself, then followed the guy out the front of the casino. They turned and slowly started down the boardwalk. Peter was conscious of the slight crowd in the early evening, and the fact that he was considerably taller than his companion.

"Just out of curiosity," Peter said, "you seemed to recognize me on the bus. But I don't remember you."

Damon laughed. "I don't really know you. I just have this ability to recognize costume types. I call them suits."

Peter was shocked, but instead he just laughed. "Well, you got it wrong this time."

Damon stared at Peter for a moment as they walked, their heels clicking on the boardwalk, people moving around them in a hurry to get places. "I don't think so," he said after a few more moments. "I can always tell an off-duty suit. And you know why?"

Peter just shook his head no, without saying a thing. This guy might be totally crazy, but he was right about the "suit" thing.

"I used to be one," Damon said. He laughed. "Hard to believe, huh?" He indicated how he looked and then patted the paunch that hung slightly over his belt. "Sure couldn't tell it by looking at me now. Which one are you, anyhow?"

Peter shook his head. "You got it wrong this time. Honest you do. I wouldn't want to be one of those idiots."

"You sure you're not one of those Fantastic Four? Or one of those mutant X-Men? Never can get their names straight."

"Sorry to disappoint you," Peter said.

"Oh, you're one of them all right. I can tell. And I don't blame you for not trusting me. I really don't. You have no reason to."

"Good point," Peter said.

They walked for a minute in silence before Damon asked, "You ever hear of the Black Bee?"

Peter shook his head. "Nope, can't say as I have."

Damon laughed. "Not surprising. I was working this area and all over New Jersey about twenty years ago." Damon glanced up at Peter and laughed. "Way before your time. Of course I only stayed 'in business' about two years. That might have something to do with you never hearing of me."

"It might," Peter said. But he didn't say that he thought the only reason he hadn't heard of the Black Bee was that the guy was making it all up. Meeting crazies like this guy was another fun aspect of being Spider-Man.

Another good reason to hang it up and get back to a normal life.

"I was working in a toxic waste dump when it all started," Damon said. "Had a good home, nice wife named

Connie, and a steady job. You know, I had been working outside for almost ten years and never got stung by a bee until that Friday afternoon.''

Peter nodded and let the guy go on talking as they walked past shops and food stands along the boardwalk. The smells were making Peter hungry, but he still didn't want to commit to a long talk with this guy.

"It was one of the biggest bees I'd ever seen. It must've been hanging around the dump for too long, I guess, and messed around with the radioactive slime too much. So I got stung by this thing, and instead of ballooning up or getting sick, I got the powers of a bee. Weird, huh?''

Peter again just nodded, not because he thought it was weird but because of how similar it sounded to how he came to be Spider-Man. Too similar, actually—almost creepy.

They turned off the boardwalk and ambled down onto the beach. Here the wind seemed stronger, and the evening colder. Peter pulled his jacket up around his neck and they kept walking.

"Look at this,'' Damon said and held the back of his hand up so that the light from the boardwalk shown on it.

The knuckles were white and looked swollen. But otherwise the hand looked fine.

Damon tapped the slightly swollen knuckles. "That's where the stingers were when I needed them. I used to knock people right out with those babies, let me tell you.''

"I'll bet,'' Peter said. "What happened? Did you have them removed?''

Damon shook his head and just studied the back of his hand for a moment before lowering it to his side. "Nope. They just retracted out of sight. One Friday night after about two years of doing my caped crusader routine, I ran into just a few too many clever gang members. Three of them kept me busy from the front while three others came up from behind me. Right down there by that shop." Damon pointed down the beach toward a candy shop on the boardwalk.

Peter nodded, now actually interested in what had happened.

"They caught me from behind with two-by-fours. By the time they were done beating on me I ended up in the hospital with broken bones, internal injuries, and a headache that wouldn't quit. Was in there for over a month."

"You ever find who got you?"

Damon shook his head sadly no. "Never could make myself put the suit back on."

Peter nodded again. He knew that feeling real well. He glanced down at his still sore arm and thought back to that fall that almost killed him. This guy was right in quitting. What was the point of hurting yourself like that? Peter moved his arm up and let the pain add confirmation to his decision to leave the costume in the closet.

They turned and headed back away from the ocean and toward the boardwalk, walking in silence for a few moments until finally Damon said, "My wife left me a year later."

"Because you quit?" Peter couldn't believe that someone would actually want another person to be a "suit."

Damon nodded. "Actually, yes, but not in the way you think. I started drinking to try to forget, to make myself walk away from all the pain and problems I saw around me. And by walking away, I also walked away from who I was."

They climbed the stairs back up to the boardwalk in silence. Then Damon went on. "Since that Friday night I've been married and divorced twice, can't seem to keep a job for more than a few months before I blow it, and I'm still drinking. I live in New York because I can't stand to be here very often, even though I love it. Too many memories."

"All because you quit being the Black Bee?"

Damon nodded. "It was a gift. Hell, it was a career, and I blew it. And along with blowing it, I destroyed my life."

"So why didn't you just go back to it?"

"After two years I tried," Damon said, holding up his hand again. "But the stingers didn't work and I'd lost most of the rest of my powers, too. It was like any other talent. If you don't use it, you lose it. I lost it."

They walked in silence down the now more crowded boardwalk in the direction of the hotel and casino. Within a hundred feet of the hotel, Damon turned to Peter and asked, "So who are you? What suit do you wear?"

Peter didn't say anything and Damon after a moment just laughed. He pointed to the entrance of a small bar and said, "I think I'll stop in here for a few drinks."

"It was nice talking to you," Peter said.

"I enjoyed it, too," Damon said. "Stop by some time when you're back in New York. I live in the Calimax Hotel."

"I just might do that."

"See ya, kid," Damon said and disappeared into the bar.

Peter wandered back through the casino and upstairs to the room knowing that his decision had been made. He was going back to New York and putting back on his "suit." Everything that Damon had said made sense to him, not just on the surface, but deep down inside. Deep down in the place where Uncle Ben's death touched him in the be-

ginning. If he could make any difference at all in the world
by being Spider-Man, it would be a difference worth making.

Before sleeping he exercised and stretched his sore arm
and shoulder. Another day and it might be able to support
him from a web. Another day after that, he wouldn't even
notice that it was weaker. The Vulture was still out there.

But three days from now Spider-Man would change that.

And true to his word, three days later the police had
the Vulture's wings clipped, his hands in handcuffs, and
were leading him off to jail.

The fight had turned out to be fairly easy. Spidey had
caught the Vulture as he was trying to rob J. Jonah Jameson
of the *Daily Bugle* payroll. Their fight covered three floors
and mostly destroyed the *Daily Bugle*'s offices, over the protests of Jonah and to the delight of Spidey. As he said to
one of Jonah's complaints, "It couldn't happen to a nicer
guy."

The end of the fight came when the Vulture tried the
same trick again on Spider-Man. Only this time Peter listened to his spider-sense and dodged the Vulture's attack
instead of letting the Vulture pull him high into the air over
the city.

The Vulture thought he had won because he would just
drop Spider-Man to his death.

But Spidey was one to learn from his mistakes. Never
again would he find himself in the air without a way of
stopping or slowing his descent. So when he had gotten
back from Atlantic City he had spent most of a night in the
lab working on a new type of webbing, one that would form

solid. And before he went to look for the Vulture he had added it to his web-shooters.

So as the Vulture neared a thousand feet above the city, Spidey surrounded the Vulture's wings with webbing and started them falling toward the ground.

Now it was time for the Vulture to cry for mercy and cry he did. But Spider-Man just swung around onto the Vulture's back and using the new webbing formed a large parachute that floated them safely to the ground and the Vulture into the hands of the police.

Later that same night, feeling good about his victory and not really wanting to do more math homework, Spider-Man found himself dangling upside down outside the window of Damon Hooks's room.

The hotel was a run-down place mostly full of drifters and those down on their luck. Damon's room seemed almost too bare to hold a man's entire life. A single unmade bed filled one corner, an old television covered a scarred dresser, and a few bottles of beer littered the floor beside an armchair.

Spider-Man shook his head, convinced now more than ever that he had made the right decision. Even though old Jonah didn't think so, the city was a safer place tonight because of Spider-Man and Peter liked that thought. In fact, he liked it a lot.

He was about to fire a web at a nearby building and swing off when he noticed Damon come out of a bar just down the street. And in the shadows where Damon was unsteadily heading were two muggers, both with guns and both looking like they meant business.

Spider-Man quickly swung down just as the two men jumped in front of Damon. Damon stopped, almost not believing what he was seeing. But it was very real—two dangerous men with guns pointed directly at him.

Spider-Man swung in behind them with the intent of knocking them down without them seeing him coming, but he once again made a mistake with his spider-sense. Thinking it was simply warning him about the danger of the two men with guns, and intensified because he was getting closer, he landed on the sidewalk behind the two men. In fact, it intensified because the sidewalk was covered with a sheet of ice. With a hard smack and cry of pain he slipped and fell on his still-sore shoulder.

Both gunmen spun and aimed at Spider-Man, but before either could fire Damon was on them. With a flurry of quick movement, faster than Spidey could regain his footing, it was over.

Both muggers dropped to the street in agony; large black bee stingers extended from their necks.

Spider-Man rubbed his sore arm and flexed his shoulder. "I've got to quit doing that." Maybe he would give the shoulder a few more days to heal and catch up on that homework after all.

Over the two sprawled muggers Damon stood staring unbelieving at his hands. Then, with the biggest grin Spider-Man had seen in years, Damon looked up at him. "They worked again."

"That they did, Damon," Spider-Man said as he moved up beside Damon. "Thanks. You saved my life." He didn't want to tell Damon that he could have handled those two just fine. It was better to let Damon think he had really helped. And in an odd way, he had. It was because of him that Peter was Spider-Man again.

And that might really have saved Peter's life in the long run.

Damon looked down at where the stingers were retracting back into his hand and then up at Spidey. He was still smiling, but now it was cut slightly with a look of puzzlement. His dark eyes looked Spider-Man quickly over, then he stepped back. "You know my name?"

Spidey laughed. "We suits have got to stick together, you know."

Damon nodded, his full smile returning to his face as he realized just who he was talking to. "Thanks. I think I'm a little too old these days to wear a 'suit,' but thanks anyway, Peter."

Spider-Man just nodded. "Take care of yourself," he said as he shot a web at a far building and swung up into the air.

"You, too," Damon shouted after him.

Fifteen minutes later Spider-Man was perched on the top of a building across from Damon's hotel. He could see Damon rummaging around in his closet and then finally pulling out an old box tied with string.

Sitting at his kitchen table and pushing aside an old pizza box, Damon carefully unwrapped the string and then pulled out an old, black costume that looked a lot like a huge black bee.

He held it up in front of him for a moment and then moved to the mirror. What he saw there made him laugh, but even from across the street Spider-Man could tell it was a good laugh. A laugh that seemed to release years of tension and pressure from the short man's thick shoulders.

With a shake of his head Damon dropped the suit back

into the box, tied the string up tight, and put it back into the closet.

Then, as Spider-Man swung off toward home and his math books, Damon Hooks slowly started to clean up his apartment.

C O O L

LAWRENCE WATT-EVANS

Illustration by Ron Frenz and Patrick Olliffe

Stuart Miller was only nine when he first saw Spider-Man. He was shopping with his mother, getting ready for fourth grade. The two of them were walking up Sixth Avenue across from Macy's when Stuart heard people shouting and looked up.

There he was, swinging across the street on an impossibly thin strand of something black, something almost invisible against the bright blue sky. As Spider-Man reached the end of his swing he raised a hand and something shot out and stuck to a cornice; then at the very top of his swing he let go of the first line, grabbed the second, and swung off down Thirty-Fourth Street toward the Empire State Building.

Stuart turned to follow, fascinated, but his mother grabbed him and dragged him away, up Sixth Avenue, ignoring his protests.

Stuart couldn't concentrate on picking out new shoes; he was imagining what it would be like, swinging up there above the crowds . . .

When his mother gave up in disgust and hustled him home, he sat in front of the TV and saw the news report of Spider-Man battling the Shocker atop the Empire State Building.

"Wow," he said.

He began to watch the news more regularly after that, and to read the newspapers and magazines.

Spider-Man was so tough, so strong, so *cool*—it was almost creepy how he moved so fast and stuck to walls and everything, and Stuart appreciated creepy things.

Stuart had been a movie-monster fan, with pictures of Dracula and Jason and Frankenstein's monster on his wall, but those were just *stories,* and Spider-Man was *real.* And he was a *hero.*

The movie posters came down, and clippings about Spider-Man went up.

Stuart began hanging around places where he thought he might see the web-slinger, and over the next five years he glimpsed his hero eleven times—in Central Park three times, in the East Village twice, and here and there around midtown half a dozen times.

On one of those occasions, when he was twelve, Stuart was just standing on the sidewalk when Spidey swung over him—right over Stuart's head—clearing him by only a yard or so; Stuart shrieked in happy surprise.

To his astonishment, at the end of his next swing Spider-Man didn't shoot a new line, but instead caught the side of the building and hung there, head down.

He then ran *down the side of the building,* as calmly as if he were on level ground, and hung there, ten feet off the ground, as he called out to Stuart, "You okay, kid?"

"I'm fine, Spidey!" Stuart called back, in a paroxysm of delight. "Spidey, I'm your biggest fan! You are so cool!"

Spider-Man smiled—Stuart could see it, even through the mask, the cheeks seemed to rise. "Thanks, kid," he said. "What's your name?"

"Stuart Miller. Oh, wow, I can't believe I'm talking to you! It's just so cool the way you swing on those webs!"

"You like it?"

"Oh, yeah!"

"Want to try it?"

Stuart stared, goggle-eyed, overcome by the thought that he might actually swing on Spider-Man's web. At last he managed a nod.

"Which way are you headed?"

"Uptown," Stuart managed.

Spidey nodded, and offered his back, indicating that Stuart should climb on, piggyback style. Grinning, Stuart did so.

"Hold on tight," Spider-Man called, and Stuart grabbed Spidey around the neck with both hands. The webbing made a "thwip!" sound as Spidey quickly secured Stuart's torso.

Then he was being carried along as if he were on a swing, swooping over the sidewalk, almost a full block uptown before he was lowered gently to the sidewalk. It felt exhilarating, terrifying, and utterly wonderful, and Stuart could hardly breathe.

Then he was back on the pavement, and the webbing went slack as Spidey let it go.

"Don't worry about your shirt," Spider-Man called. "It'll dissolve in an hour or so, and it washes right out." Then he threw Stuart a salute and swung off.

Stuart stared after him—the webbing still clutched in both hands—until Spider-Man vanished in the distance.

He wanted to go home and tell everyone about it, but his mom was busy with some church thing and his father was upstate hunting. When at last he did get a chance to tell his parents, they seemed unimpressed.

"He didn't try anything funny, did he?" Stuart's father asked.

"Of course not!" Stuart replied.

And his friends flat out didn't believe a word.

The next time Stuart saw the web-slinger, he waved and shouted, and Spider-Man waved back.

And the time after that.

The time after that, though, when Stuart was fourteen, Spider-Man didn't see him, didn't wave. Spider-Man was much too busy.

Spider-Man was feeling pretty good—there wasn't much left of the last snow except for an occasional heap of dirty slush, the daffodils were out in Central Park, and spring was very definitely in the air. Aunt May was feeling chipper, and Mary Jane had been all smiles that morning. Thanks to Peter Parker being the only photographer at the scene of the last battle the Avengers fought, he had money in the bank, for once, and just about all of his own enemies were safely in jail.

Life was good, life was skittles and beer, and it was a fine day for web-swinging, so that's what he was doing.

Sometimes, he thought as the wind came through the fabric of his mask and made his skin tingle, being Spider-Man was just about worth all the grief. A swoop, hand up, hit the button, hit the next building, grab and swoop . . .

If there was a more enjoyable way of getting around, Spider-Man didn't know what it was—assuming, of course, you didn't get sick to your stomach from all that up and down; some of his unwilling passengers had had that problem.

Right now, he didn't have any passengers, willing or otherwise; he wasn't chasing anyone or searching for anything, he was just enjoying life.

A swoop around a corner, a loop around a flagpole . . .

That was when he heard sirens somewhere to the west—the diamond district, perhaps?

Well, wherever they were, duty called—with great power comes great responsibility, as well as the fun of swinging from webs. He headed toward the sound.

The sirens were moving north on Eighth Avenue, moving pretty fast, and it wasn't until he reached Columbus Circle, where they turned onto Broadway, that he caught up.

Once he came in sight, though, he quickly spotted the trouble. It was rather hard to miss, actually.

There was a man bouncing up Broadway, clutching a valise.

He wasn't dressed up in any sort of scare-the-victim super-villain costume, but Spider-Man figured anyone taking fifty-foot leaps up Broadway with a bunch of cop cars chasing him was probably a felon, even if he was just in jeans, a black T-shirt, and a leather jacket.

And the valise was probably full of loot—diamonds, maybe.

The bouncing fifty-foot leaps made this all interesting, and put it right into Spider-Man's area of expertise.

He couldn't quite see at first how the guy did it—he was wearing something strange on his feet, though, big boxy things. Giant springs, maybe?

The police were keeping pace with their quarry, but they couldn't catch him—he spent most of his time in the air, and the bounces were too quick for anyone on the ground to grab him.

Spider-Man drew slowly closer, though. He was pleased to see that his web-swinging was slightly faster than the thief's bouncing.

Then, when he was almost in reach, the bouncer left the street. With a higher leap than any he'd managed up to that point he cleared the parapet of one of the lowest of the apartment buildings in the neighborhood, and came down on the roof.

And didn't bounce.

Spider-Man glanced down and saw cop cars starting to turn, to brake, but by the time the police could get to the rooftop, he realized, the thief might be in the building, his footwear removed—they'd have a long search on their hands.

Or he might bounce to one of the neighboring buildings.

Spider-Man, of course, could swing up there in a matter of seconds.

This, Spider-Man thought, was going to be fun.

Stuart heard sirens, but that wasn't anything unusual in New York. He didn't pay any attention.

Then the sirens stopped fairly close by, and Stuart looked up, just glancing out his bedroom window.

And froze.

Stuart was on the twelfth floor of one of the higher buildings in the neighborhood, with a good view of rooftops for several blocks in every direction.

And there was someone on a rooftop, over toward Broadway—someone wearing black and leaping about in a truly unbelievable way.

And there was a second figure, in red and blue . . .

Spider-Man!

Stuart hurried to the window to watch.

"Yo! Bouncing bozo!" Spider-Man called, to get the thief's attention. "Who are you supposed to be, one of the Super Mario Brothers?"

The young man with the trick shoes turned, startled.

"You sure don't look like Mario or Luigi in that outfit, though," Spider-Man said conversationally from the parapet, trying to keep him distracted. "No overalls, no hat—you must be Guido, the black sheep of the family, right?"

"Spider-Man!" the thief said, clutching his valise.

"No, no," Spider-Man said, as he leaped up atop a chimney and crouched there. "You can't be Spider-Man—*I'm* Spider-Man. But if you play real nice, maybe you can have a turn tomorrow, okay?"

"Get away from me!"

"Oh, hey, is that any way to be?" Spidey put the back of one hand to his forehead in a mock histrionic gesture. "I'm hurt. My little heart is broken. I haven't done anything to you." He dropped the hand and grinned down at the punk. "And if you turn yourself in to the nice policemen down on the sidewalk, right now, I won't do anything to you."

"I'm not turning myself in!" The thief clutched the valise to his chest and backed away. "Get away, you freak!"

"Whoa! Name-calling! Naughty, naughty, Mr. Bouncer." Spider-Man leapt right over the thief and landed atop an air conditioner. He lifted his hand, and pressed the stud that should have sent a stream of webbing out to snag the thief.

All that emerged was a thin dribble of goo and a brief hiss.

Spider-Man looked down at his hand, startled.

It was clear enough what had happened, of course; he'd been having so much fun swinging around New York that he'd used up his supply of web fluid.

And he hadn't brought any extra cartridges—he'd been

meaning to make up a new batch of the stuff that morning, but he hadn't gotten around to it before he got distracted by the lovely weather. All his spare cartridges were sitting at home waiting to be filled.

He grimaced under his mask. He obviously wasn't going to be able to just wrap this guy up in webbing, the way he'd planned.

He could have taken the guy out with a kick or a punch right then and there, of course, but he felt so good today that he didn't want to hurt anyone. A punch or a kick would hurt, might even give the guy a concussion or crack a rib, especially if it sent him tumbling while he was trying to use those fancy shoes.

He wouldn't hit this guy at all if he didn't have to, Spider-Man decided; he'd just keep him busy until the cops arrived, or until the guy wore himself out and surrendered. Then he'd let the boys in blue take it from there.

But meanwhile, he had to keep the guy from just bouncing away. Without his webbing he wouldn't be able to keep up with those giant leaps for very long.

If he could convince the thief to fight, instead of flee, that would give the cops time to get here.

"So, Spring-Heel Jack," Spider-Man said, "you gonna just stand there waiting for me, or are you going to use those nifty moon-boots to stomp me first?"

The thief glared at Spider-Man, then said, "Yeah, I'll just do that!" He hopped up, not in one of his superhuman leaps, but just an ordinary jump; Spider-Man guessed that this was part of restarting the bouncing mechanism.

Before the bouncing man could move again, Spider-Man suddenly leapt to a stairwell cover, then to another air conditioner.

"Hey!" the man shouted, "Hold still!"

"So you can stomp me? *Sure* I will!"

"I'll get you wherever you go!"

"Come and try, Bouncing Betty!" Spider-Man called.

Then Spider-Man bounded away again.

The thief turned and bounced after him, but by the time he landed, Spider-Man was somewhere else.

"Nyah nyah nyah, you can't catch me!"

He wouldn't hit the guy if he could help it. No one would get hurt, no bruises or anything, just a game of keep-away until the cops got there.

It might even be fun.

At first everything looked okay—Spider-Man was jumping around, and the other guy, the super-villain, was just standing there. Stuart wondered why Spidey didn't just clobber him.

And then the bad guy started *chasing* Spidey! Spider-Man was jumping all over the roof, and that guy was bouncing after him, and . . . and Spidey wasn't fighting back, he was just *running away*! He wasn't using his webbing or anything!

That super-villain must be a real badass, Stuart thought, and he wished there was something he could do to help.

Why didn't Spidey even *try* to hit him? Did he have a forcefield or something? Was he using some kind of fear gas?

This was *terrible*! Spidey, his hero, was in trouble, and all he was doing was *watching*!

There had to be *something* he could do.

And then a thought struck him.

He turned from the window and ran for his parents'

bedroom, straight to his father's closet.

He wasn't allowed in here, and if his dad ever found out about this, he'd be grounded for life, but he had to help Spidey!

There it was, in the corner behind the clothes—his dad's hunting rifle. And the cartridges were up on the top shelf.

He took the ammo box and the rifle and ran back to his own room, where he loaded the rifle with trembling fingers, watching as that bouncing bastard chased poor Spidey back and forth . . .

The police had opened the stairway door and emerged onto the roof, and Spider-Man sighed with relief. It was just about over.

"Freeze!" a cop called, drawing his pistol.

Then, as Spider-Man turned to say something to the bouncer, a sharp *crack* sounded.

For a moment he thought one of the bounce-boots had broken, or something of that sort, but then he saw the bouncer twist in mid-leap and fall heavily sideways. One of the boots fired on impact, the other didn't, and the thief was suddenly flung sideways, hitting his head against a vent pipe and leaving a smear of blood on the tarred roof.

In an instant, Spidey was beside him, looking him over.

He was bleeding from a wound in the side, unconscious—probably from the blow on the head—but still breathing. Spidey placed a hand on the man's chest and felt a strong heartbeat. He hoped that meant the injuries weren't too serious.

"Did you—" a policeman said.

"No," Spider-Man said, "it wasn't me—someone shot

him! Did you guys have sharpshooters?''

The cops looked at each other uncertainly.

''Forget it, just get him an ambulance, before he bleeds to death!'' Spider-Man looked down, trying to decide whether he should try to bandage the wound somehow, but one of the policemen was running forward, and he decided to leave it to the professionals.

Then he caught the glint of sunlight on glass in a window a few blocks away, a flash that wasn't just from the window; it was moving. He turned and stared, and realized what was glittering.

. A telescopic sight.

Whoever fired that shot, Spider-Man intended to have a few words with him. The bouncer had probably been about to give up—there'd been no reason to shoot him!

He leapt across the rooftop and headed for that window.

Stuart hesitated. He knew he should put the rifle away as quickly as he could—and he should unload it and clean it, but he didn't know how.

But he wanted to see what had happened over there.

And then when Spidey started bounding across the rooftops toward him, he wanted to show the rifle to prove it had been him, Stuart Miller, who had helped!

So he put the rifle on his bed, then leaned out the window and waved.

Spider-Man saw the kid waving, and for an instant he thought that the boy was being held prisoner by the shooter, that he was in some sort of hostage situation—but then he saw the broad grin and he recognized the boy's face.

This was one of his fans. He'd given the kid a swing on a web once. His name was Steve, or Stan . . .

Stuart, that was it.

And he was leaning out the same window the shot had come from.

Spider-Man jumped up, clung to the brick wall, and began climbing. Stuart stepped back as he clambered in the window.

"Spidey!" the boy said. "I can't believe you're really here! This is so cool!"

Spider-Man glanced around. He saw the wall covered with clippings and photos of himself and stared for a second, then spotted the rifle on the bed—an expensive hunting rifle with a telescopic sight.

"*You* shot him?" he asked.

"Yeah," Stuart gushed. "I helped you out, didn't I? Was he giving you a lot of trouble? It's my dad's gun, when I saw that guy chasing you I got it from the closet—did he hurt you?"

"He never touched me," Spider-Man said. "I was just . . ."

He stopped, staring at that wall again, at those blurry gray photos from *the Bugle*—at least half of them shot by his own automatic camera—and at the glossy color shots from the magazines.

Hero worship, that's what it was.

"I was just tiring him out," he said weakly. "You shouldn't have shot him."

Stuart's mouth dropped open in astonishment.

"But you were *fighting* him!" he said. "He was trying to kill you!"

"I wasn't in any danger," Spider-Man said miserably,

trying not to see the clippings. "He couldn't have hurt me even if he'd hit me—and he couldn't hit me."

"But . . . well, he was a bad guy, right? And I stopped him?"

"Yeah," Spider-Man admitted unhappily. "He was a crook, and you shot him, and he's lying on that rooftop bleeding because of it."

"I was trying to help you!" Stuart said, almost crying.

"I can take care of myself, Stuart," Spider-Man said—knowing that the words would hurt, would cut right into the kid's heart.

"You remembered my name!" Stuart said, brightening. "Oh, Spidey, I'm your biggest fan, man—I think you are *so cool!*"

And you shot a harmless, desperate man because of it, Spider-Man thought, but he didn't say it aloud.

And what, he asked himself, am I going to do about it?

It was his own fault, after all. He'd been showing off when he'd gone out of his way to make this kid a fan. He'd screwed up when he hadn't brought enough web fluid to take the bouncer out quickly. And this was the result, one kid shooting another.

A kid with a wall covered with Spider-Man photos.

What could he do about it?

He'd sworn years ago that he would never just let another criminal walk away, the way he let the burglar who killed his Uncle Ben go. Stuart had just shot a man.

The clippings didn't change that.

"Come on," he said, climbing back up on the windowsill.

"What?" Stuart asked.

"Come on," Spidey repeated. "We're going to go talk

to the cops about what you did.''

''No, we aren't! I didn't do anything wrong.'' Stuart backed away.

''Yes, you did. You've got to accept responsibility for what you do, Stuart—now, come on.''

''I was helping you!''

''Yeah, and you're underage and a lot of other things, so they'll probably just let you go with a warning or something, but you're still going to talk to them and tell them what happened.''

''No!'' Stuart turned and started for the door, but Spider-Man, moving faster than any normal man, grabbed him by one arm. Then Spider-Man slung Stuart over one shoulder and headed back toward where the police were waiting.

''Here's your shooter,'' Spider-Man announced, setting Stuart on the roof. ''The rifle's on his bed, in his apartment.''

The police stared.

Spidey could hear an ambulance approaching in the street below. ''How's he doing?'' he asked, nodding at the injured bouncer.

''He'll live,'' said one of the policemen.

Spider-Man told Stuart, ''Lucky for you.''

''I was trying to help!'' Stuart protested, struggling to get away from the sight of the man he'd shot. ''Let go of me!''

Spider-Man released him and stepped back.

The ambulance siren stopped, and car doors thudded.

A policeman stepped up, cuffs in hand. ''Come on, son,'' he said.

''You bastard!'' Stuart shouted at Spider-Man. ''How

could you do this to me? And I thought you were cool!''

Spider-Man didn't reply. He didn't know what to say.

He watched silently as the cops led Stuart away, as the ambulance crew hauled the bouncer off on a stretcher.

Then he began looking for somewhere private to change back to his street clothes. This was no longer a good day for web-swinging—even if he'd still had the fluid.

Somehow, he didn't think that wall in Stuart's bedroom was going to be covered with clippings much longer.

"No, Stuart," he said to the air of a deserted men's room a few minutes later, as he pulled off his fancy red boots, "I'm not cool." He flung a boot aside. "I'm not cool at all."

B L I N D S P O T

ANN NOCENTI

Illustration by James W. Fry

A toxic sunset streaks across the slack ruinous faces of Miguel and Jose as they slump at the corner of Pitt and Bowery.

"That witch shows, I'm gonna mess her up," Miguel hisses between missing teeth.

"She ain't never gonna show, amigo, this a big waste." Jose plays with his mustache in the plate glass window behind them.

"She gonna show, her old man never miss a night of whiskey." Miguel watches Jose's pathetic vanity play in the mirror, and suppresses a laugh.

Something down the block attracts his eye. "Jose, check it out, what the heck is that thing, a rat?"

Jose looks over. "Oh, man, what is it? What's wrong with its back? A dog, man, right? It's got some kinda wires coming out its head!"

Miguel sniggers. "Check it out, Jose, it be lookin' in the mirror, just like you, man."

"Shut your— Hey, here she comes, Miguel! Hide, look cool. Soon as she passes, we grab her. Forget the dog."

Is that my face? It sniffs the chill silver glass, uncomprehending. No. Not my face. I am not a dog. Head slunks down, spine telescopes into itself impossibly . . .

It seeks the wet, it seeks the dry. Something is wrong. The scales of its underside need water but the feathers get too heavy when wet. There are so many wills in it: the will to never stop eating, the will to burrow, and the greatest urge, to find the face the eyes used to see reflected back at them.

It stops dead. Fur erect; scales buckle; skin shimmies. Something is coming. It feels the backdraft of a force. It scurries to quick hide make itself small and invisible, just in time to see the

glare—the loud blue, the rude red, a blur, a SWOOSH!—a tor-
nado swirl of litter left at the tail of his passing flash. "Stop!" the
flying man cries so loudly it stabs the creature's ears. And then the
blue-red blur is gone, the refuse of its wake a dirty tissue flown in
to stick dry and cling to the creature's mouth, snatching breath.

"Stop!" The cry is Spider-Man's, and he did notice the doggish beast that slunk low into a small hole in the wall behind a fire escape, as if collapsing in on itself. But his mind is on the mugging below him: Two crooks are grabbing a woman's purse, and pushing down the old man trying to defend her. How low the low will go, he thinks. Well, trajectory's perfect for a double-web slam-dunk an' hang 'em out to dry.

It's an impossible flip off his cornice roost. The taut muscle machinery of Spider-Man's honed body twirls and lifts out of the tuck with a perfectly timed webline coursing out of the web-shooters on his wrists; a viscous squirt that instantly congeals into an iron-tough rope, strong enough to buttress his one hundred and eighty pounds. As he swings over and drops the bomb of his body, two more streams of steely web entomb the muggers. A flip, and the fulcrum of his ballast weight slams the two—with the help of a foot in each gut—into a parking meter each. Within seconds they're garroted, straitjacketed, and bound to their poles.

To the two muggers it is a frenetic dance of pain, blows of force that go along with the blue-red blur. A flurry of punches form a creature that is everywhere and nowhere, and between the gasping loss of wind and the gulp of a first breath, they find themselves bound, gagged, and helpless.

* * *

"Thank you so much," she says, bending over to pick up a fallen lipstick. Another one, candy pink, rolls to tap Spider-Man's foot, and he too bends, retrieving it for her. He glances up and is startled by the gleam of her swinging gold cross. A bit too large for humble faith, yet who would dare question it?

They rise together, her cross disappearing now behind a fold in her blouse. She is sassy, Latina dark, and just the other side of young. Her straight spine and delicate way of walking betray a finishing school, yet the cut of her jib is spiced-down by a swagger can only mean she defied her training every step of the way.

"Thank you," she says again, "for this . . . " Her hand gestures down and away to indicate the two sullen muggers, one distinguished by teeth spaced so wide he looks as though he's missing every other one, and the other's tag being an unnaturally long mustache ineptly tapered with twirling wax.

"Please," she continues, "could you help my father in-side?" They both turn to look at the old man—so out of breath—leaning into the wall to hide his weakness. A big man, a large percentage of what were muscles gone lax with the years, with hands crooked slightly into arthritic clutches.

"Daddy!" He moves from the wall like an ex-prize fighter who misses even the burn of the ropes. "I'm Sonja, and this is my father, Amerigo. You can call him Gig."

Amerigo, proudly refusing any help, pauses to look Spi-der-Man up and down in that hostile, envious way the old and impotent have when assessing the young and virile.

Sonja steers them into a nearby bar, leaving the glare of high noon in New York City behind as they allow the darkness of the tavern to take them in. Spider-Man glances back once to make sure Tombstone Teeth and the one with the 'stach are well bound. They have been speaking in rapid, angry Spanish, and something about it bothers him. He meant to ask Sonja what they are saying, but forgets in the bar.

It is early enough in the day for the low voices and clink of glasses to sound cheerful. Soon enough that cheer will sour and slide down the other side of hope, approaching the crash landing at the end of the night when a man's beer and his urine start smelling the same. Gig heads like a mule to a specific seat, and the bartender has his drink poured by the time his butt sinks into leather. A few old-timers in the bar nod vaguely but with warmth at Gig, and Spider-Man realizes the old man is a regular here.

Spider-Man approaches Gig to ask if he's okay, but Gig begins talking loudly about the football game on the tube. "Simms, bow out gracefully why don't you? I tell you, working with him was demoralizing."

"You were with the pros?" asks Spider-Man. "What position?"

"I don't know, I can't be expected to remember. Go talk to my daughter, will you? But I warn you, she'll try and get you all worked up about some stupid cause-du-jour. If you don't watch it she'll have you picking through toxic waste dumps collecting samples or busting open science labs calling you an animal liberator, and then you got all these freak monkeys and rabbits with electrode heads to take care of. Go on, go talk to her, leave me alone, will you?"

"Daddy, be nice." Sonja steers Spider-Man to the side. "I'm sorry he rants like that. He's just humiliated; he would have liked to have saved me from those muggers. He's angry at you for doing his job. He was in the pros for four years, and all it left him with is terrible arthritis; every joint's so banged up he's in pain all the time. He refused to take any sponsorships, you know, beer ads and all that, so to top it off he's broke.''

She tries to beckon him onto a chair, but Spider-Man is too aware of the glare of his presence even in this dark light, and remains poised to leave. When he first came in, he saw something like disgust in the eyes of the old drinkers. It was one of those moments when he wished his costume weren't quite so bright. They end up leaning into a jukebox, both looking absently at the tunes—''Layla,'' ''Unforgettable''—rather than at each other.

''Listen, I wish you'd swing by here once in a while and keep an eye on him. I'm so busy with my genetics work—''

''What work?'' Spider-Man perks up, curious, as if reminded of a past life.

''Oh, I used to specialize in genetics research, but I've swung full around and become an activist against such work. It's just the next time bomb ready to unleash viruses, splinter and ruin life as we know it . . .''

''I hear you. I've been reading about how they put cow genes in tomatoes to make them beefier and all that other mix and match stuff. Is that what you mean?''

''God yes, they have no idea of the Pandora's box they're opening with such experiments. Or rather they do know but don't care. It's not just vegetables, either. They're mixing cow genes with fish genes, pig genes with chicken. I went to this pig farming conference undercover posing as a buyer, you know? They're breeding what they call meat machines: animals that have a heightened desire to eat, and with a cellular structure that expands so rapidly it mimics self-replication. Next they want to breed away legs, so the poor things will just be tubes of expanding meat. Anyway, don't get me started on this or I'll try to recruit you." She laughs, delightfully.

"Well, I'd better get those crooks to the jailhouse, Sonja. And, well . . . I don't normally have the time, but I will try to look in on your Dad when I pass this way."

He looks back once over the bar: the row of rounded shoulders; the drinker's slouch; the cigarettes forgotten in fingers about to burn; and that stare. They all stare off into their own private spot, a non-spot, like looking down a drain after all the fluid has vanished—only it's memory not liquid that's irretrievable.

He sees the television, now showing one of those generic ads advertising a beautiful life-style somewhere, ads full of pouting lips and hair blown by studio fans. Above the television is a painting of the Last Supper, draped in dust and leftover Christmas lights.

The Last Supper. For a moment Spider-Man's eyes nearly tear as he looks at the row of hunched backs, clutched drinks, the wisened fight scars, the rolls of sagging flesh . . . A warrior's graveyard. A pugilist's reward. He touches his stomach—still taut, perfect, betraying no age— and stares ahead too, as if into what could be his future, with some fear but also with something surprising, something like envy.

Old-Man Gig catches his eye, and raises a shot glass to him. Winks once, and tosses it down. Spider-Man nods and turns to go, hearing voices at his back: "You know him, Gig? That Spider-Man dude?"

"Not in this life," is Gig's answer. "Wouldn't be caught dead."

*　　*　　*

Outside, his interrogation of the muggers is over-earnest, as if he is trying to recapture some flush of virility. The one with the tombstone teeth is trying to tell him something in Spanish. All Spider-Man can understand is "cora-zones"; something about a million pesos and a delivery of rotten hearts.

"Mujer muy mal, muy mal. ¿Mayans pobre? ¡Loco, bah!" Miguel spits past his lonely teeth, then smiles wide and lewd as if someone just jabbed a hotwire into his brain and he liked it. "Heh heh. Heh heh." Malignant eyes, trying to communicate something to Spider-Man about the woman, something base, an instinct born on cheap mat-tresses in two-dollar rooms. The one with the mustache reaches out with dirty fingers, toward the red spandex cos-tume, but Spider-Man deftly shifts away to avoid the grimy touch.

"Heh. Heh heh. Bueno, bueno. ¿Es caliente, no? Heh. ¿Hot, hot? ¿Tu es hombre araña? ¿Es verdad?"

When the other one also reaches out to touch Spider-Man's clinging second skin, his impulse is to web their mouths shut, and bind their grubby fingers to their sides.

He's heard enough out of their mouths. From what he can gather they were mugging her, but for what she owed them for some black market trade deal gone bad. Maybe jewelry, gold hearts or something. They called her a bad woman, and something about poor Mayans. Poor Mexican Indians. He looks at their grins, seedy and twisted as if they'd been eating dirt. Spider-Man decides to leave these two dregs for the police, and to keep an eye not on the father but on the daughter.

*　　*　　*

It watches from its hidey-hole. The smell of pounding flesh makes it salivate. It sees the fight and scurries out when they are gone. So hard to leave this familiar block. The occasional spilled beer on the sidewalk comforts it. The smell of the old men. The pounding of the flesh. Food. It is starving but it can't eat. Its very cells seem swollen, its bones ache with the expanding flesh. It craves corn. Corn, beans, fruit, flesh. Beer. Whiskey. Its impulse to consume is unceasing, but at the same time its cells swell in anticipation, bloating it on nothing. It rubs into the sandstone wall, scratching off scales, fur, and feathers along with the itch. It seems to be shedding all this, and its joints hurt as if its legs want to come loose. It's the holes that hurt the most. The holes in its flesh, especially where there are wires and metal bits. Especially now that things seem to be changing. The scales spreading, the fur dropping out. The spine buckling, taking a new shape. It uses its simian brain to consider how to stem the change. It seeks its image.

Another mercurial pool. Claws extend to pry at the mirror surface, thin as a Roosevelt dime and deep as the eye can reach. This thing that reflects a face that is not its face will not budge. It looks at its claws; curled, sad and sensitive, as if ready to paint a gesture so subtle not even its own eyes could see it. What is this memory that is not its own? It moves on, shivering on the cusp of the turn. It wants to climb. It wants to hide. The predatorial impulse insists on hunting. Food. It wants to eat, to kill, to sleep. It needs to find its rightful eyes.

Spider-Man lurks outside Sonja's window, trying not to feel like a voyeur. He can see her in her hallway, staring into a mirror. Not putting on makeup, not even really looking at herself, just gazing. As if she can't recognize her own face.

Liar, thinks Spider-Man. Liars stare into mirrors a lot,

trying to recognize themselves. He knows about these things.

He watches as she wraps a scarf around her neck, and goes out into the night. He is close behind her.

Elsewhere, a blind man sculpts eyes. He takes the ball of wet clay in his palm and rolls it. He fits it into the empty socket of his own eye. It is too small. He places it on the table with the others. He gazes outside. Why is it that those without eyes seem to stare more than anyone else? When he sold them, he believed he didn't need them anymore. He thought he'd seen enough. He drank the three thousand dollars for each eye. Drank one eye in two months. The second he drank in three weeks.

Five hours. Five hours of following the cryptic movements of this Sonja. She goes on what appears to be a date, only to leave the man in the restaurant, halfway through a meal, while she slips out the back door. Spider-Man now waits for her in an alley, and passes the time squinting at the headlines repeating on a nearby newsstand.

He sees a tabloid title about an animal rights raid and the horrible experiments they found dead in bins, and near-dead in cages. He stares at the doctored photos that show a dog with pig's hooves and a snake grafted in to replace his spine. Bad airbrush job. Something about this fake creature being the city's new "Bigfoot," and how so many people now claim to have sighted it slinking around the streets.

Spider-Man remembers reading once that some shrink said UFO sightings were man's desire to see circles, and therefore his yearning for harmony. What do dirty dog sightings signify? He sees another headline, about a man willing to sell one of his kidneys for twenty-five thousand dollars. And this story; what does it mean? But Sonja is moving on, and he can't finish reading it.

She picks something up at the loading dock of a supermarket, something from a little freezer box, and drops it off at a dark factory. She stops at a printer and argues with the night man about a leaflet. From afar it looked to Spider-Man that she won whatever she was fighting for. He hasn't figured out much, but she's beginning to look less like a sophisticated genetics expert and more like a plain old thief.

When she goes home seemingly to sleep, he goes back to check again on her rounds: the printer, the warehouse— but it's at the supermarket that something finally happens. Tombstone Teeth and Twirling Wax show up and when they see him, they wish they hadn't. They run.

Spider-Man yells at them to stop, but when they ignore him, his web-shots hit their backs, jerking them like dogs on a short leash. "Hey! You with the teeth!" he yells.

"What teeth?" answers Tombstone, rolling his gums over a sad gap.

"So you do know English!" says Spider-Man.

"Free ESL classes. Very pretty teacher lady. She is learning me."

"How did you get out of jail so fast?"

Twirling Wax spreads his hands wide. "You no give no evidence. Heh heh."

"Yeah? Hold still." They slink down like puppy dogs caught in the garbage, sighing and whining. Webbed again. And he didn't even have to hit them. He loves it when street scum train so fast.

Spider-Man opens one of the cold-storage boxes he finds on them, and sees what look like hearts. Real live hearts. Frozen hearts. And not animal hearts. He webs the contraband to their hands, writing "Evidence" on the boxes, and an arrow with the word "Fingerprints."

Spider-Man swings back over to Sonja's house just in time to see her leaving again, and he follows her to a twenty-four hour coffee shop. He drops into an alleyway where he left a stash of street clothes. Time to be that normal human—Peter Parker. He webs his costume into a ball and hides it nearby; he only plans to stay a civilian briefly. He wants to watch her in action, up close, and not miss a word. The costume doesn't allow such intimacy.

What he sees when he enters the coffee shop surprises him. He's not the only one that has another identity. She's a different woman. Gone are the conservative clothes, the demure cut of the skirt, the reasonable heels.

He slides to a spot at the counter and strains to hear her whispers. She has sidled up against a man with long earlobes who bends over his stale cool coffee. "I'm in the market," she says.

"For what?" He licks his spoon.

"Eyes."

"You got eyes."

"They're not for me."

"Outside," he orders Sonja. He turns to the waitress. "Keep it warm, Maggie. I'll be back."

"I can't wait," Maggie hisses sarcastically.

*   *   *

Outside, Peter misses some of their exchange as he hurries back into his costume, but he's already overheard enough. Before he had only hearsay and circumstantial evidence, now he has it directly from her incriminating lips.

Sonja's contact returns to his cup, and she is halfway down the block when she gives out a little yelp. Spider-Man dangles before her, upside-down.

"You really are silly," she deadpans, to cover her shock.

Down the block two boys on Rollerblades pirouette to a stop at the sight of Spider-Man. "Way awesome," says the one. "He's a dude," says the other. They lurk at the corner, trying to eavesdrop.

"Have you been to see my father? I was just out looking for him—"

"Stop with the lies, Sonja." As Spider-Man cuts her words off, something in her face stiffens. "I've been following you. I haven't put it all together yet but I know you're buying and selling human organs for some black market trade. Exploiting the poverty of people a continent away. Trafficking with laboratories doing illegal experiments on animals. That's just the bit I can guess at; I'm sure there's more. Just how many identities do you have?"

She collapses against a wall. It all comes spilling out—a relief. "Too many. But they're all true. I was a genetics researcher. Most of the work was good and ethical, but you find sick people everywhere. People obsessed like so many Frankensteins, driven to create some kind of new life. Scientists with god-complexes. They splice together the genetics of different species, they graft organs and limbs from one animal to another, all of it dressed up in scientific rationalizations, much of it even funded by research grants.

My god, you should see the ways they're cutting apart and grafting together animals . . .

"I got so sick of the hypocrisy in the business, and I joined a group of activists. But the animal 'liberators' were just as fanatical. They won't stop at labs, they want to bust into private homes and liberate pets! It's just all too pointless, it goes nowhere. Then I stumbled on the organ trade." Spider-Man watches her eyes flicker around, as if searching to snatch her next line from the thin air. "At first I just thought it was animals, but then I realized it's humans too. They find a poor family, here in the city or as far away as Mexico or Central America. They offer what doesn't seem like a lot to me, say five thousand dollars, for an eye, a kidney, a hand . . . but to the poor family it can get them out of debt and eating. So they do it. I've been trying to expose this ring, and the lab that traffics in this stuff.

"I've heard such horror stories! People wake up, feeling drugged, having lost a day of their life they don't know where, with scars on their stomachs that were never there before . . ."

"Sonja, why didn't you just go to the police?"

"Here's the thing. My real mission . . ." Her hand plays nervously on the wall. "I think my father is dying. Dying because he isn't pro anymore. I wanted to get all the evidence together. I found this one blind man who lives right down from the bar, the old man sold his eyes. I could get him to testify but I want Daddy to do it. I want him to piece the puzzle together, to do the final act, so he can feel like a hero again."

"For himself? Or for you? Are you so sure this is what he needs?"

"Please help me."

"How can I trust you, you make up a new story every time I see you?"

"I had to become a criminal to be trusted by them. Don't you do that? Don't you become like the criminals you chase, in order to catch them?" She shifts her weight to the other hip and looks slyly at him through painted lashes.

"That's what the suit is for, Sonja. It keeps me honest. The suit protects me from doing that, reminds me not to get like them. I like your Dad. I wish I could help. But it's just too dangerous to involve him. Do what you will, but I'm going to bust this ring myself now."

"It's too late. I've already planted the right clues in my Dad's mind, and one in his pocket. He's probably out there tracking them down now. I don't know, maybe you could still catch him at the bar, downing a few for courage."

It's been waiting. Some instincts recede. Others, the patient ones, rise. Past this door. Up those stairs. It needs to get there. It needs someone to open the door. Someone is coming. It tries to scurry in, but is kicked. "What the hell? Did you see that? A rat? A dog?" The voices seem far away. Its will is mutating. Its cells are creeping, as if cancerous. It pushes down the scavenger urge, tries to use the ingenious monkey bits it knows are in its blood. It needs to find a way to find its face.

Up at the top of those same stairs, a hand places an eye on the shelf to dry. The blind man hears a strange squeal, as if a pig were kicked, and looks up. He stares out the window into the black, knowing now that something circles and watches him. The sun is rising.

* * *

A certain knock opens the tavern door, hours before it's legal to open. Spider-Man finds Gig at his usual spot at the bar.

"Have a drink," says Gig, with a smile.

"No, I don't drink."

Gig looks the red and blue man up and down. "Hard to trust a man that won't drink." He takes a sip of his shot and a swallow of dark beer before continuing. "So you're here about my daughter. She try to rope you into one of her schemes to get the old man kicking again?"

"Why don't you tell me, Gig, why you figure your daughter is like she is."

"You mean why is she a pathological lying double-faced role-playing enigma? Why must she spin multiple lives within lives that may or may not be real? I don't know. Why don't you drink? Answer me that. Here, how 'bout one little beer?"

"No thanks, Gig. And yes. Why don't you take a shot at answering my question. You must have a clue."

Gig sadly pulls out a wad of yellowed news clips. "You fighters, you kill me. When you gonna give it up? Why don't you just retire? Join me and the other dead warriors, here in the bar. I'm your future self, you know. That must be why you like me, sorry cranky old man that I am." Gig is smoothing out the wrinkled clips carefully on the mahogany bar.

"Sure you don't want a drink? Here, look at these. See the guy in the crazy bodysuit? All that silly color, all those lethal gizmos, the redundant mask. That was me. I was a big time do-gooder, just like you. A golden age hero. Here, scotch is a good drink. Just a sip. It don't hurt."

"Can I look at those clips?"

"Sure. Listen, it's all my fault. I raised her while I was leading my crazy costumed life. Poor little girl. Her life was a big blur of secret comings and goings, the daddy with a mask, the daddy without the mask. The danger . . .

"Look, Spider-Man, lemme tell you something—never have kids. The hero dad is too much for a child. Things that should be gray become stark black and white for them. And when you fail, it kills them. They got you so high up there, that when you can't do it anymore, you fall too low in their eyes. Lower than they got any right to see you as. That's why she wants me back at it so bad. I gave her a whopper of a complex.

"But you know what? Now, I just want to be left alone with my guilt. Here. You take this address." He hands Spider-Man a slip of paper. "She planted it on me, about as subtle as a child, that girl is. I think this is the address of some blind man who sold his eyes, she needs him to testify. You're a young man. You're the hero. Fix this mess my daughter's in."

"Gig," says Spider-Man, handing back the crumpled yellow news clips. "Why doesn't the hero in these news photos look like you?"

"I've changed, damn it. Now get out of here if you ain't drinkin'."

Spider-Man is stopped at the door by another old drunk. "Listen, don't give Gig such a hard time, okay? So he's a little confused, and he makes up stories. We all gotta have nostalgia, you know? Memories, even fake ones. And sure, he's one cranky old fool, but lemme tell you something about Gig. You need a buck, a drink, a good word? Gig's always got one. We're a family here. A club. A desperado club, but a club. Gig's no failure. His daughter is trying to make him a hero? Well, he already is one. Get her to see that, and you will have helped him."

Elsewhere, Sonja climbs stairs, and knocks. She waited for her father to do it, and he let her down again. She scares the thing in the hallway as it tries to get past the door to slip in with her, but it doesn't make it. It'll wait. It has very patient genes, somewhere.

"Who are you?" says the blind man, letting her in. Sonja looks around the room, surprised there is so much art, so many pictures. So many pretty things he can't even see.

"I'm a friend," she says. "I've come to talk about your eyes."

"They're right on the table." Sonja looks where he points, and sees the brown clay eyes, some beautifully painted, some still wet.

Spider-Man, on his way to find the blind man, is startled by something he can't quite believe. Twirling Wax and Tombstone Teeth, out of jail again.

Gig sits with his whiskey and his brown beer, watching the television news without seeing it. A man on the next stool nudges him. "Hey, Gig, you been following this weird Bigfoot story? It's our block the thing's been sighted on. The ugly freak escaped from some science lab."

Gig looks at the tube, and sees an artist's composite sketch of the various descriptions from people claiming to have seen the thing. It looks like a dog with a reptilian back, with shark fins and scales, feathers, the beginnings of wings, and wires sticking out of its skull. The most striking thing, though, are its completely human eyes. Suddenly Gig realizes why this thing has been sighted on this block. Its eyes are looking for someone. He grabs his beer and runs out of the bar. The bartender looks up.

"Look at that. I ain't never seen Gig move so fast."

The blind man hears it first, the scratching at the door, and Sonja makes the mistake of opening it. The creature flies into the room, smashing everything in its path, a blur of fur and limbs, and hides behind a junked piano. Terrified, Sonja and the blind man back against the wall. "What is it?"

"Just stay back," Spider-Man says from the window. He comes in, trying to coax the creature out from its hiding spot, ready to web it up. But the thing attacks him, fast.

Sonja can't see much more than the blind man can, as a tornado of red and blue; fur and feathers; smashing and pounding; three rows of teeth shredding cloth; and five kinds of howls, all whirl before them.

Suddenly Gig is at the door. "*Stop!*"

Gig squats down, and splashes some beer on the floor near the creature's head. By now Spider-Man has the thing half-crippled with webbing, and holds it down to the floor. Now that it's still, it looks quite small and helpless. The creature sniffs the beer, and gazes at Gig who is low to the ground and repeating soft gentle words.

"Now you, blind man. It wants to look at you."

Sonja moves the blind man gently before it. He talks softly, and the creature is calmed. Its eyes have finally found the face they are used to seeing in the mirror. It will guide this face for the rest of its days.

"See? It was just scared. Best way to tame fear is to lie

down before it, submit to it. Don't fight it. Best way to find peace is to stop fighting.''

Spider-Man releases his grip on the animal, and it happily sniffs the skin of the blind man's caressing hands. It is starting to act just like an ordinary dog. Sonja gazes at her father curiously, and takes his hand. Even sitting, all these years, drinking peacefully in a bar, he was, and is, a hero.

"The sign of a great warrior—'' Gig whispers to his little girl ''—is knowing when not to fight. It's a good thing to be old with aching bones and phoney memories. Can you understand that, daughter? Come have a drink with your old man.''

The blind man "looks" at them all, and without a word or the help of eyes, eloquently implores for some time alone with his new companion.

Spider-Man approaches the dog-thing once more. The creature shyly sniffs him. Now that it isn't scared, and no longer perceives any threat to the blind man, it is quite a sweet beast. Spider-Man determines this animal is of no danger to anyone.

As they leave, Spider-Man hesitates before asking the blind man about testifying. The man would lose his new friend to the circus of the courts. Spider-Man will find another way to bust up the ring, without his help. He always finds a way.

Alone now with his friend, the blind man sweeps the clay eyes off the table and into the garbage can, and prepares a meal for two.

KRAVEN THE HUNTER IS DEAD, ALAS

CRAIG SHAW GARDNER

Illustration by Alex Saviuk

He looked down at Manhattan, the lights glittering as he soared through the polluted air. Once, the very act of flying would fill him with a sense of power, a feeling that he was better than everyone.

But what good is flying if you were going to die?

It was like the world had taken everything he'd done and thrown it back in his face. People had always made fun of his looks, his attitude, his lack of talent. They'd thought of him as a balding, hawk-nosed geek; he could see it on all their smirking faces! That was why he had been driven to succeed in the first place—to show them all they couldn't laugh at Adrian Toomes. And he had succeeded in a way beyond most people's wildest dreams, a way that would strike fear in all those who laughed at him, and a way that could make him rich beyond his wildest dreams.

But his dreams were never realized. No, *he* stood in the way. Over and over again, Toomes had found himself captured when he should have been king of the world!

And now, his own body had rebelled against him. Cancer was eating away at his insides, had already almost killed him once or twice.

But even cancer didn't reckon with the strength of the Vulture. Somehow, he always found new willpower to carry on, new anger to spread his wings and fly again.

And all his strength, all his anger, was pointed toward a single goal. Toward that one cursed individual who kept the Vulture from catching his dreams of wealth and power.

Toomes knew that he could not beat the cancer forever, but if he was going to enter the land of the dead, he'd push Spider-Man through the door in front of him. The Vulture laughed at the thought, a laugh that turned into a hacking cough.

There was no more time for laughter. There was no time for anything but one final, glorious act, as he felt his fingernails tear into Spider-Man's chest to rip out his arachnid heart.

What was that noise? Quentin Beck thought with a furtive glance backward. Could they have found him again, so soon? He moved quickly through the alley, eager to return to the light.

It was his own fault, he knew that now. His special effects genius had failed him, over and over again. Spider-Man had seen through every trick, had trapped him like a common criminal, but he had been trapped once too often. And the day he stopped being Beck and became Mysterio, he had sworn he would never be small-time again. No more simple movie tricks. This time, he swore his effects would not fail.

It all became real during his months in the penitentiary. There are certain strange advantages to a stretch in prison. A person can have lots of time on his hands. You hear stories, too, like one about a guy in California named Frankie Foster who had found a way to escape from prison using the kind of fanfare that Mysterio approved of: a whole wall of the prison gone, and the prisoner nowhere to be found. And, if you know how to use them, there are all the resources of the underworld at your disposal, resources that can locate items that might have been used in that other prison escape; items that would make Mysterio a free man in no time at all.

So it was that Mysterio acquired certain books; books which hinted at the possibilities of acquiring some real powers, greater than any of the special effects he'd ever used before. Well, sure, the books mentioned certain difficulties, muttering about pacts with certain particularly dark allies from, well, somewhere else. But part of that was in the way these old books were written, all flowery and melodramatic. That kind of writing hadn't stopped Frankie Foster, and he'd stayed free for months. Mysterio wouldn't let it bother him, either.

But the books were also not as clear as Mysterio might have liked, written in archaic English, or badly translated from Greek or Arabic. He tried first one incantation, then another, with no result.

And then a new book came into his possession, a slim, handwritten diary that had belonged to a mad Englishman around the turn of the last century. And that man had spoken very clearly of how one must call on "creatures from the other realms"—as he so colorfully described them— and about the sacrifices they demanded.

Well, Mysterio was willing to put up with a little mumbo jumbo, if it would let him out of there.

With the aid of this new book, the third incantation had worked. Far too well, as it turned out.

Mysterio had gathered all the necessary items into his cell, speaking the words, mixing the herbs and the bits of hair. At the proper moment he had called the guard, Sweeny, the guard he hated the most. Mysterio maneuvered the sadistic Sweeny so that the guard stood precisely at the center of the mystic symbol Mysterio had chalked outside his cell in the darkness.

Mysterio called the words quickly. Sweeny stared at him, as if about to laugh.

Instead, he screamed.

Mysterio could not clearly see the creatures that came for the guard; they had shown themselves only as a blur around that place where the guard had stood. Just beyond the bars, where Sweeny had mocked him only a minute ago, all Mysterio could see now was frantic movement, a smear of gray, then nothing.

Mysterio did not see the creatures, but he would never forget their growls. The sound was so deep that Mysterio swore he felt it more than heard it, as if those growls wanted to shake apart his bones.

And then the shadows were gone. And, with the return of light, Mysterio saw that they had taken not only Sweeny, but also an entire corner of the prison with them, every brick and bar along with half a dozen of Mysterio's fellow prisoners.

The things had been hungry. Mysterio escaped easily during the confusion that followed. But his encounter with the beasts had shaken him. For someone who had always dealt in illusion, they were much too real.

Perhaps, he thought as he made his way back to the city, he would have to find other ways to increase his powers.

It had been on the following day, as Quentin Beck stood in a subway station that he heard the growls again; growls that made him realize he had no choice. He would have to find some better way to defend himself, or he would be as dead as Sweeny.

He looked down into the darkness of the subway tunnel, sure that the creatures were near. The growls were growing, as if the things were prowling toward the light. Mysterio looked around at the others who shared the platform, but instead of fear, all he saw was boredom and impatience. Couldn't anyone else hear them coming?

There was a sudden roar in the tunnel, and the train burst into the station. Just an ordinary train, full of the same tired and angry people you always saw on a New York subway.

Beck quickly boarded the train. He didn't want to be left alone in that subway station, or anywhere.

But he knew now just where the subway should take him.

Ten minutes later, he opened the door to the little bookshop. With the grime covering the front window, he could barely tell that the place was open. But a bell chimed overhead as he pushed in the door.

This was *the* bookshop, the one that had sent him the most arcane of all the books he had read in prison. It was dirtier and darker than any bookshop Mysterio had ever seen. The place seemed to be lit by one sixty-watt bulb placed three feet away from the front door.

It was much too dark in here for Beck. As Mysterio, Beck had spent his whole life popping in and out of smoke and shadows; now he wanted nothing but light.

"May I help you?"

Beck jumped as the voice came from the shadows.

"Yeah—I—"

"Oh, I know who you are," the voice continued in the darkness. "Have you come looking for something new?"

Beck looked quickly among the shadows, trying to pinpoint the source of his interrogator. "Well, actually, this is more about something you already got me—"

"A problem with the merchandise?" The voice took on a critical tone. "Those were very special items that we obtained for you. Returns might be—problematical. Are you sure that you used them correctly?"

"Well, actually, they worked almost too well." Beck quickly explained what had happened at the prison, and the second time he heard the growls.

"Oh, dear." This time, the voice actually seemed genuinely concerned. "In that spell, did you happen to use any part of yourself?"

"Part of myself?" Beck laughed in disbelief. "I used a lock of my hair when the spell called for one."

"Oh, dear." The voice made a soft "tsking" sound. "That's the trouble with books by mad Englishmen. They're always leaving out those little details."

"Details?" Beck demanded. "What details?"

The owner of the other voice took a moment before he provided an answer. "The beasts, you see, have tasted you. They're hungry for the rest."

"Hungry?" Suddenly, Beck could think of nothing but the dark creatures' growls. "What can I do? You got me into this! You've got to find some way to stop them!"

The voice hesitated again. "I might be able to get something in a few days. In the meantime, I'm afraid I'll have to ask you to leave the shop. Some of these things can be messy if provoked."

"What? In a few days, I might not be alive. I'll force you to help me!"

"Force me? My good Mysterio, the moment you make a move against me, I think you'll find you've been talking to yourself."

So the shop's owner wasn't even here? Beck should have guessed; voice projection was an easy enough effect to achieve. But he wasn't thinking about anything except for those things that followed him.

"Give me a call in two days—if you're still around," the voice spoke abruptly. It grew softer as it continued. "In the meantime, if you have any friends with superhuman strength, now would be an excellent time to visit.''

The sarcastic voice probably thought he was making a little joke as he faded away. But Beck knew someone who fit just that description, and someone who would be all too ready to fight evil creatures.

Look out, Spider-Man, Beck thought. I'm about to give you the fight of your life.

This was worse for Peter Parker than a battle with Dr. Octopus.

He was home alone with nothing to do. Mary Jane's Aunt Anna was in town, and the pair of them had gone out for an afternoon's shopping. She wouldn't hear of having Peter tag along. "You know the way Aunt Anna is when she really starts to shop!" Peter knew it all too well. If he had to choose between a fight with a super-villain and following Anna Watson through a mall, the super-villain would win every time.

He collapsed on the living room couch. Mary Jane was really doing him a favor. The stress of a newspaper job interspersed with his recent fights as Spider-Man had totally exhausted him.

"Why don't you sit around," Mary Jane had suggested, "read a book, stare at the tube, listen to music? Relax.''

Relax. The way Mary Jane had said that last word, it had been an order. Peter hardly ever got that sort of command from his wife. It was the least he could do to follow it. Being married to Spider-Man was hard enough on her already without him ignoring her good advice.

But exhausted or not, Peter Parker couldn't sit still.

He got up from the chair and plopped down on the couch. Up again, he'd find his feet leading him into the bedroom, where he'd sit on the bed for a minute before heading for the kitchen.

Peter Parker couldn't think of anything to do.

Did he need Spider-Man to keep him sane?

What would he do if there was no Spider-Man? What did Peter Parker really want, right this minute? He was a married man now, with a decent job down at the *Daily Bugle.* But he had no life beyond that, no life besides MJ and Spider-Man.

And more and more, since the day he was bitten by a radioactive spider, Spider-Man seemed to control his life. Control his life so much that now maybe there wasn't any Peter Parker left at all.

Peter Parker stared out the window. There must be something going on, out in the city, some crime being committed, some innocent in danger, somebody who needed Spider-Man.

What should he do with himself?

So how did one find Spider-Man?

The more Beck walked aimlessly around downtown Manhattan, the more hopeless it seemed that he'd ever find the superhero. The midday crowds were thick now, extra protection against the things that followed him. But what happened as evening fell? The people would grow fewer and fewer, and darkness would be everywhere.

Beck realized this was the first time he actually wanted to see the web-slinger. Usually, that damned do-gooder showed up at the worst possible moment, in the middle of the perfect bank robbery or jewelry heist.

That was it, then. In order to snare a Spider-Man, he'd have to set up a crime. But what? He found himself jumping at shadows on street corners, and every city noise seemed to sound halfway like a growl. And he feared that, if he stopped for more than a moment anywhere, the things would find him for sure. There was no way he could concentrate long enough for one of his usual elaborate plans.

A headline at a corner newsstand caught his attention. "SIDNEY CHECK SHOWS FABULOUS FORTUNE"

Beck moved quickly to the newsstand, reading the smaller headline on the *Daily Bugle* as he approached.

"Exhibit Opens at Noon to Promote New Rooftop Restaurant at Check Towers"

There was a picture next to the headline, a photograph of jewels under glass sitting on a rooftop, right under the sun. There wouldn't be a single shadow there. It was the perfect place for a noon robbery, and the perfect place to meet Spider-Man.

For the first time since his prison-break, Beck smiled. He couldn't think of a better thing to do on a sunny day.

Then the smile fell as his eyes ran over another piece in the *Bugle* about the hunt for Frankie Foster, the so-called "Sacramento Strangler," whose body had just been identified after they put it back together. Beck couldn't bring himself to read the details of what the body looked like— his imagination was more than sufficient—but he saw enough to know that his death was not a pretty one.

Filled with a renewed sense of purpose mixed with dread, Beck went to arrange to retrieve his costume.

Peter Parker turned away from the window.

So much had happened, he thought, since that day I was bitten. And things that meant something to Peter Parker, not to Spider-Man.

There had been the deaths of those he loved. His uncle first. Later, the woman he loved, Gwen Stacey. There had been a long time when he'd thought Gwen's death had left a hole that could never be filled.

And there had been so many others. There was Gwen's father, Captain Stacey; and his Aunt May's fiancé, Nathan Lubensky. His close friend Harry, who had taken on his late father's role as the Green Goblin, one of his greatest foes. Even Kraven the Hunter, an enemy all the more dangerous for the code of honor by which he conducted all his hunts, including his pursuit of Spider-Man, whom Kraven considered the greatest catch of all.

But wait. The Green Goblin? Kraven the Hunter? They were dead, but their deaths were more important to Spider-Man than to Peter Parker. Weren't they?

Unless, Peter thought, those deaths affected them both.

Mysterio always kept some of his effects handy. He quickly arranged to obtain his costume, too, with the translucent dome that covered his head and the long, flowing robes. The whole thing fit quite compactly into the box Quentin Beck now carried, the sort of box that went with the delivery-man uniform he wore. And, as soon as the elevator left him on the roof garden, he would make a delivery of another sort altogether.

Well, actually it was more of a pickup.

The doors opened. "Roof garden," the elevator operator remarked in a monotone. "Please exit to your—"

The elevator operator stopped abruptly when he heard the shouts.

It seemed that somebody had already started the party without Mysterio. He should have realized that sort of headline in the *Bugle* would have attracted others, too. Well, the more the merrier, especially when he was hoping to attract Spider-Man.

"What the—?" the elevator man cried with considerably more emotion as the elevator filled with smoke. Mysterio stepped from the smoke a moment later, hidden within his trademark helmet and robes.

"You!" a cry came from overhead. It was the Vulture, somehow hanging in the air as he flapped his great wings.

Mysterio had no time for the scrawny bird-man now. Unless, of course, he could use the Vulture to cause an even larger distraction.

Mysterio waved graciously towards the jewels. "Certainly there's enough to go around."

The Vulture shuddered where he hung in the air, his face contorting as if fighting some silent pain. Still, his voice was strong as he announced, "I want more than the jewels, here. I've got a score to settle!"

Was he looking for Spider-Man, too? Perhaps the two of them really could work together. Mysterio turned from the Vulture and looked down at the jewel cases that dominated the center of the roof garden restaurant.

A scream came from the elevator, a sound full of pain and fear and utter hopelessness.

Mysterio spun around to look past the elevator doors. The cubicle beyond was still obscured by thick smoke, courtesy of his smoke bomb.

Smoke was as good as shadows for hiding things.

He felt the vibration through the elegantly tiled walkway at his feet; the low growl of the things that came for him. Smoke roiled forward from the open elevator doors, settling over the garden like fog, far more smoke than that released by Mysterio's device.

"What's that?" the Vulture called from where he still hovered above them all.

Maybe, Mysterio thought, the Vulture would be useful after all.

"Something we don't want to meet," he said to the bird-man. "If we go somewhere, I can explain."

The Vulture frowned down at the cases spread before them.

"Oh, of course," Mysterio remarked, "the jewels." Those dark things filled too much of his thoughts. "If you'll allow me . . ."

He ran toward the cases then, reaching within his robes for the flash bombs, stunning the onlookers with brilliant strobes of white. From now on, the only tricks he'd use would have to do with light.

He heard glass breaking as the Vulture swept down to collect the loot. Alarms started to ring. What good were alarms against the likes of the Vulture and Mysterio?

Or, for that matter, against the things that followed Mysterio? Any sense of triumph the trickster had was completely replaced by fear.

"Now!" he called to the Vulture. "Let's get out of here."

"I will need an explanation," the Vulture remarked as he pulled Mysterio from the midst of the crowd. "And I haven't agreed to any split of the jewels."

Right now, jewels were the last thing on Mysterio's mind. He looked down as the roof garden shrank below him, and saw the smoke blowing away in the breeze, as if

the dark things had already left to await Mysterio somewhere else.

Peter found himself in the bedroom. His feet had taken
him there while his mind had wandered elsewhere, thinking about death.

He turned to look at the photos scattered across the
dresser. There were three of Aunt May and Uncle Ben, including one of the two of them standing on either side of
a teenaged Peter. But the largest picture was of Peter and
Mary Jane on their wedding day. He smiled at these images
from his past. There was a lot more than death here. These
were images of life; a good home as he grew, and, he
hoped, an even better life with his new wife. So far, Mary
Jane and he had managed to talk no matter what happened. And a lot could happen when you were Spider-Man
on the side.

He thought again about Kraven and the hunt, the thing
that gave Kraven the Hunter his purpose. Well, maybe Peter
used a webbed costume to help him find his purpose, too.
He used Spider-Man to make New York City, and maybe
the world, a better place. His alter-ego also gave Peter a
place to release his pent-up feelings. And the greatest of
those feelings was the anger he held inside him, anger at
all his losses. But Kraven never seemed to have anything
but the hunt, while Peter Parker had other feelings, too,
ones that he wanted to nurture, especially those feelings
that could grow between him and Mary Jane.

Now Kraven the Hunter was dead.

And Peter?

This was why he had stayed in the apartment this afternoon, to feel the good part of him that was Peter Parker,

the part that was often lost when Spider-Man was showing off in between the skyscrapers outside.

He turned away from the photos, and saw a newspaper discarded by MJ's side of the bed. Sometimes she'd do the crossword puzzle in the *Bugle* when she had trouble sleeping.

The newspaper had been folded closed so that all Peter could see was the headline:

"SILENT BOMB DAMAGES PRISON"

"Mystery Explosion Destroys Wall. Seven Missing"

Peter quickly scanned the article below. Both Peter and Spider-Man knew that prison. And both knew the other identity of one of those listed as missing.

Quentin Beck, a.k.a. Mysterio.

Peter shook his head. He hardly looked at the newspaper any more. Maybe he'd glance at the sports page, and read the comics. But these days he was too close to the news. Heck, working as a photographer for the *Bugle*, he was there when the news happened.

Mysterio had escaped. Peter looked at the date at the top of the banner. Yesterday. Peter knew he'd be seeing his old enemy sooner or later. The way his luck ran, it would probably be sooner, and Mysterio had probably already made headlines in today's news.

He remembered seeing this morning's paper folded on the kitchen table. He walked quickly into the other room, and flipped the paper over to the front page.

But there was nothing about Mysterio here; at least not directly.

"SIDNEY CHECK SHOWS FABULOUS FORTUNE"

"Exhibit Opens at Noon To Promote New Rooftop Restaurant at Check Towers"

Wow, Peter thought. Why didn't the Check organization just make up a big sign that said "Rob Me?" If Mysterio was in town, Peter knew just where to find him, not to mention maybe a hundred other crooks and lowlifes. No matter what he had promised Mary Jane, Spider-Man was needed.

Peter froze, his spider-sense tingling. There was danger now. Had Mysterio or one of his other enemies found out his secret identity?

He turned quickly, ready to fight.

A spider hung there, in midair, directly behind where Peter had stood a moment before. A spider that might have bitten Peter's neck if he had been still another instant.

Peter almost laughed. A few years ago, a spider bite had changed his life forever. What could this new spider do, take away those powers the other spider had given him?

But he knew that was unlikely. For all the times he had wished he didn't have superpowers, that he was just plain old Peter Parker, he knew he could never go back.

Sorry, sister, Peter thought, as he pinched the strand that held the dangling spider. He carried strand and spider to the windowsill, letting the arachnid down gently on the wood. The spider quickly scuttled out of sight.

He heard a key turn in the front door lock. Mary Jane opened the door, her arms full of brightly colored bags from department stores.

"You're still here?" She looked surprised to see him. "You actually listened to me for a change?"

"MJ!" Peter protested. "You made me promise—"

His wife laughed at that. "A lot of good that does most of the time!"

"What?" Peter didn't know how to answer that. "But, MJ, I really—"

He must have looked pretty shocked at her little joke, because Mary Jane dropped her bags and rushed over to hug him. "Oh, Peter, I know you always mean well. And I knew exactly what I was getting into, Mr. Parker, the day I said 'Yes!' " She let him go and took a step back to smile up into his face. "So, do you want to see how me and my aunt spent our hard-earned money?"

Peter hesitated again. He'd love to spend the rest of the day close to this loving woman. If only other things didn't always get in the way! He looked down at the paper in his hands.

She followed his gaze, looking down at the newspaper headline. "A jewelry exhibition? That means a jewelry robbery, doesn't it? See? Now you've even got me thinking like Spider-Man!" She laughed and shook her head. "I think you can look at my clothes later."

He stood there, frozen in the hallway, staring at the beautiful woman who was his wife. Spider-Man knew he had to go, but there was a good part of Peter Parker that wanted to stay behind.

"Go, Peter," Mary Jane commanded, "before I get other ideas."

Peter tossed the newspaper onto the hall table and smiled back at her. Sometimes, he swore Mary Jane knew him better than he knew himself.

Peter kissed her quickly and headed for the roof.

They landed at last in an abandoned naval yard at the river's edge.

Mysterio had vetoed the first two places the Vulture had wanted to land. The alleys had held too many shadows. And every shadow could hide those things that demanded Mysterio's blood.

The Vulture deposited Mysterio on the cracked asphalt only a few feet from the river. The bird-man landed heavily beside him an instant later, then fell to his knees, overcome by a never-ending stream of great, hacking coughs.

Mysterio only stood and watched the other man, not knowing what he could, or should, do. But the Vulture sounded like he was dying.

Somehow, the bird-man managed to start breathing again. He rose unsteadily to his feet. "Used a bit too much of my strength," he explained between deep breaths. "I'll be all right in a minute." He shook an emaciated fist in Mysterio's direction. "Don't you think about touching the jewels!"

How could Mysterio tell him that the Vulture could have the jewels for all he cared?

The Vulture's bald head snapped up. "Wait a moment! Have you brought someone to ambush me?"

Mysterio turned. He hadn't heard anyone. But now that he stood still for a moment, he could feel the vibration.

The growls had followed him here, too. Even the brightest naval yard contained a few shadows. And in those shadows, the things had come for his blood.

The light was shifting. Even though the sun stood high in the sky, with hours to go before evening, the shadows were growing longer as Mysterio watched. If the two of them stood still for another moment, they would be swallowed by darkness.

"These are no friends of mine," Mysterio said.

"No one's taking my jewels," the Vulture announced again.

It would be a fight, then. And maybe, with the help of the Vulture, Mysterio might stand a chance.

He still held a dozen flash bombs in his arsenal. The things that hunted him wanted his flesh and blood, but they depended on darkness to survive. Perhaps, in following him through the afternoon, the dark things had grown too greedy. Out in the open, Mysterio and the Vulture had the advantage.

"Let's get rid of these things!" Mysterio called, rushing toward the growling dark. And the Vulture was with him, too, somehow once again in the air.

Mysterio darkened his helmet so that he might be able to see through the glare, and threw the first of his weapons.

The shadows before them turned to noon.

Mysterio could almost see the creatures that wanted him, for even in the light, they seemed to come from the shadows, quick moving shapes that would only pause for a moment to leave a glimpse of dripping fangs or razor claws.

But the Vulture jumped on the fast-moving things, using his airborne strength to fight back. The dark things were not used to fighting in the light. It was their turn to scream, a high, piercing noise that made Mysterio want to cover his ears. But he needed to keep the bright flashes coming, to weaken the enemy so they might have a chance against them.

He threw one flash bomb after another as the dark things changed again. They seemed to ebb and flow like they were half liquid, trying somehow to merge with the Vulture, as if his scrawny body would give them someplace to hide.

But Mysterio would not let them go. He had four of the

flash bombs left. He ignited them all at once.

The strange screams stopped abruptly. The creatures were gone, almost as if they had been vaporized by the light.

There was a moment of silence, disturbed only by the distant sound of city traffic.

"The pain!" the Vulture called as he landed in the dirt. "My pain is gone. Cancer! I'm dying of cancer, and now I don't feel it any more. Those things—whatever they were—have pushed it back. The Vulture will live a little while longer after all!"

Evil feeding on evil, Mysterio thought. He knew he was a criminal, but he was nothing compared to what they had faced today.

"I wonder if I'm cured!" The Vulture laughed. "Far too much to hope for, no doubt. But now I can start all over again!" He waved at the bright gems that had been scattered all over the yard during the battle. "Maybe I'll even share some of my jewels!"

"Oh, no," Mysterio replied. Now that those *things* were gone, he needed to think about his future. "I believe I'll be taking all of those nice stones."

"What?" The Vulture abruptly lost his smile. "You dare to question my generosity? Very well, then. I have my own plans for these jewels." He flapped his wings in preparation for takeoff.

But the Vulture couldn't fly where he couldn't see. Mysterio pulled a smoke bomb from his arsenal.

He looked up suddenly as a new shadow covered his face. "Oh, no," he said flatly. "Where were you when I needed you?"

"Is that any way to greet an old friend?" Spider-Man

called from the building above.

Well, there was more than one place to throw a smoke bomb. Mysterio drew his arm back to throw his missile at Spider-Man.

"Sorry, Spider-Man," Mysterio called. He tossed the bomb in the air, but webbing slapped down on it, surrounding the missile like a catcher's mitt.

Mysterio decided he'd had enough of fantastic confrontations for one day. It was time to get out of here. But a second strand of webbing snagged his costume, and a third got tangled up in his feet. The webbing was everywhere, tightening his arms against his sides so that he couldn't reach his arsenal.

He heard a birdlike cry of despair from the Vulture. Mysterio looked over to see that webbing had totally covered the bird-man's wings as well.

"Nice of you to keep the jewels for me," Spider-Man added as he landed between the two of them.

Sometimes these things just worked out right. Spider-Man had ambushed the Vulture and Mysterio as they had begun to fight over the jewels, trapping them before they had a chance to defend themselves. Spidey guessed if you fought enough battles, once in a while one will turn out just right.

In a way, neither villain seemed to have had much fight left in him. Spider-Man wondered exactly what had happened here. Had they fought each other? Or had there been a third party involved, perhaps someone far worse than either of the miscreants he'd already trapped?

Spidey paused a minute around the old shipyard. But this corner of New York City was as quiet as his spider-sense.

If there had been danger here, it was long gone. He guessed he could ask his two prisoners. Not that he expected them to talk much. It would be a long time before either Mysterio or the Vulture would want anything to do with him.

Besides, he'd gotten the jewels and the two villains who'd snatched them.

Spider-Man bundled the two bad guys together, making sure the webbing would last until he could summon the police to pick them up. They didn't struggle all that much. They really did seem exhausted. Quiet, too. He heard none of the usual threats and taunts that bad guys tossed his way. Strange that they would give up the jewels so easily. In an odd sort of way, they almost seemed relieved he'd captured them.

But a lot of things were different today. He had missed most of the action here, but somehow things had worked out all right. Better than all right, really.

He quickly gathered the jewels together so that he could return them to the rooftop and their rightful owner. And he thought again about all those he'd fought, and those he loved, and some of those who were gone. The Vulture, Uncle Ben, Gwen Stacey, Mysterio, and Aunt May. His wonderful wife Mary Jane.

And of Course, Kraven the Hunter.

And that's what was different today, because, before he had even put on his spider suit, he had finished a hunt of his own.

The jewels had been rescued. Mysterio and the Vulture were captured. Kraven the Hunter was dead.

But both Spider-Man and Peter Parker were very much alive.

RADICALLY BOTH

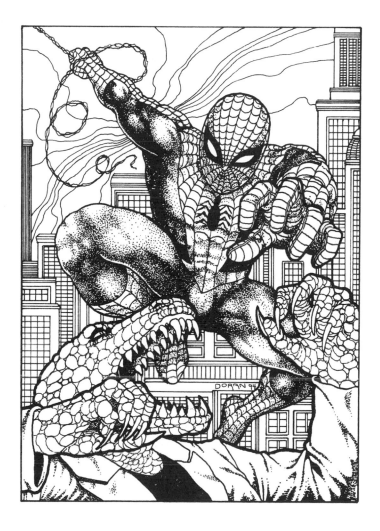

CHRISTOPHER GOLDEN

Illustration by Colleen Doran

*Of the two natures that contended in the field of my conscious-
ness, even if I could rightly be said to be either, it was only because
I was radically both.*

—Robert Louis Stevenson
The Strange Case of Dr. Jekyll & Mr. Hyde

There was a time in his life, in younger, more naive
days, when Dr. Curt Connors would have yelled "Eureka!"
upon the successful development of a new serum or formula. In those days, he had enthusiasm and humor to spare
and he spread them liberally among his many friends and
to his new wife and infant son.

But the Lizard took all that away.

In that reckless time, his experiments were daring; some
would even say he'd been tempting fate. And it turned out
that fate was not amused. Since then, his body had been
mutated into the Lizard and back so many times—his bio-
chemistry and physiology so completely altered—that even
when things seemed back to "normal," Dr. Connors would
often wonder if he could ever be the man he'd been before.

Before the Lizard.

There had, admittedly, been times when he thought
he'd won. But of late, optimism had been at a premium.
In truth, several months earlier, he had abandoned all hope
of ever completely excising the Lizard from his mind, the
Hyde from his Jekyll, the id from his superego. But, as had
happened several times in the past, in the dark depths of
the despair which came with such a terrible admission,
came inspiration.

Twice before, due to the oddest of circumstances, he
had been changed into the Lizard while retaining his own
mind. Twice before, the mind of Curt Connors had over-

come that of the Lizard. Oh, the savage creature's mercilessly evil consciousness was still there, but subjugated to the mind of its host, Dr. Curt Connors. He had even fought alongside the Lizard's greatest enemy, Spider-Man, during those periods, becoming the oddest kind of superhero—a monster with the mind of a man.

Dr. Connors knew that in order to protect his family from himself, or rather, from the thing that was within him, he would do anything. If the Lizard could not be cut from his body like a tumor, then perhaps he could create a serum which would once again allow him to remain in conscious command of his body, even after it had become the Lizard.

It was just past sunrise, and Dr. Curt Connors paced the length of his uptown Manhattan lab. The blinds were down, but cracked open so that the brightness sliced in, a fresh contrast to the fluorescent office lights that Connors had worked under all night. Noticing for the first time that the sun was up, Curt went to the window and pulled the blinds all the way open, letting the sun flood the room. Half a smile creased his face as he rubbed the ghost of sleep from his eyes.

The battered air conditioner labored noisily where it hung like a fat man's belly out one window. It was August in New York, and even at night the heat and humidity had been terrible. By one o'clock that little old a/c unit wasn't going to do much.

Of course, by then, Connors would be gone. One way, or the other.

"Stop procrastinating," he said aloud to himself.

Dr. Connors walked back to the table over which he'd stood the whole night, but took a step back when he saw the vial of serum he had concocted. It may have been a trick of the light, for it was gone now, but he was sure that the liquid in that vial had been almost phosphorescent. Ah, but now it was just a sickly green, the color of Gatorade.

He lifted the vial from the rack and stared at it for a long time. This was how it had started, all those years ago. He was confident now, as he had been then, that he had done all of his calculations correctly, that his serum would do exactly what it was intended to do. And that was the problem . . . he had always been confident. Too often, running the razor's edge of scientific discovery, confidence was little more than wishful thinking. His experiments had gone wildly wrong in the past, and Dr. Curt Connors had finally come to realize that each new serum, each new formula, each new test was nothing more than a shot in the dark.

The time had come 'round again. He could procrastinate no longer. Taking a last look at the way the sunlight glittered in the greenish liquid, Curt Connors lifted the vial and drank the four ounces of serum without taking a breath. It tasted horrible, and when he put the empty vial down he bit his lip a moment and squeezed his eyes together, warding off imaginary tears. It had been a long time since he'd cried, his body seemed somehow incapable of it now, but not a day went by that he did not want to.

He laughed softly. That had been the easy part, the serum which would enhance the chemistry of his subconscious mind. Now the hard part would begin, for the serum was untested. The only way to see if it had worked was to purposely, willingly transform himself into the Lizard.

He didn't want to do it, but the time for stalling was over. Perhaps due to some effect of the serum, his mind seemed to race now, to urge him into action. He cast aside all doubts, all fears, and took half a dozen steps to another table in the lab, where a different vial was filled with a liquid so darkly green it was almost black, its consistency more akin to oil than water.

Once his fingers had touched the vial, Dr. Connors looked away, looked out at the sun spreading across the city. He stopped thinking, turning his mind completely away from what he was doing lest the fear overcome him and he lose the courage to follow the experiment through.

He drank the transformative serum, its thick pasty texture making it difficult to swallow, leaving a terrible taste and a thick film inside his mouth. He had not even made it to the window before the change began in all its glorious pain.

God, was it ever this bad?!?

He couldn't recall whether in those times when his mind had control of the Lizard's body, if the change in form had been so violent; it was as if his entire body were tearing itself apart. In truth, quite the opposite was occurring: he grew, the scales thrust out of his flesh, the agonizing growth of snout and tail continued.

"YEEAARRRGGGHHHH!" he screamed, but in his mind, the litany went on and on, *for Martha, for William, for Martha, for William.* And for the sake of his wife and child, he resisted the urge to simply throw himself out the fifteenth story plate glass window, ending it all, the research, the pain, the despair. They had been through too much as a family for him to abandon them now.

One thing was certain, something different was happening. In the past he'd felt only the beginning of the change, save for those few times he'd been in complete control. This time, he was getting the full brunt of it, the pain increasing as his metamorphosing body grew more powerful, more able to handle the pain, as if strength and agony were growing together.

Connors fell to the ground, shuddering and writhing from the pain. His hands curled into slashing talons, and in his new mouth rows upon rows of needle teeth pushed through his gums. His spine curved, forcing him into an almost fetal position, and the tail continued to grow, muscle upon muscle bursting forth from somewhere else. Had he evolved or devolved, or was that even a facet of the answer? He would probably never know.

The pain subsiding somewhat, Dr. Connors tried to get up, but he couldn't move. His eyes were open, his heart was beating, he was breathing, and he could feel the pull of every muscle, but while his brain was sending the mental message to stand, the body of the Lizard wasn't responding.

Then he felt his mouth opening, his tongue snaking out to flicker around his nose and caress his fangs. He felt it all . . . but he wasn't doing it! In a flash, the Lizard was standing, sniffing, then rushing to the window. Its tail whipped around at extraordinary speed and shattered the glass, sending shards plummeting toward the early commuters innocently passing below . . . and Dr. Curt Connors was helpless to stop it.

Rather than asserting control over the Lizard, all his experiment had succeeded in doing was bringing his consciousness awake, so that he remained aware through the transformation and whatever destruction the creature might wreak upon the city now that it was loose again. Curt Connors was aware of every move, felt every muscle, smelled every scent, saw what the Lizard saw, but he was merely a passenger, a witness. He had no control.

In his mind only—for no matter how his brain commanded them otherwise, his vocal cords would not do his
bidding—Curt screamed in rage and frustration. He knew
that if he could control the body he would cry, as he had
been unable to for so long.

The Lizard was out the window and using the sticky
resin of its hands and feet to rapidly descend the building's
outer wall. A camera crew of some sort was gathered nearby.
Curt was torn between the natural inclination to flee and
the new urge that filled him.

Yes, he thought, kill them. Kill him. Kill us. End it.

That was not what he really wanted, but the thought did
cross his mind. No matter, however, for he was utterly, completely helpless in a way he had never imagined possible. A
prisoner within his deadliest enemy, himself.

And he knew where the Lizard would head—downtown,
to the Village, where his wife Martha and their son William
were probably still sleeping.

Unaware of the danger that was even now approaching.

Most days, Mary Jane Watson-Parker had to get up long
before Peter, and this day was no exception. The only problem with that arrangement, as far as Peter was concerned,
was that for whatever reason, once Mary Jane was up, he
found it nearly impossible to go back to sleep. So what if
they'd been out until two o'clock in the morning, it was six-
thirty now, and time to get up! He buried his head under
his pillow.

Mary Jane came out of the bathroom, one towel
wrapped around her perfect body and another swept up to
cover her long red tresses in a terry cloth turban. Peter said
nothing, only propped himself up on one elbow and

watched his wife move. He loved to watch her move, to do the smallest things, like brushing her hair.

Ain't love grand?

"Breakfast, tiger?" she asked, and though he was tempted to drag her back to bed, he only nodded and instead extricated himself from the sheets, sleepily pulling sweatpants up over his Jockey shorts.

He knew the routine. She asked if he wanted breakfast, which meant, "sweetheart, while I put some clothes on, you go make coffee and eggs, toast the bagels, and get the paper from the hallway." Meanwhile, Mary Jane clicked the TV on in the bedroom grumbling about how it was so early, *Good Morning America* wasn't even on yet. Married life; Peter absolutely loved it.

The coffee was brewing and the eggs were done when Peter heard MJ's blow-dryer start humming, his signal to stick the bagels in the toaster oven. They had to keep the glass door to the oven down when they weren't using it, because for some reason, it wouldn't turn itself off. Peter was sure it was a fire hazard of some kind, and he'd been promising Mary Jane he'd get around to fixing it . . . and he would, one of these days.

He was flipping through the *Times* when he heard the blow-dryer buzz subside. He looked up at the toaster to see that he'd let the bagels burn again! He knew Mary Jane would say, "Nobody's perfect, Peter," with that smile of hers. It was what she said every time he messed up in the kitchen.

"Peter, come in here!" his wife yelled suddenly, and he was up and sprinting for the bedroom before she finished, alarmed by her tone and hoping it wasn't another mouse. How many times could the exterminator visit the Parkers' humble abode? At this point, the guy might as well move in.

It wasn't a mouse, though, and suddenly Peter was silently taking back what he'd thought. If it had only been another mouse, all would have been right with the world. This pest was much larger, much more persistent and far more threatening than any minor rodent.

It was the Lizard, sighted by a news crew that was doing a human interest piece of some sort. Peter recognized one of the nearby buildings as the one which housed the laboratory of Dr. Curt Connors.

"Oh, man," Peter whispered. "Poor Curt." Louder, he asked, "When did this happen?"

"Just a couple of minutes ago," she answered. "He disappeared into a subway station."

"Of course!" Peter nearly shouted, smacking himself in the head, and then he was a blur of motion as he ran around the room hurriedly, slipping into his costume.

He knew exactly where the Lizard was headed, and in that moment, so did Mary Jane. She looked back at the TV and the color drained from her face.

"He's not wasting any time," she said softly. "He's going right home."

Peter had never crossed the city faster in all his years in New York. In midtown there was some fracas going on with the Avengers, but he didn't even slow down. As Spider-Man, he had struggled again and again over the years to save the lives of the entire Connors family, and today was not going to be the day he lost that struggle. He promised himself that.

Once in the Village, it was much harder to swing from

building to building, but they were so close together that for the most part he could simply run over the rooftops and jump across the narrow streets.

He arrived on the roof of the Connorses' building and climbed down the wall to enter through the top story into their living room window, as he had several times before. But this time there were bars across the sixth floor window and steel shutters inside them, closing out the world, closing out the danger of the Lizard, the loving father and husband to the people hiding inside.

Wouldn't you do the same, he thought, if the Lizard had destroyed your life, had haunted your family? And yet, Spider-Man was saddened by the sight, for the Connors had always remained optimistic in spite of the tragedies that had befallen them. They had abandoned hope now, but Peter knew that their preparations would not be much of a real defense once the Lizard arrived. They must have known it, too, and to Spider-Man that was the real tragedy.

Spider-Man scuttled along the wall until he found a window which opened onto a common hallway in the apartment building. No time for niceties, he popped the screen in and climbed through. In seconds, he was banging on the Connorses' door, realizing as he did so that it was probably barricaded on the other side. With no place in his heart for his usual witty patter, he simply pounded on the door, calling for William and Martha until finally, there came a reply.

"Who's out there?" an angry, frightened young voice asked.

"William?" he said. "It's me, Spider-Man. Are you and your mom okay?"

"For now," the boy answered gravely, and Spider-Man

thought how sad it was that the child had had to grow up so fast.

"You saw it on TV, the Lizard?" he asked, knowing the answer.

"Uh-huh," the boy, the young man, replied, and Spider-Man began calculating in his mind. The monster should have already arrived, or would arrive at any minute.

He knew almost without considering it that the Lizard would try the windows first, wanting to avoid the people in the lobby until after its murderous passion had been fulfilled.

"Don't worry," Spider-Man told William. "I'll stand guard."

With that, he slipped out the hall window again and in seconds, was on the roof, where he watched the street, surrounding buildings, and the walls of the Connorses' apartment with increasing anxiety.

Where was the Lizard?

It had been a mad, full throttle dash across Manhattan, underground. The Lizard knew every nook and cranny of the subway tunnels, current and abandoned, and the sewer system as well. The homeless people who lived under the city by the thousands clearly recognized it, but incredibly, at least to Curt Connors, they did not run from the beast, nor did it attack them.

A captive of the Lizard's five senses, Connors wanted to blink when the creature pulled itself out of the sewer, but he could not control the muscles to make it happen. Then he was looking up at his building, at his home, and he knew that his family was up there, dug in the way they had planned, behind barricades and bars that might buy them an extra minute of life.

Dr. Curt Connors thought he might go mad.

Though he could not hear any real thoughts in the Lizard's mind, Curt did sense a terrible anger once the creature had scaled the wall and reached the barred and steel-shuttered apartment windows. But instead of simply tearing and smashing his way through, as Curt had expected, the Lizard kept going, climbing up to the roof. He didn't understand. The Lizard was strong enough to peel the steel shutters away like aluminum foil, and yet . . . well, he could never profess to having understood the monster's thought processes.

Curt heard the warbling of pigeons, and the Lizard's eyes darted to one side where Mr. Cranston's pigeon coop was aflutter with nervous birds. With the agile, loping gait of a reptile, the Lizard quickly hid behind the coop. The birds shrieked their displeasure at his presence, but settled down again after a few moments.

What was the Lizard waiting for?

And then Dr. Curt Connors had his answer. Over the edge of the building, exactly where the Lizard had come onto the roof, Spider-Man appeared. And now Curt knew what had stopped the Lizard outside the barred apartment windows. Spider-Man had been inside, and the beast had somehow sensed him.

And now it lay in wait, hoping to ambush its most hated enemy, Spider-Man, the only creature on Earth it wanted to destroy, to devour, as much as it wanted to kill Martha and William Connors. It was a murderous hate that Curt could not help but sense. It enveloped him and made him feel unclean, filthy, less than human.

He felt the Lizard's muscles tense as it was about to spring from behind the pigeon coop, ready, at the very least, to tear Spider-Man's heart from his chest. Dr. Connors wanted to call out, to warn the web-slinger, but it was too late. The monster was completely silent as it leapt. The pigeons panicked then, and sensing the Lizard's attack Spider-Man leaped from harm's way, barely escaping the swish of the creature's tail (of *his* tail, though he didn't like to think of it that way).

And the battle raged.

Spider-Man turned to look back down the way he'd come, wondering how long it would be before the Lizard arrived. His spider-sense was rattling his teeth, but he searched the roof and then back down the side of the building for any trace of the Lizard and found none. His spider-sense was a little on the fritz, he finally decided, because though it was loud, it was muddled, uncertain, directionless, as though the danger itself were uncertain.

He thought briefly of Mary Jane, how she'd looked that morning coming out of the shower, and wondered, as he had many times, if this was the day he would make a fatal error. He had been asked often over the years how long he intended to keep up the superheroing business. His answer was always the same: it wasn't something he chose to do, and it wasn't something he could choose to stop doing. It was who he was.

Yeah, they'd have to kill him to make him stop being Spider-Man. And one of these days . . .

But not today, he thought as he jumped back and up, away from the sharp-taloned attack of the Lizard. Both the pigeons and his spider-sense had started screaming, and he'd realized what that meant just in time. If he'd been any slower, he'd have had new air-conditioning in the old red and blue tights, not to mention his lower back. Even in mid-jump, he was forced to whip his legs up and over his head to avoid the creature's slashing tail.

As he landed, the Lizard charged at him again. Spider-Man shot from the hip. His webbing wrapped around the savage thing but barely slowed it down. As fast as he could web it up, the Lizard was tearing itself free. They traded blows for nearly a minute, Spider-Man desperately trying to avoid that deadly tail, testing his old enemy and finding the Lizard, to his distress, more powerful than ever. He was going to have to use his brain, he decided, because a one on one had uncertain results, and with William and Martha downstairs, there was no room for uncertainty.

Then, suddenly, the savagery of the Lizard diminished a bit and it seemed to slow down, as if confused. Spider-Man's head rang with the aftershocks of the one time the Lizard's tail had connected, but he was still alert enough to take advantage of this new development. The web shooters came up and the spider began spinning, the Lizard's green scales quickly disappeared under a mound of sticky gray. It wouldn't hold him long, but Spider-Man hoped it would be long enough to get him back to the lab, where he guessed he would find the serum to transform the creature back to Curt Connors.

The webbing built up quickly, it was almost enough. Spider-Man locked eyes with the Lizard for a moment . . . and they weren't the Lizard's eyes. In fact, they weren't even vaguely reptilian. No, they were the most human eyes he had ever seen, filled with a terrible, aching sadness. They were the eyes of Dr. Curt Connors, as if that one part of him had not been transformed into the Lizard after all, or had fought to change back. Somehow, Curt Connors' mind was in there, fighting, slowing the Lizard's attack.

"Curt?" Spider-Man asked, pausing for a moment in his efforts to web the Lizard up.

And then the sadness was gone, replaced by a consuming rage, and the Lizard's eyes were its own again. It thrashed about, using claws and tail to tear at the webbing. Fearing that it would not hold, Spider-Man moved in to grab the Lizard, but at that second, its tail snapped free and slashed around to drive into his stomach at seventy miles per hour, tossing him across the roof and far out over the edge. He slammed into the bank building across the street and fell three stories before he managed to shoot a webline up onto the brick face of the building and crash out of control through the picture window at the front of the bank, scattering glass and tellers everywhere.

Wonderful, he thought. In tomorrow's *Bugle,* Jonah will accuse me of bank robbery.

Curt Connors knew exactly what had happened. When it seemed as though the Lizard might actually hurt Spider-Man, he had reached out with the force of his will, with every ounce of concentration he could muster, and attempted to usurp the Lizard's control over its body. It hadn't worked, but he had slowed the thing down, had affected it, at least somewhat. Enough that Spider-Man had seen something, had somehow begun to understand!

Spider-Man was gone now, injured at least, perhaps worse than that, but maybe Curt wasn't as helpless as he'd thought. The Lizard smashed open the door leading into the building, and pounded down the stairs. He could expect no more help from the wall-crawler, so Curt Connors reached out again, concentrating as he had before. He would take over the Lizard's form, or at least stop him from moving, from hurting, from slaughtering his family. He could not. His efforts seemed only to enrage the Lizard more.

The apartment door, 6J, was torn from its hinges and flung into the hallway. Despite the noise, none of the other doors on the floor opened. The barricade they had built up—bookcases, a fold-out sofa, and an incredibly heavy bureau that Curt couldn't imagine William and Martha moving by themselves—were thrown aside as if the Lizard were marching through irritating strands of cobweb.

The living room was empty, but Curt knew it would only be moments before the Lizard was face to face with his family. He tried with every fiber of his soul to stop the creature, but it was useless. He fell into despair. He would not give up, he kept trying despite the apparent ineffectiveness of his efforts, and yet, in a way he had given up . . . in all the ways that mattered.

He remembered Martha asking him once if he truly believed that, when the seemingly inevitable occurred and she and William were face to face with the Lizard with no hope of escape, the creature would actually kill them despite the fact that it was, in essence, a separate personality borne of his own consciousness.

"I hope we'll never have to put that question to the test," he'd told her at the time. "But don't you ever doubt it."

Now it had come to that, and Curt knew the answer as certainly as he'd known it that day. The Lizard *was* a part of him, but to the creature, Dr. Curt Connors was nothing more than a prison it had escaped. Its hatred of him was its driving passion, and if it couldn't destroy him, then his family, a reminder of its human counterpart, would have to do in his place.

The Lizard walked through the bedroom door, which was closed and dead bolted from the inside, like it wasn't even there. Martha sat, weeping, on the edge of the bed, but William, his beautiful son, soon to be a man, stood firm in the center of the room, protecting his mother against the savage beast, all of nine courageous years old.

"Go on then," William said angrily. "You're afraid of us, that's why you want to hurt us. Afraid of him, of Dad. Because you're not him. You're not my father. Kill us and get it over with, but you'll never be him."

And that did it, Curt Connors was back, fighting now as never before, screaming in his mind, trying to get through to the Lizard, attempting to steal even an ounce of control over the monster's limbs.

The Lizard reached out a hand and rested his claws on William's face, and the boy started to cry.

No, damn you! Leave my boy alone!

The Lizard drew his claws lightly across William's cheek, just softly enough so that he did not draw blood.

Stop! You can't do this, you're a part of me!

The Lizard clamped his other hand down on William's shoulder, and the boy whimpered, speaking softly, snuffling, through his tears.

"I'm afraid all right," William Connors said. "But I'm not as scared as you are."

Holding William in place with one talon, the Lizard raised the other above his head, about to tear the boy's head from his shoulders.

I will not allow this! This is my body! I am Dr. Curt Connors! I am the Lizard!

As he sprinted through the living room, Spider-Man could see what was happening—and what was about to happen. It was something he would not allow. William Connors was about to be viciously murdered by a creature who was, in truth, his own father. Spider-Man wondered if he had imagined that awareness, that part of Dr. Connors that he had seen in the Lizard's eyes, but there was little time to reflect.

With extraordinary speed he rushed into the bedroom, tore the Lizard away from its alter ego's son and threw the creature against the closet door, which sprang open, leaving it thrashing in a pile of suits and gowns. Without missing a step the hero leapt on top of the Lizard and began to pummel its face again and again and again. For once, Spider-Man had no wisecracks to offer. For once, the fear and anger and frustration of his avocation was too much for him. The thought of the danger William Connors faced, and the scars the Lizard's actions had already forever left on that small, noble family drove Spider-Man into a fury unlike any he had ever known.

And then, in mid-swing his fist was caught, held, by the powerful grip of the Lizard. But the monster didn't throw him off, didn't strike out with talon or tail. Instead, in its snarling half-voice it growled one word: "Enough!"

Spider-Man looked down at the beast, and once again, its eyes were the grieving, terrified eyes of Curt Connors.

"The serum," the Lizard growled, "working. Get to the lab."

Or at least, that was what it sounded like the beast . . .

like Dr. Connors was saying. Suddenly uncomfortable in the apartment, Spider-Man stood, for a moment unable to think. Then he helped the Lizard to its feet, to *his* feet. He had a hard time thinking of it as a monster when he knew that Curt Connors's mind was in there, that Connors had overcome the Lizard.

"Are you okay, William?" Martha Connors asked her son, and both Spider-Man and the Lizard turned to see the boy hugging his mother. Martha would not look at her transformed husband, regardless of his newly asserted control. Spider-Man could not blame her; the Lizard was the great tragedy of their lives.

The Lizard went out into the living room, but no further. Dr. Connors was waiting for Spider-Man to come along, anxious to be human again, anxious to begin anew the process of repairing his family, a process which was becoming, to them, the same as breathing.

"Are you okay, William?" Spider-Man asked, because the boy had not answered his mother.

"Totally," William said, mostly to his mom, then turned to Spider-Man and added, "He's just a big bully. Dad would never have let him hurt me, not really."

Then the man disappeared from William Connors's face, and he was simply a little boy again.

"Dad wouldn't have let him hurt me," he repeated, insistent now, as though trying to convince himself.

"Not in a million years, William," Spider-Man said confidently. "Your father loves you, you know that."

He heard a shuffling noise and looked up to see that the Lizard, Dr. Connors, had been standing in the doorway of the room, watching the exchange. He moved back into the living room, and with one scaly claw beckoned Spider-Man to hurry and join him.

"Tell him he should stay away for a couple of days," Martha Connors said, and Spider-Man opened his mouth to respond, to ask if that was really necessary. But then he realized that it was not his place. He had done his part, had been there, that was the important thing. The rest of the healing was up to them.

At top speed, he and the Lizard fled the building. Sirens wailed, growing ever closer as they descended the outer wall and slid into a sewer hole to make the best speed uptown. Momentarily, Spider-Man wondered how it was that Curt Connors also knew the city's underground so well, but decided that was a question for another day. He also wondered what, exactly, Martha was going to tell the police when they showed up.

"You lied to him," the Lizard growled several minutes later as they entered an abandoned subway tunnel.

"Did I?" Spider-Man asked sincerely.

The Lizard was silent then, and Spider-Man was glad he could not see its eyes, for he was certain that they would show the truth. The truth of life or death for a young boy, and the heart of a family.

It was a truth he was glad not to know.

S C O O P !

DAVID MICHELINIE

Illustration by Bob McLeod

I don't want to die in the rain, thought Henry Pogue. Hell, he didn't want to die at all! But he was going to. And soon.

He leaned back in his old leather chair, listening to it creak, and stared past the empty darkness of the *Smithville Gazette*'s city room to where a determined November storm flung endless raindrops at the building's wide front window. Martha had died on a night just like this. And she hadn't had any more say in the matter than he did.

He glanced at a framed picture on the corner of his desk: Martha. Even behind old glass, her eyes seemed to sparkle like a child whose every day is Christmas. He missed that sparkle, the excitement and energy she brought to everything she did. He missed their talks in the evenings after work, where even after decades of marriage he had found her always fresh and new and wonderful. He stretched forward, drew a gentle finger down the edge of the frame. The photo had been taken years ago, before a piggyback semi had jackknifed on I-19, ending her life in a rage of steel and screams and utter injustice.

He swiveled his chair to look at the cluttered wall next to his desk: a couple of regional press awards, faded tear sheets of front-page stories (''Grange Hall Burns!''), and a half-dozen letters from readers who'd found some form of comfort or profit in his words. Not a whole lot, he mused, for almost forty years. Oh, he knew he was appreciated well enough, and he pulled down a respectable salary, the *Gazette*'s editor treated him decently. But . . .

He looked back on the deserted city room. What did it matter, he thought angrily. What did *he* matter? What had four decades of covering the news in south central Pee-Ay gotten him, anyway? A few bucks in the bank, a headful of thinning gray hair, and a ravenous cancer the size of a small melon. Martha had been his anchor, his reason. She'd known—more, she'd *cared*—what being a reporter had meant to him. Without her, he realized now, that meaning had started to dim even in his own heart.

He punched a fist into his thigh in frustration. He was going to die, and with Martha gone, no one would give a rat's ass. He was no Woodward or Bernstein; hell, he wasn't even a Jimmy Breslin. It wasn't fair. A man should count, should matter. His death should ring bells, bring tears, rattle the world!

A sudden "tacka-tacka" sound startled him. He got up, groaning, and walked stiffly to the chattering teletype machine. Eventually, he knew, even the *Gazette* would switch over completely to computer bulletin boards and the like. But for now, he looked with affection at the clacking, antiquated device. He'd lately developed an abiding respect for things that endured.

Casually, he read the wire service transmission. It was yet another Spider-Man story from New York. "Bank Robbery Foiled!" that sort of thing, good for page three filler: "... appeared out of nowhere . . . enigmatic vigilante saves day . . . mysterious hero leaves citizens to wonder . . ."

Slowly, subtly, Henry Pogue straightened. Abrupt purpose gave him the strength to lift his sagging shoulders for the first time in months. He remembered that Martha used to call the glow in his eyes, "like someone fired up a lighthouse in your head." And like the cancer inside him, the glow was growing.

Through the one-way eye shields of his mask, Spider-Man saw evil.

"This is chicken feed, babe! You're gonna have to do better'n that!"

Spidey eased down the alley wall, his red and blue costume a second skin, hands and feet clinging to the dirty brick like Velcro. The scene was a familiar one; he'd seen it often enough. The kid with the knife, using his free hand to scrounge through the purse, couldn't have been more than sixteen. The woman with her back pressed to the wall, trying bravely to stem her trembling, wasn't much older. He wondered how many scenes like this would play out elsewhere in New York before the day was done.

"Thirteen bucks?" The mugger snorted, dropping the purse. "Ain't enough. Ya wanna cruise *my* alley, ya gotta pay righteous toll. One way . . ." He moved toward her, teeth an ugly grin. ". . . or another!"

"Ahem!"

Spidey's throat-clearing had the desired effect. The punk whirled, head snapping up and eyes going wide.

"S-S-Spider-Man?!"

Flipping from the wall, somersaulting agilely, Spidey landed on the alley floor just feet from the would-be robber.

"Hey, why be so formal? Just think of me as your friendly neighborhood civil service inspector. You do have a license to collect tolls, don't you? I'll just take a look, make sure it's up to date, then be on my way. Fair enough?"

The kid started to raise his knife, but Spidey moved faster. His middle fingers pressed the triggers hidden in his palm beneath his glove. With a wet whine, thin gray strands of webbing shot out and stuck the mugger's knife hand against the far wall, adhering instantly. The kid pulled futilely, giving a small whine of his own.

"That webbing will dissolve in about an hour," Spider-Man offered as he bent to pick up the purse. "Plenty of time to think up an entertaining excuse for the local beat cop."

He held the purse out to the woman, but she backed away, eyes wary. I keep forgetting, Spidey thought, that scaring bad guys can make me spooky to civilians as well. With an exaggerated bow, he placed the purse on the ground before the woman.

"No thanks necessary, ma'am. Your expression of breathless gratitude is reward aplenty." Sheesh!

Shooting a webline to the side of a building, Spider-Man pulled himself effortlessly upward. Soon, he was web-swinging between the monoliths of Manhattan, traveling high over urban canyons like a New Age ape-man, generating his own biodegradable vines. He relished the freedom, the wind whistling through the thin fabric of his costume, impeded only slightly by the webbed bundle he wore on his back. The air tasted cool and fresh, having been washed clean by the storm that had swept up from Pennsylvania a couple of days before. It was times like this that he realized, despite the frequent danger and an annoying lack of respect, what a lucky man he was. He was only semesters away from an advanced science degree, he was married to the most beautiful young actress in New York, and he didn't have to hassle with taking cabs to cross the city.

But then his shoulders slumped as his wrist launcher extruded another webline. There was only one little thing he didn't have, he thought: money!

Resolutely, he angled towards a somber stone building several blocks away, one with fifty-foot letters braced across the roof reading *The Daily Bugle.*

*   *   *

"What's this, Pete—a cobweb?" Ace reporter Joy Mercado reached from her desk as Peter passed through the *Bugle*'s day room, plucking a patch of gray from his tan Members Only jacket.

"Uh, guess I need to clean my closets more often, Joy." That's what I get for lugging my street clothes around in a webbing pack, Peter thought. "Is Kate in?"

" 'In'? That woman practically lives in her office! I'm surprised she still makes payments on her condo! And Pete," Joy added with an enigmatic grin, "she's been asking for you."

"Thanks," Peter said, studiously ignoring her mock-lecherous expression. He walked quickly to Kate Cushing's office. As City Editor, Kate was responsible for making story assignments, and as a free-lance photographer, Peter needed every assignment he could get to pay the bills.

The door was open, but he rapped politely on the door jamb anyway. "You wanted to see me, Kate?"

Kate glanced up from behind her desk. "Come in, Peter. There's someone I'd like you to meet."

The man who rose from the chair reminded Peter a little of Jason Robards—if the esteemed actor hadn't eaten in a few months. But while the visitor appeared frail, his eyes were clear, and his grip was strong as he shook Peter's hand. "Henry Pogue. Glad to meet you."

Kate continued: "We're doing a story on vandalism at the Hudson River docks. Right-wing zealots have been trying to stop imported goods that cost American jobs, and their sabotage activities have been getting more violent. We could use some pictures."

Peter felt his mood brighten; crime photos, taken with

the help of his spider powers were his specialty.

Then Kate said: "Henry will be going with you."

"What—?"

"Henry's boss at the *Smithville Gazette* is an old friend. I promised him Henry could take part in our news-gathering process for a while, to bring back a little big-city savvy. And Henry specifically requested teaming with you."

"But, Kate, I work alone! I couldn't possibly—!"

Kate's voice was clear and cool, with an edge like honed steel. "Correct me if I'm wrong, Peter, but the *Bugle* still signs your checks? *We* don't work for *you*?"

Peter sighed, then forced a smile. "Welcome aboard, Mr. Pogue."

As they left Kate's office, Peter matched Pogue's slow gait. He couldn't help but ask, "I don't get it. Why *me*?"

"I've seen your credit on pictures of Spider-Man for years, young fella. I'm hoping to use that connection."

"Oh," Peter replied, thinking he understood. "You want to do a story on Spider-Man."

"Nope," Henry said. "I want to tell the world who he really *is*!"

"Peter, tell me you're kidding!"

Mary Jane Watson-Parker, red-headed vixen of TV's *Secret Hospital* soap opera, set the Hungry Helper Frozen Dinner on the coffee table in front of her husband. Pete looked at the microwaved lasagna, creamed corn, and stewed apples with the same enthusiasm normally reserved for a pile of dog poop with a spoon in it. "Oh, yum!"

"Come on, sweetheart" —she sat on the couch next to him— "you know I have to hurry back to the studio for a night shoot. *Duck à l'orange* tomorrow, I promise! Now tell me more about this hotshot reporter from Podunk.''

''Smithville,'' Peter corrected, moving some of the pasta around on his plate. It was sticky, he discovered. ''And I can't help feeling sorry for him. He told me while we were waiting for a cab, MJ; he's got cancer, bad. Only a couple of months to live.''

Mary Jane's brow creased with concern, and her hand settled gently on Peter's arm.

''Everyone with a terminal illness reacts differently. Pogue wants to make his life count for something. He's decided to solve one of the world's big mysteries—namely, to discover Spider-Man's true identity!''

''But, Peter, doesn't he realize what that would do to you? To the human being *behind* the mask?''

''I don't think he's thought about it, hon. Henry's scared, and he's funneling that fear into obsession. He's so determined to matter that I doubt he's considered how his actions will affect anything but his legacy.''

''What will you do?''

Pete put his fork beside the plate, his appetite dampened by more than the congealing meal before him. ''Not much I can do. Keep a low profile as Spidey, I guess. I know it may sound cruel, but if I just hang in there, maybe I can . . . well . . . outlast him? Nuts. Sometimes having all the power in the world doesn't mean squat.''

Mary Jane slid closer, putting her arm around him, her head on his shoulder. Peter wished it comforted him more than it really did.

The night air was thick and uncomfortably humid. Peter felt it pressing down on him as he waited, leaning against the corner of a warehouse along the Hudson River docks.

The clean air brought in by the recent storm had apparently blown out to sea.

His spider-sense tingled mildly, like a feather brushing his inner ear, telling him that someone approached. As if he wouldn't have heard the hacking cough even before Henry Pogue had rounded the far corner.

"That sounds pretty nasty, Mr. Pogue," Peter said, straightening. "You okay?"

"No problem, Peter. Fit as a fiddle. And call me Henry. Now, where are we supposed to ambush these patriotic hooligans?"

"Don't even *think* ambush, Henry." Pete led the way down an alley between buildings. "These punks are mostly spray paint artists and malicious pranksters, but they could be dangerous if cornered. We're here to get photos and take notes, that's all!" Peter gave a sidelong glance at his companion. Henry looked disappointed, clearing his throat after hiding another cough behind a fisted hand.

"But if there's no trouble, then Spider-Man won't show up!"

Precisely, Peter thought. Aloud, he said, "I'm just a photographer. I don't *want* trouble!"

"That's no way to get ahead in this racket," Pogue muttered, but he didn't pursue it, to Peter's relief.

They reached the end of the alley and Peter looked out over the night-dark docks to where the *Toyo Maru* rested in its slip. The Japanese freighter had arrived late that afternoon and was awaiting dawn to unload a shipment of automotive parts and agricultural aids. A perfect target for the graffiti commandos, he thought.

Then his spider-sense tingled softly once again, and the low growl of an engine heralded the arrival, sans headlights, of a battered old van. The van's side door opened; Peter counted at least a half-dozen men in their mid-twenties jumping out and pulling several burnished aluminum cases after them. A chill tightened Peter's gut as he photographed the men unpacking the cases, removing gleaming black metal in the shape of arms, legs, and a head. As they began fitting the components onto one of their number, attaching chest plate and leggings, then clamping on helmet and boots, Peter realized those components had to be high-tech armor of some kind. The game had changed, he thought. Then the punks added one last mechanism to their armored member: a sleek, ebony backpack that connected to the man's gauntleted wrists with thick, segmented tubes. Tubes that could only be one thing.

Gun barrels.

"Henry!" Peter whispered hastily. "We have to get help!" He turned to the older man. "They've cranked things up a notch! Those lunatics must've found a corporate sponsor that wants to scrap the competition! Stay here! I'm gonna go call the police!"

Peter sprinted back down the alley, turning a corner that quickly put him out of sight. "So much for a low profile," he muttered as he loosened the top button of his shirt, exposing the blue and red costume beneath.

"Hey! What're ya doin' there?" Two uniformed security guards were drawing pistols as they approached the van. "You got authorization papers? An' who's that doofus in the shiny suit?"

The metal man pointed an arm in their direction. "Who you callin' doofus, pinhead!"

The armored wrist jerked slightly as its stubby barrel

made a soft "chuff." Twenty feet away, the guards suddenly twitched, then fell to the concrete in khaki-colored lumps.

"Whoa!" cried one of the punks. "Trank darts worked great! Those rent-a-cops dropped faster than a Bills quarterback in the Superbowl!"

"A speed record *you're* about to break, sports fans!"

Spider-Man watched the vandals turn as one, facing the direction of his unexpected cry. When they saw him floating in from the darkness on a webline, they gaped.

"H-Holy geez! It's Spider-Man! Raker, d-do somethin'!"

Once more, the armored man raised his arm.

"And what're you supposed to be, Raker—" Spidey spun a second webline and swung closer to the clustered vandals. "—the Dork Knight? You'll have to do better than tranquilizer darts to play with the big kids!"

But this time the wrist cannon didn't cough, it roared, sending a beam of blazing energy straight at Spider-Man. Reacting with superhuman speed, Spidey jerked knees to chest as the crackling energy spiked below him, bringing a warm, unwanted glow to his backside.

Barrels must be multifunctional, he thought, probably controlled by cybernetic triggers! Oh, man, like I need this?

Raker fired again, and twice more, but Spidey never stopped moving, his phenomenal speed and agility keeping him out of harm's way; he just wasn't there when Raker's blasts arrived. Two bolts lanced harmlessly into the sky, while the third smashed through a wall of one of the many warehouses lining the dock. An unsettlingly familiar warehouse.

Henry! thought Spider-Man. That's the building he's hiding behind! Have to move the danger away!

Arcing in midair, sending out a new webline, Spider-

Man swung toward the water and the *Toyo Maru*. As he'd hoped, Raker wasn't about to let him get away. Compact nozzles popped from Raker's metal boots, flames spat from their twin snouts, and Raker rose into the air in pursuit.

In the alley next to the damaged warehouse, Henry Pogue looked on in awe. All the stories he'd read over the years, all the headlines and the teletypes, couldn't prepare him for this. *Spider-Man.* He was actually witnessing a legend in action, like spotting the Loch Ness Monster, or seeing Sasquatch in the wild. He just hoped, as he nervously looked on, that he wasn't here to see a legend die.

Spider-Man was doing his best to stay alive, jerking his body side to side to avoid the barrage of inch-long needle-sharp nails that Raker was now firing from one of his wrist weapons.

The guy's quick, Spidey thought. And getting close! Those nails could rip me raw if they connect! I gotta take him down, now!

Even as the thought formed, he was acting, letting go of his webline and tumbling through the air to land feetfirst on the port side of the *Toyo Maru*, sticking there like a human Post-It. He twisted, launched fresh weblines from each hand, and snagged Raker in mid-flight. He yanked with all his strength. The airborne attacker, caught by surprise, twisted out of control, his mini-jets slamming him into a massive loading crane. With a low groan, Raker slid heavily to the dock, bounced once, and lay still.

A graceful leap brought Spider-Man to the dock surface, where he crouched next to his facedown opponent, cocking back a fist: "Either this backpack is a handy place to carry your lunch, or it's what supplies the power to your weapons systems! Either way, let's see what happens when I turn it into leftovers!''

But a shriek in Spidey's head halted his fist scant millimeters before it struck. Spider-sense! Of course, he thought. If this thing is a power pack, and I punch into it, that'd be like sticking my hand into an on-line generator! I'd be electrocuted!

In that moment of hesitation, Spidey's warning sense cried again, and he barely tumbled out of the way as Raker whipped a hand around, wrist barrel blazing.

Pulling himself along as fast as he could on his ropelike weblines, Spider-Man swung back towards the freighter. Behind him, Raker took to the air in pursuit once again, snarling, "I'm gonna pulp you, wall-crawler! Gonna do it the old-fashioned way, with my bare hands! And there ain't nothin' you can do about it!''

Like a high-jumper clearing a six-foot bar, Spider-Man glided easily over the rail to land nimbly on the *Toyo Maru*'s main deck. Bare hands? he thought. That means he'll have to get close—and that gives me an idea!

Looking around, he spotted a tower of packing crates stacked beside a vertical beam, part of the mechanism used to lower cargo to the docks below. A horizontal spar, wrapped with cables and ropes, jutted out at a right angle from the beam about eight feet over the uppermost crate.

Perfect.

In seconds, he was standing on the top crate. Spidey knew Raker was grinning beneath his metal mask. The way his shoulders bunched, the way his fisted gauntlets thrust forward, the guy had to think victory was a done deal.

And indeed, Raker barked a short laugh as the nozzles

of his boot jets fired hotter, their flames turning from orange to white, driving him towards his target ever faster, quickly reaching a speed meant to tear Spidey in two from impact alone. It was also a speed that wouldn't allow Raker to deviate from his projected course even if he'd wanted to.

And that was exactly what Spider-Man was counting on.

The instant before Raker's steel-hard fists would have slammed home, Spidey hopped, jumping just high enough to grasp the overhead spar. He then jerked his feet up and, as the startled Raker passed by underneath, kicked out and down with the full extent of his radiation-born strength. His heels hit Raker's back, ripping the power pack loose with a sharp squeak of tearing metal. In a sputter of sparks and hissing fire, the whole backpack spun to the deck below, skidding to clang harmlessly against the bulkhead. Spidey then watched as Raker, deprived of power, continued forward until he reached the next stack of crates, which happened to be filled with bags of designer fertilizer destined for farms in upstate New York. Raker hit with a smack and a squish, then lay unmoving in the mass of splintered wood and custom dung.

Spider-Man looked down at him, slowly shaking his head: "Sooner or later, pal, ya gotta learn: crime stinks!"

Just then, he heard the wail of approaching sirens, in the distance. Someone else must've heard the fight, he thought. Good. Cops can go after the punks that got away in that van. And I can still use calling them as an excuse for splitting from Henry! He ran off to where he'd stashed his clothing, threw them on with practiced speed, then jogged down the alley.

He slowed as he rounded a corner and saw the older man hunched over, coughing into a stained handkerchief.

He felt sorry for Henry, and a bit guilty at deceiving him. But there was little choice. It was either that, or—

Peter's spider-sense tickled his inner ear a split second before he heard the ominous crack and rumble. Over Henry's head, chunks of brick began to rain down as the wall he was standing beside leaned outward.

Oh, Lord! Peter thought. Raker's blast must've damaged the building's structure! The wall's starting to collapse!

He darted forward, unofficially setting a new world record for the short sprint. "Henry! Look out!"

Henry Pogue may have been dying, but he still resented anything that might take away his hold on life one second sooner than God decreed. Even so, he could only stare in shock and anger as a ton of mortared brick began its inexorable arc toward him.

And then Peter was there. The young man's face strained with effort, but he nonetheless seemed to be doing the flat-out impossible: he was holding up the falling wall with his bare hands! But no one could do that, Henry thought. At least, no one . . . human!

"Go, Henry! Get out of here! I can't hold this up forever!"

Though stunned and shaken, Henry was still a newsman. And decades of habit led him to slide a small camera from his coat pocket. A single flash illuminated Peter Parker's widening eyes, like a deer caught in a car's headlights, and then Henry was stumbling towards the safety of the open docks, his flight blind because his eyes never left the sight of the *Daily Bugle* photographer holding up the entire side of a building.

At last Peter jumped, a leap that carried him over fifty

feet, and he tumbled nimbly out of danger as the wall came down in a thunder of dust and shattering brick.

Henry stood silently as the night began to blink red with squad cars screeching onto the scene. Soon, there would be questions. But none would be harder-edged, or hold more potential devastation, than the one in Henry Pogue's mind as he stared at Peter Parker.

And when Peter returned Henry's look, his own eyes held no answers.

"Did you get what you came for, Mr. Pogue?"

Thin morning sun filtered into Kate Cushing's tenth floor office, highlighting the pallor of Henry Pogue's skin. To one side of her desk, Peter Parker leaned rigidly against a file cabinet, eyes fixed on Henry. Peter's face was ashen.

"I . . . got what I needed." Henry smiled slightly, then extended his hand. "Thanks for your help."

Kate smiled back warmly as she gently shook his hand. "It was our pleasure. Have a safe trip back to Smithville. And tell Mike Kaufman to write me once in a while, okay?"

"Will do."

Henry left the office, coughing once, and walked towards the elevator bank at the far end of the day room.

Peter Parker followed him. "Come on, Henry! Please! You don't know what you're doing!"

Henry hesitated, shoulders sinking. Then he turned to the younger man, looked at him with eyes that showed no malice, no fear, only an unbreachable shield of sad resolve.

"Maybe not, Peter. But I know what I *have* to do. I'm sorry."

He left Peter standing there. He did not look back.

*   *   *

"No, Mary Jane, I am *not* going to kill the guy!"

Peter sat glumly, moving pieces of duck in orange sauce around on his plate with his fork as he watched the sun set over New Jersey. In the middle of the kitchen table were cardboard cartons labeled "Manny's Gourmet Take-Out"; at the far end was his wife, equally glum, elbow on the table, her chin propped up in a palm.

"I didn't mean literally, Peter. But you have to stop him from printing that picture! If the world finds out you're Spider-Man, it'd wreck everything! Your hopes for a Ph.D., my acting career, Aunt May's life, maybe even . . . us."

Peter set his fork down and looked into his wife's emerald eyes.

"I know what it would do, hon. I've lived with this possibility ever since high school, since I first got my powers. But I'm no vigilante. I can't strong-arm some old man just to keep him quiet! That would make me no better than the lowlifes I put in jail. And besides, even if I wanted to, I . . . I don't think I could."

Mary Jane's concern softened with affection. "I know, sweetheart. And I love you for that. But we're talking lives here—ours! I don't have a solution. I wish I did. But I do know you have to do *something*!"

Peter looked out the window. MJ's argument in some ways echoed the last thing Henry Pogue had said. What was that old line? "A man's gotta do what a man's gotta do"? So damn corny, Peter thought. He shook his head and pushed back from the table.

So damn corny and so damn true.

*   *   *

Henry grimaced as he swallowed the last of his prune juice. Lord, he thought, what I'd give for a cup of coffee. Even instant!

He set his glass back on the desk and lay his fingers lightly on the Macintosh keyboard. Another reason for working at night, he thought. During the day, the *Gazette*'s offices were full of reminders of things the doctors wouldn't let him have any more: the smell of fresh ground coffee, the sweet stink of cigarette smoke on the shirts of colleagues coming back inside after a breath of "fresh air." He missed those things, along with the noise, the bustle— the sounds and smells of being alive.

He'd been tapping on the keyboard about a minute when he realized he was no longer alone. It wasn't a psychic phenomenon, more like resignation; he'd been expecting this. He looked up to see Spider-Man, half in shadow, perched on the railing that ran across the front of the city room.

"You gonna kill me?" Henry asked as he leaned back in his chair.

"Funny," Spidey answered, hopping down and stepping forward to stand in the pool of light surrounding the desk. "You're the second person to ask me that tonight."

"It's a logical progression. I've seen what you can do. What's to keep you from doing it to me to get what you want?"

"That's easy, Henry: I'm no murderer. All I am is"— he reached up to peel off his full-head mask, revealing the troubled face of Peter Parker —"a man."

"I figured you'd drop by, but it won't do any good. You're gonna to have to stop *me* to stop this story. Can't you understand? This is the scoop of the century! It's what's gonna make people remember me! It's everything!''

Peter leaned close. "You got that wrong, Henry. Celebrity is just surface shine, and glory doesn't mean beans. It's people's actions, their *deeds*, that count. Both the good deeds, and the bad. Listen, I've got a wife, friends, relatives. If my true identity got out, their lives would be be over— maybe literally! They'd have to go into hiding just to get a moment's peace! And if they didn't, my enemies would know where to find them. Most of the scum I've put behind bars would just love to rip my heart out by gunning down people that mean the world to me. For pity's sake, Henry, at least think of them!''

Henry dropped his eyes, picked up a pencil and toyed with it nervously. "That's easy for you to say. You've already made a difference! You matter to people! But, me—''

Peter slammed a fist on the desk, knocking the empty juice glass over. Henry met his gaze.

"C'mon, Henry, wake up!" Peter said. "I didn't ask for my powers! But I've tried to use them for one thing: to make the world a better place. And you say you're different? I remember what you told me while we were in that cab, about how important Martha was to you, how happy she made you for thirty years. If she was such a wonderful person, and *chose* to be with you all that time, you must have done a pretty good job of keeping *her* happy, too!''

Henry glanced at the framed photo on the desk.

"And if that isn't enough, just look around." Peter pointed to the wall of Henry's work station; the weary reporter turned to follow his finger. "Maybe you should dust off those civic commendations and reread those letters. Cripes, Henry, most folks who live *twice* your age don't touch *half* as many people!

"Bottom line is, telling the world who I am will destroy me, possibly destroy the people I love, and almost certainly destroy any hopes I have of helping anyone else in the future! Is that what you want? Is that a fair price for your fifteen minutes in the spotlight?"

A long moment of silence stretched thin, vibrating with the anxious electricity of anticipation.

And then it ended. Peter stood and stepped back, let out a long, deep breath. Slowly, he reached up to draw the red and blue mask back over his head.

"I didn't have a choice becoming what I am, Henry." Spider-Man turned and walked back into the shadows. "You do."

In seconds, just as surely as he'd sensed the other man's presence before, Henry Pogue knew he was alone again. For half an hour he sat, saying nothing, alternately looking at the computer's monitor screen, at Martha's picture, then back to the words he'd been writing. Once, he reached over to the wall, to a piece of lined paper affixed with a push pin. He brushed dust from the note. Scrawled in crayon, it was a note of thanks from a little girl for a human interest filler he'd dashed off, one that had led to the return of her lost kitten. "Earthshaking stuff. Yep, I'm a real world changer, I am."

He grinned, coughed his lungs clear, then turned back to the desk. After a moment, he opened the center drawer, rummaged in the back, and pulled out a half-empty pack of Lucky Strikes. He removed a cigarette, finding it dry and brittle. Been there since Doc Simpson gave me the bad word, he thought. He held the paper cylinder under his nose and breathed in, his eyelids lowering in remembered pleasure. He put the filtered end in his mouth. "Hey, like it's gonna matter *now?*"

But when he took a disposable lighter from the drawer and flicked it into flame, bringing it towards the cigarette, he paused. And then, with a congested chuckle, he took the cigarette and flipped it into a nearby wastebasket. "What do you know?" he said to the empty room. "Maybe I *can* still learn a thing or two."

He reached back into the drawer and took out a plain, white envelope. Thumbing the lighter back to life, he touched flame to the envelope's edge, then placed it in a wide glass ashtray Martha had bought for him on what turned out to be their last vacation together. The thin strips of photographic negatives inside crinkled and crisped, curling into delicate black ash. As they burned, he turned back to the computer, slowly deleted the text of the document he'd been working on, and started over.

Excerpt from an article in the Sunday *Smithville Gazette*, "My Night With Spider-Man," by Henry Pogue: "And while I discovered many things in my short encounter with this amazing individual, perhaps most salient was the fact that the man behind the mask—whoever he may be—is vastly more vital than the flash, the stunts, or the costume, the things most people tend to remember. Because when all is said and done, a single truth prevails: as with most things in life, it's the man inside that counts. And in this instance, that is a very wise man, indeed."

Excerpt from the *Smithville Gazette*, some weeks later, an obituary written by guest columnist Peter Parker: "Henry Pogue saved my life. The details aren't important, for I suspect that in his years he saved many lives, and few even realized their salvation. With his kindness, compassion, and courage—and with his words—he delivered people from ignorance, from deception, and from sorrow. He made decisions most of us never have to face; he put what was right ahead of what he thought *should* be right, making sacrifices that left this world a better place for the rest of us. Doing what is just is arguably the most unrewarding task in life, but to Henry it was also the most significant. So, what epitaph shall we offer? How shall we honor the memory of this man? Though I only knew Henry a short while, simplicity and veracity seemed to be the traits he admired most; I suggest we do no less in remembering him. These, then, are the words I think Henry Pogue would have approved; and in the hearts of all he touched, they are words honestly earned: He mattered.''

TINKER, TAILOR, SOLDIER, COURIER

ROBERT L. WASHINGTON III

Illustration by Stephen Baskerville

A hot, sticky wind wove its way among the skyscrapers as the gridlock traffic jam below slowly gained in noise and intensity. Spider-Man watched from above as hordes of shouting cab drivers cursed at office workers leaving too late to beat rush hour traffic. A thousand horns blared at once.

It was a typical New York summer weekend rush hour, and Spider-Man wasn't *exactly* known for traffic duty. But for two upturned faces, attached to arms swinging madly and voices raised in desperate salutation, the rush hour woes and Spider-Man were an equation of last resort. Their cries and the flashing lights of their ambulance, with its front grille smashed in and a puddle of radiator fluid pooling under it, were enough to reverse Spider-Man's path with a deceptively simple-looking triple somersault and another flight of his webbing.

Spider-Man landed lightly atop the ambulance. "What's the story, guys?" he asked amiably. "I'm not exactly Mr. Goodwrench, but I'm pretty sure you know that."

"Spider-Man, please," begged one of the two, a short, stocky man in his mid-50's whose face told of many years of grim civil service. "Time's running out. We've got a donor organ for a little girl . . . she needs it badly. They didn't even think she'd live long enough to operate, but she held on and a liver just became available."

His young partner broke in. "We didn't have time to arrange for a helicopter lift. We've *got* to get it there in the next hour and a half or it'll be too late. Even if we can get alternate transport here, in the middle of Friday rush hour—"

Spider-Man hopped to the ground. "Say no more. Where does it have to go?"

"Methodist Hospital. Park Slope, Brooklyn. You know it?"

Spider-Man groaned inwardly, but nodded. "Oh yeah."

It's a good thing a look of weary shock is hidden by a mask, he thought to himself. I *couldn't* say no, but if these guys only *knew*...

The younger man ducked into the back of the ambulance and soon reappeared carrying an oddly-shaped metal canister. He handed it to Spider-Man. "This is it. It's got a battery-operated refrigeration unit that should last another *three* hours, so you shouldn't have any problem."

"Well, not with that part, anyway," Spider-Man muttered. He took the container and hoisted himself to the ambulance roof one-armed. Using his webbing, he casually wove a makeshift sling for the canister around his arm. "Great. Or maybe I should say 'cool.' Or maybe not," he amended, looking at the pained faces of the two men in response to the lame pun. "Seriously guys, don't worry. It'll get there."

And, shifting the sling around to hang off his back, he was off with a series of standing leaps from ambulance roof to bus roof to car roof to truck roof, increasing in height and length with each bounding step.

Gotta build up speed and height quickly, Spider-Man mused. I'm going to need the time to figure out how to get past that Little Problem. Heading downtown, he shot out a web to catch onto a nearby building.

The air began to whistle past his ears as he quickly accelerated and surpassed his previous web-slinging velocity; flexing his arm muscles, he yanked at the webline, increasing the angle and speed of his motion.

He cut across Eighth Avenue, Seventh Avenue, Broadway and the impressively-named-but-rather-plain-when-you-came-down-to-it Avenue of the Americas, effectively crossing the whole of Times Square in a near-beeline, a move impossible except by air.

He hit midtown moving even faster, using his stomach muscles and hauling his shoulders into the efforts of tugging in the line on his downswings, spacing out his arms for even greater descent angles as he worked for yet more acceleration. He passed the shopping complex known as A&S Plaza, then the Flatiron Building.

As he neared the Washington Square Arch, the weight of the canister on his back began to bruise even his muscles. Its corners pulled thin holes through the soft sling as the webbing dried and dug into his back. He ignored the pain, however, and gave no sign of discomfort as his downswing took him just over the slightly shrunken version of the Arc de Triomphe in Paris.

Below, he spotted several drug dealers fleeing from the small park—they had probably seen him, he thought. Their flight was halted by some of New York's Finest. If the bust made it into the papers, he knew the *Daily Bugle*'s story would read "SPIDER-MAN DOPE DEAL FOILED BY QUICK THINKING COPS!"

Swooping over East Broadway, he spotted one of New York's rarest sights, a New York City bus in continuous motion on a thoroughfare *not* clogged with traffic. Appraising the scene below and ahead of him, he calculated his chances and finally deciding to make the attempt, despite the risk.

He twistflipped off at his downswing, did a series of somersault rolls to take away some of his momentum, and landed easily on top of the bus. One handed, he swung down to peer into the driver's side window.

"Okay, now, don't panic," he said to the driver. "Just keep driving."

"Umm, okay, sure, but, uh, don't you usually—" began the driver. He mopped his forehead nervously with a towel.

"I don't have time to explain. I've got a life to save. Where's this bus going?"

"World Trade Center. A life at stake?"

Spider-Man nodded. "A little girl. I've got less than an hour, and I've still got to get to Brooklyn."

The driver turned and called to his passengers, "Sorry folks, but this bus just went express. Next stop, WTC."

"Thanks." Spider-Man said. Reaching into a small pouch underneath his costume's waist, he pulled out a token he carried for just such an emergency. He offered it to the driver.

"It's on me," the driver said. "It's worth it for the story!" Pulling out a token of his own, he deposited it into the fare box.

"Thanks again." Smiling, Spider-Man hauled himself back up onto the roof. The bus lurched forward, accelerating, and just beat a red light. This should save more time than I'd lose cutting back across town, Spidey thought, holding on and catching his breath.

Minutes later, they reached the World Trade Center stop. Spider-Man leaped off the bus with a wave, snaring a high edge of the nearest of the twin towers, shooting another web on his upswing at the second tower, and repeating the process to gain altitude.

Then, swooping down and across the Bowery District, body still curling madly to work up speed, he began to look around more actively, taking time between casts of his weblines, slowing as the difference of not casting on his maximum acceleration began to cut in. There weren't enough skyscrapers to swing from, he realized. The buildings in this area weren't tall enough.

Turning to throw a webline as he approached the South Street Seaport Area, he found himself with a wicked surprise—the last building he always used on this route had vanished, replaced with a huge open construction pit.

He found himself tumbling and threw out a webline that just barely extended to another building in time. He shifted the sling around to his stomach and swung around. Two more webswings and he touched down half a block over, where a new highrise was in its initial girders-only stages. From here he could see Brooklyn . . . and the nearest way across was the subway bridge.

He quickly scaled the construction work, then laid a thick, nearly liquid sling of webbing between two girders. He leaped to the sling's center and dragged it back until it began to stretch.

"Gotta get my angle just right . . . only one shot," he muttered.

Carefully shifting himself and sighting, he finally let loose. The web launched him into the air with the sound of a thousand rubber bands releasing.

Carefully shifting and adjusting his freefall slingshot as best he could, his thoughts came in a constant stream: think up, think up, think *up*, I'm going to make it . . . what's *that?!*

A D train headed for Brooklyn bolted across the bridge below him with a sound like a thousand. Instinctively Spider-Man shot out a webline to snag one of the cars—and abruptly found himself jerked along like a kite at the end of the string. Only he was a very heavy kite and gravity was just about to seize him.

Swiftly he reeled himself in before he could fall and be dragged along behind the train. As he touched down on the roof of the rearmost car, he checked the clocks on the enormous spire of the Williamsburg Bank Building behind him.

Plenty of time left. He could make it.

The D train left the bridge and slowed, approaching the station. Spidey began a low, easy series of webswings along the brownstones and annoyingly low buildings of the area. They didn't matter now. He was close enough to hoof it if he had to.

Then his spider-sense went off, and an instant later a flying metallic object cut through his web. He tumbled to the ground, shocked, then did a flip and landed on his feet. Luckily he hadn't been very far off the ground.

Whirling, Spider-Man faced a man hovering overhead via shoulder jets and looked into the strange metal goggle helmet of the mercenary known as Chance.

"What do *you* want?" Spidey demanded. "Listen, I've got an errand to run. Go play that new trading card game all the kids are into now. I hear they only play for each other's cards, but eventually, they gotta be worth some— Hey!"

A stream of darts shot from Chance's wrist launcher. Spidey jumped out of their way.

"Sorry, Spider-Man, but I don't have time for monologues. I've wasted enough time trying to catch up with you since you left the ambulance. An employer has paid me well for the contents of that canister, so let's not play games, shall we?"

He opened fire again.

Dodging in a series of superhuman backflips, Spider-Man jumped to the side of a brownstone, heading toward the hospital, now only a few blocks away. "Forget it, Chauncy. I'm paid for door-to-door service, bum mercenary whomping included!" Spidey threw another webline at a nearby brownstone.

"Tsk, tsk. You should have figured I know my way around you by now," Chance offered calmly. He flew toward Spider-Man, bringing to bear what appeared to be a small rocket launcher.

Spidey felt a sharp tingle in his spider-sense.

Chance fired a battery of whirling razor-sharp discs in a scatter pattern. Spidey ducked as best he could, but one cut his webline and forced him to the ground once more.

"Well, a guy can hope!" Spider-Man resumed his course with a series of leaps.

"Of course a man can hope. Hoping for the best is what taking chances is all about. But this time, I'm afraid Chance is against you."

When Spidey looked back, Chance fired a grenade. But all Chance's software could not account for the feeling like a thousand needling tendrils streaming from Spider-Man's head as the crosshairs focused on him. Spider-Man leaped to the side.

True to Chance's tracking software, the grenade exploded exactly where Spider-Man would have landed, erupting a cloud of greenish fog. But Spider-Man was coming to ground just to the left of his original destination, with plenty of time to get in a breath before holding it as the cloud expanded in a roiling, flattening sphere.

"No *way*, Chance! Nothing's going to slow me down! As

long as I don't breathe this stuff in, whatever it is—"

Leaping towards the next rooftop and out of the gas, Spider-Man felt his stomach tighten in anxiety. He felt the canister slide from his back and tumble towards the ground.

Chance gloated: "But I don't need to slow *you* down. If I can slow down the canister, oh, say, with a special corrosive gas formula to dissolve that affair you carry it with, you can be on your way with my returns."

Spider-Man bounded back toward the canister, but couldn't stop Chance from snatching it in midflight and reversing his jets entirely into a full backward thrust. "That's better. I'd thank you for your help, but frankly, you've taken me far out of my way."

"You'll be headed into next week if I have anything to say about it! Give me that!" Spider-Man threw a webline at Chance's rapidly fleeing form, just barely catching Chance's right boot.

Chance stopped in midair as his shoulder jets matched power with Spider-Man. As the desperate moment stretched, Spidey saw Chance reach for an oval object the size of a soda bottle. Twisting and pushing a button in one tip inwards, he lobbed it at the last of a nearby row of buildings.

"Forget about . . . playing catch . . . I'm not . . . interested!" Spider-Man grunted as he began to haul in Chance.

"Well, I don't think you want to catch an incendiary device that powerful. You'd burn to a crisp, like the people inside that building will."

"You wouldn't—" Spider-Man began, but a rapidly spreading sheet of flame engulfed the building before he could finish. Looking back between Chance and the fire, he finally let go of Chance and raced towards the building. There had to be dozens of people trapped inside, and he had to save them first. Then he would hunt down Chance and see justice rendered.

Chance jetted away.

"How could you do this to a *child*?" Spider-Man screamed at his back. He dove into the burning building.

For once, luck seemed to be with Spider-Man. As he moved quickly through the building, he discovered it almost deserted. Most of its residents had to be caught in rush hour, and the few teens and retirees were easily helped along or lowered to safety out a window via webbing.

Moving into the last of the top floor apartments, however, he was dismayed to discover a man in his late fifties trapped under a collapsed support beam. A warning tingle in his spider-sense told him the floor was about to give way. Moving quickly, he tossed the beam aside, then felt the floor beneath him shift sickeningly. The support beams were giving way. As quickly as he could, he looked the man over for serious injuries.

"Doesn't seem too bad," he said reassuringly. "Now if we can just get you out of here before the place comes down around us . . . " He lifted the man over his shoulder.

But the floor had other ideas. Spider-Man leaped toward the window, but too late. The floor fell out beneath his feet. Gotta twist, he thought. Maybe I can break the old man's fall—

They tumbled toward the rubble below. Working desperately to shield the man's body from the impact, Spider-Man prepared to shoot web to cushion their impact.

But before he could, he felt himself strike something soft but resilient. He bounced a little and realized they'd landed in a mesh net. Then he looked up and, to his surprise, found Chance hovering there.

But his surprise reached its peak when Chance flicked a switch on his belt, releasing the series of electromagnetic metal balls that ringed the net, freeing them and allowing approaching paramedics to take charge of the victim Spider-Man had rescued.

Chance continued to hover just out of Spider-Man's reach. "Look," he said, "Maroni didn't say anything about a child. Just that he wanted me to retrieve these medical supplies, no questions asked. What's all this about?" He lowered the canister to the ground as he spoke.

"Medical supplies? That's a donor liver for a little girl in there! Why would Maroni steal a donor liver . . . of course!" said Spider-Man, struck with an inspiration. "It's for himself, right?"

"Donor *liver*? Yeah, he's sick, he was bedridden when he—Hey! I get it! He needs a transplant."

"But he's like a million years old," Spidey broke in. "He started out shining shoes for Al Capone! Besides, he's got a record a mile long. Donor organs are regulated through a federal program. He couldn't possibly get one any other way without suspicion, so . . ."

"So he tracked down an incoming specimen that matched his blood and gene type," Chance finished, "and hired me. Not an unreasonable thought."

"Well, I guess that's it then." Spider-Man faced Chance from a few dozen feet away. "Your sleazy boss wants to let some poor kid die so he can hang on to his pile of dirty money just a little while longer. I just want to give the kid back her shot. The hospital wants this liver in the next fifteen minutes tops, according to the clock on that bank. What do *you* want?"

Chance's face was unreadable beneath his goggle helmet as he reached into a belt pouch and withdrew a silver dollar. "I want tails," he said, tossing the coin in the air with a flourish.

The coin pinged to rest atop the canister. Spider-Man couldn't read it from his position. Chance looked at the coin, then at Spider-Man.

"I also wanted to complete my assignment, but my employer failed to account for you in the picture. Wish I'd been able to catch up with you."

Disbelieving, Spider-Man approached the canister. He glanced at the coin's face as he moved to take the canister. *Heads.*

"I don't believe it!" he said. "You really risked a little girl's life versus some old crook's on a coin toss!"

Chance laughed as his shoulder jets took him speeding off into the evening. "Did I? It takes a special kind of man to trust in Chance completely. Perhaps if you did . . . "

"It takes a special kind of stone cold jerk! If I *ever* have a half a—"

"Half a Chance, Spider-Man? Right now you don't even have half a clue. But we'll see what the future brings." Laughing, he jetted off into the distance.

Spider-Man picked up the silver dollar and looked at it. Chance had lost his call, all right. How could he have done otherwise with a two-headed coin?

Shaking his head, Spider-Man grabbed the canister and sprinted for the hospital. He still had a little girl to save.

THUNDER ON THE MOUNTAIN

RICHARD LEE BYERS

Illustration by Tom Lyle and Scott Hanna

Davy was looking for blackberries when he started feeling nervous. At first he didn't know why. Then he noticed the forest had gotten quiet. A crow had stopped cawing, and nothing rustled through the brush.

Farther up the mountain, hidden among the rows of dark green pines, something chattered. Though the noise wasn't exactly like the bang of Dad's guns, Davy could tell it was shooting. Then something boomed like thunder, again and again. A giant's footsteps, shaking the ground, pounding closer.

It could only mean that the bad men—the people Dad called the barbarians—had come at last, just as Davy had always feared they would. He knew he should run or hide, the way he'd been taught, and if there'd only been the shooting, maybe he could have. But the awful thud of the giant's feet froze him. He dropped his bucket.

A rifleman in a camouflage jacket stepped out from behind an oak, saw Davy, and pointed his gun right at him.

Then something red and blue streaked down from the sky. An arm whipped around Davy's waist. Before he could even think of trying to break free, the man who'd grabbed him jumped, carrying him halfway up a tall spruce, somehow sticking to a part of the trunk where there was nothing to hold on to. Guns clattered.

Still holding Davy so tightly it hurt, the red and blue man raced through the trees, jumping and swinging from one to the next. Branches bounced and leaves rattled. Far below, the ground flashed by in a blur. Davy held his breath. He was sure they were going to fall, but they never did. The red and blue man was as surefooted as a squirrel.

At last, the man jumped back to the ground, a thirty-foot drop. Davy cringed, but the grown-up's legs soaked up the shock for them both. It was no worse than flopping down on his bed.

The man let him go. "We're safe now," he gasped, his chest heaving. "I'd sense it if we weren't."

For a second, the mountain rocked. When Davy got over the dizziness, he moved away from the grown-up and looked him over. Lean and muscular, the stranger wore a tight costume with spiderweb designs on it. A mask hid his whole head, even the eyes. He looked almost as scary as the shaking ground had felt. Davy wanted to run, but having seen how strong and fast the man was, he knew he wouldn't get away.

"Take it easy," said the stranger. "Don't you recognize me? It's your friendly neighborhood Spider-Man, champion of justice, defender of the oppressed, and national spokesperson of the I Hate Barney Support League. Man, I have got to hire a publicist."

Davy wanted to answer—this spiderman might get mad if he didn't—but he couldn't think of anything to say. He trembled.

"Hey," said the masked man. His voice was softer now, the joking tone gone. "You really *don't* know me, do you? I mean, you've never even heard of me, have you?"

Davy shook his head.

"Well, I promise, I'm a nice guy. I just dress spooky. And I'm sorry if it frightened you when I grabbed you and carried you off. But I had to get you out of the way of some genuine bad guys, namely those creeps who shot at us."

Davy started to feel better. Maybe *this* stranger wasn't dangerous. He had carried him away from the awful footsteps and the shooting, and he didn't have a gun or knife. In Dad's stories, the barbarians always did. "Uh, okay. I mean, I believe you. And, uh, thanks.''

"No biggie," said Spider-Man. "It's all part of the service. What's your name?''

"Davy." Now that he'd gotten over being scared, he felt dumb. Shy. "Or David. David Carter.''

"Nice to meet you, Davy." Spider-Man held out his hand. Davy hesitated, then shook it. The stranger's fingers felt strong as steel, even though he didn't squeeze hard. "I need you to take me to your house, okay?''

Davy jerked his hand back. "I can't.''

The masked man cocked his head. "You mean you're lost?''

"No. But—but my dad told me never to lead strangers home. I'm not even supposed to talk to you.''

"And maybe that's a smart rule," Spider-Man said. "But sometimes you have to make exceptions. Big, nasty things are going down, and I'm hurt, see?'' He lifted his left arm.

Davy gasped. Spider-Man's shirt was torn, the skin beneath it cut. He wasn't bleeding badly now, but blood spotted the red and blue costume all the way down to the knee. Its coppery smell mixed with the stink of sweat.

"Don't panic," Spider-Man said. "I'll live, but this is a problem. So will you help me? Please?''

Davy ran his fingers through his hair. He knew he wasn't supposed to break Dad's rules, no matter what. But he couldn't just turn his back on someone who'd helped him, not when the guy was hurt. Feeling trapped, he finally said, "All right.''

"Great," said Spider-Man. "Give me a second, then we can go." He pointed his hand at his side, and gray thread shot out and covered the wound. For a second, Davy felt sick. It looked like the costumed man was squirting the stuff out of his body, the same way a real spider pulled webbing out of its butt. Then he made out the shape of some kind of spray gun under the stranger's glove. "There. Not the world's greatest bandage, because it'll dissolve, but it'll do for a little while. Do you mind if we hoof it from here? I feel a little too woozy for another Tarzan routine."

"That's okay," said Davy, wondering what a tarzan was. "It's this way." He led him down the slope. Before long, they found one of the game trails that ran down to the lake.

One by one, the birds started singing again. A breeze blew, carrying the smell of pine, and a doe ate grass on a faraway ridge. Every so often, Spider-Man stiffened, and sucked in a hissing breath.

"We're almost there," Davy reassured him.

"Glad to hear it. And thanks for trying to keep a poor, decrepit hero's spirits up." Davy decided that it didn't matter much that Spider-Man kept his face covered. He could usually hear a grin in the stranger's voice.

Spider-Man pulled up the bottom of his mask and wiped at the sweat on his stubbly chin. "You know," he continued, "no offense, but you sure are quiet. If I were a kid tramping through the woods with a weird guy like me, I'd be asking questions nonstop. And it would be cool, because we superdoers love to yack. Except for the eleven secret herbs and spices in the web fluid, I'll tell you anything you want to know."

Davy's cheeks got warm. He *was* curious, more curious than he'd ever been before, but he was also afraid that anything he said would sound stupid. "Are you and the other men from New York City?"

"More or less," the man in the costume replied. He sounded surprised. "What made you ask that?"

"I don't know," Davy said. "Except, I was born there."
He tried to imagine it sometimes, millions of people living
together. None of them would ever get lonely or run out
of things to do. Sometimes he even dreamed about running
away and living there himself.

But he knew he never would. He was afraid to. Dad said
the city was a dirty, dangerous "hellhole." Sometimes it
sounded kind of crazy, but if the giant and the gunmen
had come from there, it must be true.

Spider-Man said, "When—" He turned. "Something's
wrong. Stay behind me." He somersaulted over Davy's
head, landing in front of him on the trail.

Dad's voice yelled, "I've got you covered! Let the boy
go!" Looking around, Davy spotted him kneeling behind a
stump. The late afternoon sun gleamed on his gray hair,
round, steel-rimmed glasses, and the barrel of the shotgun
he was pointing at Spider-Man.

The costumed man said, "Did you think I was holding
him prisoner? Doesn't *anybody* outside the Big Apple know
who I am? I haven't been this depressed since Ben Grimm
beat me out for that Hair Club for Men endorsement."

"I know you," Dad said, "and it doesn't matter." Davy
was shocked by the shakiness in his father's voice. He'd
never heard him sound so upset, even when he talked
about the bad times. "Turn around and go back the way
you came."

Davy swallowed, then said, "Please don't send him away.
He didn't make me bring him. I wanted to."

"What? I told you never to do that!"

"But he's hurt!" Davy said. "And he saved me from the
barbarians!" Spider-Man glanced back at him. "They shot

at us, and one of them walked so hard it shook the ground!''

Dad said, ''My god! Are you all right?''

''He's fine,'' Spider-Man said, ''but he almost wasn't. You've got some dangerous characters running around up here. If you're smart, you'll want to know about them. So how about this deal: you give me whatever first aid you can and something to eat, and I'll give you the lowdown.''

Dad hesitated. Davy cried, ''Please!''

His father said, ''You have to promise never to tell anyone about us or our place.''

Spider-Man shrugged. ''Fine. Whatever.''

''All right, then,'' said Dad, standing up. Davy saw that Dad's high boots and faded jeans had gotten all dusty again and that the lines in his face seemed to be etched deeper than ever. ''Get over here, son.'' Davy did. Dad glared at Spider-Man. ''Follow us.'' He turned and started down the trail.

''Thank you,'' said Davy, running to keep up. Up close, Dad smelled like gun oil. ''I—''

''Quiet!'' his father snapped. ''For now, I don't want to hear another word out of you. I particularly don't want to hear you talking to *him.* You and I will have this out later.''

Davy cringed.

Five minutes later, they came to the path home; it was a rocky slope that showed no trace of footprints. Dad hesitated before climbing up, stopped again before going the last few feet, then pulled aside vines and opened a steel door.

The front of the cave was the biggest part, so Dad had done a lot of work to make it nice. The floor was flat and had a carpet. Shelves with books, CDs, and a stereo ran along the walls. The air-conditioning felt almost too cold after the heat outside.

"Wow," said Spider-Man, looking around. "I was expecting a shack. I thought you were some kind of paranoid Adirondack hillbilly. Now I'm guessing you're a paranoid survivalist vacationing in his secret bunker. Unless you're a super-villain in civvies. Your average evil mastermind is big on underground lairs. Seriously, this is impressive. Where do you get electricity?"

"From the wind and the sun," Davy said proudly. "And—"

"I told you to be still," his father said. "Get the first aid kit, a pan of water, and clean washcloths." He turned to Spider-Man. "You sit."

"Have you considered switching to decaf?" the masked man asked. Dad glared. "Okay, okay, I'm sitting." Davy watched with concern as Spider-Man walked past the shop, with its workbenches, lathe, potter's wheel, and half-finished wood carvings, and started to lower himself into one of the chairs at the kitchen table. Halfway down, he grunted and froze, then dropped the last few inches.

Davy brought the first aid stuff. "Now go fix some sandwiches," Dad said, kneeling. Spider-Man stripped away the wispy remains of the web bandage, then pulled up his shirt. Dad looked at the cut and poked the skin around it. The stranger jerked.

"Do you know what you're doing?" he asked. "It feels like you're trying to bust a piñata."

"Don't worry," Dad said, "I took a course. I think that besides the gash, you cracked a couple of ribs."

"Swell," Spider-Man said. "But I guess I shouldn't complain. If I hadn't already been dodging the bullets when that bozo nailed me, he probably would've splashed me all over the hillside.''

Davy guessed "that bozo" was the giant. He shivered.

"I can hold you together with tape," Dad said, lifting a washcloth out of the water. Drops pattered back into the pan. "But I wouldn't recommend doing anything strenuous or you're liable to tear yourself apart again. Now, explain what's going on."

"Okay," said Spider-Man. "It was a dark and stormy night—"

Dad made a disgusted spitting sound.

"All right, I don't actually know what the weather was like, but a couple of years ago, the Army got hold of an extraterrestrial soldier's energy weapon and carted it off to a lab near here for study. And they wound up mighty impressed. The gadget had the firepower of an aircraft carrier, plus an all-but-impenetrable force shield to keep the operator from getting a boo-boo."

Davy sliced bread. He had to saw hard to get through the crust. The fishy smell of iodine filled the air.

"Unfortunately," Spider-Man continued, "the lab had a disgruntled employee named Kenneth Warren, who stole the gizmo to sell to the highest bidder. The FBI caught him before he unloaded it, but they couldn't get him to tell where he'd stashed the thing."

Surgical tape "scritched" off the roll.

"*They* couldn't," Spider-Man said, "but the moron eventually spilled his guts to a lowlife named Hillyard he met in prison. Told him he'd buried the zap gun on this mountain, and built a pyramid of white rocks to mark the spot. You guys haven't seen it, have you?"

"No," said Dad. "Davy?"

"No," Davy said, too. He would have remembered a white pyramid.

Spider-Man sighed. "It figures. Anyway, Hillyard had ties to a mercenary band called Barton's Raiders, and he passed the info along to them. Four of them came up here to retrieve the ray gun for themselves."

Davy brought over the food and a glass of water. Spider-Man pulled up the bottom of his mask, gulped half the drink, then took a big bite of sandwich. "What is this," he asked, "tuna salad?"

This time Davy remembered that he wasn't supposed to talk, but it would have felt rude and mean not to answer. "Trout," he said. Dad scowled.

"Well, it's good," Spider-Man said. He gobbled another mouthful. "Anyway, now we've reached the part of the story where yours truly comes in. One of the mercs told some snitch a little about what was going on, the snitch told a reporter friend of mine, he told me, and, intrepid soul that I am, I set out to keep the weapon from falling into the wrong hands. Looking back, I kind of wish I could have found it in my heart to pass. I've been on their trail for three days. I've hardly eaten and haven't slept at all. And when I finally tracked the Raiders here and tried to throw a net over them, I found out just an eentsy bit too late that they'd brought along a super-strong thug called the Rhino for backup. He butted me a good one, so I made a strategic withdrawal, at which point I spotted Davy here standing in the path of the onrushing goons. I scooped him up and carried him out of harm's way, and here we are.

"And now you know why I need to use your phone, or is it your radio? It may not do my rep a lot of good, but seeing as how I'm wounded, I want some backup."

Dad said, "We don't have either one."

Spider-Man set down his empty plate and glass, wiped his mouth with the back of his hand, and pulled his mask down. "But you must have a car nearby."

"No."

The stranger shook his head. "It's really amazing. If bad luck were good luck, I would hit Lotto every week. Okay, then I need you to hike to where there is a phone while I keep the lid on here. Call the state police, the Army, the Avengers, Underdog, and Dudley Do-Right, whoever'll come."

"That's out of the question," said Dad. "I've already helped you as much as I agreed to. As soon as you feel able, I want you to leave."

"Look," Spider-Man said, "I know there's at least a slim chance you could run into the bad guys, and ordinarily I wouldn't ask a civilian to do anything dangerous. But this is important. The Raiders aren't happy-go-lucky good-guy commandos out of some Schwarzenegger flick. They're butchers. They work for organized crime and some of the slimiest governments in the world. If they get the weapon, a lot of innocent people will suffer because of it."

Dad said, "But not here. As soon as they find what they came for, they'll go away."

Spider-Man said, "I don't believe this. I understand that you'd rather keep your little post-apocalyptic hideaway here a secret, but—"

"You don't understand anything," Dad snapped. "This is our *home*. We live here all the time."

Spider-Man said, "You're kidding." He looked at Davy. "Except, that would explain why you didn't know me, and why you're so shy. How long has it been since you talked to anyone besides your dad?"

"Six years," said Dad. "We came here just after his mother died."

"I'm sorry," Spider-Man said. "How did it happen?"

"Marjorie and I were mugged," Dad said. "Not a block from our building, in broad daylight, by a bunch of kids. They already had her purse and my wallet, but one of them stuck a knife in her anyway. Evidently he just wanted to."

Davy's eyes stung, and the room got blurry. It usually happened when he thought about his mom, but he knew it wouldn't happen to Dad. Much as his father missed her, he hadn't even cried at the funeral.

"Afterward," Dad continued, "I felt like I'd taken off a pair of blinders. I saw things I suppose I'd tuned out before. There was nothing unusual about Marjorie's death. It was just one symptom of a universal plague. So are serial killings, hate crimes, gangs, child abuse, drugs, governmental gridlock and corruption, the failure of the schools, the breakdown of the economy, and the decay of the infrastructure.

"Civilization is crumbling. Everyone who tries to live in the rubble is at the mercy of the new barbarians. Maybe I could have risked my own life that way, but not Davy's. So I liquidated my assets and turned this place into a refuge."

Spider-Man asked, "And you've never been back even once?"

"There's no need," said Dad. "Nature supplies most of what we need, and we've stockpiled the rest."

"Yeah, but . . . look, society has *always* had problems. Read some history. But when good people—and most of them are good—work together to fix what's wrong, they usually manage to live decent lives. And even when they can't, they feel a *duty* to help each other out."

"I don't," said Dad. "Not when it's pointless. Don't you understand, it's too late for your world! There'll be mayhem and destruction whether your friends the mercenaries get the alien gun or not. The one meaningful thing I *can* do is protect my son, by keeping our heads down."

"Funny you should mention heads," the masked man said. "I don't mean to insult you—and heaven knows, a guy in my racket has no business questioning anybody else's sanity—but hasn't it ever occurred to you that when you moved to a cave you were acting wacky? Could be you weren't running from big-city violence as much as your own feelings: grief, guilt that you couldn't save your wife. Believe me, I've been there, I understand the temptation. But Marjorie wouldn't want you to throw away—"

"Shut up!" Dad cried out. "You don't know anything about her or me."

"Maybe not," said Spider-Man. "But let's talk about your kid." Davy flinched. "What kind of life can he have stuck up here? You had your shot at friends, a career, a wife, and children. He never will. And when you're gone, he'll be alone."

"You make me sick," said Dad. His face was red, and a vein stuck out on his forehead. "You'll say anything to suck me into your miserable game of cops and robbers, won't you, even if it upsets a little boy?"

Spider-Man said, "You are without a doubt—Skip it. I won't say it in front of your kid. Let's cut to the chase. Reading between the lines here, trying to pick up on every subtle nuance, I'm getting the feeling you're a little reluctant to call 911 for me. Is that about the size of it? Then I guess I'll just have to wrap this job up solo after all. What the heck, it'll look good on my résumé." He stood up.

Davy said, "Don't go!"

"I have to," Spider-Man said. "It's in my contract. Remind me to fire my agent."

"But the giant hurt you once already!"

"A freak accident," the man in the costume said. "I was weak with hunger. The Rhino came at me from behind, at the worst possible moment." His voice got squeaky: "I was a victim of soycumstance!" He waited as though he expected Davy to laugh, then sighed. "Tough room. Look, I promise, I'll be fine. If I can find the zap gun before the heavies, I won't have to fight. I'll just schlep it out of here. And if not, well, I'll handle it, that's all. You take care of your dad, and stay inside for the next couple of days." He squeezed Davy's shoulder, then walked out. The metal door clicked shut behind him.

Davy got ready to be yelled at. But Dad just went into the shop and started moving the tools on the pegboard around. His hands shook. Once he dropped a hammer. It clanked onto the floor.

Davy moved around the cave, picking up things and putting them down. The AC was still blowing, but now the room felt stuffy. At last he said, "I wish we could have helped him."

Dad turned. "We didn't owe him a thing."

"But he got me out of trouble!"

"And we repaid him by taking care of him."

"I still don't want anything to happen to him. I like him."

Dad's mouth twisted. "You don't know anything about

him, or the ugly place he comes from either. And that's the way we're going to keep it."

Something tied a knot in Davy's chest. "I know a little," he said. "You don't want me to remember anything but Mom, so I pretend I don't, but I still think about the other kids in our building and at preschool. The dogs in the park. Nice things."

"You're remembering a dream," said Dad. "Someday you'll understand that."

"But—"

Dad looked him in the eye. "Who do you believe in, Davy? Who do you really care about? A stranger in a clown suit or your own father?"

Davy swallowed. "You."

"Then you'll forget that freak and everything he said. None of it had anything to do with us."

Davy said, "All right." Dad stared at him a moment longer, then went back to the tools.

For a few minutes, Davy really did try to forget, but it didn't work. Once he'd thought something, how could he *un*think it? And suddenly, everything looked different.

He guessed that even though he had some happy memories, he'd always more or less believed Dad, that "society" was a terrible place. But Spider-Man was nice, and said most other people were too. If that was true, then how bad could their world be?

Davy knew his father was a good man. A smart man. But maybe he'd run to the mountain not because it was smart but out of some kind of fear.

And if Dad's ideas were *wrong*, then it would be just as wrong for Davy to leave Spider-Man to fight the Raiders by himself. Or to let the bad men steal the zap gun to kill helpless people like his mom.

Nervously he waited for Dad to go into the bathroom, then slammed the door to his own bedroom. With luck, Dad would think he was inside. Then he tiptoed to the gun rack, grabbed the bolt-action Remington 700—the heaviest rifle he could handle—and a handful of ammo, and hurried out of the cave.

The sun had nearly disappeared behind the mountain to the west. The air was cooler, and shadows stretched along the ground. Usually Davy didn't mind the dark, but usually it didn't have gunmen and—what had Spider-Man called them?—super-villains running around in it. When a bat flew over his head, he jumped.

Heart thumping, he set off down the slope, jogging to get as far as he could before he lost the light. He wished he knew where the nearest phone really was. Since he didn't, he guessed he'd head for the cabins on the far side of the lake.

Gunfire crackled in the trees below him. A monster's footsteps shook the ground.

Spider-Man and the barbarians were already fighting again. Which meant there was no way Davy could get to a phone in time for it to make a difference.

The shockwaves in the earth shivered up his legs. He wanted to run home. He knew Spider-Man would want him to. But he'd sneaked out here to help the masked man, and maybe if he got closer to the fight, he'd see that there was something he could do.

Sweaty hands gripping the rifle, he sneaked down the hill, ducking from one patch of cover to the next. Fallen leaves slid under his feet. His toe bumped a pine cone and sent it rolling.

The shaking got stronger, the shooting louder. His nose stung from the smell of gun smoke. He ran to a hemlock, peeked around it, then gasped and jerked back. A gray giant, with two horns like the rhinos in Dad's nature books, was flailing around right in front of the tree! Didn't Spider-Man say the Raiders had hired someone called the Rhino?

Davy's heel caught on a root, dumping him to the ground. He banged his elbow, and pain jabbed up his arm. For a second he could only lie there shivering. Then, somehow, he made himself crawl forward.

When he looked out again, he saw the other fighters. Spider-Man jumped and flipped around the Rhino. Two tough-looking riflemen in fatigues ran back and forth trying to get a clear shot at him. Snarling swear words, a third Raider squirmed in the webbing that stuck him to an oak, and a fourth lay unconscious on top of a pyramid of white stones. The marker was smaller than Davy had expected, and half hidden between two bushes besides. It was no wonder he'd never spotted it.

Even though two of the gunmen were already out of the fight, Davy didn't see how Spider-Man could win. The vigilante's punches didn't seem to bother the Rhino, and he couldn't dodge the giant's fists and horns and the Raiders' bullets forever. Davy had to help him. He took the Remington's safety off.

But he didn't even like hunting animals, would never have learned if his father hadn't made him. He'd sure never wanted to shoot a person. As he tried to aim at one of the Raiders, he felt sick to his stomach. And when he squeezed the trigger, his hands jerked.

The shot missed. The two Raiders turned, the muzzles of their assault rifles swinging to cover him. Spider-Man shouted, "No!" Grabbing the Rhino's armor-plated shoulder, he jumped over the villain, landed in front of the Raiders, and knocked out each one with a single punch.

The Rhino turned and charged, head down. Spider-Man tried to jump out of the way, a second too late. The points of the horns didn't stick him, but the blow threw him across the clearing. He crashed into a pine tree, then fell to the ground.

"Spider-Man!" Davy screamed. The man in red and blue didn't move. Davy fumbled with the bolt of his rifle, trying to load another round.

A big gray hand grabbed Davy's forearm and lifted him into the air. Another yanked the Remington out of his grip and threw it spinning away. "A kid," said the Rhino. His voice sounded like rocks grinding together. "Huh. I don't usually kill kids, but nobody snipes at me and gets away with it." His fist tightened. Davy imagined his body squishing, bone snapping, bloody flesh oozing out between the giant's fingers. He felt numb. Couldn't move. Couldn't breathe.

A gun banged. Bullets pounded the Rhino's back and bounced off whining. The barbarian grunted and staggered a step, then caught his balance.

Looking over his shoulder, Davy saw his father firing his M-16-A1. Bandoliers made an X on his chest, and a .44 Desert Eagle, a Gerber combat knife, and four hand grenades hung from his belt. "No, Dad! Run!" he yelled.

The Rhino turned. Dad was getting ready to fire again. Now Davy was scared that *he'd* get shot instead, but Dad's aim was as good as ever. He didn't hit him.

The giant said, "What is this, amateur night?" He

started forward. Davy worried the Rhino would use him as a shield, but he didn't even bother. He just leaned into the ammo like he was walking against the wind.

Dad's face was white as paper. When the Rhino got close, he started to back up. Suddenly moving as fast as a striking snake, the giant caught up with him and slapped the rifle out of his hands.

Backing up again, Dad grabbed a grenade. "I swear, I'll do it!" he said, his voice breaking. "I heard you say you were going to kill Davy anyway."

"Go for it," said the Rhino. "That little toy won't hurt me either. As soon as I squeegee the kid off my suit, I'll be good as new."

Dad looked like he was going to cry. He pulled out the Desert Eagle. The pistol shook.

The Rhino chuckled. "You know, in a way, this is a hoot. But I've got a death ray to dig up, so I think I'll be nice and put you turkeys out of your misery." He stamped. The shock threw Dad off his feet. As he tried to get up, the Rhino lowered his head.

"Hey, Zero!" someone called. "I'd back off if I were you. I'm pretty sure the boy can take you."

Spinning, the Rhino tossed Davy aside. He could tell the giant wasn't interested in hurting him, just getting rid of him. But the fall still knocked the wind out of him; he might even have some broken bones if he'd landed differently. Looking between the barbarian's legs, he saw Spider-Man get up. To his horror, the injured man looked wobbly, and the white strip of bandage that showed through his torn shirt was turning dark.

"This is good," said the Rhino, his voice thick with hate. "You went down too easy before. I didn't get to hurt you enough." His right foot pawed the dirt.

"My, my," Spider-Man said. "Slip in a couple of cheap shots and we get all cocky. In case you've forgotten, gruesome, ol' Spidey *always* creams you in the end. Mainly because you have the same keen wits as a sack of ferti—"

The Rhino charged.

"—lizer," Spider-Man finished calmly. He stood in the Rhino's way until the last possible second, then, so suddenly that Davy almost missed it, cartwheeled aside. The giant tripped on a strand of webbing the masked man had strung a foot above the ground.

The Rhino crashed headfirst into the same tree that Spider-Man had hit. His front horn stuck in the trunk. As he strained to yank it out, Spider-Man jumped to the Rhino's side, and began hammering punches into his back and ribs.

With a crunch and a shower of splinters, the horn tore free. The tree started to fall. Davy watched it for a second, making sure it wasn't dropping toward him or Dad. When he looked back, the Rhino was whirling, head low, swinging his horns. But Spider-Man wasn't next to him anymore.

Glaring, the Rhino turned back and forth. Davy was just as confused. Where had Spider-Man gone?

Suddenly, he swung out of a tree on another webline. His feet slammed the Rhino's wide, flat face—the only part of him his thick suit didn't protect.

The Rhino stumbled backward. Letting go of the swing line, Spider-Man somersaulted and landed behind him. When the giant turned, he shot webbing into his eyes.

The Rhino struggled to rip the threads away. Spider-Man danced around him, punching. The blows banged like an axe splitting wood.

The web blindfold tore loose, taking skin with it. The

Rhino spun and snapped a punch at Spider-Man's stomach. Perhaps the smaller man hadn't expected him to get his eyes uncovered so fast, because he didn't dodge. The blow doubled him over and threw him backward.

The breath caught in Davy's throat. He was sure Spider-Man would go down again, but he flipped twice and landed in a crouch. "Congratulations!" he said. "You actually tagged me. Just a wimpy little love tap, but still, that's one in a row!"

The Rhino lowered his horns and charged. This time Spider-Man ran to meet him.

Just before they slammed together, the man in red and blue dropped to one knee. His right fist flashed at his enemy's nose. A loud *crack!* echoed through the woods.

Davy understood what Spider-Man had tried. He'd added the power of his punch to the force of the Rhino's charge. But which fighter had it hurt worse? Davy was afraid his new friend had broken every bone in his arm.

For a second the two foes were as still as statues. Then the Rhino fell. Even that shook the ground a little.

"Oh, yeah," groaned Spider-Man, climbing slowly to his feet. "This was fun." His left hand held his bloody side. He shook the right, used it to rub his stomach, then shook it again. "I haven't enjoyed anything this much since my last root canal."

Dad scrambled over to Davy. "Are you all right?" he cried.

"Yeah," Davy said. "I'm sorry I—"

Dad hugged him. "God, when I realized what you'd done, I was sure I'd lost you too!"

Spider-Man limped toward them. "Hello again, gang. Say, is this a Kodak moment or what?"

Dad gave Davy one last squeeze. Before looking up, the grown-up wiped at his face, smearing stripes in the dirt that had stuck there. "How badly are you hurt?" he asked.

"I have definitely been better," Spider-Man replied. "But the bleeding's slowing down, and it doesn't feel like any new bones or major organs are busted, so I'm pretty sure that one day, I'll play the accordion again. I know, I shouldn't say that as if it were a good thing."

Davy and Dad got up. "Is this mess really over?" Dad asked.

"Yeah," said Spider-Man, "I'd say so, pretty much. Now I tie the mercs up, take the zap gun, and find that phone I keep nattering on about. With luck, we'll have a SWAT team equipped with tranks and a pair of handy-dandy electrified titanium shackles here before the Rhino wakes up. One nice thing about Zero—aside from the fact that he can't even *spell* IQ—when you finally do manage to put him out, he generally stays that way for hours."

"I knew you'd beat him," Davy said.

"Really?" Spider-Man said. "I wish you'd let me in on it. Actually, I can only take half the credit for this win. Down-to-the-bone stupid as the Rhino is, if your dad hadn't distracted him, he probably would've noticed me coming to. And made sure I didn't."

"I guess I did help," said Dad. He sounded surprised. "I helped save my boy."

"Absotively," Spider-Man said. "And now if you'll excuse me, I'd better start mopping up." He squatted beside a khaki duffel bag one of the Raiders must have dropped and dug around inside it. "Hey, jackpot! An entrenching tool and rope too."

Looking dazed, Dad sat back down on the ground. Davy plopped down beside him.

"Was he right?" asked Dad after a while. "Is it awful for you here?"

Afraid of hurting his feelings, Davy said, "No. But it would be nice to live where I could have friends."

"It's strange," his father said. "Six outsiders came up the mountain today, and all but one of them were scum. Logically speaking, that should confirm every idea I had about society. But I don't *feel* like it does." Fresh tears ran down his cheeks, but he grinned too. "I feel like I've been acting wacky."

"Do you have any boxes?" Spider-Man asked. "Whenever I move, it takes a bunch." He finished tying one Raider and moved on to the next.

C O L D   B L O O D

GREG COX

Illustration by Ron Lim

The worst winter in years had left Manhattan buried in snow and ice. A pebbly, translucent layer of frozen sleet glazed every exposed surface, from lampposts to skyscrapers, while chilling winds seemed to come from every direction so that no one, not even Spider-Man, could avoid them.

I don't believe this, Spidey thought; thirteen major snow storms in as many weeks. Shivering, he clung upside down to the frosted facade of the Flatiron Building. His skintight costume covered every inch of his body, but barely protected him from the nonstop blasts of wind and snow. On nights like this he wished he could exchange superpowers with the Human Torch; that hothead probably never worried about the windchill factor.

Maybe I should call it a night, he thought. Fourteen stories below, Fifth Avenue was almost deserted. The arctic weather had driven most New Yorkers indoors, crooks and potential victims alike. The image of a quiet evening at home sipping hot chocolate with Mary Jane in their warm, snug apartment grew more appealing by the minute. Great power means great responsibility, sure, but even during a blizzard?

Suddenly, however, he felt a familiar sensation: an electric tingling that seemed to radiate outward from his brain to his skin—his spider-sense alerting him to danger. Instinctively, he glanced up over his shoulder and spotted a large icicle, over two feet long, hanging precariously from a ledge several stories above his head, its sharp point aimed right at him. Battered by the storm, the icicle broke free from the ledge with a muffled crack. It hurled towards Spider-Man as his spider-sense kicked into overdrive.

He had only seconds to react, but he checked the street below first. Years of high-altitude battles with the likes of the Vulture and the Green Goblin had trained him to always watch out for innocent bystanders who might be harmed by falling masonry or pumpkin bombs. To his horror he saw a homeless man, wrapped in a tattered yellow raincoat, pushing a junk-filled grocery cart down the snow-caked sidewalk. Apparently unaware of the plummeting spear of ice, the old man walked directly in its path—unless, of course, the icicle impaled Spider-Man first.

At best, Spidey thought, it's likely to make a shish kebab of us both.

He wasn't about to let that happen. Heedless of gravity, he leaped to one side, feeling a rush of wind as the deadly icicle dived past him. His gloved fingers and the soles of his boots reached out to stick onto an adjacent section of the wall, but the ice-coated stonework resisted his natural adhesiveness. For a brief heart-stopping instant he felt himself slide down the side of the building. No, he thought desperately, not now! Pressing his palms strenuously against the wall, he secured himself more firmly, halting his downward slide. In all, he'd only slipped a few inches, but was there still time to save the old man?

Spider-Man snapped into action. A line of sticky gray goo streamed from one of his web-shooters and grabbed hold of the icy spike, snatching it away from the unsuspecting man less than a heartbeat before it would have crashed through his skull. Instead it swung into the west wall of the Flatiron, splintering harmlessly into hundreds of tiny ice crystals that fell to join the frozen mess piled high on the sidewalk.

Despite his mask, a puff of fog formed in front of Spider-Man's mouth as he breathed a sigh of relief. Far below, the man in the raincoat struggled to push his cart through the endless snowdrifts, oblivious of his narrow escape. Spider-

Man watched quietly as the man slowly made his way uptown.

Maybe, Spidey decided, I am needed tonight after all. He thought wistfully again of Mary Jane and central heating (not necessarily in that order), then shot a webline across the street and pushed off from the Flatiron. What the heck, he thought, it couldn't hurt to swing around a bit more before heading home.

Blood, his body screamed at him. He needed blood.

Morbius, the Living Vampire, soared on the night winds. His outstretched arms extended before him while a ragged cape of torn violet fabric flapped about him like the wings of an enormous bat. His deathly white skin was pulled tightly over the bones of his face. Yellow eyes glowed red around their centers. Wild, unrestrained hair twisted in the wind like a gorgon's snakes, as midnight black as the leather bodysuit he wore only when hunting human prey, the suit he wore tonight. Saliva dripped from his fangs, freezing as it fell to earth.

Blood. His hunger grew steadily as he flew over the city. Ever since a reckless scientific experiment transformed him into a pseudo-vampire, Dr. Michael Morbius had been torn between his conscience and an unquenchable thirst for human blood. After years of gruesome atrocities, and ceaseless remorse, he had vowed to feed only upon the blood of the guilty, upon those whom he thought deserved to die. New York City, with its crime and corruption, usually provided him with more than enough evil blood to sustain him . . .

But not tonight. As Morbius swooped and glided upon the air currents, he found the city streets empty of criminals. It was the damned weather. He had no doubt that acts of violence and cruelty—acts worthy of a vampire's vengeance—were taking place every hour, even as he searched fruitlessly through the back alleys and shadowy corners of Manhattan, but the blizzard had forced all the human predators indoors and out of sight. They were safe, blast them all, and he was starving.

Blood. It was more than just a hunger; it was an addiction. His entire body ached with need. Thirsty veins pounded in his temples; his skull felt as if it were ready to collapse under the constant, pulsating pressure. His eyes watered and throbbed. Acid churned in his gut and scalded the back of his throat. From head to toe his skin felt raw and irritable as an itch crawled over his flesh, an incessant, nagging itch that he could not scratch but could only wash away with the hot, pumping lifeblood of another human being.

The winter wind pelted his exposed face and hands with ice-cold flakes of snow. Morbius barely noticed the sub-zero temperature. Feverish, he felt himself burning up from the inside out. He had to find a deserving victim soon. A rapist, a mugger, even a burglar . . . anyone he could kill without too much remorse.

Wait! What was that? Morbius spotted a suspicious shadow in a dead-end alley between two deserted office buildings. He glided lower to get a better look, coming to rest on the weathered stump of a broken stone gargoyle. Perched several yards above the floor of the alley, Morbius saw an elderly man, gray-haired and lined with age, huddling next to a grocery cart by a graffiti-covered wooden fence at the far end of the alley. The old man squatted on the snow-decked pavement, trying hard to pull as much of his body as possible into the shelter of a dilapidated, timeworn raincoat.

Disappointment and rage surged through Morbius. This was no villain, he realized, no social menace worthy of extinction. The poor soul shivering beneath him was just another homeless derelict, more sinned against than sinner. Morbius shifted his weight upon the gargoyle preparing to take flight once more and resume his hunt. He would depart now, this very minute.

He didn't move.

Morbius stared at the helpless old man. Despite himself, his lips peeled back, revealing his fangs. His tongue caressed the razor-sharp points of his teeth.

Blood.

"No," Morbius whispered to himself, horrified by his own instinctive reaction. "Not another innocent. Never again."

The throbbing in his temples crashed like waves upon a rocky shore. *Who'd have thought the old man had so much blood in him?* Morbius grit his teeth together, forcing his jaws shut. He tried to look away. "He's done nothing," he argued with himself. *Nobody will miss him.* "He doesn't deserve this." *How do you know?* "I won't do it!" Morbius vowed, even as he felt his sanity slipping away. Clutching his stom-. ach, biting down on his lip, his eyes grew wider and more reddened as he contemplated the old man in the snow, so cold, so vulnerable, so full of . . .

Blood!

With a feral snarl, Morbius launched himself from his perch and flew towards the old man. His intended meal must have heard the vampire's howl, because the man looked up suddenly, his wizened, soiled face filling with mortal terror as he saw a fanged, white-faced demon reaching out for him from the sky. The old man shrieked for help while groping frantically for something in the pockets of his coat. Morbius didn't care what his victim was doing.

All deliberate thought had fled his mind, banished and usurped by an overwhelming urge to satisfy his hunger—no matter what. He hardly noticed when the old man yanked a gun out of his coat and pulled the trigger . . .

The temperature kept dropping and the storm was getting worse. Swinging uptown, roughly in the direction of his Upper East Side apartment, Spider-Man found travelling increasingly difficult, even for him. High above 34th Street, his left web-shooter jammed and he had to hastily shoot a line from his other wrist in order to avoid falling half the length of the Empire State Building. Granted, the local weatherman had predicted up to eighteen inches of snow, but Spidey doubted that would be enough to cushion so long a drop.

Crawling carefully onto the nearest rooftop, he inspected the malfunctioning device on his left wrist. After a few minutes of tinkering he got it working again, but the web it produced, he noted with concern, quickly turned hard and brittle in the cold. This is getting genuinely dangerous, he thought. Maybe it really was time to stop patrolling the city and head home as quickly as possible.

Then, over the roar of the wind, he heard a hoarse scream, followed by the unmistakable sound of several gunshots. Spider-Man quickly pulled his glove down over the repaired web-shooter and, hoping for the best, jumped off the rooftop in the direction of the shots.

Thankfully, the frozen web-shooter worked once more and he did not end up splattered on the pavement.

Minutes later, he had followed the alarming sounds to the brink of a tall office building overlooking a narrow, dingy alley. Looking down, he instantly took in the tense scene unfolding many stories below.

He recognized Morbius first. He'd battled the vampiric scientist several times before, and had even joined forces with Morbius on rare occasions. He felt sorry for Morbius; like too many of Spider-Man's foes, such as Man-Wolf or the Lizard, Morbius had never intended to become a monster. At times Spider-Man had even believed Morbius to be cured or reformed. Now, though, the vampire clearly menaced a helpless victim, an old man backed against a snowflecked fence, waving a gun in one hand and screaming bloody murder.

Oh My God, Spider-Man realized with a start, it's the guy from Fifth Avenue, the one I saved from the icicle.

Morbius had the man cornered. The vampire stood only a couple of yards away from his victim. He clutched his chest with one clawed hand while his other hand stretched long, taloned fingers towards his prey. The homeless man kept pulling on the trigger of his gun, but he had obviously run out of bullets. Spider-Man guessed that he'd shot Morbius at least a few times first, not that it mattered much. Spidey knew from experience that bullets would not stop Morbius; at best, they could only slow him down.

It's up to me now, Spider-Man thought grimly. Sorry, Doctor, this time I'm putting you away for good.

"Morbius!" Spider-Man shouted to get the vampire's attention. He scurried headfirst down the wall until he was close enough to the floor of the alley to jump the rest of the way. Twisting smoothly in the air, he landed firmly on both feet, a short distance behind Morbius. "Step away from him, Morbius!" Spider-Man clenched his fists and raised them. "I'm warning you, step away from him now."

Hissing angrily, Morbius spun around to confront Spider-Man. Despite all the times they'd met in the past, the vampire's face still shocked Spidey, especially the way it looked tonight. Morbius's eyes were crazed and fiercely bloodshot, his nostrils flared like an animal's, while spittle dripped from his chin. The expression on his bone-white face seemed more lupine than human, and the only sound that escaped the vampire's throat was a low, hungry growl.

This looks bad, Spidey thought. Sometimes Morbius could be reasoned with, but he had a sinking feeling this wasn't one of those times. Yet he had to try, for everyone's sake. Beyond Morbius, Spider-Man could see the old man, still terrified, cowering behind his grocery cart. Spidey could only hope the man wasn't afraid of spiders too.

Morbius brought his clawed hand away from his chest. Spider-Man saw three bullet holes in the leather suit but no wounds and only a smidgen of blood. He's healing already, Spidey deduced. Lucky me.

"Listen to me, Michael," he began. "I know you can't help yourself, but this has got to stop." No sign of comprehension showed in the vampire's bloodred eyes. Morbius snarled at him through bared fangs. "Let me help you." Spider-Man took one cautious step towards Morbius. He reached out an open hand. "Don't fight me this time . . ."

A warning tingle told Spider-Man the time for talking was over. Morbius lunged, slashing out with his claws. Spidey jumped backwards to avoid being raked by the vampire's inch-long talons. Then he leaped again, over Morbius's head, landing between the vampire and his prey. Morbius is fast, he recalled, but I'm more agile. Hopefully, he could stay out of the way of those fangs and claws long enough to bring Morbius under control.

Letting loose with both web-shooters, Spider-Man

sprayed a heavy, gray net over the vampire's head and shoulders. Howling in fury, Morbius tore into the web with his hands and teeth, shredding the net into sticky, knotted ribbons. But while he was distracted by the web, Spidey went on the offensive. Getting a running start, he hurled himself feet-first at Morbius. Spider-Man's boots smashed into the vampire's chest, sending him sprawling backward. At the same time, Spidey bounced off his enemy, landing nimbly on all fours in front of the grocery cart. God, this snow is cold, he thought, as his hands and feet sunk into the chilly white mess. His fingertips felt numb.

Spider-Man sprung again at Morbius. One good punch to his head, he thought, and maybe I can wrap this mess up. The vampire moved too quickly, however, ducking out of the way of Spidey's fist and taking to the air. The ragged fringe of his cape caught the wind as Morbius glided above the alley. I hate bad guys who can fly, Spidey thought glumly. Where's an air-traffic controller when I need one?

Then again, who needs to fly when you can run up the side of a wall? Spider-Man chased Morbius by racing up the nearest building until he was almost eye-level with the hovering vampire. He fired a line of webbing at Morbius's face, but the vampire easily evaded it by soaring higher. Then, only a second after a sudden buzz of spider-sense, Morbius came at Spider-Man like a blood-sucking divebomber. Spidey twisted to get out of the way but his feet refused to stick to the ice, and he slipped and stumbled to regain his footing. He snatched onto a windowsill to steady himself, only to feel a clawed hand swipe at his back. Sharp, frigid fingernails tore gashes in both his costume and the flesh beneath. Wincing in pain, Spider-Man looked up and saw Morbius swooping down for another swipe at him. With his free hand, he tried to shoot another web at his attacker; unfortunately, the web-shooter chose that moment to jam up again.

Great, Spider-Man thought. There was only one thing left to do. Letting go of the windowsill, he dropped several stories to the floor of the alley. One boot landed on a crusty patch of old snow, and Spider-Man twisted his ankle, almost falling headway into the snow. As if sensing weakness, Morbius dived at Spider-Man even as Spidey fought to stay on his feet. The vampire's eyes glowed with madness. A mouthful of fangs opened to take a huge bite out of Spider-Man.

At the last minute, though, Spider-Man stomped his good foot through over a foot of snow, connecting at last with the solid pavement underneath. Thus braced, he met the vampire's charge with a powerful blow of his own. He swung his fist into Morbius's chin, stunning the vampire long enough for Spider-Man to grab onto the purple cape and toss both cape and vampire across the alley and, quite deliberately, away from the man behind the grocery cart. Morbius landed in a heap on a snowdrift.

Then the angry vampire stood up, shook the white powder off his shoulders, and stared at Spider-Man with sheer homicidal bloodlust in his eyes.

I'm in trouble, Spidey concluded. Experimentally, he put his weight on his bad ankle and was rewarded with a sharp stab of pain. The arctic wind numbed the wounds in his back, but as the bitter chill penetrated into his bones, Spider-Man would have preferred the cuts to the cold. The weather is working against me, he thought, but Morbius seems oblivious to the storm.

Still, Spidey conceded, at least he's forgotten the old guy for the moment. He's after my blood now.

His wild black mane whipping about in the wind, Morbius advanced toward Spider-Man. His nostrils quivered, perhaps smelling the fresh blood dripping from the gashes he'd clawed into Spider-Man's back. Spidey aimed his last working web-shooter. A stream of webbing sluggishly spewed from his wrist, wrapping a thick cable around Morbius's legs. The vampire slashed at the snare, and Spider-Man could hear the freezing webbing cracking apart almost as fast as Morbius tore it asunder. Spidey aimed again, hoping to reinforce the cable with more webbing. Nothing happened, except for a spurt of fluid followed by a slow, grinding noise from the mechanism on his wrist. The grinding rapidly turned into silence. It was official now: both web-shooters had frozen up.

Next winter, Spidey promised himself, I'm only fighting vampires in Florida. Assuming I get out of this with any of my own corpuscles left.

In minutes, Morbius reduced the cable to fragments of flaking gray debris. Spider-Man considered leaping away, but rejected the strategy. Between the ice and his lame ankle, he'd just end up flat on his back. Forget agility; he would have to depend on his spider-strength.

Morbius pounced. Spider-Man gripped the vampire's wrists and shoved him away as far as he could. Still, despite the hollow bones that allowed him to fly, Morbius was unnaturally strong as well, and he put all his might into pressing past Spider-Man's defenses. They grappled face-to-mask while the biting wind tossed snow at Spidey and threatened him with frostbite. Morbius snapped at Spider-Man's throat, only inches away. He twisted and fought to free his arms from Spider-Man's grasp, but Spider-Man kept his fists locked around Morbius's wrists and refused to let go. If he gets those claws free, Spidey knew, his canines will be in my neck before I know it.

But how much longer could he hold on? Through the tears in his costume, the wind felt so cold it burned. Every time he had to shift his weight to counter Morbius, his ankle gave another tortured yelp. He was losing ground and he knew it. The fangs kept getting closer and closer. He could feel the vampire's fetid breath; it was hot and smelled like a butcher shop. He hoped the old man had run for safety while he and Morbius wrestled, but he couldn't spare a second to look. If not, he reassured himself, maybe my blood will be enough for Morbius tonight. The old guy might actually live to see the morning.

Abruptly, Morbius stopped pushing against Spider-Man's arms, and Spidey almost tumbled forward into the vampire's grasp. He spotted the feint in time, though, and held on to his position. Then Morbius charged at him again. Every muscle Spider-Man had strained to keep the vampire away, but he was fighting a losing battle against fatigue, injury, and the endless, unforgiving cold.

I'm not going to make it, he realized. In the movies, the sun would conveniently rise about now, frying the dastardly vamp in the very nick of time. In real life, Spidey knew, the dawn remained hours away. Goodbye, Mary Jane . . . Goodbye, Aunt May . . .

Morbius leaned forward, his hungry mouth drawing nearer. Spider-Man repelled him once more, but felt his knees start to buckle. Then, a familiar buzz rushed over him: his spider-sense at work. What in the world, Spidey thought, puzzled. Like, I really needed a danger warning now?

Automatically, he risked a glance upward. His eyes grew wide beneath his mask. There, directly overhead, was another spear-like icicle vibrating in the heavy wind—then suddenly it broke off with a loud *snap!* and plummeted earthward.

Once again, he had only seconds to act. Throwing all of his weight onto his good leg, he spun around, out of the path of the icicle, and tried to shove Morbius to safety as well. Unfortunately, Spider-Man succeeded only in throwing himself off-balance. Something tore in his ankle, and he collapsed into the snow. Morbius, seeing his foe fallen at last, howled in triumph—until the falling icicle stabbed him in the back like the fang of some gigantic ice-demon.

The vampire's howl turned into a scream of agony. The point of the icicle burst through Morbius's chest. He dropped to his knees, then toppled over lifelessly onto the frosted pavement.

Gasping from exhaustion, Spider-Man pulled himself upright. He limped toward the crumpled black form. The severed base of the icicle protruded from the purple cape draped over Morbius. My God, Spider-Man thought. Was the Living Vampire dead at last? Spidey had to admit that a part of him wished that Morbius really was gone forever. But, no, upon closer inspection Spider-Man saw the skewered body take deep, uneven breaths. Morbius wasn't dead yet. He might not even be unconscious for long.

This is it, Spidey thought. My one chance to stop him, once and for all.

He seized the exposed end of the icicle and yanked it free from the vampire's back. Morbius groaned weakly, his body convulsing. Spider-Man rolled him over so that Morbius's chest was exposed. He positioned the bloody icicle like a wooden stake over the vampire's heart. "I'm sorry it's finally come to this, Dr. Morbius," he said.

His memory raced back over the years to his first encounter with Morbius. It was during a part of his life that he wanted to forget but knew that he never could. An experimental serum had mutated Spider-Man even further, transforming him into a six-armed freak. I found a cure eventually, he recalled, but what if I hadn't? He contemplated the fanged, pointy-eared monstrosity he was about to destroy. I could've ended up like him, Spider-Man realized. Science turned Peter Parker into a human spider just like it changed Michael Morbius into a living vampire. He looked again at Morbius's inhuman visage. There but for the grace of a few stray atoms and chromosomes . . .

Spider-Man lifted the gore-stained icicle away from Morbius. Shaking his head wearily, he hurled it across the alley. I can't do it, he decided. I can't just kill Morbius in cold blood. But what am I supposed to do instead?

Pain! Morbius woke to an excruciating pang between his ribs. Confused and disoriented, he found himself lying on his back in a snowbound alley. How did I get here? he wondered. He lifted his head slightly and saw a lean, athletic man in a red and blue costume standing over him. Stylized black lines radiated from the eight-legged emblem on the man's chest. Morbius recognized the symbol instantly.

Spider-Man!

In a rush, the night came back to him. He remembered it all: the hunting and the hunger, the old man, the fight in the alley. He had just been about to rip out Spider-Man's throat when something had struck him from behind.

Thank God, he thought. I must have been insane. He shuddered when he realized how close he had come to committing not one but two inexcusable murders. But what-

ever shock had rendered him unconscious had also re-
stored his senses—at least for the moment. He still needed
blood, now more than ever, but he could think again.

But first he needed to escape. Morbius peered up at
Spider-Man. Looking lost in thought, the wall-crawler appeared unaware at first of Morbius's awakening. Something
must have alerted him, though; before Morbius could make
a single move, Spider-Man turned his masked face toward
the vampire. "Morbius?" he said suspiciously.

There was no time to waste, Morbius knew. He had already lost the advantage of surprise so he lashed out vio-
lently instead. He kicked Spider-Man in the knee, then
rocketed to his feet. Spider-Man grunted, clutching his leg
as though in torment. Morbius grabbed onto Spider-Man,
lifting him bodily over his head before flinging him savagely
at the fence sealing off one end of the alley. Spider-Man
crashed into the wall, snapping the wooden planks into
splinters. The superhero rose from the wreckage, but he
looked dazed and unsteady.

Morbius stretched out his arms. His cape spread out
behind him. He felt the roaring wind lift him off the
ground and he banked into the air currents, letting the gale
take him up and away. He glanced briefly back at the god-
forsaken alley where the monster within him had come so
close to damning him once more.

"Thank you, Spider-Man," he whispered. "I won't forget this." As he joined the storm rampaging far above the
streets of the city he resolved that he would not waste this
second chance at redemption. I will find evil blood, he
vowed, if I have to hunt all night and all winter.

*   *   *

Spider-Man watched Morbius disappear into the clouds. With his web-shooters out of order and his body about to collapse, he knew he would never be able to catch up with the flying vampire tonight. "We'll settle this another night, Morbius," he muttered. "You can't hide from me forever."

Still, at least he'd kept Morbius from killing one more person. He turned his gaze away from the sky and checked out the man he'd fought so hard to save. Sure enough, the old guy was still huddling behind his cart, which had somehow overturned during the chaos of the battle. Probably when Morbius threw me into that fence, Spidey guessed. He suspected he was probably covered with bruises, not to mention splinters. Hope MJ's got plenty of Bactine ready, he thought.

He stepped towards the old man, who flinched at his approach. "Calm down, pal," Spider-Man said reassuringly. "Everything's fine now." He took hold of the capsized grocery cart and effortlessly put it back on its wheels. Kneeling down in the snow, he looked the other man in the eye. "What's your name, friend?"

"Wilson," the man answered. Up close, Spider-Man saw frost in Wilson's whiskers and an ugly, untreated scab below one ear. Otherwise, he looked unharmed. Frightened and chilled to the bone, yes, but still intact and in full possession of his blood. Spider-Man stood up, unsure what to do next. Morbius was gone and unlikely to return, yet Spidey hated to leave Wilson out in this ghastly snowstorm with only a beaten-up old raincoat to keep him warm.

"Look, Wilson, don't you have anyplace you can go?"

"No," he said tersely, shaking his head. Spider-Man noted that the man's ill-fitting sneakers were already soaked through with melted slush. His own costume wasn't much better.

Spider-Man sighed. He knew that not even the Avengers and the Fantastic Four combined were likely to solve the homeless problem before spring finally arrived for the hundreds of Wilsons in similar straits all over the city. Nor did he know what chain of circumstances, what mixture of tragedy or personal weakness, had brought this man to his wretched situation. On a night like this, he figured, it didn't matter. There but for the grace of whatever, etcetera, etcetera . . .

Spider-Man knew he had to do something. He watched the snow falling relentlessly from the sky and, after a few minute's thought, an idea occurred to him.

First, he warmed his web-shooters under his armpits until they were functioning again. Then, raising his arms as high as he could, he weaved a dense and intricate net of webbing across the width of the alley. The web caught the snow and Wilson, gradually understanding Spider-Man's intentions, scrambled underneath the web to escape the avalanche of icy flakes. Spider-Man kept on spraying his webs, adding layer after layer to the net until eventually his reserves of web-fluid were exhausted. Beneath his mask, he smiled, satisfied with his accomplishment.

In time, the frozen webbing would dissolve, he knew, but not before a solid sheet of ice formed over the lattice of webbing he'd constructed. The ice would remain when the web disappeared. It wasn't a permanent solution, but at least it put a roof over an old man's head on the coldest night of the year.

"Take it easy, Wilson," Spider-Man said. "Try to stay warm." The homeless man grinned back at him.

Content that he had finally done his part tonight, Spider-Man headed home.

AN EVENING IN THE BRONX WITH VENOM

JOHN GREGORY BETANCOURT AND
KEITH R.A. DeCANDIDO

Illustration by Mark Bagley and Sam DeLaRosa

It is better that ten guilty persons escape than one innocent suffer.

—Sir William Blackstone

"Spider-Man! *Hey, Spider-Man! Down here!"*

There is a moment at the end of a web-swing when you hang, caught between Earth and sky, gravity and momentum. Everything is laid out like a picture postcard before you, and time almost stands still.

"Spider-Man!"

Spider-Man sighed, the perfection of the moment shattered. He shot a new webline, swung around, and landed on the corner of an office building forty feet above the Ninth Avenue sidewalk. Who had been shouting for him? His spider-sense hadn't gone off, which meant there was no immediate danger. He scanned the crowd below and spotted a group of homeless people. A black man with dreadlocks was jumping up and down and waving at him. Despite the summer heat, the man wore a tattered olive green overcoat and a scarf. Probably crazy. Still, Spider-Man knew better than to fluff the man off; the homeless saw a lot of things people didn't give them credit for noticing.

The man ran toward him, bringing a smell like rotting meat. His clothes, frayed and filthy, had seen better decades. Nevertheless, Spider-Man lowered himself to within ten feet of the pavement on a webline.

"What's the hubbub, bub?" he asked.

"Chasing me," the man gasped. "Been after me all across the country, man—he gonna *kill* me!"

"Who?"

"Venom!"

Spider-Man felt an unnatural chill in the ninety-degree heat. "Did you say Venom?"

"Uh-huh. He tryin' to *kill* me, man! See, I lived in the city underground—back in San Fran. He used to protect us, but he don't no more. He went *nuts*, started wiping everyone out. I'm the last one left and now he's after me. You *gotta* help, man! I'm a *witness!*"

"How'd you escape?"

"He was tearing into my best friend, Harold. Gave me a chance to get out. Been running for *days*. Almost got me once, but I jumped a train."

"So much for my quiet afternoon," Spidey muttered. Venom was an alien symbiote that had merged with a bitter, nearly insane man named Eddie Brock. He'd been at odds with Spider-Man for a long time, but they'd come to a truce when Venom relocated to San Francisco. There, Venom had pulled himself together, made himself the guardian of an underground city of homeless people, decided to spend his life protecting the innocent, and seemed to settle down. Venom might be crazy, but there had always been a definite method in that craziness . . . and it didn't include chasing innocent people across the continent and killing them. Unless Venom really *had* gone completely around the bend— but he wouldn't believe that until he saw it. No, Spider-Man decided, the homeless man's story didn't quite add up.

"Where is Venom now?" he asked skeptically.

"Dunno, man. Last time I saw him was Kansas. But he's gonna find me, man, he *always* does!"

"Listen, uh—"

"Josias."

"We'd better get you somewhere safe, Josias. I'm going to take you to the local precinct house." Spidey went through his mental map to locate the nearest police station and the quickest way there.

Josias took a step back. "No cops!"

Spider-Man sighed. "Look, the police are equipped to protect you if Venom shows up. He *is* a fugitive, so they want him behind bars, too."

Josias still looked reluctant, but slowly nodded. "Okay, man."

Spidey leaped down to the street and turned his back. "Hop on."

As Josias did so, Spidey thought, He's *definitely* let too much time lapse between baths. Then again, running from a lunatic symbiote didn't exactly leave time for showering.

Captain Frank Esteban ran a hand through his thick black hair, then gazed up at the red-and-blue-costumed figure perched on his office wall just below the ceiling. Spider-Man seemed perfectly at ease with his knees bent and his feet and shoulders flat against the wall. Definitely weird, Esteban thought. He'd never seen a costume up close like this before.

It was going to be one of those days, he thought, wiping the sweat from his brow. The building's air conditioning had gone out again, and the small fan on his desk and the three open windows did little to cool the room. They certainly did nothing to dilute the stench of the dreadlocked man now slouched in the one guest chair.

"So let me get this straight," Captain Esteban said slowly, looking up at Spider-Man. "You want me to whip out the big guns against Venom *plus* provide police protection for a homeless man just 'cause he *says* he's being chased?"

Spider-Man shifted uncomfortably on the wall as if he knew how ridiculous that sounded. "That's basically it, yeah."

Esteban shook his head. "I can think of a dozen reasons to throw both of you out on your ears. You got any evidence of this threat? Any proof Venom's on his way here and means to hurt Josias?"

Josias leaped to his feet. "You gotta help me, man, you gotta! He'll kill me! He—"

"Quiet!" Captain Esteban said, frowning angrily. "Sit down and shut up!" He nodded when Josias slumped meekly into his chair. "I've had enough of this," he went on. "You keep saying he's gonna kill you, but you won't say why. You're not exactly helping your case."

Josias began muttering to himself. Esteban sighed. It wasn't *going* to be one of those days, he thought. It already *was* one of those days.

"Look," Spider-Man said, "can you keep a secret?"

Esteban felt like he was in high school again. "Depends."

Spider-Man sighed, seemingly weighing his options. Then he finally said, "Josias told me he's from the underground city in San Francisco."

"I never heard of any underground city."

"You wouldn't have; like I said, it's a secret, but it's there. A section of San Francisco got buried in the 1906 earthquake, then the city built Golden Gate Park over it. A bunch of homeless people discovered it a few years ago and set up a community there, complete with a ruling Council. Venom's been acting as their protector."

"So?"

"I'm one of the few outsiders who even knows that underground city exists. If Josias knows about it, then he's got to be a resident.''

"Okay, let's say I buy that—at least the possibility,'' Esteban said. "Any way to check his story out?''

"Not really. I only know the place exists because I helped stop a threat to it a while back. I've never even seen it, and the San Francisco Police Department doesn't know about it, so I don't know how we could communicate with the city short of flying out there and searching for a way in.''

"All dead now,'' Josias muttered from his chair. "Venom killed them, man. *Dead.* All *dead.*''

Esteban shook his head and said, "Okay, fine. Just wanted to make sure I had it right for the paperwork. You costumes don't have to deal with that stuff.''

"Captain,'' Spider-Man said, "Venom *is* a legitimate threat. Do you remember what happened the last time he was in town?''

"I had to identify my cousin's body.''

Esteban saw Spider-Man wince under his mask. "I'm sorry.''

"Part of the job.'' He frowned to hide his discomfort, then pushed the intercom button on his desk. "I want to see Lieutenant Nahmod,'' he said.

A few seconds later a knock sounded at the door. "Come,'' Esteban called. Lieutenant Nahmod, wiping sweat off his dark forehead, stuck his head in.

"Yes, Captain?'' he said with a Pakistani accent. He took in Spider-Man on the wall and Josias in the chair, but said nothing about them.

"We got a potential situation here.'' Esteban nodded to Josias. "He claims Venom pursued him from San Francisco and is now trying to kill him.''

Nahmod paled. ''Oh boy.''

''Yeah. I want him cleaned up and held pending my instructions.''

''Right.''

Josias leaped to his feet. ''No, man! You gotta stop Venom! He'll get me if you leave me here!''

''Shut *up!*'' Esteban thundered. ''If you can't control yourself, I'll have you arrested for disturbing the peace and you'll spend the next month in jail! Got it?''

Josias shut up. Nahmod took his arm and led him from the room, shutting the door behind them.

Esteban rose and paced. ''I want you to know I got real problems with your friend's story.''

''Me, too,'' Spider-Man said. ''I know he's not the most reliable—''

''He's not reliable at all! He may even be certifiable!''

''But the threat is real.''

''The threat is *potentially* real.''

''I won't argue the point. I thought it was better to be sure.''

''I agree one hundred percent.'' Esteban sat behind his desk once more. ''It's gonna take some doing, but I'll get your friend his police protection, at least for the next few days.''

''If Venom is really after him, that's not going to be enough,'' Spider-Man said. ''I think I'd better—''

''I don't care what you think,'' Esteban said, ''I want you at the safe house, too.''

''*What?*'' Spider-Man dropped from the wall. ''Did you say—?''

''You were expecting me to tell you to take a hike, right?

I've heard it all, too. 'Vigilantes have no place in this town' and 'Civilians shouldn't interfere with police business, even if they do wear costumes' and 'That Spider-Man is a menace' crap, right?''

"Basically, yeah."

"Forget it. This isn't the *Daily Bugle* or the DA's office. You may've dumped Josias on me, but you ain't gettin' off the hook that easy." Esteban rummaged through the papers on his desk and managed to locate a blank index card. He scrawled a Bronx address on it. "I want someone there who knows what Venom can do and how to stop him."

"I guess this wouldn't be the best time to mention that I've never actually beaten Venom before."

"Maybe not, but you drove him out of town. That's more than anyone else has done." He held out the index card. Spider-Man took it. "This is the safe house. Give us three or four hours to get Josias out there. And stay inconspicuous—not much point in hiding someone, then sticking a guy in bright red leotards on the roof. Didn't you used to have a black costume?"

Spider-Man winced again. "Uh, yes, I did. Venom's wearing it now."

"Oh." Good one, Esteban, he told himself. "Well, just try to stay out of sight, then. At least till after dark."

"Unless Venom shows up." Spider-Man leapt to one of the open windows. "Don't worry, Captain. You've done the right thing." Then he swung away on a line of webbing.

Unless Venom shows up? Esteban thought. I'm counting on it. He remembered his cousin, a beat cop fresh out of the Academy who just happened to be in the wrong place at the wrong time when Venom plowed through a building in pursuit of Spider-Man. Esteban remembered the broken body on the slab in the morgue, and knew he had to see Venom brought to justice—dead or alive.

"We're looking for a friend."

Shotgun Sally looked up from her cardboard box and squinted. The sun hit the alley the wrong way and caught her in the eyes. She couldn't make out much beyond the shape of the man before her. He had blond hair and seemed to be dressed in tatters and rags, like her. He had to be one of the homeless, too, not a cop. But that didn't mean he wasn't dangerous—he could be after her squat. Or worse.

"Who you want?" she asked. Sally slowly moved her right hand deeper into her box, searching for the knife she kept for protection.

"Black guy. Name's Josias. He just got into town."

Sally ran that through her mind. An image clicked. Black. Dreadlocks. Ugly guy. Kept muttering about Venom coming to kill him.

"Spider-Man," she said slowly. "Spider-Man took him to the cops."

"Which precinct?"

She shook her head. *Pre-cinct.* The word seemed meaningless.

"Can you point the way?"

She slowly turned and pointed uptown. "There."

"We thank you. Here, get something to eat."

He reached toward her, and Sally recoiled. Where was her knife? Only slowly did she realize he had money in his hand. She snatched it.

A twenty dollar bill. She stared at it. Where did he get that kind of cash? Maybe he had more—

She looked up, but he was walking away. His clothes seemed to be crawling all over his body. As he turned the corner, she could swear he looked just like a cop now, blue uniform and all. But hadn't he been a homeless guy?

Then he was gone. She blinked. Had he been real? She fingered the twenty dollar bill. Real enough. She scrambled to her feet. *Food—*

Detective Sergeant Vance Hawkins arrived for the walk-through of the safe house just before four o'clock. It was a two-story row house in a line of nearly identical buildings in the Castle Hill section of the Bronx: small, nondescript, and completely forgettable. The street didn't get that much traffic and the neighbors tended to mind their own business. He parked in front, took his satchel from the back seat, and walked up the six slate steps to the front door. After he let himself in, he bolted the door.

The safe house was exactly as he remembered it: front hall, a door to the left leading to the living room, a door to the kitchen straight ahead. He went into the living room and dropped his satchel on the card table. There were half a dozen plastic folding chairs, an old TV, a small sofa, and a floor lamp. At least the TV had cable. Two weeks ago, he'd had to babysit a minor gang member here. The kid had turned state's evidence on the other members of Hell's Platoon, and District Attorney Tower ended up putting away a couple of very nasty characters. Compared to this, though, that job had been a cake walk.

Venom . . . I'd like to see him behind bars.

Quickly he explored every room of the house. At least the cleaning service had been here since he left: the few dirty dishes they'd left in the sink had been washed and left to dry in the drainer, the floors vacuumed, and the beds upstairs neatly made. He nodded. Exactly as expected. He checked his watch; everything had gone on schedule so far.

In the living room, he removed his walkie-talkie from the satchel. He pushed the send button and said, "Hawk to chickens. Coop clear."

"Roger that," came the reply. "Chickens coming in. Over."

Hawkins went to the front windows and adjusted the miniblinds so nobody could see in. Peering between two thin slats, he watched a gray van pull up behind his car. Three officers in plain clothes got out of the back, along with Josias Doe. Hawkins wrinkled his nose at the thought: Josias No-Last-Name stank when he'd been brought in. Now, showered and shaved, with his dreadlocks trimmed, and in clean clothes, he looked almost normal. Only the frightened way he kept looking around called attention to this group of four buddies seemingly out to visit a friend.

There were other police officers stationed outside as well, Hawkins knew. He'd check in with them later. If Venom showed up, he'd be in for a real surprise. The New York Police Department was not to be trifled with.

Hawkins crossed to the front door, unbolted it, and let the four men inside. The three other officers headed for the living room. Hawkins stopped Josias in the hall.

"A few ground rules," he said firmly. "You stay inside at all times. You can watch TV in the living room or sleep in one of the bedrooms upstairs. You're to be accompanied by an officer at all times. Do not go outside. Do not open the blinds or look out the windows. Clear?"

"Clear," Josias said.

"We'll send out for dinner in a couple of hours. There

should be soda in the icebox if you're thirsty. Or there's water."

"Okay."

Hawkins moved aside. Josias went into the living room and flopped onto the sofa. He stared raptly at the TV even though it wasn't on. At least he's quiet, Hawkins thought. He could put up with quiet crazies.

"Got a present for you, Hawk," Detective Sergeant Stephen Drew said with a grin. They'd been partnered at the safe house several times before, most recently last week with the gang informant.

"Oh?" Hawkins said.

"Here." Drew pulled a holster with an odd looking gun out of his own satchel and passed it over. "Check it out. The latest anti-Venom hardware."

It was a bulky metal pistol, but unlike any Hawkins had ever seen before. It was light, for one thing—about half the weight of his 9mm—and its barrel flared like an old-fashioned blunderbuss.

"Ray gun?" he asked.

"Sonic," Drew said, "but not frequencies humans can hear. Supposed to hurt dogs as well as Venom, so be careful where you point it."

"Right. He doesn't do loud sounds too well—or fire, either."

"Yeah," Drew said, "but a flame-thrower would be a bit impractical."

"True." Hawkins started to undo the 9mm holster under his left arm, thought better of it, and strapped the sonic gun's holster under his right arm instead. Picking up his satchel, he pulled a chair from the card table and went to the far corner of the room. There he pulled out a pencil and a crossword puzzle book—"More difficult than the *New York Times!*" the blurb promised, along with, "All new MENSA-level questions!" He had his doubts.

Tricky pawn move (2 wrds). He counted spaces, then wrote "en passant." He hadn't played chess in years; such games bored him. But he certainly remembered the rules. *The Emperor Claudius's first name.* "Tiberius." He'd read *I, Claudius* in high school: Tiberius Claudius Drusus Nero Germanicus Caesar, that was his full name. Occasionally it amazed him how much trivia he had stored away over the years; a trick memory, his friends used to say, but it just came naturally. He sighed, then rapidly filled in the next ten questions. At this rate I'll finish the book by dinner, he thought.

"Hey, Hawk."

Hawkins looked up. "Yes?"

Drew grinned at him. "Up for a little low-stakes action?" He riffed a deck of cards. Hawkins noticed Persons and Sakamoto were already pitching dollar bills into a plastic jar and taking chips from the kitty.

"Not this time," he said with a little smile. "Sorry."

"Your loss," Drew said.

Hawkins just shook his head. He had learned years ago not to play poker with fellow officers. He counted cards and knew the odds tables as well as any professional gambler. He couldn't help but win. It wasn't sporting, and once he'd been accused of cheating when he won several hundred dollars. One such experience had been more than enough. These days he stuck to crossword puzzles, acrostics, and mental games. Should've been a yuppie, he thought. Why couldn't he get partners who obsessed over Trivial Pursuit?

He glanced over at Josias, who was still absorbed by the

blank TV screen. "Someone turn it on for him," he said. "He's giving me the creeps."

Drew obliged, but kept the sound off.

Josias began to giggle just as Hawkins finished the rest of the crossword puzzle in short order. When Hawkins looked up, though, instead of a dumb sitcom, he found Josias engrossed in pictures from a bloody train wreck in Louisiana. That disconcerted him more than he wanted to admit. He narrowed his eyes. Have to keep a close watch on this one, he thought.

The precinct house bustled with activity. Small, hot, and overcrowded, it was the perfect place to infiltrate, Eddie Brock thought. Nobody would have the time or energy to take more than a second glance at him.

Disguised as a policeman, he strode through the main doors as though he owned the place, cutting through crowds of victims filing complaints and reports, past the lockup area, and straight to the desk sergeant. There he paused and waited to be noticed.

"Yes?" the sergeant said after a moment. She didn't look up.

"I'm supposed to report here?" Eddie said.

The woman squinted at the nameplate. "Officer Badger, is it?"

"Yes, Sergeant. I'm supposed to help out with the Venom case."

"Where's your paperwork?"

"It was supposed to be here already. I was sent over from the Fifteenth."

The sergeant sighed. "Figures. Well, the paperwork'll catch up. We're plenty short-handed right now." She riffled through the papers on her desk, found a form, and quickly filled it out. "Give this to Stan, Room 403. Relief shift's going out to the safe house at seven-thirty. He'll get you fitted out and introduce you to the others."

"Thanks."

"Glad to have you aboard, Badger."

Spider-Man arrived at the safe house just before five o'clock. Over the last few hours he'd stopped home for a late lunch, restocked his web shooters, and left a message for Mary Jane letting her know where he'd gone.

The trip out to the Bronx had taken longer than expected, then he had trouble finding the right address. Now, though, he perched on the roof of an apartment building across the street from the safe house, watching and waiting.

It was pretty nondescript: he wouldn't have looked at it twice if he hadn't already known this was the place. Although there were several cars and a van parked out front, the place showed little sign of habitation. The shades had been pulled down on the second floor and the blinds drawn on the first. The air conditioner hummed, though, so he figured people had to be inside. When a trickle of sweat ran down his back under his outfit, he longed to join them. It had to be over a hundred degrees out now, he thought. Probably a hundred and twenty in the sun.

He gazed up the block. Few people braved the streets in this heat and humidity; a couple of kids sat out on steps toward the end of the block, and opposite them, working his way forward, a man with a plastic bag seemed to be searching everyone's garbage for deposit cans and bottles. A couple of cars drove past, then a truck pulled up and parked two houses down. A middle-aged man in gray overalls locked it up and went inside.

A mild tingle of his spider-sense made Spider-Man tense. It couldn't be Venom, though. Venom didn't affect his spider-sense. Slowly he realized the tingle involved the man collecting cans and bottles. He was still rummaging through the garbage and talking to himself—or rather, Spider-Man realized, he was talking to the lapel of his shirt. Realizing he had to be a cop covering the outside, Spidey sank back a bit. Nothing to do now but wait, he thought.

Seven o'clock came. Hawkins decided to check in with Andrew Lipinski, the most junior officer of the team, now stuck playing the homeless guy scavenging outside. Hawkins picked up the walkie-talkie and said, "Rags, this is Hawk, come in."

Lipinski's voice came over the speaker. "This is Rags. Webs at two o'clock, and I found three dollars worth of cans and bottles in the garbage cans. Over."

"Congrats, Rags, you've doubled your pension. Shout if there's trouble. Hawk out."

Hawkins couldn't help but smile. "Webs at two o'clock" meant Spider-Man had been seen above. Hope he doesn't have a wife to go home to, he thought. At this rate, it could take all night.

Thankfully his own shift ended soon. He glanced at the others. Their poker playing continued unabated—Hawkins was perversely pleased to hear Drew's cursing intermingled with Persons's cheering and gloating. He hid a little smile as he went back to his crossword puzzle book—three more puzzles and he'd be finished.

He went through them quickly, then glanced at his watch. Just before seven-thirty. Where was their relief? They should have checked in by now.

As if on cue, Sergeant Karen Doyle's voice came from his walkie-talkie. "Queen Hen to Hawk," she said. "Come in, Hawk."

Hawkins picked up the walkie-talkie again. "Hawk here, Queen Hen. What's your ETA, over?"

"Two minutes. How's the egg?"

"A little cracked, but okay. I'll open the henhouse door. Hawk out."

Hawkins rose and stretched. "Time to wrap it up, guys," he said.

Grumbling good-naturedly, the other officers finished their hand, then began to cash out their poker chips now that relief was in sight. Shaking his head, Drew scooped the chips and cards back into his satchel—each shift was responsible for its own entertainment, after all.

Josias rose and went into the kitchen. Hawkins heard the icebox door open, then the pop of a soda can opening.

"Check on him," he said to Drew. Then he went and looked out through the front door's peephole. Karen Doyle and four others were just coming up the steps. He undid the deadbolt, then opened the door for them.

Doyle entered first, followed by Tom Cavetti. A new guy, a burly blond, followed them, then Carlos Augustan and Mary Brzytov. Hawkins spotted the telltale bulges of sonic pistols beneath their light jackets and briefly wondered how Esteban had pulled off requisitioning enough weapons for both shifts to get their own.

"Any sign of Venom?" Doyle asked.

"Not yet," Hawkins said. "I'm starting to wonder if he's going to show tonight."

"He will," said the third officer, the new one. He

looked vaguely familiar to Hawkins, which was odd. Had they met before? He raised his eyebrows and looked at Karen for an introduction.

"This is Ed Badger from the one-five," Doyle said. "He's on loan. Ed, this is Detective Sergeant Vance Hawkins."

"Pleased to meet you," Badger said. "How's Josias?"

Drew appeared in the doorway. "Been pretty quiet," he said before Hawkins could reply. "Then again, if I had Venom on my ass, I'd be quiet, too."

Everyone laughed. Especially Ed Badger, Hawkins noticed. His bad feeling about Badger got worse the longer he looked at him. Frowning, he tried to figure out where he'd seen the man. He hadn't been around the precinct before, of that Hawkins was certain—anyway, Doyle said he was from the Fifteenth. So where—?

Shaking his head, he moved toward the living room to get his satchel. So much for my trick memory, he thought with a mental snort. Maybe he needed to treat it like a puzzle, try to force the connection. Red is to apples as Badger is to—

Brock.

It hit him like a sledgehammer, dredged up from some ancient trivia game: in certain Scots dialects, badgers were called brocks. It's him. He found us. Hawkins felt his mouth go dry.

Badger—Brock—*Venom*—was still in the hall, trapped behind Doyle and Cavetti, who were chatting amiably with Drew, trying to talk him into leaving his cards and poker chips for their use.

Hawkins took a deep breath. Take it slowly and calmly,

he thought. No sense rushing and putting everyone in danger.

Josias had returned to his seat on the sofa, he noticed, bringing a can of Diet Coke and a bag of pretzels with him. He'd be safe there for the moment.

Hawkins picked up his satchel, stepped out of Brock's line of sight for a second, and drew his sonic pistol. Would it work? He hoped so. He didn't even have time to warn Spider-Man or call for back-up.

Swallowing, he stepped out into the hall, covering his pistol with the satchel. "Coming through!" he called. "Dinner's waiting for me!"

Obligingly, they cleared a path to the door for him. The second his line-of-fire was clear, he dropped the satchel and whipped up the sonic pistol.

"Freeze, Brock!" he said in a loud voice.

Hawkins heard several voices—"Christ, Vance, are you nuts?" "Hawk, what the hell're you doing?"—but kept his eyes right on the blond-haired officer.

Then behind him Josias shrieked, "*It's him!*" which perversely relieved Hawkins, since it confirmed his own suspicion.

"It seems we've been discovered," said Badger. "We're sorry for the deception, but it was necessary. As this is."

His clothes started to shimmer, shift, and reorient themselves into the more familiar ebon shape, with the spider emblem on the chest, the huge teeth and slavering tongue in the mouth, and those awful, hollow white eyes. In seconds Venom stood before them.

Hawkins swallowed and found his mouth suddenly dry. "This is a sonic pistol," he said with more conviction than he felt. "You will step back and raise your hands or I will fire."

Venom raised his hands. A section of his black suit streaked away from his chest, wrapped itself around Hawkins's gun hand, and tried to jerk the pistol away. Hawkins pulled the trigger, but didn't hear anything.

Venom must have, though—he screamed and staggered back. But he didn't release his grip on the sonic pistol; instead, he jerked harder and the pistol flew from Hawkins's grip. It seemed to vanish *into* Venom's body.

Then Venom reached for Hawkins.

Detective Sergeant Hawkins had only a moment to scream.

The first indication Spider-Man had of anything wrong in the safe house came when one of the plainclothes officers went flying through the front window in a spray of glass and miniblinds. Spidey hadn't felt so much as a tremor in his spider-sense, so he knew Venom had to be the cause.

Moving with superhuman speed, Spidey shot weblines on either side of the falling cop. Whipping his wrists back and forth in a long-practiced motion, he formed the webs into a sort of cushion where they hit the ground. It softened the officer's impact, but Spider-Man didn't have time to give him more than a glance. He swung down toward the row house.

To his left, he heard the officer posing as the homeless can-collector (who had been in the process of being relieved by another *faux* homeless man) bellowing into his walkie-talkie for assistance.

Spider-Man leapt through the gaping hole in the front window. Inside, several cops were struggling with balls of black goo attached to their shooting hands. Strands of black connected the balls of goo to a costumed figure in the middle of the room: *Venom.*

Spider-Man launched himself at Venom and punched the symbiote in the side of the face with all his strength. Venom's head snapped back, but then he shook the blow off.

"So, Spider-Man," he said. "Once again you've broken our truce. We're *very* disappointed." A piece of the alien suddenly protruded from Venom's chest and slammed into Spidey's stomach. Then he struck Spidey backhanded across the face.

Is he getting stronger? Spider-Man wondered as he rolled with the blow as best he could, striking the far wall with a disheartening *thud.* Venom always threw off his fighting style. Normally he fought using his spider-sense—a sense Venom neutralized.

But that didn't matter. He had to stop Venom once and for all. He rushed forward—and again Venom sent him crashing back head over heels. The plaster wall shattered from the impact. His vision swam and he heard a clear ringing tone in his left ear.

Hearing cries of pain, he forced himself up once again. The officers needed him. He couldn't let them down.

He shook his head, trying to clear his vision. The ringing in his head lessened. Venom was retracting the globs that had engulfed the cops' hands—hands now empty of the sonic weapons. Venom had torn the pistols loose and absorbed them, Spidey realized.

Venom turned and strode through the doorway into the next room. Spider-Man staggered after him, through the small empty dining room and into the kitchen.

The back door stood open; Josias had fled. Spider-Man forced himself to leap forward and block Venom's way.

He straightened. "You can't have him," he said with more firmness than he felt. "Give it up, Brock."

"We won't be cheated of our justice!"

Venom expanded, turning into a battering ram, and suddenly charged. Spidey leaped, spraying a blockade of webbing across the doorway, but he hadn't moved fast enough to halt Venom's rush. Venom struck Spider-Man another glancing blow and went through the webbing as though it were paper.

Spidey tumbled and hit the refrigerator, then gave a low moan: he'd forgotten what a chore fighting Venom could be. He felt dizzy and sick from pain, and the ringing in his head returned worse than before.

By the time he climbed to his feet and made it to the back door, the world seesawing wildly around him, Venom had vanished. Spider-Man staggered back in to check on the cops, but one of them—a blond-haired woman—waved him off. "We're all right. Get after him! We'll call for backup!"

Spidey didn't wait. Shaking off his dizziness as best he could, he jumped out the window, fired a webline to the roof next door, and pulled himself up. Venom and Josias couldn't be so far ahead of him that he wouldn't spot them if he got high enough, he thought. Maybe fresh air would clear his head—

He heard a scream from several blocks over. Quickly he shot a web across the street and scurried across, then crossed to the third block over. A scream sounded—wasn't that Eddie Brock's voice? Then he remembered the two officers who'd been outside posing as homeless scavengers.

Perhaps they'd given chase and found Venom. If so, their weapons must be working.

He reached the roof of an overlooking house just as a pair of explosions shook the glass in the windowpanes around him. He steadied himself. Below, Venom and the two officers faced off in the middle of the street. The two officers were shaking their hands in pain. Their sonic pistols were gone—but a pair of three-foot-deep potholes now broke the pavement between them and Venom. Venom must have done something to make their pistols explode, Spider-Man thought. Overloaded them, perhaps?

"Whoopsie," Venom said to the officers with a sneer. "Did we have a bit of a misfire there, boys?" Despite his words, Venom sounded a bit shaky to Spider-Man. "Pity, 'cause we don't give second chances. On the other hand," he said, his voice growing stronger, "we know you were only doing your jobs. So we'll let you go. Besides, justice still needs to be carried out!"

Spider-Man shot a web and swung to the ground behind Venom. "Justice? Is that what you call it?"

Venom whirled with a hiss.

"I thought your shtick was safeguarding innocents now, Brock." Spider-Man knew he needed to stall for time—if he could pull himself together, maybe he could mount a proper attack on Venom and give Josias enough time to get away again.

"And we haven't changed our tune, Spider-Man," Venom said. "This doesn't concern you. This is a private matter between ourself, Josias, and the Council. No one else. Not you, and not these police officers." Venom disgorged the weapons he'd absorbed, then webbed them up with the alien's organic webbing. He started to move off.

"Tell them to stay out of my way—advice you'd do well to take yourself. While we swore not to kill you, we will brook no interference. Josias *must* come to justice!"

"Oh no you don't," Spider-Man muttered, giving chase.

It wasn't easy to keep up with Venom. For one thing, night was falling, and this area wasn't as well lit as a typical Manhattan street. For another, the buildings were too low for any real web-swinging; he had to trail Venom on foot, and he kept losing sight of his target in the shadows. It also took all of his concentration to keep from falling when dizzy spells hit.

From the direction Venom took, Josias was headed toward the interchange where the Cross Bronx Expressway, the Bruckner Expressway, and the Throgs Neck Expressway all met. Josias probably figured he could lose Venom in the latticework of exit ramps.

Of course, Josias had also probably figured he could lose Venom in a cross-country chase, then figured he could stay hidden with secure police protection. No, Spider-Man thought, Josias would only survive the day if he stopped Venom.

Forcing down the cobwebs that muddied his brain, he pushed himself on.

Josias had just picked a direction and fled. He didn't know if he could keep ahead of Venom, but no way would he stick around that safe house. All those cops and Spider-Man hadn't been able to protect him.

Josias was running out of options.

Then he saw a highway exit ahead. *Maybe I can lose him there.*

Or maybe Spider-Man would stop him.

Of course, Spider-Man hadn't stopped Venom yet.

Josias cut across a patch of overgrown plant life between roads, pushing through bushes and waist-high weeds. Then he tripped over a tangle of roots and came crashing to the ground. He tried to get up, but couldn't seem to get his legs to work.

"Having a little trouble, Josias?"

Josias froze. *Venom.*

He tried to sit up, failed, then looked down at his ankles—a strand of the alien creature had tripped him, not a root.

He looked up to face Venom. The man who had come to call himself "Protector" looked pretty woozy. Maybe those cops did some damage—Josias allowed himself a flicker of hope.

Then he saw the red and blue figure coming up behind the symbiote, and the flicker became a spark.

Spider-Man slammed full tilt into Venom's back. From the web-slinger's reputation, Josias expected some kind of snappy comment, but Spider-Man said nothing, he merely kept hammering into Venom, not letting up for a moment. Venom released Josias and, with a roar, turned to face his enemy. The two traded blows, circled, traded blows again. Neither seemed to be gaining any real advantage—they were both staggering.

The hell with it, Josias thought. He rose and ran as fast as he could.

Spider-Man saw nothing, heard nothing, felt nothing but the fight, a constant barrage of punches, kicks, slaps, and more punches. He was a red-and-blue blur, not pausing, refusing to give Venom a chance to recover.

Suddenly, Spider-Man felt familiar tendrils wrap around his legs, and before he could do anything about it, they threw him clear. The symbiote cried, *"Enough!"*

Spidey crashed into the door of a rust-laden car that must have been abandoned on the side of the road ages ago. His head pounded mercilessly, and it took all of his willpower to keep from falling unconscious. He tried to focus past his fluttery, swimming vision on Venom.

"We warned you, Spider-Man! We warned you not to interfere! This is *not* your concern! You vowed to leave us alone!"

Every word a struggle, Spider-Man replied, "I—I said I wouldn't go—after you as long as—as long as you continued protecting innocents! I don't consider mass murder to be—a good job of that!"

"What are you blathering about?"

"I—won't—let—you—kill—Josias!" Spider-Man gathered every last ounce of strength and climbed to his feet.

"Josias will suffer the same fate as all of his kind do—justice at our hand!" Venom turned and sprinted away, calling, "This is your final warning, Spider-Man. Do *not* interfere with our hunt again!"

Spider-Man didn't get it. Venom kept saying "justice." That didn't sound like mass murder. Nor did calling Josias "his kind"—from anyone else, that might come across as a racist remark, but Venom was only prejudiced against people he considered to not be innocent. So "his kind" could only mean someone guilty.

Once more Spider-Man ran after Venom.

This time he caught up with him under one of the Bruckner's entrance ramps. There Venom had cornered his prey. Shiny black tendrils reached out, seized Josias, and smacked him around like a cat playing with a cornered mouse. When he saw that, Spider-Man knew Venom had changed. Venom specialized in killing people quickly and efficiently. He'd never gone in for brutalization.

"Is this how Harold felt, Josias?" Venom demanded.

Spider-Man drew up, remembering Josias had described his best friend Harold as another of Venom's victims. How would Josias know how his friend had felt?

Sirens grew louder in the distance. Spider-Man struggled to stay on his feet. He moved on sheer force of will.

"Let him go!" he cried.

Venom whirled. "Amazing. You should be unconscious or dead by now. We admire your tenacity, Spider-Man, but you're *really* starting to bore us. Heed our warning—Josias will be brought to justice."

"Only one—being brought to—justice is—you!"

"Your hypocrisy disgusts us. You have the gall to call yourself a hero, yet you do everything you can to protect this scum!"

"You're talking about yourself, Venom, not Josias. I won't let you kill him!" He leaped forward in a tackle that took Venom down.

Venom had to let go of Josias to push Spider-Man off. "Listen to us!" the symbiote cried. "We don't wish to kill Josias—unless the Council decrees it!"

Spider-Man paused. "What?"

"We are *not* here to pass sentence. We only want to bring Josias back to face judgment before the Council."

Spider-Man found himself lost in a fog that had nothing to do with his head injuries. "Can't—be—true—Council—dead!" he gasped.

"Don't be ludicrous," Venom snarled. "The Council

sent me after Josias after he killed Harold McWilliams and ran away."

Killed Harold McWilliams? Ran away? Spider-Man's head swam. Concussion. I must have a concussion. Venom started to blur—or was that the alien changing form? So hard to focus. Josias killed Harold?

"He told me—*you'd* killed—everyone underground."

Then Venom laughed. Spider-Man stared at him in surprised confusion.

"And of course," Venom said, "you believed him. It makes *far* more sense to believe that we murdered those we have sworn to protect on the say-so of a fugitive. You disgust and insult us, Spider-Man. Now, if you don't mind, we have a murderer to bring in."

Venom turned, then cried, "*No!*"

Spidey realized that there wasn't anything to see. Josias had once again taken advantage of the distraction to flee. As he'd taken advantage of Spider-Man ever since he flagged him down on Ninth Avenue that morning.

"I'll help," he told Venom.

As one, they loped forward. One way or another, Spider-Man thought, Josias would face justice.

Josias ran up the ramp toward the highway. Behind him, he heard that awful voice: "You can't escape us, Josias! We will not rest until you've been caught and brought back!"

Reaching the highway, he paused, staring at the steady stream of traffic. It was dark now. If he could make it across, surely he'd be able to hide till morning.

Maybe he could make his way back to the docks in New York, jump ship to Europe or South America, or anywhere else. Now that he was cleaned up, it wouldn't be so hard to find a job, would it?

The police sirens were getting louder. He could see their lights flashing on the streets behind him when he looked back. Then he saw a dark shape starting up the highway ramp. Venom.

He had to move. He had to get across the highway.

Car after car zoomed by.

He paused, looked back, saw Venom—and then panicked and ran.

He never even saw the station wagon that hit him.

"Blast," Venom said when they neared Josias's body sprawled out on the Bruckner Expressway. Traffic had stopped in both directions; curious onlookers craned to see the accident. "He should've stood trial."

Spider-Man couldn't believe Venom actually said that. Maybe he *had* changed for the better.

Not that it mattered now. Sirens wailed, approaching quickly. On the other side of the highway, traffic slowed to a crawl as drivers gazed in fascinated horror at the bloody scene. An instant later several police cars pulled up the ramp. Venom would now be stopped, Spider-Man thought. Time for the big guns. If Spidey could only keep his head from spinning.

"Once again, we must take our leave, Spider-Man," Venom said. "We're willing to let you off the hook for breaking our agreement this time, since you were obviously taken in by this murderer. Next time, though, we may not be so forgiving."

Spider-Man called on the last reserves of his strength.

He straightened. "You're not getting away that easily, Venom," he said.

Behind him, he heard a sudden skid of tires and the crunch of steel colliding with steel. Glass shattered, and a child screamed—though whether in pain or fear, Spider-Man couldn't tell.

He turned. Venom would have to wait. He sprang over the divider to the scene of the crash. A subcompact had rear-ended a minivan, doing extensive damage to the car. A couple of children in the minivan seemed hysterical, but unhurt. The drivers were already cursing at each other, trying to assess blame at the loudest possible volume. They didn't need Spider-Man's help.

As he turned back toward the other side of the highway, several cops pointed guns at him. One yelled, "Don't move, web-head!"

He looked around. Venom was nowhere to be seen.

Another cop car screeched to a halt nearby, its swirling lights lost in the kaleidoscope of red that surrounded Spider-Man.

A familiar voice called, "Lay off him, he's with us!"

"Who the hell're you?" the cop who had yelled said.

"Esteban, NYPD. Spider-Man's working with us to protect a witness."

"You mean the guy we called the meat wagon for?"

A pause. "Looks like, yeah. Damn."

"Didn't do such a hot job protectin' him then, huh?"

"You try going up against Venom." Esteban glanced at Spider-Man with concern.

"I'll pass, thanks," the cop said, then walked back towards his car, gesturing to the people around him. "All right, back in your cars, folks. Show's over."

Esteban approached Spider-Man. "You okay, pal?"

"Been better."

"Did Venom do Josias?"

"No, he got hit by a car on the road."

"Damn." Esteban paused. "You, uh, you need a lift somewhere?"

Helluva thing to tell the wife, Esteban thought—I gave Spider-Man a lift home. Well, not home as such. The masked man asked for a lift to midtown; he would take it from there. Secret identity and all that.

They had waited until the paramedics loaded Josias's body into the ambulance and the woman driving the station wagon gave her statement. Then Esteban had led Spider-Man to his car and they'd headed west on the Bruckner toward Manhattan.

Spider-Man wasn't up to much in the way of conversation, Esteban found. He had to be hurting under his costume; perhaps a mild concussion, certainly lots of cuts and bruises. Still, sitting quietly in air conditioning seemed to do him some good. He was lucid enough by the time they crossed the Triboro Bridge to the FDR Drive to explain what he learned about Josias.

"I feel like this was such a waste, y'know?" he finished.

"How you mean?" Esteban asked.

"Here I went and busted my butt thinking I was protecting an innocent man from a killer. Instead, I helped a murderer escape justice. For someone who's supposed to be the good guy—"

"Look, sometimes there ain't any good guys or bad guys," Esteban said. "If you hadn't done anything, Venom would've caught the jerk and brought him back, and they probably still would've killed him. Josias'd be just as dead and Venom would be just as on the loose.''

"I suppose.''

Spider-Man didn't sound very convinced. So Esteban tried another tack. "Venom threw one of my men—a good guy named Hawkins—through the safe house window. He wanted to thank you. If it wasn't for your web pillow, he might be dead now.''

Spider-Man looked at Esteban.

"Think about that next time you're feeling useless.'' He took the 49th Street exit. "Any place you want me to let you off?''

"The corner's fine,'' Spider-Man said. "I think I can web-swing from here.''

"You sure?''

"Yeah. I heal fast. Take care of yourself, Captain. And thanks.'' Spider-Man opened the door and climbed out. Then he shot another of those weblines and swung away.

Sighing, Captain Esteban turned left on Second Avenue, headed for the Midtown Tunnel. Helluva thing to tell the wife, all right.

FIVE MINUTES

PETER DAVID

Illustration by Rick Leonardi

The cinnamon rolls had been carefully baked (although they had originated from a Pillsbury container, the intention was nonetheless sincere) and frosted with orange icing. She brought them into the bedroom where her husband was sleeping late. Tiny candles inserted into the rolls flickered valiantly to avoid flaring out.

She put the plate down on the nightstand next to the bed, gently waking her husband with a whispered "Happy Anniversary" in his ear. With a smile he rolled over to respond, and as one thing led to another, somehow breakfast in bed was forgotten. The orange frosting was now hopelessly mingled with candle wax, a lazy trail of black sooty smoke rising from the rolls. They were, in short, inedible, although the couple in the bed didn't especially care.

There were a few faint streams of light peeking in through the drawn window shades, but otherwise the room was dark.

Mary Jane's still-warm body was curled up against her husband, her head tucked on his shoulder. Her fingernails traced a lazy line down the front of his bare chest. Her palm stopped briefly over his heart and felt the rapid beating finally slowing down.

"Oh good," she murmured. "You're still alive."

"True," replied Peter. "But if I hadn't been, then what a way to go."

"Happy anniversary," she said, and nuzzled her lips against his cheek. "Hope we got it off to a good start."

"Day's certainly gonna be downhill from here."

At that moment, as if to add emphasis to Peter Parker's words, they heard raised voices from below them. Angry shouting voices of a couple bickering.

Peter moaned softly and shoved his head into his pillow.

"There they go again," he said. "Why don't the Swansons just get a divorce already?" They'd never been formally introduced; Peter didn't even know their first names, but he'd taken note of their last name on the mail slot downstairs the first time that he'd been awoken late at night by one of their screamfests. Morning, evening, anytime could potentially be disrupted by their fights.

They had a child, also. A little girl, about five years old. Peter wondered what it was like for the kid to be in that sort of situation, day in, day out.

"Maybe they still have a hope of saving the marriage," Mary Jane suggested. But she didn't sound convincing, even to herself.

They heard a door slam. One of the Swansons had gone out. Perhaps both. Either way, good riddance, as far as Peter and Mary Jane were concerned.

Peter sighed, and then glanced over at Mary Jane. He saw the concern on her face. "What's wrong, hon'?" he asked.

"I don't ever want to get like them," she said softly. "Not ever."

"Don't worry."

"Not *ever*," she repeated.

"I said don't worry, and I meant it." He rolled over and kissed her. It was lingering, but not quite satisfying, because he wanted more, and she started to give it to him . . .

Then, in the far distance, they heard a siren. Several of them, and a horn blaring. Some sort of emergency vehicles were hurtling down the street.

Peter sat up, his brow furrowed.

He felt a tug on his arm. "Honey . . . come on," said Mary Jane, trying to pull him back down into bed.

"There's a siren . . . "

"I know, honey. We live in Manhattan. There's sirens all the time."

"Yeah, but this one was close. Maybe there's something I should be doing . . . "

"Peter, come back to bed." Her voice was cajoling. "I'll make it worth your while."

His bare feet were on the hardwood floor. "MJ . . . "

"Peter . . . " She paused, no longer sounding cajoling, but instead trying to cover disappointment and even frustration. "There are thousands of people in this city who are paid to handle emergencies. Firemen and cops and ambulance guys, and whatever. And you know what? They all get time off. They get paid, and still get time off. Shouldn't you? At least five more minutes to ourselves."

"But it's nearby . . . "

"Five minutes."

"But . . . "

He paused. There was no answer, but he could feel a chill in the air. "Hon'?"

"Please?" came her whisper in the darkness. Her fingers gently ran the curve of his spine. "Five minutes? Just to cuddle and hold each other and not be like those people downstairs? Five minutes in the warmth, in our bed? God, Peter, I dated guys who would have killed for five minutes with me, and here I'm begging you . . . "

He sighed and rolled back into bed. He took her face in his hands and kissed her gently. "You don't have to beg," he told her, feeling like something of a creep. He held her tightly. "Five minutes won't kill anyone. Hell . . . make it ten."

But it was five.

Because as warm as she was, as giving as she was, his mind was still wherever the destination of that siren might have been. Finally, aware that his mind was not in accord with his body, she gave in to the inevitable, Mary Jane got up and said simply, "I'm going to go shower now."

By the time she came out, Peter was gone.

Spider-Man swung in the direction he'd heard the sirens going. Tucked securely under his web belt was his camera. Whatever was going on, photos for the *Daily Bugle* would certainly not be out of line. Perhaps they'd even be a means of salving the guilt he was already feeling for running out on Mary Jane.

In the distance, on Madison Avenue, he saw a cluster of flashing lights around 79th Street. That seemed the likely place. He fired a webline, and swung in a dizzying arc down Broadway. The air rushed past him, an exhilarating, liberating experience.

There were police cars clustered around, and a fire truck, but Spider-Man saw no sign of a fire. Perhaps it was a false alarm. Swell. Mary Jane would just love that.

Then he spotted the ambulance.

As Spider-Man descended toward the street, he saw the body bag being loaded into it. Whoever was going into that ambulance was going on a one-way trip.

People in the crowd were pointing and shouting at Spider-Man, but he gave it no heed as he dropped from the sky, landing lightly next to one of the cop cars. He recognized an officer named Mead, a cop with a few years under his belt (and the rolls of fat to accompany it) and one of the few cops on the force who didn't seem to mind Spider-Man sticking his nose into police business. He appeared to regard Spider-Man and his super-powered brethren with both curiosity and amusement.

"What happened?" asked Spider-Man.

"We lost one," said Mead. "Guy tentatively identified as," and he glanced at a notepad, "Ted Thomas. Business going down the tube, so he decided to take a long walk off a short window. Too high for ladders, and he jumped before the fire eaters could get the cushions set up."

"Aw man," said Spider-Man. He saw an area cleared out, saw a large red splotch on the ground, and looked away. He sighed. "Family?"

"Wife, two kids."

"Aw man," he said again. "Wasn't there anything anyone could do? Talk him out of it? Anything?"

"Well," Mead said, looking Spider-Man up and down. "Chances are you could have saved him, I guess. If you'd gotten here, I dunno, five minutes earlier . . . "

Spider-Man took a step back as if he'd been slugged. His masked face, his all-covering costume, did nothing to hide the effect those words had on him.

Mead regretted it instantly. "Hey, man, I didn't mean nothing by it," he said consolingly. "That's the way things sometimes come down, y'know? That's the breaks. Nobody's blaming you. You can't be everywhere."

Spider-Man was nodding. "Yeah . . . yeah, sure," he said, but he wasn't really listening.

He was thinking about warm flesh pressed against his, which now seemed very cold.

"I'm sorry," Mary Jane said again for what seemed to her the hundredth time.

Peter sat at the living room table. He was playing solitaire.

"I've told you, you have nothing to apologize for," he said. He unconsciously put a black jack on a red queen.

"Then why do I feel like you're still blaming me for something?"

He looked up at her, his face expressionless. "I don't know," he said.

She sat there, her hair still damp. "Look . . . we both said we were taking the day off to celebrate. So how about we go out and do something."

"I don't feel much like celebrating."

"Damn it, Peter, you *do* blame me."

"No, I don't."

"Who, then? Yourself?"

He said nothing at first, but then muttered something very softly.

"What was that?" she asked.

"Nothing."

She crossed the living room, pulled out the chair across the table, sat down and looked at him squarely. Her green eyes blazed like an angry cat's. "*What* did you say?"

He met her gaze and now some of the resentment started to seep through. "I said *I* had wanted to go."

"You mean this morning."

"Yes."

"And I stopped you."

"Yes."

"And now that man is dead."

"Yes."

"So it's my fault."

He said nothing.

Mary Jane slammed her hands down on the table. "I can't believe this! Some stranger decides to kill himself and it's *my fault!*"

"No, it's my fault for listening to you!" he shouted, unable to contain himself anymore. "If I'd gotten there five minutes sooner, he'd be alive!"

"If! If! God, Peter, listen to yourself!" She shook her head, her wet hair slapping around on her shoulders. "And if the fire department had gotten there sooner, they might have saved him! Or if the police had talked him down, they might have saved him! Or if his business dealings hadn't gone sour, he'd never have gone out the window! Or if he'd decided to go into another line of work, he'd never have had a business to go bad, and on and on, forever and ever. Peter, you'll make yourself crazy keeping up this way. How much are we supposed to second-guess ourselves? How far back in the second-guessing do we go?"

"Just to this morning," he said, staring at her coldly.

Her hands trembled, and then her right hand swung as if on its own. He dodged it, of course, with only the most minimal of movement, and she missed him clean.

Mary Jane glared at the man to whom she had been curled up, skin to skin, barely an hour before. She had wanted that moment to last an eternity. Now it seemed hard to believe that it lasted an eyeblink.

"I made a vow," he said. "Years ago. I swore that no one would ever be harmed again through my inaction. And here I am, all these years later, and I haven't learned a thing. I heard the sirens. I knew something was happening. But I ignored it, and now a woman has no husband and her children have no father."

"Okay." Mary Jane bobbed her head quickly. "Okay,

Peter. Fine.'' She was speaking so fast that the words were tumbling over one another. ''So let's just cover all the bases, then. If you want to do this, then do it right. How about if you start carrying a police band radio. Or maybe we can get phone taps on all the suicide help lines, so you can listen in and pitch in there. We can have fire alarms ring here.''

''Stop it.''

''Or . . . I know!'' She sounded almost giddy. ''How about if we give a big spider-signal to the commissioner of police so that he can shine it on a passing cloud whenever you're needed!''

''Stop it!'' he shouted. ''I take this seriously!''

Her hands were trembling. ''And what about me, Peter? What about what I want? When do you take *that* seriously, huh? What do you want from me, Peter?! What the hell do you want?! I love you and I wanted to be with you, and you're punishing me for it! You're *punishing* me! It's not fair!''

He stared at her for a long moment.

''No. It's not,'' he agreed.

And then he walked out.

Joe Robertson looked up from his desk in surprise. He put down his pipe, leaving it behind in his office, before entering the smoke-free area that comprised the city room. He stopped at Joy Mercado's desk, which was occupied, but not by Joy, who was out on assignment.

He looked down at Peter Parker. ''What are you doing here, son?''

Peter didn't glance up. He seemed utterly engrossed in tapping a pencil on the desk blotter. ''Nothing,'' he said.

Joe sat on the edge of the desk. "Correct me if I'm wrong, but as I recall I talked to you about an assignment today, and you said you were going to be busy celebrating your anniversary."

"I know."

"Did I get the date wrong?"

"No. We celebrated, and now we're done."

Joe glanced at his watch. "All done by 10:30 in the morning? Come on, son. Where's the stamina?"

Peter shrugged.

"Ah, the shrug. Most common weapon in the arsenal of teenager communication. Of course, you're in your twenties, son, so you don't have an excuse."

This time Peter didn't shrug, although he had to fight the impulse to do so. Then, after a moment of thought, he turned to Robertson and said, "How long have you been married, Robbie?"

"Twenty-four years."

"Wow." He considered that. "Twenty-four years."

Joe laughed softly. "You make it sound like a jail sentence when you say it that way."

"I'm sorry. I just . . . well, it just sounds like a very long time, that's all. Do, uhm . . . do you and Mrs. Robertson ever fight?"

"From time to time," he said drily. "A little fight now and then is good, though, son. Clears the air. Keeps the lines of communication open. Certainly better than letting things simmer and build up."

"Yeah, I know. But what about big fights? I mean . . . " He shifted in the chair. "Did you ever have a fight where you think . . . maybe lines were crossed. Maybe there was no coming back?"

Joe nodded slowly. "On occasion."

"And what did you do then?"

"I came back."

"Oh." Peter looked down once more.

"Look, son," said Robbie, shifting on the edge of the desk. "Hopefully you've got a lot of years ahead of you. Hopefully you'll have more fights, and more chances to make up. Maybe coming here to cool off was a good idea. Just so long as, sooner or later, you go back and resolve things. That's what's important."

"I guess. But . . . " He paused. "I think it'd be better if I waited a while. Maybe . . . I dunno . . . go to a movie or something."

"Whatever you think best, Peter. But I've seen you and Mary Jane together. I think you'll manage to stitch together whatever's torn you apart. And you know what? Believe it or not, something that seemed so major to you today could very well be, years from now, insignificant. You might laugh that you got so worked up over it."

Peter envisioned the blood-stained street. The look of anguish on Mary Jane's face, and the loathing he felt for himself and his inaction. And the anger for Mary Jane that he simply couldn't shake.

At that moment, Betty stuck her head out of Jameson's office. "Oh! Peter! I thought I saw you!" she called. "Your wife's calling. Said she hoped to catch you here. I'll switch her over!"

"No, don't do th—!" Peter started to say, but it was too late. The phone was ringing. He stared at it as if it were sounding a death knell.

Robertson patted him on the shoulder and gave him a thumbs-up before heading back to his office. Peter sighed.

He didn't know what to say, but letting the phone ring made him feel like an idiot.

He picked up the receiver. "Yeah?" he said, his voice flat.

He wasn't sure what he expected Mary Jane to say, but it certainly wasn't, without preamble, "Are you alone?" She spoke with a sense of urgency on par with a spy hurriedly relaying secrets to home base.

"Yes."

"Good. Have Spider-Man get his blue butt over here."

Now, for the first time, he realized that she wasn't in the apartment. She was in the street. He could hear traffic, the sounds of shouting, cars screeching to a halt nearby. She had to be on a pay phone.

"What's going on?" he demanded. "Are you okay?"

"I'm fine, thanks for asking," she said, and it was hard to tell if she was being sarcastic or not. "But there's a problem with the Swansons."

"The people downstairs? What kind of problem?"

Clearly she was trying to stay calm as she said, "Mr. Swanson says if he doesn't get what he wants, he's going to blow Mrs. Swanson's brains out in the next five minutes."

Ron Swanson's right hand was trembling as he kept the gun aimed at his wife. His left hand was pressing the phone hard against his ear. "You're running out of time!" he shrieked into the phone.

He was in his late thirties, with thinning hair and fraying patience. He had removed his glasses because he was sweating so much that they were sliding off the bridge of his nose.

Crouched in the corner of the apartment were his wife,

Rose, and their daughter, Janie, who was clutched to her mother's bosom. Mother and daughter were slim and blonde. Rose used to boast that her daughter's hair had validated her own. No one would ever again question that she was a natural blonde.

Once upon a time, Ron had found that amusing.

Now it was just another one of the many irritating things that his wife said.

So easily did love turn to loathing. What charmed one day, appalled the next.

He wasn't entirely sure where and when it had all gone wrong. It just had, that's all. Those things happened. It was probably because she had been unable to share his vision. He had seen the deterioration of the world, of the way things were. Every night he came home from a hard day's work, looking for a little commiseration. A little understanding.

But he hadn't gotten that, oh no. No, he'd gotten sighs, and exasperated looks, and "Oh, Ron, enough already." and "What do you expect *me* to do about it?" He hadn't expected her to solve the world's ills, for crying out loud. He just wanted someone he could unload on, the way women were always saying they wanted men to do. To be forthcoming and tell her what was on his mind, and did she listen or appreciate? Hell, no.

And she'd started shrieking at him and belittling him, and finally this morning, she'd said enough, that's it, we're done, let's get the divorce papers, I've had it.

He'd had it as well. But he knew what was going to come down next. She was going to dump him and go off with his angel, his little love, his Janie. She would go off and live the fabulous life of a divorcée while he supported them and saw Janie only when she felt like letting him . . . which he was quite sure would be hardly ever.

She didn't want him around? That was fine with him.

But she wasn't getting Janie.

When he came back with the gun, he had treasured the look on her face. The shock. But then the shock quickly turned to contempt as she became convinced that the gun was a fake. A quick shot into the wall convinced her otherwise. Unfortunately it also served to alert the neighbors, and the next thing he knew the area was crawling with cops, and there were guys all over the place. He just wanted to take his daughter and go, already, just go. That's all he wanted. He didn't want to harm anyone.

But now look what had happened. Just look.

And it was all *her* fault.

"You better get that car here for me!" he shouted into the phone. "You better! And you gotta let me go! Me and Janie! That's the deal! You got two minutes now! Two!"

"You got it, Ron," came the voice of the cop on the other end. "We're arranging for it now. Right now. Just give us a little more time."

The shades were drawn and he was staying clear of them. He'd seen enough cop shows to know that much.

From the floor, Rose summoned up her defiance and said, "Ron, this is pointless. Give it up. They're not going to let you go. They're not."

"They will if they know what's good for them. And for you," he said darkly.

Janie was whimpering against her mother, and Rose stroked her hair and said, "It'll be okay, honey. I promise. It'll be over soon."

Ron sidled over to a window shade and peered out. He

saw no car. What he did see were S.W.A.T. members being deployed.

The car might still be coming, though.

The car might . . .

No.

At that moment, total despair seized him. Rose was right. Once again, once again she had to go and be right.

All his anger, all his vituperation boiled over, and suddenly he reached over and grabbed her by the back of the hair. He hauled her to her feet, keeping the gun muzzle buried in her neck. The phone, which was a cordless, was still propped on his shoulder. "I'm gonna kill her!" he was screaming, as he felt his entire world spiralling away from him.

"Ron, the car's on its way," the cop said over the phone.

"No it's not! You're lying!" His heart was pounding, his pulse thudding against his temple. His world was becoming a haze of red. Janie was still whimpering, terrified. He ignored her, moving toward the window because he now knew without a doubt that he was going to kill Rose, just blow her away and send her dead body plunging to the ground, and if after that they came in and shot him down, well, that was fine, he was dead already.

"You're lying, and it's been five minutes, and you're just trying to screw with me, and I'm gonna die but I'll take her with me, I swear to God I will—!" and now he was right near the window, but they couldn't see him because the shade was drawn, and he cocked the hammer of the gun . . .

And a gloved hand smashed through the glass, knocking aside the shade, moving like lightning. As if the hand's owner knew precisely where the gun was without even looking, steel-like fingers snared the gun and crushed it before the hammer could fall.

Ron let out a yelp and at that moment Rose slammed her head into his face. He staggered and Rose shoved him away.

The window burst inward, glass flew as Spider-Man leaped through the opening. He landed a couple feet away from Ron and stood facing him.

Ron yanked out a switchblade he had as backup, but he never even got the chance to flick it open. Inside of a second, Spider-Man had fired his webbing and hopelessly gummed up the knife.

Frustrated and mortified, Ron threw the switchblade at Spider-Man. Spider-Man batted it aside with no effort, took a quick step forward and slugged Ron before he could get his guard up . . . not that his guard would have made much difference. Ron spun like a top and thudded to the floor, not five feet away from his daughter.

Spider-Man started toward him to make sure that he was down for the count. Then, to his surprise, the little girl threw herself across the sprawled body of her father.

"Don't you hurt my daddy!" she cried out. "You're a *very bad man!*"

Spider-Man stopped in his tracks, puzzled and not sure how to handle the outburst.

Rose dropped down next to her daughter and held her close. "No, Janie," she said. "Spider-Man is a good man. He helped us."

"He hurt daddy, and I hate him," said Janie resolutely.

At that moment the door was kicked open and the police charged in. Spider-Man took that as his cue to head back out the window, and within moments he was swinging away over the rooftops.

Peter poked his head into the apartment later that day. Mary Jane was seated quietly on the couch, her legs tucked under her as she read a book. She barely glanced up at him. "Hi," she said.

"Hi." He cleared his throat. "I, uhm . . . got some pictures from earlier. Me and the Swanson thing. Sold 'em to the *Bugle*. Jonah was happy. Said it showed Spider-Man interfering with a police operation. Made his day."

"That's nice," said Mary Jane, and she turned the page of the book.

"Got the money for 'em here. Thought maybe we'd go out or something. To dinner maybe."

"That's nice," she said again, and turned another page.

"You don't read that fast."

"I just look at the pictures."

"There's no pictures in that book."

"Takes less time that way."

He paused a moment. Then he sighed. "Look, what's it going to take, huh? Am I supposed to apologize now? Tell you that your calling me made up for this morning? We're all even now, is that it? Lose this life, save the other, and that makes it okay? Okay, fine. I'm sorry. We're all even. We . . ."

He heard a slight choking noise. He moved closer.

There were tears dribbling down her face.

"Aw, c'mon now . . . don't start," he said, feeling that first wave of helplessness that usually seized him in moments like this.

"You . . . you have no idea what it took for me to call

you, do you?'' she said, her voice quavering.

"I . . . don't know. I figured that you . . . no. I don't. I mean, I figured you saw that there was this thing happening, and you called me, and that was that.''

She turned to face him, her cheeks glistening. "I saw you come crawling down the side of the building, and pause outside the window, and then go leaping in there . . . God, Peter, it was so frightening to watch.''

"Frightening?'' He was genuinely puzzled. "Why? It was just one guy with a gun.''

"Oh, just one guy. I see. So when am I allowed to be scared for you, then. At least two guys with guns? How about one guy with, like, a really big gun, or half a dozen guys with small guns? Tell me the requirements so I'll know when it's allowable to be worried that my husband is going to get a bullet in him?''

"MJ'' —he gestured helplessly— "this isn't anything new. Not for me. Not for us. I've been doing this for ages, and—''

"And I can't help thinking about the law of averages, Peter,'' she said. "That, sooner or later, your luck is going to run out. That, sooner or later, you'll be a second too slow . . . or make a split-second decision and it's wrong . . . and that's it, it's over, and it was all pointless because your Uncle Ben will still be dead and you'll be right next to him in the ground, and I won't have you anymore.''

"That's not going to happen.''

With fierceness in her voice, she said, "You tell me that eye to eye. Face to face.'' She jumped up and took his face in her hands, and gazing into his eyes said, "Tell me right now, with utter confidence, that it could never, ever happen. Not ever.''

He tried. He truly did. His mouth moved, but the words wouldn't come out.

She sighed and released him. "Thank you. Thank you for being honest." She turned away, and now she made no effort to keep the tears back. "You hate me for this morning and you have every right to. Because I was being selfish. I was. I was being selfish. I thought about you leaving our warm bed and hurling yourself into some new danger, and maybe this would be the one. Maybe this would be when some punk got lucky, or some revenge-crazed nutcase finally hit on the ideal plan to snuff you out. Maybe this would be the day, this day, our day, our anniversary, and all I'd have left of you is a warm empty spot on the bed that would be cold in five minutes. A man died because I love you so much that I wanted to keep you safe with me. And when I was calling you at the *Bugle* to tell you about the Swansons, my finger was trembling as I dialed. I thought, What if this is it? What if I'm now sending my own husband to his death? What if . . . I dunno . . . what if God is so angry at me for being selfish, that he punished not only some poor stranger, but now he's going to punish you too, and I didn't know what to do and . . ."

She couldn't say anything more, because her body was so racked with sobs.

He tried to think of what else to say, but there was nothing else. There were no words.

There would only be time. Time to come to terms with what had happened, and to let the salve of successes ease over the pain of failure. Time to let scales be balanced somewhere where such things are maintained; where the incomprehensible finally makes some degree of sense.

He took her to him, and kissed her wet face, and he

started to cry as well. They held each other tightly, each seeking forgiveness for each other and for themselves.

They kissed more and more fiercely, to try and burn away the hurt and frustration, and he picked her up as if she weighed nothing and carried her to the bedroom.

And there they remained, shutting out the rest of the world, taking joy in each other, in being alive, in being there for one another.

And they did so for a time, for all too brief a time.

To be precise: For two hours . . .

. . . and five minutes.

BIOGRAPHIES

Stephen Baskerville recently completed a one-year tenure as inker/finisher on *Web of Spider-Man*. Currently he is providing inks for the *Black Cat* miniseries and finished art for the *Spider-Man: The Arachnid Project* miniseries. Previous inking credits include *Gene Dogs*, *Sleeze Brothers*, and a variety of toy and TV tie-in comics for Marvel UK; *G.I. Joe*, *Transformers*, *Captain Planet*, and a variety of X-Men custom comics (for clients such as Pizza Hut) for Marvel; *The Hitchhiker's Guide to the Galaxy* for DC; *Ray Bradbury's Tales of Terror* for Topps; and several bits and pieces for Fleetway's *2000 A.D.* He lives in London, England.

John Gregory Betancourt is the author of eleven science fiction and fantasy books, including the acclaimed *Johnny Zed*, *Rememory*, and *The Blind Archer*, as well as dozens of short stories and nonfiction essays. He has two collaborative novels forthcoming in 1995: the YA fantasy *Born of Elven Blood* (with Kevin J. Anderson) and the *Star Trek: Deep Space Nine* novel *Devil in the Sky* (with Greg Cox). In 1993, he and his wife, Kim, were World Fantasy Award finalists for their independent publishing venture The Wildside Press. Currently he lives in New Jersey, where he collects cats and computers with equal success.

Richard Lee Byers is the author of the novels *Netherworld, Dark Fortune, Dead Time, The Vampire's Apprentice, Fright*

Line, and *Deathward,* as well as the YA books *Joy Ride, Warlock Games,* and *Party Till You Drop.* His short fiction has appeared in numerous magazines and anthologies, including *Phobias, Dark Seductions, Confederacy of the Dead, Grails: Visitations of the Night, Freak Show, When Will You Rage, Larger than Life, Excalibur, Friends of Valedmar, Fear Itself, Death and Damnation, Elric: Tales of the White Wolf, Dark Destiny,* and *The Ultimate Superhero.* A resident of Tampa Bay, the setting for much of his fiction, he teaches Fiction Writing at Hillsborough Community College and has taught Writing Horror and Dark Fantasy at the University of Tampa.

Greg Cox is the author of *The Transylvanian Library: A Consumer's Guide to Vampire Fiction* and has co-edited an anthology of science fiction vampire stories titled *Tomorrow Sucks.* Not surprisingly, his favorite spider-villain is Morbius, the Living Vampire, hence the antagonist in his story. With John Gregory Betancourt, he has written a *Star Trek: Deep Space Nine* novel, *Devil in the Sky,* to be published in 1995. He has also contributed short stories to Bantam's *Further Adventures of Batman* anthologies, and he decided to write for this book to see how the other half lives. Greg lives in New York City, where he works as an Associate Editor for Tor Books.

Peter David is a prolific author, having in the past several years written nearly two dozen novels and hundreds of comic books, including such titles as *Aquaman, The Atlantis Chronicles, Dreadstar, The Incredible Hulk, The Phantom, Sachs & Violens, Soulsearchers & Company, Star Trek, Wolverine, X-Factor,* and the various Spider-Man titles.

He has written several popular *Star Trek: The Next Generation* novels including *Q-Squared, A Rock and a Hard Place, Vendetta, Imzadi,* and *Q-in-Law,* which have spent a combined six months on the *New York Times* best-seller list. His other novels include *Knight Life, Howling Mad,* the "Psi-Man" and "Photon" adventure series, a "classic" *Star Trek* novel and a *Star Trek: Deep Space Nine* novel, and novelizations of *The Return of the Swamp Thing, The Rocketeer,* and the *Alien Nation* teleplay "Body and Soul." He also writes a weekly column, "But I Digress . . ." or *Comics Buyer's Guide.* David is a long-time New York resident with his wife of seventeen years, Myra (whom he met at a *Star Trek* convention), and their three children, Shana, Guinevere, and Ariel.

When he was young and impressionable, **Keith R. A. DeCandido**'s parents gave him J. R. R. Tolkien, Ursula K. Le Guin, Robert A. Heinlein, and P. G. Wodehouse to read. He was doomed. He has been both a writer and editor in the science fiction, fantasy, comics, and library fields since 1989, with his writing appearing regularly in *Publishers Weekly, Creem, Library Journal,* and *Wilson Library Bulletin.* For over four years and well over 100 episodes, Keith has been a host and producer of *The Chronic Rift,* the acclaimed New York City cable-TV talk show on science fiction and comics. He lives in New York City with his lovely and much more talented wife, Marina Frants.

Tom De Haven's novels include *Freaks' Amour, Jersey Luck, Funny Papers, Joe Gosh, U.S.S.A., Sunburn Lake,* and the King's Tramp fantasy trilogy: *Walker of Worlds, The End-of-Everything Man,* and *The Last Human.* He has scripted several graphic novels, including *Neuromancer* (based on the William Gibson novel) and *Goldfish* (based on the Raymond Chandler story) both for Marvel, and *Nightmare Alley* (part of the Neon Lit series for Avon). He also wrote the text for *Pixie Meat,* an album of illustrations by Charles Burns and Gary Panter. He recently finished writing a film script based on *Freaks' Amour* for director Alex Proyas (*The Crow*) and is completing the script for *Green Candles,* a 280-page graphic novel to be published in 1995 by DC/Paradox Press. In 1987, he contributed several scripts to the animated TV series *The Adventures of the Galaxy Rangers.* The recipient of two National Endowment for the Arts creative writing awards, De Haven is a professor of American Studies and English at Virginia Commonwealth University in Richmond, where he lives with his wife and two daughters.

Colleen Doran was born in 1963 and has been a professional illustrator and cartoonist since age fifteen. Her work has appeared in over 250 comics, books, and magazines, among them *Amazing Spider-Man,* Walt Disney's *Beauty and the Beast,* Clive Barker's *Hellraiser, Captain America,* Anne Rice's *The Master of the Rampling Gate, Nestrobber, Valor,* and lots more. She is the creator of the series *A Distant Soil* and the publisher of Aria Press, with a line of books, comics, prints, and other merchandise featuring the work of Colleen Doran. She wonders intently if anyone ever reads these back-of-the-book bios; if so, all of you send her a dollar to prove it.

Ron Frenz has been working as an artist for Marvel for eleven years, which began with a run on *Ka-Zar the Savage* and also included two years on *The Amazing Spider-Man*, where he was first partnered with writer Tom DeFalco (also Marvel's editor in chief). Since then, he and DeFalco collaborated on a seven-year run on *Thor*, and they are now working together on *Thunderstrike*. The shorter half of Dead Fly Studio, Ron lists his turnoffs as "standing on line and insincere people."

Rocketed to Earth as an infant, **James W. Fry** escaped the destruction of his home planet and grew to adulthood in Brooklyn, New York. In 1984, seduced by the irresistible combination of insane deadlines and crippling poverty, he embarked on a career as a free-lance illustrator. James's credits include *Star Trek* and *The Blasters* for DC Comics, *Moon Knight* and *Slapstick* for Marvel, and most recently Topps Comics's *SilverStar*. Himself a leading cause of stress-related illness in comic book editors, James's greatest unfulfilled ambition is to get one full night of guilt-free sleep.

Craig Shaw Gardner is the author of over twenty books, including *Dragon Sleeping, A Bad Day for Ali Baba, Revenge of the Fluffy Bunnies*, and the *New York Times* best-selling novelizations of the movies *Batman* and *Batman Returns*. He feels that comic books warped him from an early age, and can still remember picking up *Fantastic Four* #1 at the local drug store. (He didn't start reading *The Amazing Spider-Man* until issue #2.)

Christopher Golden's first novel was *Of Saints and Shadows*. Its sequel, *Angel Souls & Devil Hearts*, will appear from Berkley in summer 1995, along with a pair of YA thrillers,

The Bikini Killer and *Beach Blanket Psycho,* to be published
by Bantam, and a novel based on Marvel's *Daredevil* for
Boulevard/Byron Preiss Multimedia. He is an
entertainment journalist, specializing in the comics and
film industries, and won the Bram Stoker Award for
nonfiction in 1993. Golden was born and raised in
Massachusetts, where he still lives with his wife, Connie,
and son, Nicholas.

Stan Lee, the chair of Marvel Comics and Marvel Films
and creative head of Marvel Entertainment, is known to
millions as the man whose superheroes propelled Marvel
to its prominent position in the comic book industry.
Hundreds of legendary characters, such as Spider-Man,
the Incredible Hulk, the Fantastic Four, Iron Man,
Daredevil, and Dr. Strange, all grew out of his fertile
imagination. Stan has written more than a dozen best-
selling books for Simon & Schuster, Harper & Row, and
other major publishers. Presently, he resides in Los
Angeles, where he chairs Marvel Films and serves as co-
executive producer for Marvel's many burgeoning motion
picture, television, and animation projects, including the
new *Spider-Man* animated series on the Fox Network.

Rick Leonardi was born in Philadelphia. He started
working at Marvel in 1980, and set himself up as one of
their premiere fill-in artists, providing issues of *Daredevil,
Uncanny X-Men, The New Mutants, Amazing Spider-Man,
Spectacular Spider-Man,* and many others. He broke the
trend by becoming the regular penciller on *Cloak &
Dagger,* and currently provides the art (with Al
Williamson) over Peter David's stories in *Spider-Man 2099.*

Ron Lim got his start on the alternative press comic *Ex-Mutants*, then moved on to prominence as the artist on Marvel's New Universe book *Psi-Force*. He has since lent his artistic talent to a variety of comics for Marvel, including *Spider-Man Unlimited*, *The Silver Surfer*, *Nightwatch*, *X-Men 2099*, and several *Venom* titles, including *Lethal Protector*, *Death Trap: The Vault*, and *Nights of Vengeance*. He also provided the chapter heading illustrations for Diane Duane's new Spider-Man novel *The Venom Factor*.

Bob McLeod was born in Tampa, Florida in 1951 and now makes his home in Emmaus, Pennsylvania. He attended the Art Institute of Fort Lauderdale in Florida, then moved on to an apprenticeship at Neal Adams's Continuity Studios. Starting out as an inker for Marvel in 1974, he moved on to penciling in the early 1980s, working on several Spider-Man titles. In 1983, he co-created *The New Mutants* with Chris Claremont, and worked on the title first as penciler, then as inker. He penciled DC's *Action Comics* for several years. His latest work is the recent *Venom: The Enemy Within* limited series written by Bruce Jones.

David Michelinie was born in Nashville, Tennessee, where he grew up reading science fiction and playing guitar. He eventually graduated from the University of Miami with a degree in television and film, after which he spent a year writing bad television commercials. This earned him a prestigious industry award and an abiding contempt for people who actually enjoy this sort of thing. Realizing the error of his ways, he turned to fiction and has to date published one novel and more than 500 comic book stories, including tenures on both *Web of Spider-Man* and *The Amazing Spider-Man.* He currently chronicles Superman's adventures in *Action Comics.* In his spare time, he likes to abduct aliens—fair is fair.

Ann Nocenti lives in upstate New York and Manhattan. She writes fiction, film, and journalism. Her short fiction has appeared in Titan Books's *Forbidden Planet* and Arcane/Eclipse's *Words Without Pictures* anthologies. She is currently working on a screenplay-reading series for the Nyuorican Poets Cafe in New York City called "The Fifth Night." She wrote *Longshot, Daredevil, Someplace Strange,* and many other works for Marvel, including several stories in *Marvel Comics Presents* and a dozen or so Spider-Man comics. Her latest comics work is *Kid Eternity* for the Vertigo imprint of DC. Her next Spider-Man project is the upcoming "Eureka" trilogy.

Patrick Olliffe came to Marvel three years ago after slaving for four years in the alternative press. His proudest accomplishment from those early days was an adaptation of Mary Shelley's *Frankenstein* (with Martin Powell) published by Malibu. These days, as the taller half of Dead Fly Studio, he is the artist on Marvel's *Warlock and the Infinity Watch* and his pencil work has shown up in *Nomad, She-Hulk,* and *Thor Corps.*

Brooklyn-born **John Romita Sr.** started drawing at age five. He attended a city high school that later became Art & Design, and then studied illustration at night. He got into comics "temporarily" in 1949, and stayed in the business for forty-five years (and counting). After tours at

Atlas, DC, and Marvel doing Western, romance, war, mystery, and superhero comics, notably a lengthy run on *The Amazing Spider-Man* in the 1960s, he is currently Executive Art Director at Marvel Comics.

Alex Saviuk attended the School of Visual Arts in New York City and studied sequential art with Will Eisner, renowned creator of *The Spirit*. He began his professional career in 1977 at DC Comics, illustrating *Green Lantern, The Flash, Aquaman, The Atom, Hawkman,* and, last but not least, *Superman*. In 1986, Alex began working exclusively for Marvel starting with *Iron Man, Defenders of the Earth,* and others. He has been associated with the Spider-Man titles since 1987, notably a seven-year run penciling *Web of Spider-Man*, and the art chores on the new *Spider-Man Adventures* title. Alex presently lives in Florida with his wife, Jodi, and their two children, Daniel and Erica.

Dean Wesley Smith has been a Spider-Man fan since issue #1, so much so that in the mid-70s he started his own comic store, finally selling it to go into writing full-time. As a fiction writer he has three novels and over sixty short stories to his credit. He is also the editor and co-publisher of *Pulphouse: A Fiction Magazine* and has four Hugo Award nominations for Best Editor. In 1989 he won a World Fantasy Award with his wife, Kristine Kathryn Rusch, for their work on *Pulphouse*. But even with all that, he still reads Spider-Man comics every month.

Robert L. Washington III was born in Minneapolis, Minnesota, and was quickly quarantined to Detroit,

Michigan. After attending a clandestine academy for the
academically inclined/socially disadvantaged in nearby
Bloomfield Hills, he escaped to New York University, and
was eventually released to the University of Michigan
under his own recognizance. After discovering the
startling disparity between the cost of beginning a
professional filmmaking career (film + actors + editing
+ sets + costumes + effects = $50,000+) vs. beginning
a professional writing career (paper + typewriter
[borrowed] + postage = $3.50 avg.), he repudiated
the crass concerns of professional cinema for the
significantly increased profit margin of professional
prose. After breaking into comix via *Clive Barker's
Hellraiser, Epic Lite,* and *Marvel Year in Review,* he weaseled
his way into writing *Static* for Milestone Media and
creating *The Shadow Cabinet* for that company. He
currently works free-lance and counts grumbling about
the money he could be making in screenplays among his
hobbies.

Lawrence Watt-Evans was born and raised in
Massachusetts, fourth of six children, in a house full of
books. He taught himself to read at age five in order to
read a comic book story called "Last of the Tree
People," and began writing his own stories a couple of
years later. Eventually a fantasy novel, *The Lure of the
Basilisk,* actually sold. Several more novels and dozens of
stories have now been published, as well as articles,
poems, comic book scripts, etc., covering a wide range of
fantasy, science fiction, and horror. His short story "Why
I Left Harry's All-Night Hamburgers" won the Hugo

Award in 1988. His most successful novels to date have been the Ethshar fantasy series, beginning with *The Misenchanted Sword*. He's married, has two children, and has settled in the Maryland suburbs of Washington, D.C.

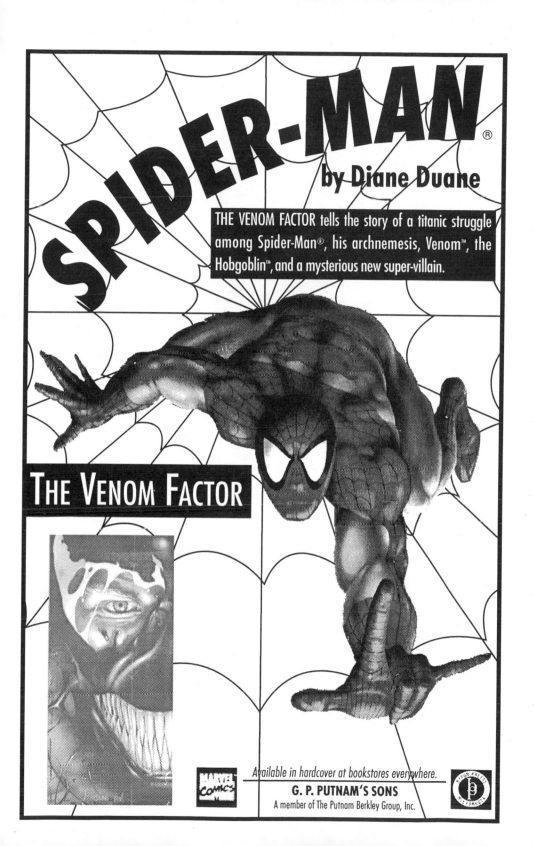